Pursuit

Naomi Metzl

Published by Midnight Sunrise Publishing

ISBN 978 0 9924 3039 9

Midnight Sunrise Publishing

For Gran
And all you have ever done for us

Also by this author

Marble Road
Waiting for the Silver Lining
Catching Liberty
Cloaks of Silver

That time of year thou mayst in me behold
When yellow leaves, or none, or few, do hang
Upon those boughs which shake against the cold,
Bare ruin'd choirs, where late the sweet birds sang.
In me thou see'st the twilight of such day
As after sunset fadeth in the west;
Which by and by black night does take away,
Death's second self, that seals up all in rest.
In me thou see'st the glowing of such fire,
That on the ashes of his youth doth lie,
As the death-bed whereon it must expire,
Consumed with that which it was nourish'd by.
This thou perceivest, which makes thy love more strong,
To love that well which thou must leave ere long.

William Shakespeare
Sonnet LXXIII

$$\sim 1 \sim$$

SWEET SIXTEEN

"Senna!"

Sienna's smile was impossible to contain. Just the sound of Flynn's voice made her feel whole again. Then she saw the others and her heart deflated. This wasn't the plan.

Ever since they'd slipped up, since Flynn's friends found out they were dating, they'd found it almost impossible to catch up alone, only succeeding when they snuck into each other's rooms at night.

"Hey, Senna," said Ashton, his voice a sneer, as she walked up the long drive towards them. James and Myra smirked. "So glad you could finally make it."

They were hanging out in the garage, pawing over Flynn's father's expensive cars. They all came from rich families, but Flynn's had the best cars. Flynn stepped towards Sienna. As she slid into his embrace, she became aware, once more, of the pervasive darkness that lurked in his absence. "Sorry. Took me ages to find something inspiring. Then I lost track of time."

"Lucky I'm not a jealous guy," Flynn replied in a laughing voice. "Pretend you love me more than your camera, even when you find somethin' other than me to immortalise." His lips were near her ear. His warm breath spilled down her neck as his hand caressed her hair, easing her head into the crook of his neck. "Show me when we get home."

"Get a room."

Sienna didn't have the chance to roll her eyes at Ashton's comment. Flynn shifted, a glint in his eye as he pressed his lips to hers. Her response was enthusiastic. When Flynn kissed her, she became something more than whole. She felt alive.

"Where we going?" asked Sienna, pulling her lips just far enough away to speak.

"Kingsford. Dumplings. Your favourite," said Flynn.

Sienna caught the annoyed looks of the others. It was her favourite. Relaxed and informal. Everything dining with her parents wasn't. But that was exactly why she didn't want to go.

"Don't deny me. Your birthday. Only the best." Flynn's eyes held hers. "They hate it," he whispered. "Wanna get burgers. Make 'em pay for ruinin' our plans."

When Flynn smiled, Sienna's lips curled with his. He was her one weakness, but also her one strength. The two were so deeply entwined they could never be separated.

"Your olds around? Which car we taking?" asked James, his eyes roving between the Lexus, Mercedes and BMW.

"We're taking my car," said Flynn. James and Ashton groaned. "Then don't come."

Ashton glared at Flynn. James and Myra exchanged glances before shrugging and heading over to the shabby Suzuki jeep, forcing Ashton to fall in line. The car was more than twenty years old. A sixteenth birthday present from Flynn's father. His parents had always promised him a car, but the make was retribution for being caught joyriding in his father's car with Ashton a few months ago. Flynn's father expected him to complain. Beg for something better. Flynn's gracious thanks and insistence on having his driving lessons in it, angered his father to the point of violence, but that only spurred Flynn on.

"We could always consider legal means of transport," suggested Sienna, even as she took the L-plate off the car.

"Everyone, get in," called Flynn, unlocking the doors. He turned back to Sienna, one hand on her waist, the other tucking a stray strand of hair behind her ear. "That's for our adventures," he whispered. "Not sharin' that with these louts."

The city's network of buses, trains and ferries had become their own adventure land. Over the past few years they had trekked to almost every reachable pocket, discovering the different flavours. In each one, they picked out a house and sketched out the lives they'd lead. For a few hours, possibilities arose within them, almost daring them to believe. It only lasted until they meandered back home to the futures that had already been so strictly mapped out for them. Their lives were not their own. They never would be. But while they were young and could run free, they would.

When Sienna nodded her final assent, Flynn's eyes sparkled in response. They were such a magnificent blue and made Sienna mourn her flat brown eyes. She hoped their child would inherit his eyes. Their other traits were similar enough not to worry about. Flynn's curls were tighter, but the sandy blonde colour of his hair was almost exactly the same shade as Sienna's long wavy locks. His skin tanned while hers burned, but underneath was the same pale white. But none of that really mattered. If their child had Flynn's smile, Sienna would be happy. Flynn's smile was her smile and she was sure she never smiled without him.

Ashton sat defiantly in the front passenger seat. Flynn squeezed Sienna's hand as he walked her to the back door. They didn't challenge Ashton, keeping up the charade they'd only been dating for months, rather than years, and that Flynn's only interest in her was physical.

Sienna slipped into the middle of the back seat as Flynn slid behind the wheel. The rumble of the engine finally brought some joy to the others' faces. Flynn turned and flashed Sienna another brilliant smile.

"You're my life," he said, his finger sweeping under her chin.

"Life of my life," Sienna replied, ignoring Ashton's exaggerated cough and the glances Myra and James were exchanging from either side of her.

"On lookout, Senna," called Flynn, as they pulled on to the road.

Sienna sat forward at Flynn's call while the others talked happily. She was their navigator on these road trips. Able to spot things at a distance and with a photographic-like memory of the city's streetscape, she had helped them avoid many potentially sticky situations. The only time Flynn had been caught was when she had not been with him.

The Sunday evening traffic was heavy due to the warm weather and lengthening days, but they made it to their destination without any hassles. If Flynn looked slightly older, the risks would've been negligible. Sienna's uncle had been teaching them to drive on his farm since they were twelve.

When they sat down at the restaurant, Flynn confiscated all the menus and proceeded to order Sienna's favourite dishes. Ashton didn't try to hide his scowl, while James and Myra smirked, but Flynn ignored them, giving Sienna the confidence to do the same.

Flynn took a single candle out of his pocket when the food arrived and stuck it in a bowl of rice. "Happy birthday, Senna. Sweet sixteen."

Sienna quickly blew out the candle, her face burning under the gaze of so many eyes.

"Too bad about the never-been-kissed part," James muttered to Ashton, causing a ripple of muffled laughter around the table.

"I don't know," said Flynn, intertwining his fingers with Sienna's. "There're a few places I haven't kissed yet."

Sienna's faced flushed as the others laughed. Flynn silently reassured her he was only joking, but it was the others she was worried about. James, Ashton and Myra were Flynn's friends not hers. Myra and Sienna went to the same school, but they rarely spoke. Sienna hardly spoke to anyone.

"Where we going for dessert?" asked James, as they walked back to the car.

"Newtown?" suggested Myra.

Flynn let the others decide their next destination. He took Sienna's hand and leant her against the bonnet of his car, the streetlight illuminating them in the darkened laneway. They kissed as the others debated. Flynn would eat anything and Sienna didn't do sweets. Flynn occasionally tried to change that. He wanted to buy her sweet things. For him she tried, but found it hard to break her ban on anything she considered unhealthy. Flynn laughed at the flaws in her reasoning, but never once asked her to change.

Sienna heard the occasional gagging noise from Ashton. They paid no attention. Neither of them had any hang-ups about public displays of affection, and the more it annoyed the others, the further they pushed it.

"Newtown!" cried James. "Get in the car. We're going to Newtown."

Flynn brought Sienna's lips to his to kiss her passionately as the others groaned. With a final chuckle, they got in the car.

They travelled via secondary roads most of the way. Flynn held Sienna close as they walked to the chocolateria. For him, she shared some of the brownie and iced chocolate he ordered. Myra watched her as she ate, only finishing half of her own dish. James didn't complain when she pushed the leftovers his way.

"Time to take you home," Flynn said to Sienna, when everyone had finished eating.

"What?" cried Ashton. "I thought we were making a night of it!"

"I am makin' a night of it, loser," replied Flynn. "But in case you can't work it out, not all celebrations are a group affair. You wanna stay, be my guest. Just make your own way home."

Flynn grabbed Sienna's hand and headed back to the car. The bustle of the main road quickly gave way to the quiet of the night as they turned into the side street. It was broken only by the heavy footfalls of the others hustling after them. Sienna scoffed. They were like sheep, always following Flynn around, never prepared to take risks unless he was there to get them out of trouble.

"Give me the quickest way, Senna," said Flynn, as soon as they were in the car.

"Quickest is right on to King," replied Sienna. "Safest is a U-turn back via the side streets."

Flynn immediately threw on his right blinker. It was late and traffic was light, but slow. Flynn weaved impatiently in and out of it to get ahead.

"Ah, company," said Sienna, as an unmarked police car pulled alongside them at the traffic lights. The officers were assessing Flynn. When he turned and flashed them one of his grins, they signalled for him to pull over.

"Your old man's going to be real pissed this time," said Ashton. "We ain't near enough to your place to make up some shit about taking me home."

"We ain't gettin' caught," said Flynn. "What's the best way, Senna?"

"To home? We're on the wrong side of the harbour. Bridge, then hope to lose them on the north side," Sienna replied. "But if we run and get caught, we're in deep."

"You can do it. Trust me?" asked Flynn seriously.

"With my life."

"Good. The rest of you shut up."

Flynn drove slowly when the lights changed, putting on his blinker and pulling over. His rear number plate was partially obscured by material that could passed as accidently hanging from the boot. Sienna played the role of anxious passenger, her head flicking back and forth as they waited for the driver to get out of the police car. She watched the cop's every step, measuring them against the traffic flowing around them.

"Now!" she cried, as the cop leant down at the back of the car.

Flynn swerved in front of a passing car and sped off.

"Slow," Sienna instructed, as they approached an intersection. They had the red, but she could see a gap in the cars approaching on the perpendicular. "Floor, now!" Flynn complied with no hesitation. "Steer right."

Sirens were closing in on them, but they were almost at the bridge, moving swiftly around the cars as though the road was their own personal obstacle course. Once on the bridge, Flynn cut loose, accelerating recklessly. There were two police cars behind them, but they were holding back.

"Gun it!" cried James, as Ashton cheered.

The adrenaline was starting to pump through them. Flynn laughed and Sienna smiled.

The exit was clear. Flynn veered off, managing to get around the meandering cars that were threatening their escape. They were only five minutes from home now and had enough of a break to have the advantage. All they had to do was get the car inside before the cops caught up with them.

"Left here," said Sienna. "Right. Down the lane. Left."

"You're my hero," said Flynn.

They were only two streets from Flynn's house and could no longer see or hear any police cars. The roads were wider down the last stretch, and Flynn put his foot to the floor. Sienna reached down for the remote. A flash of light caught her attention.

"Left!"

The look of exhilaration slid from Flynn's face as he swerved to the right. A car reversing recklessly out of its driveway kept coming. Flynn accelerated harder, pushing to get past it. Sienna's brain did the physics in a second. They weren't going to make it.

Now they'd have to run for it, knowing they'd be caught.

The impact slammed them against each other. Sienna could see Flynn frantically turning the wheel to the left to swing them around, but she had the strange feeling the car was no longer on the ground.

There was just enough time for Sienna to register that getting away was no longer the issue when the second impact hit. She couldn't count the number of hits after that. All she felt was her body being slammed against seats and people. Pain shot through her, but it was strangely abstract. She thought she screamed, then realised it was Myra whose cry was piercing the silent, suburban air, before it was replaced by the sound of smashing glass and twisting metal.

The world continued to spin and shudder even though Sienna was sure the car had finally come to a rest. She felt strangely disembodied. Straining her ears against the blackness that pressed in on her eyes, she searched for the one sound that would make the situation right again, but all she could hear was the pitiful groaning of the car's broken engine.

Then the panic set in. Myra's scream had been silenced. There was no laughter from Ashton or James.

Flynn! Flynn! Talk to me!

Sienna tried to scream, but there was nothing. Nothing from her mouth. Nothing from Flynn. Nothing but nothing.

Gasping, panicked voices began to swirl in the air. Sienna could sense the movement of people rushing to rescue them. She waited desperately for news, for someone to call Flynn's name, but there was only one word that registered in her brain. Dead. It was repeated over and over. Cautiously. Furiously. Forlornly.

They were all dead.

Even though everything was black already, Sienna felt her eyes close. She was dead. It was a painless realisation. She wondered where she was if she could still hear the world she'd just left.

Purgatory.

It was the only explanation.

But where she was meant nothing. All she wanted to know was where Flynn was. In life or death, she needed to be with him.

The screaming began again. Someone was calling her name. She felt a hand take hers.

Flynn had found her.

Sienna managed to smile then, knowing nothing could ever tear them apart. Not death. Not heaven. Not even hell.

~2~

FORTUNE

The small plane taxied to a stop. Sienna took a deep breath and closed her eyes. She'd been wrong. This was purgatory. Not really alive, but definitely not dead. Forced to live in a world that kept spinning despite Flynn's death. And now, after months in hospital and a series of painful surgeries, she was being exiled. Back to the uncle who'd raised her until she was ten.

The other passengers rose as one. Sienna stayed seated, but turned to face the aisle. Once it was clear, she stretched out her legs, both hands under her left knee to support the cast that felt desperately heavy despite its lightweight composition. Hobbling to her feet, she attempted to lift her bag out of the tiny overhead compartment, but was quickly ushered out of the way by the flight attendant. Sighing heavily, Sienna grabbed the headrests and used them to swing on her good foot up the aisle. The flight attendant muttered behind her, but Sienna ignored her and the plea to wait for assistance down the stairs. A man with a wheelchair was waiting for her.

"Where're my crutches?" Sienna asked, looking around as the last of the passengers crossed the scorching tarmac into the terminal.

"We'll give them to you in the terminal," the man with the wheelchair replied, pushing it forward.

Sienna turned around. The flight attendant was on the bottom step with her bag and crutches. "Seriously, I can take it from here." She swung the duffle bag over her head and grabbed the crutches, shuffling away as quickly as she could to prevent further intervention.

The door of the terminal was open. Sienna staggered through it, sighing with relief as the air conditioning embraced her.

"Sienna!"

The tin-shed terminal was filled with people greeting new arrivals and farewelling the departing, so Sienna didn't spot Uncle Cole until he was right next to her. "I thought you fractured a rib in the accident," he said, grabbing the duffle bag, almost pulling her off her feet in the

8

process. Three, thought Sienna. "You shouldn't be carrying this," he continued, throwing the bag over his shoulder. "How'd you get to the airport this morning?"

Sienna shifted on her crutches, looking away from her uncle's demanding gaze. "Car," she finally sighed.

"So your parents drove you?" He sounded sceptical.

Sienna closed her eyes. "No, Pete did."

"And who's Pete when he's at home?"

Two minutes. That's all it had taken before the battle between her uncle and parents reignited. Just like old times.

"I don't know. Some guy in their office that stuffed up and got stuck playing chauffeur. You didn't actually expect them to take me themselves, did you?"

"No, I guess not," Uncle Cole sighed, shifting to Sienna's side, and placing one hand on her back. With his other hand out in front, he led her through the crowd as though she was an under-siege celebrity.

"This it?" asked Uncle Cole, picking up a large black suitcase from the pint-sized carousel, leaving just one forlorn-looking orange case silently touring the arrivals hall.

"Would've had to have chartered the whole flight to bring more."

Uncle Cole grabbed the suitcase by the handle, completely ignoring the four wheels dangling from its base. Sienna followed him as he marched out into the sunlight, but staggered back at the sight of the patrol car waiting out the front. Was it not possible to pick her up in a normal car?

"I couldn't get time off with such short notice," said Uncle Cole, looking down at the uniform barely hidden by his open jacket.

It was strange the lies he told. Her exile to Fortune had been planned while she still unconscious. And he was the sergeant. If he wanted an afternoon off, he could take it, but Sienna was sure he hadn't taken a holiday in six years. Any time off he'd had was to deal with her.

They drove through Westloch at a leisurely pace, Uncle Cole scanning intently, always on the lookout for trouble. Sienna had never liked Westloch. With a population of almost thirty thousand, it had all the essentials – hospital, university, shopping centre – but she felt it lacked soul. Fortune was quainter. Just forty kilometres outside

Westloch, it was close enough to access all its facilities, yet far enough to feel like a different world.

Uncle Cole took the posting to Fortune from Sydney six years ago – after she tore their little family apart. Sienna didn't know where Aunt Daphne ended up. They'd never spoken of her again.

The first indication that they'd reached Fortune was the population sign. Sienna had watched it steadily increase over the past six years, many crediting it to Uncle Cole's tough, no tolerance policing, which had made him as loved as he was despised.

"I moved since you last came to visit," he said, turning off the main road before they reached the centre of town, and down a quiet cottage-lined street. "Not as much space as the farm, but it'll mean less travel to school."

They pulled into the driveway, stopping in front of the garage. Uncle Cole's regular car sat on the street, the windscreen dusty. The front yard was small, contained by a waist-high brick fence with a path that ran up the middle to the porch. It was a small brick cottage. From a quick glance down the side, Sienna had the feeling the whole house could fit into the largest room of her parents' home – a three-storey, harbour-front house her father's parents bought them as a wedding gift. They had often congratulated themselves for managing to put up with it for so long.

"You're room's at the back."

Sienna nodded and hobbled up the little hallway behind Uncle Cole. The lounge room sat on the right. Uncle Cole closed to the door to the room on the left, so she guessed that was his bedroom. The hallway opened up to the kitchen, which had a small square table and four chairs plonked in the middle of it. The room looked ominously unused. Her bedroom came off the kitchen, beyond which the hallway started up again, leading to the bathroom and laundry, then out to the backyard.

Uncle Cole opened the door to her room and placed her bags on the floor next to the bed. It was furnished with the mismatched items from her farmhouse bedroom, the only addition was a second-hand desk. The room had a welcoming feel, everything inviting use, unlike most of the furniture in her parents' home. Only the single bed looked impossibly small compared to the queen bed she'd so often shared with Flynn.

"I have to get back to work. You'll be right til I get home," Uncle

Cole said, his keys dangling restlessly off his finger.

Sienna nodded and slumped down on the bed. Her eyes were heavy and her body ached with so much movement just three days out of hospital. The front door clicked closed as she reached into her bag, pulling out painkillers, a bottle of water and her wallet. Once she'd taken the drugs, she pulled Flynn's photo out of her wallet. Tears immediately filled her eyes, overflowing with her attempts to restrain her sobs, but they would never be contained and when she finally cried out with the agony of Flynn's loss, her broken ribs screamed in unison.

Senna!

Sienna gasped, jerking awake. Her pillow was wet beneath her cheek. Flynn's cry didn't sound like him, but he was the only one who called her Senna. His cry in the dark – from somewhere inside his car – marked the start of every new day. It was the cry of terror he never got to make before his life was torn from his body and her life was torn asunder.

Hobbling to the cupboards, Sienna sought something to ease the aching rumble in her stomach. She'd been able to sustain herself on the food Uncle Cole had brought home each night until now, and though she didn't care to eat, her steadily returning appetite was getting too much to ignore.

Bare probably exaggerated the state of the kitchen cupboards; just enough to make a coffee. It was grating, knowing it was her fault, a by-product of her parents' disgust over her diet and overweight state when she came to live with them – just one of their many complaints about how she'd been raised. She hadn't seen Uncle Cole cook since and he almost never shopped for groceries any more. It was going to be a problem. She had no intention of replicating his current diet, which seemed to consist entirely of take-out. The last thing she needed was to get fat again and give her parents yet another reason to attack him.

Shuffling down the street, swinging between her crutches like a drunken pendulum trying to escape its mounting, Sienna was impressed that she found the shops with ease, considering how little time she spent in town during her other visits. What was less easy was negotiating the trolley while on crutches. She had to push it with her torso, and risked losing her balance every time she reached out for it after its wonky wheels sent it off course. Getting things off the top shelves was possible with the assistance of a crutch, but she gave up trying to grab things from the bottom shelves after almost falling twice, settling for grabbing whatever alternative was in reach. However, despite those struggles, she was still caught off-guard when it came to transporting her shopping home.

Come on, Senna. You, me. Two leg–two crutch race.

Flynn's voice sounded more like her own, but she still found herself nodding, hurriedly wiping her eyes to disperse the tears that fell with any reminder of him. Imagining Flynn next to her, a cast upon one of his legs, she threw a crutch into the trolley, hobbling forward in a way that didn't match her imagination. Within five minutes, she was panting. It left her relieved to hear the repeated bleeping of a siren behind her, despite the threat of Uncle Cole's anger over the food.

Pivoting awkwardly on her good leg, Sienna stuttered at the sight of two unfamiliar policemen stepping out of the patrol car.

"You do know it's an offence to steal shopping trolleys, don't you," said the older cop.

He was a surly-looking white man in his mid to late thirties. The second, younger cop grinned before his face turned serious, though it remained friendly. What struck Sienna most about him though was the fact that he was clearly Aboriginal. She'd never met an Aboriginal cop before. It was odd in ways she couldn't articulate.

"It's only stealing if you've got no intention of returning it," Sienna retorted.

"Shopping trolleys aren't allowed more than a block from the shops," the older cop replied, folding his arms.

"I've got no other way of getting the shopping home. I'll bring it back."

"So says every delinquent," the white cop muttered. "You're taking it back now. We'll drop you home and next time you find a way to shop without stealing."

The white cop looked familiar and Sienna wondered if he knew who she was. Not putting it past Uncle Cole to set up this kind of test, she chose compliance over complaint. The younger cop grabbed the trolley as she turned it around, passing her the other crutch. He kept pace with her as they walked back to the supermarket.

"So you're new in town?" he asked.

Sienna nodded, turning to assess him. He smiled as soon as he caught her gaze. Her body forgot to move, leaving her hanging on her crutches as she tried to comprehend what she'd just seen. It looked like …

"Still getting used to those things, huh?" asked the young cop, amusement in his voice when he turned to see her metres behind him. "I'm new too. Got here two months ago."

Sienna moved forward again, trying hard to walk with trembling limbs and gasping lungs. "You like it?" she asked, forcing conversation to cover her confusion.

"Yeah. I'm from the city, but this is nice. Different. Kinda peaceful. Haven't gotten sick of the fresh air yet."

They'd reached the supermarket. Sienna dared to look back at the young cop. He wasn't smiling. Her body shuddered as she took a deep breath, her heart returning to a normal pace as she told herself she'd just imagined it.

"Hurry up," snapped the older cop. He'd driven to the shops and was now waiting impatiently for them by the open boot.

The young cop swept his hand through the trolley, attempting to grab all the bags, but missed one. Sienna reached for it, regretting her eagerness when she realised it was the heaviest one. Forcing herself to continue, not prepared to display weakness in front of these cops, she wasn't upset when Jackson grabbed the bag from her and plonked it in the boot.

"So am I really in trouble for this?" Sienna asked, clicking in her seatbelt as the young cop slid into the back of the patrol car with her.

"Where do you live?" replied the older cop, ignoring her question.

"Oh, um, I don't think I know," Sienna said, trying to remember if Uncle Cole had ever told her the address. "I can probably direct you."

Both cops raised their eyebrows, but neither asked the obvious question. Sienna looked out the window, counting streets and turns in reverse, hoping not to get them lost. The older cop scowled as he drove and Sienna wondered if he was always this grumpy or just felt very strongly about abandoned shopping trolleys. It was a complete contrast to the younger one, who looked entirely at ease as he took in the passing scenery. That was until they pulled up in front of her house.

"So you're Sienna?" the young cop asked.

Sienna took a deep breath and nodded. The older cop turned away, but she still saw the disheartened look on his face.

"Great! I was wondering when we'd get to meet you," exclaimed the younger cop. Sienna nodded absently, her eyes still on the older cop, who was stepping out of the car. "That's Ian by the way. I'm Jackson."

"Hey," Sienna replied softly, instinctively reaching out to shake Jackson's hand, but she wanted to rip it back again when he smiled. It hadn't been an illusion. When he smiled, it was Flynn she saw. His lips. His spirit. His love for her.

Jackson did not appear to notice her discomfort as he jumped out of the car and grabbed the groceries from the boot. Sienna struggled with her crutches, shuffling out of the car. She had just found her feet when Ian opened her front door. Gripping her crutches tight, she hurried after them.

"Want me to help unpack?" Jackson asked, placing the bags on the kitchen bench.

"No, she doesn't," Ian snapped from the doorway.

"I'm fine," Sienna replied softly, squeezing past Ian and next to the groceries to try and wrestle back some control of the situation.

Ian left immediately. Jackson followed him, but at the kitchen door he turned and threw Sienna a bright smile before disappearing. A gasping sob escaped Sienna's chest as she slid to the floor, trying to determine what vengeful force would send the ghost of Flynn's smile here to torture her.

CONSEQUENCES

The room was dark as Sienna blinked open her crusty eyes. Her afternoon sleeps weren't getting any shorter, but they now gave her the energy for a semi-active evening. Rolling over, she spied Flynn's photo on the floor and quickly retrieved it without allowing herself to look at it.

Cooking dinner kept her mind occupied, but it could not stop the visions of that night from flickering in her mind like a television playing in the background. Sometimes the volume would spike, a scream cutting through the vacant night. The images had her full attention then – until she could close her eyes and turn down the volume again.

It surprised Sienna when she looked down to find her spaghetti bolognaise dinner sitting before her. She had no memory of cooking it beyond putting the pasta on to boil. The pleasant taste was even more unexpected. She'd found no comfort in food since leaving hospital.

There was a lot of food left over. It seemed rude not to offer it to Uncle Cole, despite knowing he wouldn't want it. Even keeping the leftovers risked annoying him. The sound of him arriving home left her in a state of confused anxiety.

"You cooked," said Uncle Cole, stomping into the kitchen.

"Sorry," Sienna replied quickly.

Uncle Cole looked around the kitchen, his gaze falling on the open cupboard. "Do I need to return any stolen shopping trolleys?"

It wasn't a joke. Sienna shook her head. She'd learned to take a backpack with her to the shops.

"What pizza?" asked an officer, strolling into the kitchen, phone in hand.

"I'll – um – better just chuck this out."

The officer moved over to the stove, his phone slipping into his pocket, as his nose flared over the saucepans. "What? Why?"

"You don't keep your mistakes. You get rid of them," said Sienna.

"Family motto," muttered Uncle Cole.

"In my world, this ain't a mistake," said the officer, spooning spaghetti sauce into his mouth. "Let's eat this, Chief."

The officer didn't wait for Uncle Cole's answer. He grabbed plates from the cupboard and dished up two large servings, finishing off the food. Sienna lingered by the bench, unsure if she should leave, before her uncle's glare got her to the table.

"Chief got you Diet Coke. Hope that's your thing. And I'm Ryan, by the way."

Sienna opened her mouth to say hi, but the words never came out. Ryan ate heartily. Uncle Cole looked at Sienna for a moment before starting his dinner.

"I have tomorrow off," said Uncle Cole, after seeing Ryan out. Sienna got the feeling he hadn't stayed as long as planned. "Might be a good chance to show you around town."

"You mean I've missed something in my treks?" asked Sienna with an attempt at a smile, though it faded when she saw her uncle's face.

"How's your leg? When's the cast supposed to come off? I'll need to make an appointment for you at the hospital."

"It's already made."

"What? They made an appointment for you out here already?"

"No. My appointment's back in Sydney. I mean the date's all sorted and the plane tickets."

"So you're just staying til your cast comes off? I thought it was permanent this time."

"Permanent until the exile's lifted," replied Sienna. "Didn't you talk to Arthur or Janice about it? It's been sorted for ages."

The confusion on Uncle Cole's face propelled Sienna to her room. Returning, she handed her uncle, who'd moved into the lounge room, a five-page itinerary.

"You're supposed to go back by yourself?" Sienna threw him a quizzical look. "For the check-up – for the cast – they've only booked tickets for you."

"Who else would they book tickets for?"

"Me, Sienna! Me! So you had *someone* with you."

Sienna shifted awkwardly on her crutches.

"This all should've been done through me. I won't have your parents organising your life without even talking to me about it. They want you to go to Sydney for check-ups, then they can pay for me to go with you.

"The only reason you ended up ever living with them was because I got posted out here. And I would've brought you with me if I could've," stormed Uncle Cole. "They don't want you. This makes it blatantly obvious," he added, waving her itinerary. "Look at this, you're here for two years until they decide what degree you should do. Law, apparently, is the front runner."

"So?" That had always been her parents' plan for her. Flynn's parents had had the same plan for him too. Now that Flynn was gone, Sienna found herself wanting to fulfil the destiny that had been set out for them.

"You've become some sort of academic genius? Can now read faster than a snail? Write better than a five-year-old child?"

Sienna gasped, swallowing hard on the lump in her throat. Uncle Cole had never cut her down like that before.

Uncle Cole slouched back in his chair. Sienna pivoted on her crutch to escape when her eye caught a photo on the wall. It was of her and Flynn. Flynn had come with her to Uncle Cole's every holiday he could and when he couldn't she had tried to get out of the trip to stay with him. Out there on Uncle Cole's property was where she and Flynn had learned to drive. Uncle Cole had given them lessons, but forbade them from driving without him. They'd always disobeyed him.

"You okay?"

Sienna felt Uncle Cole standing behind her. Lifting her hands to her face, she found it wet with tears.

"Just didn't expect – never knew you had any photos of him."

"He was a nice boy."

Sienna nodded and tried to walk away, but felt herself captured in her uncle's arms. The warmth was overwhelming. It made her think of the arms she missed so much. Uncle Cole held her tighter as her sobs became more unrestrained.

Flynn. Flynn. Flynn. Please, Flynn, come find me. Take me with you. Please, Flynn.

"You look like crap."

Sienna managed a half-smile in response to her uncle's morning greeting.

"You get any sleep?" She shook her head and grabbed a bowl for cereal. "I'll take you around town today. Show you where everything is. It's my last day off til the New Year. We worked out the Christmas rosters a while ago."

That was an excuse. Uncle Cole always worked Christmas, but at least he and Aunt Daphne had celebrated it. They'd even made Sienna feel special. Not like Arthur and Janice. They had a strange version of Christmas that involved lecturing her on how she shouldn't expect anything because she already had more than enough.

"Um, when is Christmas?" asked Sienna.

"Day after tomorrow. Today's the twenty-third."

Sienna could only nod. It seemed impossible that three months could have passed since that terrible day. That Christmas could even exist now that Flynn no longer did.

"Will show you how to get to the station first," said Uncle Cole, as they hopped in the car.

It was a place Sienna knew well. She'd always helped out there in her holidays, and with just three turns they had arrived.

"Morning, Chief. Checking we haven't burnt the place down in your absence?"

Sienna's heart thump erratically at the sound of Jackson's voice. She kept her head down, swinging after Uncle Cole and hurriedly taking a seat at a small table.

"Coffee?" asked Jackson.

Sienna nodded, but didn't look up. Jackson slid her coffee across the table, dropping his head until it was in line with her lowered gaze. As soon as their eyes met, he smiled. Sienna could not return it, staring at him as she attempted to pierce through Flynn's smile to the man behind it. It was so easy when he wasn't smiling. There were almost no similarities between them then.

Flynn, at sixteen, had still looked very much a boy. His blue eyes sparkled, making his face glow as he pushed his tussled, curly hair off his face. He was scruffy-looking and rebellious. He was everything

Jackson wasn't.

Jackson's skin was as dark as Flynn's had been pale. His hair was short and neat and his eyes were so dark they were almost black. They didn't sparkle outwards, they shone inwards and Sienna was sure looking into them would be to journey into Jackson's soul. But for all those differences, there was that smile. Flynn's smile. Her smile. The smile she hadn't been able to smile without.

"Your coffee's getting cold," said Jackson, nodding at her mug.

Sienna took the chance to look away, staring into her mug as she drank. "Urgh, that's gross."

"I told you you'd prefer hot chocolate," said Uncle Cole, while Jackson laughed into his cup.

Hobbling to her feet, mug in hand, Sienna was met by another of Flynn's smiles offering to take it. Her hand shook, spilling her undrunk coffee on the table.

"What's your problem?" growled Uncle Cole, taking the mug from Sienna's hand and throwing it in the sink. "Too good for country coffee? Honestly!"

Sienna shakily pulled her crutches under her arms, hustling out of the kitchen as Ryan entered. Jackson came up behind her, yanking open the door to the reception, smiling gallantly as he did.

"Stop smiling it me. Please."

Too jittery to wait for Uncle Cole, Sienna swung her way home, taking a wrong turn and an extra fifteen minutes to get there. When she slumped heavily down at the dining table, she noticed a hand-drawn map pointing out all the sights of interest in the town. The map was limited, detailing little more than their house, the shops, school, and police station. And the pool.

It was the one thing Sienna truly loved about her parents' house. She wondered if the price of her exile included the installation of a pool. It was doubtful, but her parents had never had any issue spending money on her. It was time they never wanted to give.

The water was delightfully cool against the heat of the day. Sienna wallowed in the shallow water, her mind clear. This was one activity not intricately tied to Flynn. He never enjoyed swimming and had little confidence in water over waist-height. Sienna only ever got him in ocean once. He never spoke about his fear of water. His passing mention of the methods his father used to teach him to swim was all she needed to know.

Sienna stayed until the pool closed, loving the weightlessness of her body and the respite from the clumsiness of her cast. Throwing clothes over her swimmers gave a refreshing coolness to the warm wind as she swung down the street. When a siren whooped behind her, the hint of enjoyment she'd been close to experiencing dissolved into despair.

"Get in," said Ryan, as he pulled up next to her.

"Uncle Cole ask you to find me?"

Ryan didn't answer. He just waited. They were barely a block from the pool and there were people everywhere. With an annoyed growl, Sienna hobbled into the car.

"You're going to give me a reputation before anyone even knows me."

"You already have a reputation," Ryan replied. "That smash was big news – even out here. Four well-to-do kids wiped out in a high-speed police chase. Only survivor, the Chief's niece and the daughter of Arthur and Janice Hollingsworth." Sienna's stomach turned. She'd expected to be as anonymous here as she'd always been when she'd lived with Uncle Cole. "What I'll never understand is why you kids didn't just pull over. What was the point? Was a bit of trouble really worth dying for? Sometimes you just have to face up to your mistakes and the consequences – not try to outrun them."

Sienna choked on the laugh that escaped her. "You think Flynn ran because he was scared of the consequences? Scared of the cops? The courts? Richard Matthews was the only person allowed to discipline Flynn and he only suffered consequences for wanting to be a good person, not for breaking the law."

"Yeah, well, I guess he suffered the consequences this time."

"Sure. If being free is a consequence."

~4~

POLICE LIFE

Sienna checked the calendar hanging on the wall beside her desk – the days dutifully crossed off by her uncle, though she didn't know when. Bile swirled in her mouth. She didn't want to face Christmas without Flynn. Life without Flynn.

Last year they had disappeared, escaping their families after a cursory festive greeting. It'd been perfect. Catching a train to the Blue Mountains, away from everyone who knew them, they dreamt of yet another future they would never live. Sitting on the edge of a large cliff-face, Sienna had envisaged the rock giving way. Now she wished it had. Or perhaps she wished she'd had the courage to ask Flynn to drop down into the canyon with her.

The house was silent. A note on the kitchen table was her only greeting.

Come to the station when you get up. We can have Christmas there.

Sienna sighed. A police Christmas. Uncle Cole was sure to have a present for her. He'd be disappointed if she had nothing in return, but present buying had been the furthest thing from her mind. She didn't even have a spare card. Moving to the cupboard, she gratefully spied the brownie mix she bought to thank him for taking her in. Hopefully, he would consider it a worthy Christmas present.

Sitting dressed, ready to go, waiting for the brownies to finish baking, Sienna wondered if it was possible for her life with Uncle Cole to return to the happy world of her early childhood. Aunt Daphne was gone. No one ever told her where. She just disappeared in the haze of tears the day Sienna went to live with her parents.

No one ever told Sienna why she'd been raised by Uncle Cole and Aunt Daphne either. Sienna knew why they'd stayed silent. Their eyes had spoking the words their mouths refused to.

They didn't love you. You weren't good enough.

Her parents insisted she already knew why – Stephen was sick. Whatever illness it was, Sienna had never seen any sign of it. He was six years older than her and he'd never presented as anything other than a model of physical fitness.

In her bitter moments, Sienna nicknamed Stephen 'Oscar' – the golden boy her parents prized. That bitterness was something she only developed from the age of ten. And that was the problem. She wasn't the girl Uncle Cole raised any more. And he wasn't the man who raised her. Being tossed to him now was almost as foreign as being dumped with her parents had been.

Beads of sweat began forming over Sienna's body the moment she stepped outside. The swinging motion created by her crutches gave some relief in the form of artificial airflow, but it couldn't draw the moisture from her palms that slipped over the handles, causing the tops of the crutches to slam painfully into her armpits. It made the embrace of the police station's air-conditioning very welcome.

"Oi!" cried Jackson, as Sienna tried to push open the door to the office. He tried to hide his smile, but the effort seemed only to amuse him. "Can't just burst in here without the access code."

"I have brownies," muttered Sienna, looking away.

"Entry granted!"

Jackson took the bag from Sienna and led her to the little kitchen where Uncle Cole quickly joined them, his face lighting up when saw the brownies.

"Merry Christmas," said Sienna. "Sorry it's nothing special."

"You're the best present," muttered Uncle Cole. "I'll make you a hot chocolate this time."

"What about tea?" replied Sienna. Uncle Cole held up a box of very cheap-looking tea. "It can't be worse than the coffee."

"And the Chief said you were completely pessimistic about life," said Jackson slyly, ignoring Uncle Cole's glare. "That has to be the ultimate act of optimism right there."

Sienna's eyes turned involuntarily Jackson's way. Even beyond his looks, Jackson was nothing like Flynn. His mannerisms, style and outlook were different in nearly every way. There was only one similarity and Sienna was starting to believe it was her ultimate damnation.

"Well, Merry Christmas!" said Jackson, holding up his mug and smiling brightly. "Thanks for my present."

"I think they were for me," growled Uncle Cole.

Sienna kept her head down as a chair scrapped angrily against the lino floor.

"Hint number five-oh-four for surviving in Fortune: don't get between the Chief and his brownies."

Jackson smiled conspiratorially when she looked up, but this wasn't a joke she could share in and was glad when Uncle Cole returned.

"That's for you," he said, placing a well-wrapped present on the table in front of her.

"Wow, thanks Uncle Cole," Sienna gasped, unwrapping a leather-bound journal. "This is really nice. It's just like the one Stephen usually gets me for my birthday."

Uncle Cole scoffed, his head shaking just slightly. Sienna wondered why it was such a big deal that he had the same taste in gifts as the rest of her family.

"You want to stick around? Help out?" asked Uncle Cole.

Sienna glanced at Jackson and shook her head. It would've helped pass the day, but this was not the day to spend with the ghost of Flynn's smile.

"Am I smiling too much again?" asked Jackson brightly.

Uncle Cole muttered something, but Sienna couldn't make it out.

"Sometimes," she shrugged, not wanting to admit it made her want to gouge her eyes out.

"Thought so," nodded Jackson, though he continued to grin. "Could just tell me to get lost. Want me to go?"

When Sienna shook her head, Jackson jumped up and cleared the table, the smile never sliding from his face. Sienna turned away.

"You want me to drop you home?" asked Uncle Cole.

"No, I'm fine," said Sienna. "It's good exercise."

Uncle Cole nodded and walked her out, holding the door open for her.

"Happy New Year," called Jackson. "Won't see you. Driving home tonight."

"Where's home?" asked Sienna, feeling a stab in her heart as his smile met her eyes.

"Western Sydney. Doubt you've ever been there," Jackson added smugly. Sienna hated the assumption, but said nothing. "Can take you with me. Visit your family if you like."

"If her parents had wanted to see her, it would've been in her itinerary," said Uncle Cole.

The comment confused Jackson, but he seemed aware enough to know not to ask the logical question. He just waved and promised to see her next year. When he walked off, Sienna felt that promise bind to her heart. Jackson's very existence was torture, yet the idea that he could disappear – and with him the last living reminder of Flynn – was somehow more painful.

***

Sienna woke with a start. Her heart was thumping so hard it hurt her chest. Tears stung her eyes as visions of the crash spun in front of her. The painkillers she'd been using to blacken her sleep since the accident had run out more than a month before they were supposed to, but she didn't dare tell anyone. Now her days were filled with physical as well as emotional pain. Her leg throbbed constantly, intermittent stabs of pain breaking the monotony.

But it wasn't physical pain that washed out her eyes each morning. Having spent nearly every night for the past four years sharing a best with Flynn, waking without him was like him dying again, day after day.

When Sienna finally got herself moving, she decided to bake before going to the station. Another two hours survived.

Cookies stowed in her backpack, Sienna was about to leave when her phone beeped.

Miss you lots Sen. Everything is crazy busy at the moment. Wish you were here. Love you so much. Mum & Dad.

No call this week, thought Sienna, shoving her phone in her bag. Her phone conversations with her parents were basically longer versions of that text. The same words of love and desire that had sucked her in as a child. They were the only reason she'd turned her back on her life with Uncle Cole and Aunt Daphne – and they'd turned out to be a lie. Yet still, her heart yearned for a way for them to be true. The only thing that prevented her from regretting her childish belief in those words was that they were the reason she met Flynn.

"Oh good, more cakes and bakes," said Ian sarcastically when he let Sienna into the office.

She ignored him, putting the cookies in the kitchen before settling into the task Uncle Cole had set up for her. It was never very taxing, but it occupied her mind and passed the time – all she sought from life.

"You done?" asked Uncle Cole three hours later. Sienna nodded. "Want me to take you out for a late lunch?"

"Just wanna sleep," said Sienna, yawning. Afternoon naps were another solid part of her routine.

"Hey!" cried Jackson, strolling into the office. "Long time, no see."

Almost a month apart and his smile was as painful as the first time she saw it. Sienna suspected Uncle Cole had been purposely rostering him on the later shifts – or sending him out on jobs.

"I'll make you a coffee," said Jackson.

"Nah, I'm fine," said Sienna, but Jackson was already putting the pod in the machine.

"It's great having you around again, Sen," said Uncle Cole warmly, grabbing a cookie and making an instant coffee.

He didn't use the coffee machine at home either. Sienna bought both of them on the credit card her parents gave her when she started high school. They'd questioned her about the purchase; her explanation of needing decent coffee immediately accepted. Their only concern had been that she'd spent so little – and that was believing she'd only bought one machine for the house.

"Was starting to think I must've really offended you when I didn't see you when I got back," said Jackson, placing their coffees on the table.

"Just coincidence," murmured Sienna.

Uncle Cole glanced at her before walking out.

"You don't really like me, do you?" Jackson sipped his coffee, watching her over the top of the cup.

"No, you're fine. Seem friendly," replied Sienna unconvincingly. Jackson chuckled. "It's just hard – you remind me of someone."

"Your ex?" asked Jackson. Sienna's arm wrapped around her stomach. The accuracy of his guess was sickening. "Aw, sorry. I just broke up with my girlfriend too. Day before New Years'. How's that for a great New Years' Eve?"

"We didn't break up."

Jackson started to ask a question, but cut himself off. "Oh, shit. I'm sorry." There was silence for a moment before he spoke again. "How do I remind you of him?"

"You have the same smile," Sienna squeaked, tears slipping down her cheeks. When she found the courage to look up, Jackson wasn't smiling.

"I know what you're going through," he said kindly, reaching out for her hand.

"I don't even know what I'm going through," snapped Sienna, pulling her hands into her lap.

"So you don't think I understand?"

"I don't know. You might, but I don't. And I don't want to."

"Your parents want to talk," said Uncle Cole, walking into Sienna's bedroom. He never knocked when they were annoying him. Sienna glanced at the phone in his hand. "I told them you were in the shower, but that I would hurry you along."

Sienna pressed her tongue into her teeth and shuffled to the side of her bed. Uncle Cole helped her up, holding her crutches. They still hadn't had a real conversation since she arrived, not like they used to when she was little. Sienna often felt like Uncle Cole stared at her, as if trying to find the person she used to be, but he wouldn't. That girl disappeared six years ago. And the girl she became after that died with Flynn. She didn't know who the girl was who now inhabited her body.

"We need to figure out Sienna's schooling," said Arthur as soon as he picked up the phone. He didn't say hi.

Sienna and Uncle Cole exchanged confused looks. There was only one high school in Fortune.

"We think Sienna should go back to her old school," said Janice. "There's no way she's going to make any useful life connections out there."

"And how is she supposed to get to school there when she lives here?" asked Uncle Cole, his face twisting with disgust.

It made Sienna uncomfortable, like he hated where she came from.

"She can board if she has to," said Arthur.

"Do you want to go back to that school?" asked Uncle Cole angrily, turning on Sienna as though she'd been involved in the ridiculous plan.

"No," replied Sienna petulantly. She'd always hated that school. It was the place that had taken her away from Flynn. He'd been sent to the nearby boys' school, but to them it had felt like separate worlds.

It took longer than it should have for Sienna's parents to give up on the idea of her returning to her old school. Their eventual concession was that she attend the private school in Westloch. It was a suggestion Sienna was much more amenable to.

"Why insist she travel for over two hours a day when there's a perfectly good high school a ten-minute walk away?" cried Uncle Cole.

"I won't leave her education at the mercy of the least qualified teachers in the state," snarled Arthur.

"It wouldn't be any different in Westloch," Sienna sighed wearily.

"Great, so you've infected her with your snobbish attitudes. At least when she lived with me, she was more tolerant, not cloistered from the world in some privileged bubble," said Uncle Cole, throwing his arms in the air and slumping back in his chair.

Sienna turned away and stopped listening. Truth was she'd never rated any teacher very highly, but her opinions had always been a source of conflict; rarely viewed by anyone in her family as more than a personal attack.

The phone abruptly hung up. Sienna's head snapped up, but Uncle Cole wouldn't meet her eye. They just sat in silence. Neither of them were new to this.

"She can go to the local school," said Janice the moment Uncle Cole answered the phone fifteen minutes later. "But it'll be on you if she doesn't live up to her potential."

Uncle Cole looked thoughtfully at Sienna. She waited for his retaliation – to explain how there was no potential to live up to – but he just agreed.

"Fine, but if she's going to the public school, you're going to have to fund it," said Arthur.

"Excuse me?" said Uncle Cole, jumping to his feet, towering over the phone sitting on the coffee table on speaker as though it was Arthur. "That is not the arrangement."

Sienna waited for details on what the arrangement was, but Uncle

Cole grabbed the phone, taking it off speaker as he walked into his bedroom.

Whatever the arrangement, Sienna knew this argument wasn't about it. Her parents hated to lose. So despite being prepared to pay tens of thousands of dollars to send her to her old school, they would quibble over spending a fraction of that just because Uncle Cole got his way.

"Ready?"

Sienna didn't have an answer. Or a uniform. She'd tried to dress plainly, but knew it wouldn't make any difference. New kid. New school. She was going to be noticed.

Uncle Cole had made breakfast for her despite rarely eating at home. Sienna thought it sweet, but when his kindness extended to an offer to drive her to school she suspected an ulterior motive. The soft smile sitting on his lips when she agreed made her feel like she'd eaten guilt for breakfast rather than toast.

"What are you doing?" Sienna asked, when Uncle Cole hopped out of the car with her at the school.

"Coming with you," replied Uncle Cole, surprised. "I know you're used to doing everything alone, but I don't abandon my kid."

No. He walked her right to the office, waiting with her as the secretary dealt with the other lost students.

"Hi, Lisa. How's everything? I just want to enrol my kid," said Uncle Cole's proudly, his arm slipping around Sienna's shoulders, as they stepped up to the counter.

Lisa's eyes roved over Sienna in a strangely maternal way that made Sienna's gaze flick between her and Uncle Cole. Sienna was glad when Lisa handed her forms to fill in. The embarrassed giggling of Lisa and hushed voice of Uncle Cole only heightened Sienna's suspicions. When another student entered the office, they pulled away, their faces overly passive.

"What's that?" asked Uncle Cole, pointing at the forms.

"My name," said Sienna.

"Not out here, it's not. Enrol under Smith."

Sienna tried to explain that she had to enrol under her actual name, but Uncle Cole didn't want to listen.

"But she can put a preferred name. We'll use that name in all her classes. We'll only use her other name for official documentation," said Lisa in a hurried voice, placating Uncle Cole. "Does she need a uniform as well?"

Sienna nodded, dutifully putting her preferred name down as Sienna Smith. It was what she'd been called through most of primary school anyway.

Uncle Cole checked the form before glancing at his watch. "You can handle the rest, can't you?" Sienna nodded. "Good. See you tonight. Have a good day."

"But we need to settle the fees. Pay for the uniform," called Lisa, as Uncle Cole walked towards the door.

"She has the credit card," said Uncle Cole in a tight voice before disappearing.

Sienna handed over the credit card. Lisa smiled, her eyes widening with curiosity as she took in the Hollingsworth name. Sienna doubted it meant anything to her. She'd never met anyone who cared for that name until she moved in with her parents.

"Good. Now we just have to sort out your enrolment," said Lisa cheerily.

Sienna was passed over to the deputy principal. They didn't have her school records from Sydney, which was apparently an issue, but Sienna couldn't understand why. The school was so small that the choice of senior subjects was limited. To appease her parents, she selected legal studies. For her own pleasure, she chose art. It had been the only subject she had come close to doing well in previously. The other selections were a matter of picking the least painful options.

By the time her enrolment was sorted and she'd changed into her uniform, it was recess. Swinging to a quiet section of the schoolyard, Sienna took out her timetable and school map. The last thing she wanted was to get lost. It should not have been possible. The school was tiny compared to her previous high school, but there were stairs to navigate and she didn't want to walk up or down any more than was absolutely necessary.

"That's her."

The whispers started as soon as Sienna arrived outside her English classroom. No one bothered to lower their voices as they discussed who she was. There were some very random guesses, but it didn't take long for their suppositions to slip closer to the mark.

"She's the Chief's daughter. Saw her arriving with him this morning."

"Nah. He doesn't have kids."

"Mistress?"

"Love child."

Everyone giggled.

With every guess, the group had moved in on Sienna and now surrounded her as though she would engage.

"So you really the Chief's daughter?" asked one of the boys, stepping forward, his arms crossed over his chest.

"No," Sienna replied.

"That's not what we heard," said another boy, moving next to the first boy, continuing the process of surrounding her.

It was more comical than threatening, but neither would entice Sienna to spill her guts. "Well you would know."

"See, I told you," hissed one of the girls, causing the boys to take a step back.

"Let me through."

The crowd parted, allowing their teacher to open the classroom door, but as they filed in he spotted Sienna and held her back at his desk. She was mortified when he turned her to face the class and asked her to introduce herself.

"I'm Sienna," she said, deciding against using a surname. She had started to hobble away when her teacher chirpily asked where she'd come from. "Sydney," she replied, still moving towards a desk.

"So what brings you to Fortune?" asked the teacher with a smile.

Sienna could not help but turn and glare at him. "I moved here."

The class laughed. Sienna ignored them and shuffled awkwardly towards a spare desk away from other students. Keeping her head down, she stayed quiet the whole day. She sat away from other students at lunch and kept away from them in class. The sound of the bell at the end of the day was blissful. She was tired and it took her a while to realise that this was the first day since she left the hospital where she had not slept during the day.

Swinging out the school gates, Sienna was caught short by the sight of a police car parked out the front. When Jackson stepped out of the car, she was angrier than if it had been her uncle.

"Chief thought you might be tired," chuckled Jackson.

"He did or you just thought it'd be amusing?" snapped Sienna.

She didn't wait for an answer and ignored Jackson as he trailed the car behind her while she hobbled down the street. It only took a block before he screeched off. Sienna could hear people talking behind her, but determinedly ignored them.

When Sienna finally threw herself on the lounge, she looked at her watch. It took less than five minutes for Uncle Cole to burst into the house.

"Sen? Sienna? You home?"

Sienna didn't move, waiting for Uncle Cole to find her.

"I don't send my people out to do things for you to have their efforts thrown back in their faces. I knew you'd be tired so I sent Jackson to pick you up and give you a lift home."

"In a police car!"

"So? Everyone knows you're my kid. It's not like they're going to think you're under arrest."

"I can walk home," said Sienna firmly.

"So you're embarrassed by me? That it?"

Sienna couldn't answer. Maybe she was, but she was determined not to be transported by police car to and from school.

"I'll take that as a yes," said Uncle Cole, already turning for the door. "That's interesting given I'm the only one who's ever wanted you."

That depressing sentiment was only confirmed by the arrival of a hotel booking – along with airline tickets for Uncle Cole – for her trip to Sydney to remove her cast. The original plan had been for her to stay at home. Without Flynn, the rejection was much harder to handle.

CAST OFF

Uncle Cole sat casually at the dining table. Sienna knew what was coming, but would not give in. Breakfast was cordial, but when he eventually asked if she wanted a lift to school, she found the courage to say no. Uncle Cole stared at her, testing her resolve. If he'd held it much longer, she would've caved.

The slam of the front door jolted Sienna's heart, but she shook it off. She was used to disappointing her family. And with a good night's sleep behind her, that little victory gave her more energy than she was used to. She pushed down the street on her crutches with force and speed that bordered on recklessness.

The achievement of feeling close to alive was too great not to share. Grabbing her phone, Sienna had dialled Flynn's number before reality hit. The sound of it ringing made her want to vomit. Dashing to the bathroom, she was still trying to control the hysterical sobs tearing through her chest when the bell rang.

The day passed slowly. Sienna spoke to no one. No one spoke to her. Comments were made, but she ignored them. People talking behind her back wasn't new either. When the final bell rang, she made her way gratefully to the gate. It shouldn't have surprised her, but the sight of the police car waiting outside made her stagger back in horror.

"I'm not getting in that car," said Sienna, as Jackson got out looking apologetic. "Just tell him you drove me home, okay."

Jackson looked ready to comply. He was getting back in the car when Ian stepped out. Sienna moved back, but Ian grabbed her arm, pulling her off-balance. Another arm wrapped around her waist as she was half-dragged, half-carried to the car. Sienna struggled at the door, but Ian shoved her in. He didn't even sit her up properly, pinning her to the backseat with his body.

"Drive!" Ian yelled at Jackson.

Jackson obeyed, driving quickly, while Ian continued to forcefully restrain Sienna. It took just a couple of minutes to reach the house. Ian pushed Sienna away from him, but she didn't dare move.

"Well, get out," Ian spat, pushing her again.

Sienna tried to, but her legs were tangled. Even her arms were stuck in her crutches. Ian offered no assistance. It was only when Jackson opened the door and untangled her limbs that she could move. Sienna's hands shook so much she couldn't get the key in the front door.

"I'm sorry," said Jackson, pushing open the door for her.

"Please don't come back tomorrow. Just leave me alone," cried Sienna, her voice wavering.

No one was waiting for her the next day, but it didn't matter. The damage was done. The whole grade was talking about her. And after finally realising she wouldn't respond to them talking around her, they started speaking directly to her. They wanted to know what she'd done to get herself hauled off by Ian. Her answer of, "Nothing, just a misunderstanding," was quickly accepted. Sienna wondered how often other people had similar misunderstandings. Only two girls asked her if she was okay. Sienna brushed off their concerns.

"Well I'm Amber and this is Amy. You want to eat with us?"

Sienna nodded. There were about ten kids in their group. Amber introduced them, but Sienna could barely keep up. She learned Jono's name first. He asked the most questions and was never put off by her short answers.

It quickly became clear that Uncle Cole was the most interesting part of her life. They skirted around the topic for a while, clearly hoping she'd spill the beans, before eventually coming out and asking what their relationship was.

"He's my uncle," replied Sienna.

"Then why's he telling everyone you're his kid?" asked Liam. "It's what everyone in town thinks."

Now Sienna felt even guiltier. Uncle Cole was claiming her publicly even though everyone knew the trouble she'd been in. It was such a contrast to her parents. Many of their acquaintances never realised they had a daughter.

"I've lived most of my life with my uncle," said Sienna. "So it's kinda true."

"But aren't your parents like super rich?" asked Jono.

Sienna raised her eyebrows and turned away. Amber jumped in and asked a question about their history homework, sparing Sienna further interrogation, but not for long. Now that she had opened up, and with someone from the group in each of her classes, there were always questions being slipped into the conversation. But Sienna had always been good at keeping things to herself.

"How you settling in at school?" asked Uncle Cole casually one night. He hadn't joined Sienna for dinner, but she sat down with him in the lounge room, examining her homework while he watched television.

"It's okay," shrugged Sienna, dumping her maths textbook back in her bag. "As good as school gets, I s'pose."

Uncle Cole nodded thoughtfully. "Made any friends?"

"Don't know about friends," said Sienna. "Just sitting with a group."

"That's good. Who're the kids?"

"I dunno," replied Sienna.

"You don't know their names?" asked Uncle Cole sceptically.

"Some first names. Amber. Jono. Liam. I don't know. Seriously. I'm terrible at names."

"I want to know who your friends are, Sen," said Uncle Cole firmly. "I'm not having you hanging around with delinquents. There're still too many kids in this town that know nothing but trouble and I don't want you being friends with them. You've already caused enough problems associating with people like that."

Sienna was grateful that her trip to Sydney came about before Uncle Cole could do too much digging into her limited social life. When they boarded the flight, she was even more thankful that he had insisted on accompanying her. It didn't matter that they hardly spoke. Just the way he squeezed her hand as the plane jetted down the runway or pointed out non-existent patterns in the ceiling as they landed made all the difference. It even helped dispel her annoyance at his refusal to pay for the taxi from the airport to the hotel. This trip was organised by her parents, he argued. If he'd had his way, she would've had her cast removed in Westloch.

While Sienna agreed with the sentiment, it still felt rude. Her parents had booked them into a beautiful suite overlooking Manly beach. It was a lovely, but painful, gesture. Perhaps they'd seen the photos she had taken there. The photos of Flynn she'd taken there.

Maybe they thought it would comfort her. They just didn't know her well enough to know better.

"You have a message, Ms Hollingsworth," said the man at the check-in desk.

Uncle Cole scowled, but said nothing. Sienna took the piece of paper. She didn't recognise the writing.

Dear Sen, hope you like the room. Wanted you to wake up somewhere nice while you were here.

Love Mum and Dad

Sienna felt like scrunching up the paper. For all she knew they had outsourced the task of writing the note. Maybe someone else even made the call to the hotel. Holding on to the paper, Sienna let the words travel through her, wishing for a way for them to be real. She wanted her parents to love her as much in practice as they did in theory. They could always say the right things to the right people, but it never extended to being there when she needed them.

Only Uncle Cole was at the hospital with her. Only he would give up that many hours. Most of it was spent waiting. Waiting for x-rays. Waiting for the doctor to examine the x-rays. Waiting for someone to tell them her cast could come off. Waiting for someone else to cut it off. But when they started, Sienna wished they had waited longer. The sound of the saw triggered something in her mind. There were no images, just emotions. Feelings she couldn't come close to describing were suddenly shuddering her body and spasming her lungs.

"Look at that bench over there, the one with all the instruments," said Uncle Cole, his voice tinted with fascination. "I was thinking how cold and clinical it was, but there's a story there – thousands of them. I was trying to work out how I'd capture that."

Sienna felt like she was betraying Flynn taking the bait, but she didn't want to break down in front of hospital staff. The scene was uninspiring. She couldn't think of an image she'd less like to capture. They discussed the harshness of the light and the coldness of the scene, how they could change it to make something worth drawing. Before they had found the solution, the cast was off and they were free to go and wait in another room.

Sienna slipped off the table and almost collapsed. It was like she didn't remember how to walk. Uncle Cole had to keep an arm around her to hold her steady. He was encouraging and joking as she walked unsteadily to her specialist appointment.

"Come on in, Sienna," said Dr Wells, forty minutes later.

Uncle Cole insisted on being in the room during the consultation. Sienna would've preferred he stayed outside, not wanting him to know anything more about the accident, but when Dr Wells asked her to strip for a physical examination, she was suddenly thankful for his presence. With a squeeze of her hand, he stood with his back to the curtain, acting like her personal security guard.

The examination was more painful than Sienna expected. Her ribs were still tender and her leg didn't feel like it belonged to her body. Dr Wells seemed to have a checklist of spots to probe, each making Sienna wince, yet when she was allowed to dress he assured her everything was healing well.

"You're a very lucky girl," said Dr Wells gravely, helping her off the examination table and into a chair. "It could've been a lot worse. You'll need to strengthen your leg, but take it slow. Build it up. I'll give you exercises. Make sure you do them or you'll risk permanent injury."

Sienna nodded, but didn't look up. She was barely even listening. She was waiting for Dr Wells to ask her about the accident. His daughter had been in the same grade as her. She might've been dating Ashton. It was only chance that Keisha wasn't with them that night. Sienna wondered if Dr Wells knew that and if Keisha was struggling to survive as well.

"We'll schedule a follow-up for three months," said Dr Wells, remaining unwaveringly professional. "We need to make sure that leg heals properly."

"She can't go traipsing back and forth to Sydney every few months," said Uncle Cole. "Is this really necessary?"

"Yes," answered Dr Wells firmly, turning to Uncle Cole, his back ramrod straight. "Sienna suffered very severe injuries. It's a miracle she survived at all. After three lots of surgery follow-up is required."

"By you?" asked Uncle Cole, leaning forward in his seat. "Sienna lives five hours away now. It'd make much more sense to have her treated locally. Surely you can arrange to have her care transferred to a doctor in Westloch."

Dr Wells looked uncomfortable as he measured Uncle Cole's stern gaze. There was no reason for him to refuse, so Sienna knew his hesitation was related to some demand her parents had made of him.

When the silence continued, Dr Wells gave in.

By the time they made it back to the hotel, Sienna was dead on her feet. Uncle Cole helped her into bed, her eyes struggling to stay open.

"I was going to go over to the beach for a swim," said Uncle Cole, stroking her hair. "Want to join me?" Sienna shook her head. Even if she'd been full of energy, she wouldn't have been able to face it. Perhaps Uncle Cole understood as nodded. "Want me to stay?"

"And be bored watching me sleep? No, you should go."

Uncle Cole kissed her head. Sienna was sure she was asleep before he left the room.

"I don't know why she didn't call you back. Maybe she doesn't want to speak to you."

Sienna blinked sleepily. Disorientated by the darkness of the room, she stumbled clumsily out of bed and opened the curtains. Light glittered through the window, prickling her into greater consciousness.

"No, she doesn't want to see you. I thought you'd realise that by now," snapped Uncle Cole. "Money won't buy you everything."

He must be speaking to her parents. The words gathered more coherently in Sienna's brain. She reached for her phone. There was no missed call. Now they lie about calling her and make out that she's the one who didn't want to speak to them. Sienna was about to throw the phone back in her bag when she saw the message. She had voicemail. Great. Now technology was conspiring to make her look like a terrible daughter.

"Hi, Sen. Just wanted to see how the appointment went and if everything has healed properly," said Arthur's voice. "Your mum and I would love to meet you and your uncle for dinner tonight. Give us a call when you get the message."

Sighing, knowing how annoyed her parents would be, Sienna rang her father but it went straight through to message bank. Uncle Cole was still yelling.

"Mum!" Sienna cried, as soon as Janice picked up the phone. "I'm sorry. I swear. My phone didn't ring. It went straight to message bank. I only just saw the message."

"Sienna, what? Why are you so frantic?" asked Janice.

"I missed Dad's call," replied Sienna.

Everything went silent. Janice started speaking just as Uncle Cole burst into the room.

"Who are you talking to?" he asked.

"Mum," replied Sienna weakly. "I missed Dad's call."

Uncle Cole glared at her. He would think she was caving.

"You still there, Sen?" asked Janice. Sienna just managed a reply, her eyes never leaving Uncle Cole. "Can we meet for dinner? We'll pick you up. Say about seven-thirty."

There was no right answer, but her parents had paid a lot of money for this trip. She owed them one dinner. "Sounds good," she answered meekly.

Uncle Cole threw up his hands in disgust. His tirade was the same as always. They didn't care. They didn't love her. They thought they could buy her off and pretend it was love. He was determined not to go. But when seven-thirty arrived, he was dressed and ready. He even roused his mood, though as they went down in the lift to the lobby she saw the strain in his eyes.

Arthur and Janice smiled as they approached, though there was something closer to disgust in their eyes when they looked at Uncle Cole. It made Sienna step in closer to him. When Arthur and Janice tried to hug her, she felt like she was being strangled by an octopus, Uncle Cole refusing to release his grip on her waist.

Dinner was awkward. Sienna was too scared to talk, fearing anything she said would start a fight. But where her answers were short, Uncle Cole's were full. He gave such a rosy account of their life in Fortune that she started to doubt her own experiences. Maybe she'd been unfairly hard on Uncle Cole, her feelings tainted by the bitterness of her continued existence.

"Well it sounds like you made the right choice moving out to Fortune," said Janice stiffly.

Sienna focused on her food rather than respond to the blatant lie her mother spoke. They had sent her to Fortune. She'd never had a say. Same as always. Uncle Cole must've understood because his arm was soon around her shoulders, squeezing her gently. When he dared to profess how happy he was to have back, dinner descended into a strange contest between him and her parents, each of them trying to prove how much they loved her. Yet rarely did any of them look her way.

"I'm sorry you didn't have a very good trip," said Uncle Cole, as they arrived home. "How about we go out to dinner tonight. Just you and me. We can celebrate you walking again."

"Yeah?" asked Sienna. "I saw a Vietnamese place in Westloch."

"I was thinking the pub." Sienna slumped in disappointment. "Oh, right, I remember, my type of food isn't good enough for your refined tastebuds."

"No, it's not – I'd really like that," replied Sienna hurriedly.

Uncle Cole was appeased, but only just.

"See, this is nice," said Uncle Cole, as they waited for their food. "You don't have to cook all the time."

"It's a good skill," replied Sienna, trying not to argue. He would only take it personally. Even the sight of her salad seemed to upset him, muttering that steak wasn't unhealthy and even served in a lot of expensive restaurants.

Uncle Cole ate quickly. When he noticed Ryan at the bar, he dashed off with a promise to return soon, but Sienna could see him being cornered every time he took a step her way.

"Hey! Can I join you?"

Sienna looked up to see Jackson standing next to her table. His smile faltered as she stared at him. It hurt to look, but Sienna forced herself to. She needed to confront Flynn's smile. Her punishment. The constant reminder of all she didn't have to live for.

"Got two legs again." Jackson pointed at her legs.

Sienna nodded and Jackson sat down, obviously taking her yes to apply to his earlier question as well.

"What are you doing here?" Sienna asked, trying to be polite.

"It's kinda compulsory. Have to make a showing to be part of the team. Just like Friday nights at your place." Sienna was thrown. She knew he, Ryan and Ian all came over every so often, but hadn't realised it was always on a Friday night. "But you being here gets me away from them for a while."

"Why do you need to get away from them?" asked Sienna, looking back towards the bar.

Jackson looked like a child who'd said too much, laughing and rambling in an incoherent manner, as he ruffled his hair. "You look tired," he said suddenly. "Want me to walk you home?"

"Get me out of here and I'll love you forever."

Jackson smiled broadly and Sienna hoped he hadn't taken her statement the wrong way. He might have been the nicest person she'd met in Fortune, but that meant nothing. Possessing Flynn's smile would never be enough. Until he could be Flynn, she could never look at him that way.

~6~

FORWARD MARCH

It surprised Sienna how little changed with the removal of her cast. As her last outward link to the accident, she felt like more of her pain should've disappeared with it. All she was left with was a festering darkness brewing within her. It was heavy and made even the simplest tasks demanding. School was the only place she didn't feel quite so burdened. She started to find her place in the group, spending most of her time with Karina and Liam, as they shared the most classes. But the big group meant Sienna didn't have to commit too much of herself to any one person. If Karina was away, it was easy to sit with Amber and Amy. When conversation got too personal, she was able to pretend she was talking to someone else in the group.

The group also helped fill the endless hours after school. Someone was always doing something. Sienna never cared who or what. But hanging out in public allowed Uncle Cole to find out exactly who her friends were. It was no surprise when he objected to some of them. Liam's brother was in gaol on drug offences and the police were always being called out to Amy's place because of her drunkard father, or busting up the parties Sam's brothers organised.

"What do you want me to do about it?" asked Sienna.

"Find better friends," demanded Uncle Cole.

"But they're part of the group. I can't avoid them."

"No kid of mine's hanging out with delinquents like that."

"But it's not even them. And don't you think most of the other parents will think your kid's the real delinquent?"

"You come straight home after school and you don't go anywhere on the weekends without telling me where you're going, who you're going with, how long you're going for. And I say you can go. I brought you here to straighten you out, not to have you end up in front a magistrate. You never behaved like this before."

"Because I was a little kid! I'm sixteen now. I'm not going to sit at home by myself and play dolls. I deserve some freedom."

"When you've earned my trust, then I'll give you some freedom, but while you're hanging out with people like that, I can't trust you."

"What possible trouble could we get into in this town? There's nothing to do! We don't even have cars."

"As I recall, that's never stopped you and your friends before."

Sienna gasped, her lungs trying to suck in air as her throat constricted. Visions she'd been getting better at blocking out burst in front of her eyes, forcing her to her room.

"You coming down to the river this afternoon?" asked Liam. "I'll keep teaching you to play guitar."

Liam confident smile faltered slightly. Amy started coughing, breaking his gaze. Sienna felt sick. Amy had suggested the week before that he had a crush on her. It didn't matter that Liam was sweet and cute. Her whole body was repulsed by the idea of him touching her.

"I can't. I'm not allowed to go out after school any more," said Sienna.

"Why?" cried everyone simultaneously.

Sienna could only shrug. She couldn't possibly tell them the truth. It surprised her when they kept talking about how unfair her situation was. Sympathy wasn't something she'd ever received before. Most people assumed she had an easy life because her parents were rich. Even her family felt the need to constantly tell her how well off she was.

When Sienna moved in with her parents, they mistook her tears as her mourning her carefree lifestyle, never realising Uncle Cole had often been stricter than them and that he always followed through on his punishments. They took her shock at what other kids at her new school had for jealousy, so cut back what they gave her so she could appreciate what she had – yet they never took anything from Stephen.

Trudging home, Sienna's eye was caught by the overflowing letterbox. They never got much mail, so she was shocked to see her name on the large envelope. There was no return address and the postage stamp was smudged. She was about to open it when her phone rang.

"We need to talk about your credit card," her father said sternly.

There was another sigh. A conference call. This had to be bad. "Log in. I want to go through all of it."

Sienna made her way to her desk in silence. Her parents huffed in an agitated manner, but there was no point explaining how much slower the internet was in Fortune.

"Okay. I'm in," said Sienna, holding in her own sigh.

"We didn't think you'd be the one to exploit this," said Arthur. "I really can't see what there'd be in Fortune to spend so much money on. Let's start back a couple of weeks ago, what's that fifty-dollar charge at, what, the take-away store? And all those transactions at the supermarket — every two days."

"It's food. Groceries," said Sienna, trying not to sound sarcastic.

"Aren't there any in the house?" asked Janice.

"Not unless I buy them," replied Sienna defensively. "Stuff's more expensive here."

"What about your uncle?" asked Janice. "Is he eating this food?"

"No, it's just for me. I don't have to shop as much now cos I can carry more back, but when I was on the crutches, it was hard."

"Why aren't you eating what your uncle eats?" asked Arthur, his voice terse but a little less angry.

"I don't like it. I'm sorry. He did offer to bring me home dinner every night, but I don't like it."

"Bring?" asked Janice. "What do you mean?"

"He doesn't like eating at home," sighed Sienna.

"Fine, then what about the other stuff?" asked Arthur, giving up that point much quicker than she expected. "I know you're probably trying to make friends, but what are you doing? Buying for everyone."

"It's not like that. I need cash," cried Sienna. "I'm not going to take a cash advance off a credit card, am I? When I get low, I offer to put our drinks or something on the card and they give me cash. What else am I supposed to do?"

"What about your allowance?" asked Arthur.

"What allowance?" asked Sienna. Her parents must be on crack. "I've never had an allowance in my life."

"Is it worth asking about when you were living in Sydney with your uncle?" asked Janice.

"Depends on what you want the answer to be," retorted Sienna.

"Well at least you haven't been touching your savings account," sighed Arthur heavily.

"What savings account? I don't even have a bank account," muttered Sienna.

"Yes, you do," replied Janice. "We set it up for you when you were a child. A savings account for when you turn eighteen and your everyday account."

Sienna let her head drop on to her arms. Her parents were having a whispered argument, but it was clear they were laying the blame with Uncle Cole.

"Sen, you still there?" asked Janice. "Sorry, we should've worked this all out a long time ago. Can you please just swear that you've never had another bank account."

"Can't I just get a job?" asked Sienna. "Then we don't have to do all this. I can pay for it all myself. You shouldn't have to pay for me anyway. I don't even live with you. I'm nothing to you."

"You're our daughter! That's what you are to us," snapped Janice. "Listen, we'll sort this out."

"I don't even know what we're sorting out!" cried Sienna. "Just let me get a job. Then there'll be nothing to sort out."

"We want you to focus on school. You've got the rest of your life to work," said Arthur firmly. "We're going to set you up a bank account, probably a joint account. We can fix it up properly when you're here. We'll put a weekly allowance in that and you can use it for what you need. Then just use the credit card for emergencies. Is that okay?"

"Please, just let me get a job," said Sienna.

"Maybe just don't tell your uncle about this, okay," added Janice, ignoring everything Sienna said.

Collapsing on her bed, Sienna's hand fell on the large envelope. She picked it up with little curiosity. Probably more instructions from her parents, and she couldn't work out why she hadn't realised that before.

Pulling out the contents, Sienna almost choked. Her body recoiled, hand over her mouth. She kept staring at the photo. It was sickening, yet entrancing, forcing her to look. Her fingers reached out to the image, though not daring to touch it. By the time her mind was able to fully comprehend the sight of Flynn's body lying sprawled in a pool of blood across the bonnet of his car, she was rushing to the toilet.

The vomiting didn't stop when the food ran out. Sienna was sure her body was trying to expel its blood the way Flynn's body had his. By the end of it she could do nothing more than lie with her head across the toilet bowl, her body empty of everything but life.

When Sienna eventually staggered back to her bedroom, she kept her eyes closed, turning the photos upside down and shoving them into the envelope. She was still gasping for air when she realised there was a note. It was typed.

Even the lucky ones need to face the consequences of their actions.

It took a while for Sienna to realise she was shaking. Her arms wrapped around her chest as she tried to hold herself together, wondering who thought she'd been cruising through the aftermath of that night too easily. Both her parents and Uncle Cole had the contacts to do it. And the will. But there were others too. Four families had been destroyed that night. And they all blamed her. They were connected enough to acquire crime scene photos. Or perhaps it was some rogue cop. The ones who had tried to pull them over and believed she should have died too.

Whoever it was, they achieved their aim. Nothing could remove that image from Sienna's mind. She tried reading, but the words always formed into the shape of Flynn's broken body. When she cooked dinner all she could taste was blood. Even when she finally fell asleep, the image came back to haunt her.

Determined to prove her memory of the photo was worse than the reality, Sienna pulled them back out of the envelope. There were ten in all and helped fill the void of ignorance that had swallowed everything after the first hit.

Ashton's arm had been flung through the open front passenger-side window, his head smashing through the windscreen. Blood smeared the windscreen and bonnet from the deep cuts in his neck that had nearly severed his head. James was thrown through the back passenger-side window before being pinned between the car and a telegraph pole. Myra had been tossed around the car, her contorted body coming to rest across Sienna's broken leg, her head lying on Ashton's seat.

The last two photos were of Sienna. She was the only one still in her seat. The only one who'd been wearing her seatbelt. It was what saved her life after their car first hit the car that pulled out in front of them before being catapulted into the air and then two parked cars. They only came to rest when they hit the telegraph pole.

No one realised Sienna had survived until half an hour after the crash when her fingers had twitched. They had taken those photos assuming she was dead.

Sienna forced herself to look over the photos every day, though for most it was just a cursory glance. The only ones that held her gaze were those of Flynn. His body had the physical appearance of him, but it wasn't him. Not really. Whether it was his soul or something else that disappeared, leaving behind only his lifeless body, was a mystery. All Sienna knew was that it wasn't the Flynn she'd loved. Not all of him anyway.

Sitting on the lounge, Sienna spread the photos out on the coffee table. Uncle Cole wasn't due home for hours. He'd picked her up from school after she'd been sent home for looking so ill. Since receiving the photos, she'd lost three kilos and been sent home four times.

A knock at the front door made Sienna flinch. She didn't move, knowing it would stop if she ignored it, but trying to stay quiet caused the pain to build up inside her. When the knocking finally stopped, sobs of agony burst from her chest, as her fingers traced Flynn's broken, lifeless body.

"Sienna? Are you – oh my God! What are – how'd you get these?"

The photos were snatched out of Sienna's hands. It was only then she realised Jackson was in the room. She felt horribly exposed and was not comforted by his embrace. She waited for the inevitable questioning, but he stayed silent. He just held her tight, his chin resting on her head.

"I came by to see if you were feeling any better," he said, when she stopped crying. "And I broke up with my girlfriend."

"But that was ages ago," replied Sienna, annoyed at herself for speaking, and pushed away from his embrace.

"The one after that." Jackson's smile faltered slightly as he lounged back, though his eyes watched her intently.

"Can't believe you managed to find another one so quickly. In this town, I mean," Sienna added, then regretted not having the courage to be rude when Jackson smirked in response.

"The Chief doesn't finish til nine and he and Ryan are planning to go to the pub after their shift. Want me to stick around? I've got a movie." Sienna nodded slowly. "You hungry?"

Sienna shook her head and Jackson gave her a guilty look. "You are?" she asked, her voice just above a whisper.

Jackson nodded enthusiastically, jumping from the lounge and holding out his hand.

It was impressive the way Jackson was able to make a tolerable dinner out of what was in the house.

"Just eat what you can," he said, sitting back on the lounge.

Sienna argued that they couldn't eat in the lounge room. Uncle Cole would flip if he found out, but Jackson was adamant no one would ever know and if they didn't start the movie they wouldn't finish it before Uncle Cole got home.

The movie selection didn't thrill Sienna. She'd been hoping for some kind of action movie. Anything but a romance. It wasn't long before her tears returned. She reached out for the photos that Jackson had placed upside-down on the table. Jackson grabbed her, his hold not one of comfort.

"Don't think of him like that. He was more than that. Don't ever think of him that way," he said, as Sienna struggled against him. But it was too late. She'd already lost those other images of Flynn. "Where'd you get them?" Sienna didn't answer. "You steal them?" She shook her head. "Given them?" Sienna nodded. Jackson sighed. His hold slowly loosened as her body relaxed, but he watched her closely as they shifted back to the opposite ends of the lounge.

"This is really horrible," said Sienna, turning away to avoid crying again. "Why would you want to watch this?"

"Well, if she'd started crying – which she would have – then I would've had to comfort her."

"Like you did me?"

Sienna turned slightly so she could see Jackson's face. He smiled like an indulgent big brother – a smile she'd never received from Stephen. "No, not quite like that."

"Oh. That really work?"

"Like clockwork." Jackson's hands swept proudly back, interlocking behind his head

Sienna found herself smiling at Jackson's claim. It felt alien. "So what happened tonight?" she asked, suddenly feeling like a very poor consolation prize.

"The Chief. Was in a terrible mood. Didn't let me leave early – well, on time, really. Usually does," Jackson added. "So I was late and she was mad. I tried to make it up to her, but I think maybe she saw through my cunning plan."

"I should probably get to bed. You know, school night and all."

Jackson smiled and nodded. Sienna reached out for the photos, but he snatched them off her and shook his head.

"They're mine," said Sienna, holding out her hand.

"You should never have seen these. They're crime scene photos."

"They were given to me."

"By who? Some cop who thought you got off too easy?" asked Jackson. Sienna couldn't answer. She really didn't know. "These – no. They should never have been given to you. I won't let you stare at the mangled corpse of your boyfriend. I'm sorry he's gone and I know it hurts, but this won't help." Sienna wanted to ask if he was going to tell Uncle Cole about the photos. "I'll lock up when I go," said Jackson, his face full of concern. "You don't have any more, do you?" Sienna shook her head, but could see the doubt in his eyes. "You can call me if you need me, okay. I know what it's like being all alone out here."

With the photos gone, Sienna found herself slowly emerging from their horrific haze. More rational thoughts started to flow through her mind. The first realisation sent her to the shops and into the kitchen. A lack of baked sweets might not have caused Uncle Cole's recent bad moods, but she'd done nothing to bring him out of them.

The cake disappeared so swiftly Sienna was soon back at the shops. Wandering down the aisles, wondering what else she could bake to keep Uncle Cole onside, it took a while for her to notice Liam, Karina and Jono sauntering towards her in an overly causal manner.

"If you can't hang out with us, we decided we'd hang out with you," smiled Liam.

In the supermarket. The only place she was allowed to go by herself. Sienna smiled in spite of herself. They walked around the store several times, up and down every aisle, joking and laughing as she slowly filled her trolley. It wasn't until she saw the unimpressed faces of the staff that she insisted they leave.

"You want me to help carry this home?" asked Liam.

"I'm really not allowed to hang out," replied Sienna.

"You won't be. I'll catch up with Karina and Jono after. You'll just be walking down the street with me. That can't be against the rules."

Sienna didn't want to admit the truth, so shrugged and let Liam take half the bags from her hands. It was reckless. The chance of being seen was high, but that wasn't what worried Sienna. It was the way Liam smiled at her and walked so close they kept bumping into each other. It was the way she wanted him to.

"Is he really that strict?" asked Liam, when Sienna suggested it was best he didn't come in. "What's he gunna do if you hang with us?"

"Tell me I can't. Yell at me," said Sienna.

"Yeah, but isn't he doing that already?" asked Liam with a cocky grin. It was a relief not to see Flynn on his lips. "Come on, can't be worse than this. Holidays are coming up. You gotta get out of the house. Sam's having a big party at his place."

"Me coming to that would only get it shut down in like five seconds flat. No joke."

"Okay, well don't come to that then," laughed Liam. "Is he really against you hanging out with us?" Sienna grimaced. "Just some of us, huh. Me?" Sienna nodded tentatively. Liam laughed loudly. "You realise you're the only one out of all of us who's been in trouble with the cops, right?"

"He got really pissed when I pointed that out," smiled Sienna.

"We don't care about any of that," said Liam sincerely, his hand reaching out to tuck a lock of her hair behind her ear.

Sienna's heart almost stopped. Her stomach flipped with revulsion, but there was a hint of desire there too. "I don't care about any of that stuff either," she replied breathlessly.

"I know," smiled Liam, his fingers brushing hers as they returned to his side. "You're pretty cool for a rich, white, city chick."

Sienna pulled back, before trying to hide her shock. Of course, she knew Liam was Aboriginal. Half their group was. But his comment made her reconsider everything she'd thought about him and if she attributed any of his qualities directly to his race. Perhaps she had, but not consciously. She would never have dreamed of saying such a thing, because with that one line he'd just divided her from him in every way.

Rich to his poor. White to his black. City to his country. It made her feel like an outsider not just a newcomer.

"It's a compliment," laughed Liam, as Sienna silently processed his remark. "I'll see you next week, okay."

"You don't have any leftovers, do you? I'm starving."

Jackson didn't wait for an answer, peering into the big bowl of salad Sienna had made for her dinner.

"Haven't eaten yet, but there's plenty," Sienna answered. She knew Uncle Cole was in the kitchen too; Ian and Ryan in the lounge room setting up for their usual Friday night. "You want some too? I can make enough for everyone."

"I don't think your parents will view that as an appropriate use of their money," said Uncle Cole, moving around Sienna to retrieve glasses from the cupboard. "We're going to order pizza."

Jackson didn't join Uncle Cole in the lounge room, defiantly grabbing two plates and splitting the salad. When Sienna offered him a bread roll, he immediately accepted, putting their plates on the dining table and grabbing the butter from the fridge.

"Aren't you going to go in with them?" asked Sienna.

"Not supposed to eat in the lounge room, remember," replied Jackson, sitting himself at the dining table. "I mean, unless you join me."

"No thanks."

"Yeah, not exactly my idea of a top Friday night either," whispered Jackson, checking behind him as Sienna sat down. "Wouldn't be here if my career didn't rely on it. Need to find another girlfriend. It's the only excuse they'll accept for not hanging out with them all the time. Don't know how Ian and Ryan's wives put up with it. They're never home. And the Chief's like some kind of permanent bachelor."

"You don't think he sees anyone?" asked Sienna, trying to sound nonchalant, as she raised her eyes but kept her head bowed.

Jackson smiled broadly. "It's not worth my job to answer that."

"Can I ask you another one?"

"As long as it doesn't relate to the Chief's sex life," smiled Jackson cheekily. Sienna's heart pierced at the sight.

"Um, you – after you broke up with your girlfriend, you – how long? I mean, you go out with her for a while?"

"Three years," replied Jackson seriously, forking his salad.

"But then you just went out with someone else. Did you like her? I mean, how long before you can like —"

One of Jackson's hand was immediately around Sienna's, his other wiping her cheek. She hadn't realised she was crying.

"There's no answer to that question. You're allowed to move on," said Jackson. Sienna slowly shook her head. "You think Flynn would've wanted you to be unhappy? To mourn for him for the rest of your life?"

Sienna honestly didn't know. All she wanted in the world was to be with Flynn. The idea of him meeting someone else, wherever he was, made her sick.

"Is this about Liam?" asked Jackson, his arm now around Sienna's shaking shoulders. Sienna's eyes snapped up. "These streets have eyes, remember. And I know his brother. Liam talks about you a lot."

"I thought his brother was in gaol."

"He has another one," replied Jackson harshly, pulling back and resuming eating. "So what happened? You kiss him or something?"

"No!" cried Sienna angrily, slouching back and crossing her arms. "I just – he touched – my hair – he touched my hair and I felt something."

Jackson was trying not to laugh. "You felt something?" he finally asked. Sienna nodded, her eyes down. "And that's why you're so upset?" She nodded again. "Aw, you're the sweetest girl ever."

Jackson got down on his knees and hugged Sienna, arms and all.

"Ah-hem."

Sienna jumped and Jackson sat slowly back in his seat with a look of mild disgust.

"Chief sent me to see what happened to you," said Ian.

"We're just having dinner," Jackson answered in the unfriendliest voice Sienna had ever heard him use. It seemed unnatural for someone who was perpetually smiling.

"Yes, I can see that," said Ian, before turning and leaving.

"You want to go for a walk?" Jackson asked, before Sienna could speak.

"Maybe you should —"

"No, screw this crap. I hate it."

Sienna grabbed her jacket, but suggested she ask her uncle. Jackson seemed unimpressed by her need to ask.

"Where're you going?" asked Uncle Cole, not even looking away from the television.

"Jackson and I were just going to go for a walk," answered Sienna, already knowing it was a lost cause. Ian was smirking and Ryan looked grave. Uncle Cole stared intently at the television.

"I think you should clean up the mess in the kitchen then go to bed. Jackson has plans for tonight. It's rude of you to hijack them," said Uncle Cole in a firm voice, never turning away from the television.

Jackson opened his mouth, but Sienna shook her head. She returned to the kitchen and started washing up.

"She was upset! I was just being nice," cried Jackson.

"I'm telling you this for your own good. Stay away from her. That sweet and innocent act is just that. An act," snapped Uncle Cole. "She's so used to getting her own way that she walks in here expecting me to say yes to everything. She needs to learn that everything she wants isn't just going to be handed to her on a platter like it was for the past six years."

Curled up on her bed, Sienna was surprised by her lack of tears. Even holding her photo of Flynn didn't produce the usual sobs of despair. She felt hollow, like the darkness that had been lurking within her had started to spread, gouging out her insides as it went along.

"You're not to be friends with Jackson Halley," Uncle Cole commanded the next morning.

"Is there anyone in this town I am allowed to be friends with?" Sienna asked, defiantly crossing her arms as she turned from the toaster to face him.

"He's a good cop. Being associated with someone like you is only going to get him in trouble. I didn't bring you out here to inflict you on other people. You need to learn respect. You need to learn your place."

"And where is my place?"

"Certainly not as the princess your parents made you. You've got a lot of work to do just proving you belong in society. All you've done for the past six years is disrespect laws. Just because you've always gotten away with it doesn't mean you always will. I'll charge you as surely as I would anyone else. I'm here to set an example. You need to be that example.

"Now you stay away from Jackson. You come straight home after school and you don't lurk around the supermarket like a delinquent. You want this magical dream of being a lawyer, then you'd better start studying, because I assure you, it's not going to happen the way you're going."

That was one point Sienna couldn't refute. No one got into law without hard work and she'd only studied when she had Flynn around to help her. She always got things when he explained them – except maths – that was beyond even his brilliance. But now it was just her, she wanted to give up within a minute. Reading was slow, but she usually got it by the third time. It was trying to put her thoughts into words she struggled with. If she could've drawn her answers, she was sure she would've been okay.

That was how Uncle Cole and Aunt Daphne had taught her to communicate as a child when words had failed her. She learnt nearly every medium through them – drawing, painting, photography, even pottering – but few people beyond them had ever appreciated those works. And they certainly wouldn't help her now. Just thinking about picking up a pencil brought forth a rush of images from that night, demanding to be immortalised.

The weekend of study left Sienna unprepared for her complete failing in class on Monday. Understanding what they'd done last week didn't allow her to learn the new stuff and write at the same time.

"Hang with us this afternoon," said Liam, as they walked towards the school gates at the end of the day. "C'mon. You'll have fun. Chief's gunna yell at you anyway. Make it worth your while."

Sienna instantly agreed. It was only when Liam smiled that she remembered why she should've thought to say no.

They hung out by the river. Sienna kept a constant eye on her watch, only daring to stay an hour; the threat of conflict quickly overwhelming her daringness. She didn't even have an excuse for not being home on time, but it wouldn't have mattered. The house was empty, and when Uncle Cole arrived home he said nothing about her afternoon activities.

Sienna tested her luck again the next day with the same result. Each day, she became a little more daring, finally deciding that if Uncle Cole caught her, she'd claim they were studying.

When the last week of term rolled in, Sienna gave up all pretence. She stayed out so long she was often one of the last to leave; her newly acquired study habits falling by the wayside.

The last day of term was unseasonably warm. Everyone was restless for the end of the day. They were planning to head down to the river. A few of the kids were even talking about swimming. Jono and Sam arrived later than the others and in a very buoyant mood.

"Something refreshing to celebrate," said Jono, pulling a can of beer out of a plastic bag as he plonked down on the grass with the rest of the group.

Cheers erupted as hands lunged into the bags. Only Sienna and Amy didn't drink.

Liam had his guitar and insisted Sienna sit with him while he played. He was good and Sienna loved watching his fingers flit across the strings. Sometimes he played a tune in the background, giving their conversation a playful melody. Other times it became a group sing-a-long that only became rowdier as the sun slid lower in the sky.

"Hey!" cried Sienna, when someone suddenly grabbed her arm. She would've guessed it was Jono, but the sight of Ian yanking her to her feet was much worse.

Ryan confiscated the alcohol and ordered everyone to disperse. Liam jumped up and shoved Ian, but it wasn't enough to loosen his grip. Sienna tried to pull away, but Ian responded by dragging her towards the police car. Liam and Amber were chasing them, hurling abuse. Sienna scrambled to regain her feet, but couldn't, and had no way of resisting Ian throwing her in the car.

"Move on or I'll arrest all of you!" cried Ryan, as they clambered around the car, cursing and swearing.

Ian forced the seatbelt across Sienna's body, but it didn't stop him physically restraining her as Ryan drove. Sienna tried not to be intimidated, but it was difficult. Ian was being deliberately cruel, holding her tight and smiling menacingly. When they reached the police station, he again dragged her, refusing to let her find her feet. It was only when they reached Uncle Cole's office that Ryan stood her upright.

Uncle Cole appeared genuinely surprised by her arrival. When Ryan explained where they'd found her, Uncle Cole's eyes narrowed in fury. Perhaps he really had no idea what she'd been doing after school.

"I thought I explained to you about having to be an example in this town!" he cried.

"I haven't done anything wrong," said Sienna. "I was just sitting by the river. There's no law against that. Not even a rule."

Anger flared in Uncle Cole's eyes. "There're laws against underage drinking."

"I wasn't drinking. Breath test me if you want." Sienna leaned forward and blew in her uncle's face. His response was swift and stinging. It took her a second to realise he'd slapped her.

Ryan was suddenly standing in between her and Uncle Cole. When she eventually looked up, she noticed Ryan's concern. He didn't say anything though.

"Go home. You're grounded for the entire holidays. You're not leaving the house," spat Uncle Cole.

"Sure you trust me to walk home by myself?" Sienna retorted, though her voice wavered vulnerably.

"You'd better or I swear you'll spend every second of your holidays in this police station."

PLAYING WITH FIRE

Sienna lightly rubbed the side of her face as she walked home. There had been something that hinted at regret in Uncle Cole's eyes as he'd followed her out of the station. A token. But one she didn't know how to cash in.

"You know I can't see you," said Sienna, not slowing her strides as she approached Liam, who was waiting at the end of her street. "I'm grounded big time."

"You were grounded before," noted Liam, walking with her. But things had changed. She'd never been hit before, yet didn't want to say so, knowing it wasn't like that for everyone. "It's no different. Just you choosing to listen. Besides, I'm pretty sure the Chief only grounded you, not me."

"What's that supposed to mean?"

"Did he ban visitors?" asked Liam with a cunning smile.

When Liam, Jono and Karina climbed through Sienna's bedroom window the next day, Sienna had the feeling they were enjoying breaking into the Chief's house. They hung out in the lounge room, watching movies and chatting. When lunchtime came, Jono and Karina offered to go and get food, saving Sienna from explaining the fight she'd had with Uncle Cole when she'd tried to go grocery shopping earlier that morning.

Liam, Jono and Karina came by every day. Sometimes they stayed half an hour, other times half the day. Sienna enjoyed their company, but hated that when they left her world became much darker than it had been before they arrived. Perhaps it was the hunger pains that plagued the days they didn't bring food. Maybe it was just the emptiness in her heart. Whatever the cause, she hated it.

Whenever she was alone, she curled up with Flynn's photo. It still brought her to tears, but it was different now. It wasn't just his absence she was mourning. It was the realisation that he was fading away. Her mind could no longer recreate the exact tone of his voice. She could hear his words, but not the inflections. Even his face was becoming fuzzy. The features she believed she could never forget were disappearing. She was losing him for a second time and it was as painful as the first.

"I didn't know you missed me so much when I was gone."

Sienna jumped. Concern clouded Liam's face as he climbed through her bedroom window. He sat next to her on the bed, gently taking Flynn's photo from her hands.

"You still miss him?" Liam asked. Sienna nodded. "That's okay, you know."

Liam's arms snaked around her, something more than friendship in his embrace, and it made her stomach twirl. When their eyes met, she knew he was going to kiss her and tried to push out of his arms, but he pulled her back into him.

"I know it's weird. I won't make you do shit you don't want, but you like me, right?"

Sienna nodded. She wanted to clarify, but didn't have the words. Liam smiled and kept holding her close.

Karina and Jono didn't come by in the second week of the holidays. Liam visited every day and somehow Sienna always ended up in his arms. He played his guitar as she sat in his lap. They watched TV and curled up on the lounge together. They held hands, and as the week progressed, Liam's kisses moved from her hair to her cheek and then to her lips.

The feelings Liam invoked were beyond Sienna's understanding. He couldn't be compared to Flynn. He wasn't close to being in that league, but that didn't stop her body from reacting to his touch. When she'd been with Flynn she'd never been attracted to another guy. It made her wonder what this was, without wanting the answer.

Liam met Sienna at the school gate on the first day of term and held her hand as they walked to roll call. His tales of sneaking into the Chief's house gained him, Jono and Karina a lot of cred.

"So you hanging out with us this arvo?" asked Jono.

Sienna knew she should say no. She could justify them coming to her place, but the dread of going back to her empty home and the waiting sadness was enough to override her other senses.

Uncle Cole anticipated Sienna's actions and was waiting for her in the main street. As soon as she turned the corner, he beckoned her.

"You only said I was grounded til the end of the holidays," said Sienna, deciding on a pre-emptive strike.

"Old rules still apply."

"What about the rules you break?" Sienna replied. Uncle Cole's eyes narrowed menacingly before softening completely. "Send me back. It's okay, they'll take me. They'd be happy thinking I can't hack it without them."

"They don't want you," Uncle Cole said, his hand clenching and unclenching as his eyes surveyed the street intently.

"And you do?"

"Go hang with your friends," he mumbled, pulling off his police cap and running his hand along the rim. "But you break a single law and you'll be grounded until you're twenty-one."

Sienna, Liam, Karina and Jono quickly became their own subgroup. And with Karina and Jono already a couple, it was easy for Liam to coax Sienna into mimicking them. Sienna felt safe with Liam, knowing her heart wasn't at risk.

"Hey, got big Friday night plans?"

Sienna turned to greet Jackson as he wandered into the kitchen, but before she could speak he flashed her a friendly smile. They hadn't seen each other lately and the sight of Flynn's smile was as painful as it had been the first time she saw it.

"Nope," she mumbled, turning away.

"But I thought the bans had been lifted."

Sienna was tossing up whether or not to explain when a muffled knocking sound came from her room. Jackson immediately moved forward, holding his hand back to keep her behind him. When he flung open her bedroom door, Liam froze. Jackson quickly pulled the door shut and dragged Sienna down the hallway and into the laundry.

"You're playing with fire," said Jackson seriously. "If the Chief catches him here."

"He's been coming over since the holidays."

"So you're really together?" asked Jackson. Sienna shrugged non-committedly. "You okay with that?" The concern in Jackson's voice was so touching Sienna found tears stinging the corners of her eyes.

Jackson's arms were immediately around her, pulling her to his chest. "Just don't rush into anything, okay. Don't let him push you into stuff you're not ready for. You don't have to get over Flynn straight away." Jackson stepped back and brushed her cheek. "You okay?"

Sienna got through her first nod before freezing.

"Bed. Now."

Uncle Cole's voice cut like ice. Sienna was impressed by Jackson's defiant stance as she crept to her room. She quickly ordered Liam under the bed. He was slow enough that he would've been caught if Uncle Cole hadn't been so angry.

"Jackson Halley is off-limits. I thought I explained that to you." Uncle Cole's stance in the doorway made it look like he was big enough to be the door.

"He was just asking how I was," replied Sienna for Liam's benefit.

"And that required hugging?"

"Not every day's easy, okay." Sienna was surprised by the way her voice broke. She was even more amazed by the way her uncle's face softened.

"I know what it's like to lose people. You need to talk, come see me. I'll listen to you. Jackson's here as my guest, not your friend."

"Why can't he be both?"

"He's a twenty-year-old boy. His mind's only on one thing and he's not getting it from my kid."

When Sienna didn't argue, Uncle Cole stomped away. Sienna closed the door behind him, turning to see Liam slowly emerging from under the bed, a hesitant smile on his face.

"Whoa, he's intense. You okay?" he asked. Sienna smiled and nodded, liking the way things seemed a little less bleak when he was around. "Think we're safe?"

"For a couple of hours."

Turning on the stereo to cover their voices, Sienna pulled her quilt on to the floor so they could be hidden from immediate view. Liam's hand was immediately on Sienna's cheek, gently moving their lips together and their bodies to the floor. The pleasure coursing through her made it feel like she was sitting outside herself, watching it unfold.

"You ready?" asked Liam, his hands moving to unbutton his jeans.

Sienna found herself sliding back into her body, trying to work out how they had arrived at this point so quickly. "You have protection?" she asked instead of saying no.

"It's okay. I'll pull out. I swear," replied Liam breathlessly, pushing up Sienna's skirt, his lips seeking to capture hers.

"Nup, no condom, no way," Sienna said, shuffling away and pushing down her skirt down.

Liam sat back, glaring. "Then what was with the cock-teasing?"

Sienna crossed her arms over her chest, before spotting her top and pulling it on. She shifted towards the bed, then thought standing in the corner would be safer. Liam groaned, swiping his t-shirt from the floor. He hesitated at the window. Then, with an agitated sigh, he was gone.

If he'd asked, Sienna might've told Liam why she couldn't risk falling for that line, but that might've also risked him thinking she'd take the same chance with him.

Flynn had warned her they needed to stop, but she'd held him closer, promising it would be fine. It was their first time. And she couldn't let him go.

Barely six months after her periods started, they stopped. Flynn stole a pregnancy test to be sure.

Sienna had wanted to come straight out to Uncle Cole's, but Flynn was convinced that if they ran away, there was less chance they'd be able to keep the baby. Arthur and Janice took the news better than either of them expected. There was no violence, but there was no support either. All Sienna heard for the next forty-eight hours was how bad a parent she would be. As if to prove the point, her parents turned up with a six-month-old baby; handing it to them with a baby bag and a demand to take care of him until his mother arrived.

No one told them how long that would be. No one stayed to help them. Screaming when he arrived, the baby didn't stop for the next four hours – when he finally tired himself out. But the reprieve barely lasted fifteen minutes and he was so distressed he could barely take a bottle.

The mother – a woman Sienna recognised from her parents' company – arrived six hours later in a state almost as fraught as her son's.

"I hope you get rid of your baby before you can torture it the way you did mine," she said, ripping her son from Sienna's arms, crying as she held him close.

"It's a trick, Senna," Flynn said when he was sent home that night and told not to return if he didn't want his parents to find out.

It might have been true, but without his support, Sienna didn't have the strength to believe she wouldn't abandon her child as soon as thing got tough – the way her parents abandoned her.

Caught up I those memories, it wasn't until Monday morning that Sienna realised her most imminent concern was not falling pregnant to Flynn. The sight of Liam waiting at the school gates made her heart stammer.

"I'm a prick, yeah?" he said, leaning against the wall. Sienna nodded. "We okay?" She nodded again. Right then, she'd do anything to be okay.

"You coming to Sam's party this weekend?" asked Liam at lunch on Thursday. "Starts tomorrow night. Ends Sunday. We're going to be one messy grade on Monday."

Sienna's response was non-committal. She would never be allowed and didn't want to go behind Uncle Cole's back. Despite all the tension in their relationship, he was still the only person who could be relied on to give her a home.

"Just tell the Chief you're staying with me and Amy this weekend," suggested Amber.

"You know it'll get shut down in five seconds if I come."

"Only if you tell the Chief what we're doing," said Sam. "We've kept this one real quiet. They were getting shut down quick anyway. The olds all think we're hanging at each other's places. I'm betting we don't get raided."

"Okay, I'll see if I can come," smiled Sienna. "Gonna have to really grovel."

Sienna was glad her parents had given her some independent spending money. Brownies from a packet weren't going to cut it for this. Thankfully, Fortune was home to the best bakery in the district.

"This for you or the Chief?" asked the owner, who had watched Sienna walk back and forth in front of the counter four times.

"Chief," said Sienna. "I need a favour."

"Ah. That's going to cost you. How big a favour?"

"Huge," smiled Sienna.

The owner nodded and waved Sienna to the counter. "You'll want one of these," she said, pointing to the apple strudel. "First thing he ever bought from here. Still talks about how it made him realise he'd made the right decision coming to Fortune." Sienna grinned and willingly submitted to letting the lady make the most appropriate selections. "You taking these home or the station? You'll need more if you're taking these to the boys."

This woman was a genius. If Sienna was going to bribe Uncle Cole, she'd need the whole police force onside.

"You want something," said Uncle Cole, as soon as Sienna walked into his office with the treats held out in front of her.

His voice wasn't agitated and Sienna thought she could be in with a chance. It made her wonder if it was the treats or because she was asking permission for once.

"So can I go?" she asked sweetly.

Uncle Cole rolled his eyes and nodded. Sienna couldn't believe it. She rushed forward and hugged him tight. His arms wrapped around her, returning the embrace tenderly. It was the nicest moment they'd shared in such a long time. It reminded her of why, once upon a time, she'd really liked living with Uncle Cole. When she'd been his little girl.

"I'd better go serve this up then," Sienna smiled.

"You wouldn't have let me have it if I said no?" asked Uncle Cole wryly, trailing behind her to the kitchen.

"Maybe," Sienna replied cheekily.

They both laughed. It caught everyone's attention. By the time they'd made it to the kitchen Ryan and Ian were with them, scavenging what Uncle Cole left behind. Ryan said thank you. It even sounded genuine. Ian waited until they were alone before he said thank you, but it sounded more like a threat.

"Missed out, huh," said Jackson, walking into the kitchen as Sienna cleaned up.

"You think I'd do that to you?" replied Sienna. "I pretended I was having some and saved it for you. Would've been nothing otherwise. They're vultures."

Jackson gratefully accepted the food and let Sienna make him a coffee, but he didn't talk the way he usually did. As soon as Jackson was finished, Sienna cleaned up and left, a feeling of sadness swirling through her. Jackson's smile was still torture, but he somehow felt like the closest thing to a real friend she'd made in Fortune and it pained her not to be able to talk to him.

~8~

PARTY

Sienna met Amber at the end of her street on Friday afternoon. Liam, Jono and Sam had organised scattered rendezvous points and times to transport them out to Sam's farm in secret. Only a few older brothers were in on it, acting as chauffeurs. Amber, Sienna, Amy and Karina congregated at a park not far from school. If anyone noticed them, they'd see nothing suspicious. Jono's brother arrived fifteen minutes later. When the coast was clear, they jumped in the car.

Sam's parents were away, so he'd been able to transform one of the paddocks up the back into a giant campsite. He, Jono and Liam had all skived off school to set it up. At the centre was a huge bonfire, which was already blazing against the rapidly darkening sky. Liam found Sienna as soon as she arrived and led her to a two-man tent.

"This is ours," he said with a suggestive grin.

Sienna tried not to let her face betray her lack of enthusiasm. There was no way she was having sex with him surrounded by so many school friends. When Liam put her bag in the tent, she suggested they get a drink. She was disappointed by the lack of non-alcoholic options. Liam handed her a bottle of beer. She took a sip, but had to repress a shudder. She and Flynn had drunk regularly from the age of eleven; a ready supply of alcohol in both their homes.

They hadn't been drinking that night. Not yet. But it was still something Sienna associated so strongly with Flynn that it felt wrong without him. She also trusted Flynn. He took care of her if she felt sick and never took advantage of her if she got drunk. She didn't trust Liam that way.

It was a good night though. The girls danced and guys wrestled. Someone kept putting food on the barbeque and someone else infrequently took it off. But as the night wore on, the short-comings of the camp set-up became more apparent. It wasn't as though anyone was above going bush, more that with a bucket of beers in them, the boys thought it'd be fun to ambush the girls trying to relieve themselves. But the girls banded together to protect their privacy. It was a strangely bonding experience.

"You couldn't even get them back if they caught you," said Amber. "They'd be proud of a picture of their dick going viral. If only one of them had a deformed one. Then they'd be scared. How's Liam's?"

"Not disfigured in the slightest," replied Sienna.

They all laughed.

"So you guys serious?" asked Amber.

"Not that serious," Sienna replied. "He wants to, but …"

"Yeah, I didn't think – I mean, it'd be really hard after – it's different if you just break up with a guy."

"Very different," nodded Sienna.

Amber squeezed Sienna's shoulder. It felt foreign. No one other than Flynn had offered her sympathy in six years.

With Liam happy to hang out with the boys, Sienna stayed with Amber, Amy and Karina. They danced and chatted – mainly about boys, occasionally about their futures. There wasn't a lot of ambition in the group besides Amber. She was the school's resident genius and wanted to be a doctor. Sienna's claim of wanting to be a lawyer generally matched everyone's view of her.

When Amber and Amy started talking about going to their tent to sleep, Sienna looked nervously over at her little tent. Liam was still drinking with Sam and Jono, but she was sure he would turn in at some point. It was a relief when Amber suggested she stay with them.

They slept until late in the morning, the smell of food on the barbeque gently rousing people. The boys were particularly slow moving, so the girls took their chance to head to the bushes in peace. It meant everyone was in a buoyant mood as they pushed down their breakfast, but as the afternoon wore on there was a feeling they were living on borrowed time. This was the longest one of Sam's party had gone for in over a year.

"Hey, come for a walk," said Liam, moving behind Sienna and wrapping his arms around her waist. She nodded and let him take her hand. "Can't believe the Chief hasn't checked up on you yet."

"Yeah, well, we'd better hope I'm back at Amber's when he does. Ain't going to end well if he finds me here."

With his free hand, Liam rubbed Sienna's hand that he was

holding, then pulled her into him as he leaned back against a large tree. She didn't resist when he started kissing her. He was drunk, but gentle.

"You wanna take this back to the tent?" he asked.

"There're people everywhere. They're going to be watching us."

"Don't be stupid!" laughed Liam. "They're all pissed. Besides, we'll be discreet."

Sienna wasn't convinced, but Liam took her silence for consent. She didn't look around as they ducked into their tent. Liam had a sleeping bag laid out on the floor. He stripped off his jeans and t-shirt in the process of lying down. As soon as Sienna laid next to him, he pushed her top up her body and pulled her tights from under her skirt.

Sienna looked around, reaching over Liam for the other sleeping bag and throwing it over them like a quilt. Liam immediately rolled on top of her.

"I brought condoms," he said, reaching into his bag and pulling one out.

"Too many people," said Sienna, shaking her head, feeling Liam's weight on top of her increasing by the second. "Don't you want it to be nice? Somewhere private?"

"Jeez, it's not our wedding night. Don't worry, you'll like it."

Liam didn't sound angry and Sienna hoped she could hold him off long enough for something to interrupt them, though another part of her thought she should just get it over and done with.

Liam kept the condom in his hand as they made out. He seemed to be happy to take his time after she asked him to go slow, but when his hands moved under her skirt, she knew her time was up.

The way Liam's hands roamed over her body helped the argument that she should submit, but the way the other part of her brain tracked every touch of the condom packet on her body told her she wasn't ready for this.

"Go slow, okay," she whispered.

"Of course," Liam replied, his fingers looping around the side of her underwear.

Sienna's heart stammered, realising Liam had misinterpreted what she meant.

"Hey, hey! Getting some, Liam!"

Liam spun off Sienna, taking the top sleeping bag with him. His fingers were still holding her undies, pulling them partway down her leg. Jolting up, Sienna was confronted by at least six guys – Jono and Sam included – huddled in the mouth of the tent, phones out in front of them.

"Give us a peak!"

Sienna quickly pushed her skirt down. Liam reached over her. She shifted into huddle under him, but what she thought was a consoling hug was him unclasping her bra. She realised just in time, her arms crossing over her chest. But that just shifted their focus to her skirt. With so many hands grabbing at her, it was impossible to fight them off. As soon as one of her hands left her chest, Liam snatched her bra from under the other one. Sienna rolled over, but her hands could only cover so much and the boys' hands were starting to roam.

"Fuck off! Leave her alone!"

More hands joined the mix, but these ones pushed down Sienna's skirt and yanked her to her feet, pressing their bodies to hers.

"I got her stuff."

A sleeping bag wrapped around Sienna's shoulders, but the bodies stayed close as they pushed through the boys and darted into another tent. Only then did Amber step back. Amy held out Sienna's bag. Sienna grabbed it, retreating to a corner of the tent and dressing hurriedly.

"You okay?" asked Amber, taking Sienna's hand and sitting her between her and Amy.

Howls of laughter surrounded the ten. Sienna shivered, pulling her knees to her chest. She'd never been scared of guys like that before. Never felt so vulnerable or helpless. Amy and Amber each wrapped an arm around her.

"I told Jono to delete the footage," said Karina, stepping into the tent, laughs and cries of 'chief slut' following her. "They're being stupid cos they're drunk."

Sienna didn't believe that.

"You want to go home?" asked Amber.

It was a stupid question. There was no way back into town without a lift. Sienna was tempted to call Uncle Cole, but couldn't trust him to take her home without arresting every boy at the party.

Sitting to the side of the tent entrance, Sienna stayed awake – on watch – all night. She must've fallen asleep at some point, waking with a start at the sound of engines revving.

"Don't get too excited. Just them racing," said Amber.

Sienna peered out of the tent. The area was deserted, everyone down the hill, cheering as two cars set off along a dirt track that disappeared around the edge of the property. Liam was there, beer in hand, unsteadily insisting the he, Jono and Karina were in the next car.

"Let them kill themselves," said Amy dismissively, following Sienna's gaze.

A year ago, she might have, but the hate she felt towards them reminded her too much of the hate she'd felt for Ashton, James and Myra. She'd wished them dead more than once. Myra, body contorted sickeningly, Ashton's head flopping off his body and James' crushed torso just wasn't what she'd imagined.

When the cars again skidded to a stop, Liam yanked open the door, pulling at the driver. Sienna, just managed to wedge herself between Liam and the driver's seat.

"You can't. You're drunk," she gasped.

"Fuck off. You're not the Chief," said Liam, trying to push Sienna out of the way.

"I wanna drive," said Sienna, grabbing the steering wheel to keep her feet. "Speed racer, remember. I'm the one who outruns the cops."

Liam's face broke into a broad smile. He ran around to the front passenger seat, as Jono and Karina scrambled into the back. Sienna's heart thrummed erratically as she revved the engine, the tyres spinning underneath them as they took off. Sienna was just ahead of the other car until halfway around the track when the back of the car slid out on a loose patch of gravel. She recovered quickly, but found her mind on a different, darker track. She was more aware of the trees, fences and ditches, and how easy it would be slam the car into them. It would hurt, but only for a second.

A flash of light brought Sienna's attention back to the race. The other car was getting ahead. Liam and Jono were yelling at her to go faster, but it was a tight corner and the other car had the advantage. Sienna eased off the accelerator just in time. Dust blew up in front of her as they rounded the corner, the other car sliding across the dirt. Flashes of red and blue danced in front of them. Slamming on the brakes, Sienna felt the car turn sharply to the right. She spun the wheel, lifting her foot from the brake for a moment, then slammed it down hard.

Bracing for impact, Sienna was disorientated by stillness of the car. When the dust cleared, she saw the police car just inches from the bumper.

"Woohoo!" cried Jono, bashing excitedly against the back against Sienna's seat.

The door swung open. Arms seized Sienna's, yanking her against her seatbelt. Angry curses were spat in her face as the seatbelt was released and she was dragged from the car and slammed against the bonnet. Her arms were pulled roughly behind her back and handcuffed.

"Sienna!"

Sienna turned, but she saw nothing as she was bundled into the back of the police van. There was a lot of shouting, but she couldn't make out the words over the constant banging on the side of the van.

The trip to the police station was vicious. Sienna would've bet it was Ian driving. He swung roughly around corners, throwing her around the van. On the third corner she hit the side of her face against the bench. She tried to brace herself, but the bumpy road meant she only earned herself a greater collection of bruises.

Uncle Cole was beyond words when Ian marched her into his office. He paced the room, glaring at Sienna at every turn as the commotion of more people from the party being brought into the station drifted into the room. "What happened to her face?" he finally asked.

"Must've happened in the accident, Chief," Ian lied.

"Then get her to the hospital and get a blood test," spat Uncle Cole. Ian grabbed Sienna's arm. "And drive slowly!"

Uncle Cole's mood hadn't improved by the time Sienna returned. Half the party was there now, including Amber, who rushed in after her.

"Hey, I got your stuff. You okay?" asked Amber.

Sienna nodded as Uncle Cole grabbed the bag.

"This would've been at your place, right?" he snapped. Amber didn't answer. "Get out of here. I've got enough delinquent youths to deal with already."

So many, it seemed, that dealing with Sienna would have to wait. She was walked out to the cells and sat down on one of the cots.

"You're not going to ask me to remove the cuffs?" asked Ian, his voice amused.

"Is there any point?" Sienna retorted.

"I would've enjoyed seeing you beg."

As soon as Ian left, Sienna shuffled he arms under her body so that her hands were cuffed in front of her. It was thirty-six minutes and eighteen seconds before the door opened again.

"You okay?" asked Jackson, kneeling in front of her and unlocking her cuffs. "You're in so much trouble."

"With the law?"

"Around here, the Chief is the law. You should know that by now."

"Then do I get my one call?"

"Who do you want to ring?" asked Jackson.

Want was a strong word. Sienna didn't want to call Stephen, but she wanted to imagine he'd be a supportive big brother when she told him about what'd happened at the party.

"I'll call him. Better the Chief doesn't know about this right now."

For the next seventeen minutes and forty-one seconds, Sienna waited for Jackson's return and news of her brother's reaction, but the call wasn't needed. Uncle Cole came instead, throwing open the door and standing to the side.

"If I could charge you with something, be sure, I would," he said calmly. Too calmly.

"There's no law against driving on private property. You taught me that."

"Just get out. I don't want to know you right now."

Sienna didn't move, disorientated by the shocking lack of consequences. Uncle Cole walked off, the cell door left wide open.

~9~

RICHIE SNITCH

Sienna packed slowly. When the front door slammed, she crept out to the kitchen. The house was silent. Uncle Cole hadn't spoke to her since her release. It was the same treatment she was expecting to cop at school, so tried to make sure she arrived right on time. The teachers weren't as thoughtful.

"That was some driving," said Liam, coming up to her as they waited outside the locked classroom. Everyone was milling around, talking about the race. "Wish we'd always known you could drive like that."

Sienna shrugged. Seeing him alive reminded her of why she hated him so much that she fought to keep him from a gruesome death.

It was an automatic reaction to join the group at lunch, but Sienna wasn't impressed when Liam sat next to her.

"We're not going out any more," she hissed, when he tried to take her hand.

"Huh?"

"We broke up the minute you undid my bra."

"Oh, yeah, right. I forgot. No one gets that kind of thing from the Chief's kid," Liam retorted, smirking as he turned to Sam and Jono.

Karina's hand covered her mouth to hide her laugh.

"That the only reason you went out with me?" asked Sienna. She'd kept her voice soft, but Liam hadn't and she could tell the whole group was listening, watching from the corner of their eyes.

"There another reason?" Liam grinned as he shared low-fives with Sam and Jono, the group chuckling nervously, waiting to see if she would react. She didn't and the ribbing died down.

"You okay?" asked Amber, as they packed up at the end of the day. "It's not personal. The Chief made lots of enemies when he first came. Came down real hard on Liam's and Sam's families. They don't care that he's helped them out too – just that he's willing to arrest them."

"It's fine," shrugged Sienna. She'd never wanted to get involved in small town politics.

Amber nodded and they walked in silence to the gates.

"Trouble," muttered Amber.

Sienna looked up to see Jackson pushing off the side of the patrol car parked outside the school. "You'd better come with me," he said gravely, placing a gentle hand on Sienna's arm. She immediately pulled back. "It's your brother. He's here."

"Shit," sighed Sienna, sliding reluctantly into the police car.

The moment they walked into the police station, Sienna could hear the arguing.

"I should fucking report you!"

"For what? Trying to keep the kids in this town alive?"

"Get off your righteous high-horse. You had her handcuffed in a cell! She's sixteen!"

Sienna walked into Uncle Cole's office ahead of Jackson. Everyone turned as one. Stephen folded his arms and huffed, glaring at her. Sienna looked away, focusing her eyes on the corner of Uncle Cole's desk.

"Why the fuck did you do it, Sen?" asked Stephen angrily. "Didn't you put everyone through enough last year? All your friends die and you get back in the car and start fucking racing again. Why?" Sienna's eyes widened at the question, believing the answer was obvious. "I thought you would've grown up a bit. Not spend a whole weekend drinking and racing fucking cars."

"I wasn't drunk," said Sienna, her voice soft and shaky. "You took a fucking blood test. What was the result?"

"She didn't have alcohol in her system," Uncle Cole answered, sounding disappointed.

"So you decided to race that car in a stone-cold sober state of mind? You have a death wish or something?" snapped Stephen.

"I was the only sober person in that car! Who do you think should've been driving?" cried Sienna.

"You shouldn't have even been in it!" yelled Stephen. "This is why Mum and Dad didn't want you going to school with these kinds of people."

"Why'd you even come here?" asked Sienna, not bothering to

correct the ridiculous flaws in his logic.

When the silence continued on, Sienna stormed out of the office.

"He cares," said Jackson, following her out to the foyer.

"Yeah, right," Sienna retorted, the feeling in the car returning – the yearning to make it all stop.

"I don't have anywhere for you to stay."

Uncle Cole's words struck terror into Sienna's heart as he and Stephen stomped into the foyer behind her.

"Let's go," said Stephen, shoving Sienna in the shoulder.

"I'll walk with you," said Jackson.

It was a silent walk. Uncle Cole was waiting for them, having driven home. Stephen paced away from them, following Uncle Cole into the lounge room, leaving Sienna standing on the porch.

"Come on, we'll cook," said Jackson, nudging her inside. Uncle Cole and Stephen were already arguing.

"There's nowhere for you to stay," said Uncle Cole.

"He can have my bed," sighed Sienna, stopping at the lounge room door. "I'll take the lounge."

"I'm not having you kicked out of your own bed in your own house. He has the money to stay in a hotel."

"And here I was thinking that, as your nephew, I might be shown some hospitality," cried Stephen.

Sienna saw Jackson open his mouth and shook her head, continuing to the kitchen.

"I'm not a great cook. Won't be anything nice," Sienna muttered, hoping Jackson might take the hint.

"It'll be fine," Jackson smiled.

Stephen and Uncle Cole continued their arguing.

"Don't tell me it's cos they care," said Sienna, when they had everything cooking; the sudden stillness of the kitchen providing space for the angry words to float in.

"Okay. But I will say that I kinda wish you were my housemate. You cook good and we get along pretty well. You're like the little sister I never had."

"You're like the big brother I never had," replied Sienna.

Jackson didn't respond. Stephen was standing right behind her.

"I thought I could just pull the cushions off the lounge and sleep in your room," said Stephen, stepping awkwardly forward. "Uncle Cole's gone out."

"Yeah, okay," said Sienna, expecting him to last a couple of hours at most. "You hungry? We made enough."

"Yeah, thanks."

Jackson smiled and started a generic conversation with Stephen. Sienna was impressed by how easily they spoke. She'd never had such a free conversation with Stephen in her life. Stephen never sought to include her. Only Jackson spoke to her, but she didn't know how to join in.

When they sat down for dinner, the conversation ceased. Jackson ate quickly. He offered to help clean up, but Sienna assured him she'd be right.

"I said I'd try and drop in on my girlfriend tonight," said Jackson, pushing away from the table. "Had a feeling today'd be frantic. Might grab a movie." He winked, before biding them farewell.

"What's that about?" asked Stephen, picking up their empty plates.

"It's how he scores," answered Sienna softly.

Stephen nodded thoughtfully. "Is that the kinda stuff you want to talk about with me?"

"You don't talk to me at all," replied Sienna. "Never have. I just thought – you know, maybe one day – maybe we'd have something. If it hadn't been for all the shit that happened on the weekend, I would've had my head together enough to know not to call you."

"What do you mean? We're glad you called, Sen. Glad you were finally brave enough to confide in us about the shit Uncle Cole puts you through."

That wasn't what she'd wanted to confide in him about, but was glad they didn't seem to expect any more dirt on Uncle Cole. And now she understood why the tent thing happened, she was determined never to tell them about it.

"So you heading back tomorrow now that you got me sorted out," she asked, setting up Stephen's makeshift bed.

"Had been planning on staying a couple of days," replied Stephen flatly. "Had been expecting a bed here, too, but I guess warm welcomes aren't the norm in Fortune. Would've thought all the money Mum and Dad were pumping into this place would've gone a bit further."

"What money? They give me a hundred a week. How far do you think that goes? Groceries are expensive. And it's not like I'm going to blow what I don't spend on another bed. I hate this shit. Uncle Cole doesn't earn the money you guys do," snapped Sienna, regretting her outburst. If she'd kept calm, she might've found out what the deal was between her parents and Uncle Cole.

"Hey! I always thought we took this photo. Did you swipe it?" he asked, picking up a picture of him, Arthur and Janice at Disneyland that sat on her desk. "That was such a great trip. We thought that was going to be the start of the best times ever."

"What times?" asked Sienna, sliding into bed. She remembered the trip, but her memories were all of her parents being disappointed with everything she did.

"That was right after you came back to live with us. Mum and Dad wanted to celebrate," said Stephen.

"And then they realised it was the worst decision they ever made."

"No! How could you say that?"

"Where are they, Stephen? They aren't here."

"You want us all to move out to Fortune?"

"Sure, if they're going to keep claiming they want me around. Why ship me out here if they're so stoked to have me in their family?"

"You're the one who wanted to come out here!" said Stephen.

"I got exiled," Sienna retorted. "What choice did I have? Of course, if they can't even handle having me around as a kid, they're not going to want me as a teenager. I only bring the great Hollingsworth name down."

"That's not true."

"Easy for you. You're the golden child. Try being the one no one wants. I don't even care. Doesn't matter. I'm never going to be good enough."

"It's not like that, Sen. It's really not," urged Stephen in a soft voice, but it wasn't very convincing.

"It just – doesn't matter. I don't care. One day I might do something worthwhile to someone," Sienna muttered, but knew she'd already found that someone and wished more than anything that she could be with him again.

Stephen was already up the next morning when Sienna woke. He looked concerned. Sienna saw him putting his mobile in his pocket and guessed he'd been speaking to their parents.

"You going to school today?" Stephen asked.

"Unless they've cancelled it," muttered Sienna.

Stephen nodded thoughtfully. He seemed to always be in deep thought and Sienna couldn't help but think she really was the dumb one in the family. She was never that pensive.

"You going home today?" asked Sienna.

"I told you, I'd been hoping to stay for a couple of days."

"Why?" asked Sienna. "I don't want to seem rude, but why?"

"Because you're wrong about so many things and I'm not going til I've sorted them out. You think we abandoned you and it's not true."

Sienna turned and looked at the fridge door, noticing tiny dents she'd never seen before. Stephen didn't know anything of being abandoned.

The hope that school would be a pleasant distraction was shattered the moment Sienna walked through the gates. The whistles and cries of 'Chief's slut' indicated the footage had spread beyond the grade. Those who hated Uncle Cole were triumphant in her humiliation. Everyone else just avoided her.

Sienna didn't tell Stephen. His presence now felt like a spy mission, because despite his claim of wanting to sort things out, all he'd done was join his parents' anthem of missing her and wishing she lived with them. But she'd fallen for that line before, and there was no Flynn to make the mistake worthwhile this time.

"You want to finish that up. Mum's going to call soon," said Stephen, dumping the rest of the unwashed plates next to the sink. "You shouldn't even be doing the washing up. It's his job."

"I made the mess," Sienna said, piling the plates in the sink. "And there's no reason not to continue washing them til they call."

"Mum and Dad take time out of their day to call you. Don't you think you should show a bit more respect?"

"They call you every day. My scheduled call time is Wednesday at seven-thirty."

The phone rang. Stephen marched into Sienna's room to answer it. The calls this week all started this way – Stephen reporting in, discussions about the office, then the stunted attempt at conversation with her.

"Mum, can you calm down," said Stephen, walking back out to the kitchen, putting his laptop on the table. Neck cricked to keep the phone in place, he tapped away for several seconds before grabbing his phone again, his other hand slamming down on the table. "Yep. I'll see you tomorrow." He hung up and glared up at Sienna. "Want to explain this?" he asked, spinning the laptop to face her.

Dramatic Demise of an Heiress

Sienna didn't need to read any more to know that Stephen's last words to their mother didn't mean he was flying home.

"You might need to see this too," said Uncle Cole from the doorway, holding out a newspaper. His other hand was holding his phone. No way he was going to forgive her now if he'd just copped an earful from her parents.

Stephen threw the paper on a clear patch of table, flicking angrily through to page six, where there was half a page dedicated to the party.

"Well I guess there's one good thing about you falsely laying claim to Sienna as your daughter. At least here they attribute her bad behaviour to you. Also doesn't mention anything about providing the entertainment."

"Why don't you claim the bits you're proud of and leave to rest to me," Uncle Cole snapped, turning and stomping out of the house.

Sienna wanted to rush after him, imagining that if she apologised they'd both turn back into the people they used to be, but though he'd still claim her, he couldn't forgive her.

Stephen was gone before Sienna woke, but returned with their parents by the time she was dressed.

"Where do you think you're going?" asked Arthur, when Sienna walked out of her room in her school uniform. It was the first thing he said to her.

"School," she replied, moving around everyone to make lunch.

"Not today," Arthur snapped.

Today they needed to talk. Sienna was marched into the lounge room. She slumped down into the armchair and waited for Uncle Cole to join them, but he didn't appear and no one mentioned him.

"Let's start simple. Why were you even there?" asked Arthur.

"It was a friend's party," retorted Sienna, leaning forward and throwing her arms up. "Am I supposed to exclude myself from all social occasions for the rest of my life?"

"Ones like this, yes!" spat Arthur.

Sienna crossed her arms and slumped back in her seat. She was surprised to find Stephen move to the arm next to her, his hand gently squeezing her shoulder.

"Fine, but you said you hadn't been drinking."

Sienna glared in disgust. "Right, the blood test cleared me, but cos there's a picture of me with a beer in my hand I must've been drunk."

"Then you explain it!" growled Arthur.

"I was dancing," cried Sienna. "With lots of other people. Last time I checked, not a crime. I had a beer in my hand. You're so brilliant, you work it out."

"Why were you holding it if you weren't drinking it?" asked Janice, her voice dripping with disappointment.

"You tried not drinking at a party?" replied Sienna, trying hard to keep the sarcasm out of her voice, resulting in it cracking vulnerably.

"The other photo?" asked Janice.

Sienna looked away. She didn't want to discuss that. She didn't want to justify being with a guy who wasn't Flynn or admit how helpless she'd felt, trapped under Liam as the others groped and cheered.

"Well?" asked Arthur.

"Figure it out yourself," cried Sienna, trying to rush from the room, but Stephen caught her hand and pulled her back.

"I just can't believe you'd do something like that," sighed Arthur, shaking his head.

"Like what?" gasped Sienna.

"Did you think it'd end there? What do you think happens when you expose yourself like that? Boys cry 'show us your tits' and you do?"

"I hate you!" spat Sienna. Stephen restrained her as she tried to leave. "I hate all of you! Why's it always my fault?"

"Because you're the one making the bad decisions," said Arthur.

"I'm allowed to go to parties. I'm allowed to dance and try and have a good time!" cried Sienna. Arthur opened his mouth to argue, but she yelled over the top of him. "I'm even allowed to kiss a guy if I want. Why don't you ever ask why those guys burst in on us? Or why he pulled my clothes off me just cos they asked him to?"

Stephen's grip loosened slightly and Sienna pushed him away, running out of the house and down the street. At the river, she finally turned around. There was no one behind her. Typical. They'd all claim they came rushing out because they cared so much, but it was a lie. If the Hollingsworth name hadn't appeared in the papers, they would've let it slide.

Striding along the river, Sienna contemplated if she had the strength to hold her head under the water until she drowned, scoffing at the idea that they would even mourn her.

She continued her march long after the track disappeared, pushing through the light shrub. The river passed under the freeway, before eventually reaching the railway line. The tide was up, so there was no way under the bridge without going into the river. The bridge over the river was narrow and would force her on to the tracks to cross it. Choosing the safer option, Sienna turned right and trekked along the wide gravel path next to the tracks. A train sped by minutes later, its horn blaring loudly, and Sienna was suddenly flooded with regret that she'd played it safe.

Tired of walking, Sienna slumped to the ground. Another train would eventually approach. The westbound train always passed through Fortune two hours after the eastbound train. It gave her time to contemplate the pain of being torn apart by tonnes of metal, but perhaps she owed Flynn that much. To die as painfully as he had.

The distance bustle of a train caught Sienna's ear. She was standing before she knew it, inching towards the tracks. Her heart pounded erratically, trying to get in its lifetime of beats. The train's horn blared. It was deafening, but she could almost hear her name in its sound, calling her to it. She took a deep breath and closed her eyes.

The whoosh of the train knocked Sienna to the ground. Tears spilled down her cheeks. She'd failed.

"What the hell are you doing?"

Sienna flinched. She wasn't alone. Trying to move, she realised she was tangled in Jackson's body. He was holding her tight and she could feel his heart thumping. He stood them up, holding her close as he moved them back from the tracks. He slumped down with her at the fence that separated the rail line from the narrow country road beside it. Sienna had no idea where she was.

"You scared me so much. I wouldn't have made it in time. If you'd taken that step ..."

"How'd you find me?" she asked, deciding against sharing her disappointment.

"Don't know," Jackson replied hesitantly, as if only now realising his well-timed arrival was a little odd. "Just drove. Had a feeling." Sienna nodded. "I'd better get you back."

"No!" she cried, wrestling until she'd pulled out of Jackson's grasp. "Please, just let me go. Pretend you didn't find me. They won't come looking for me anyway. Please, Jackson."

Jackson shifted towards her, but she backed away. Lunging forward, he grabbed her hand, pulling her down to the ground. She sat next to him, but he kept a firm grip on his hand.

"Why didn't you tell me what that little shit did to you on Sunday?"

"I don't care what Liam did. It's over. I hate them. How could they think I'd go flashing boys while they took photos of me?"

"You're not still dating that prat, are you?" snarled Jackson. Sienna shook her head. "Good."

"You see the video?" asked Sienna.

Jackson nodded. "We went to the school. Seized phones."

"Guess I'm not going to have any friends on Monday."

"They weren't your friends to begin with. No boyfriend, no friend, would ever do that. God, Flynn never did that to you, did he?"

"No!" cried Sienna, jumping to her feet. "How could you ever think that?"

"Because you seem to think it's okay."

"I never thought it was okay. I've never been scared like that before. If Amber – if there weren't other people around, I don't know where they would've stopped."

"What they did to you – that's assault. It's illegal. Yet you seem to forgive them more easily than you do your parents."

"They blamed me! They came all the way out here just to tell me how worthless and pathetic I am. They've taunted me my entire life, telling me they love me and want me, but they don't. And Uncle Cole, he tells me he wants me, that I'm like he's own kid, but he won't forgive me for being my parents' child. For believing they wanted me."

Sienna's chest was heaving as two tears tracked down her cheeks. Jackson said nothing.

"My parents love Stephen. I've watched the way they treat him. All I ever wanted was for them to be my parents too, but they don't want me and I don't even know why."

Jackson stepped tentatively forward. He brushed Sienna's cheek and smiled softly. It was sweet and calming and made her step forward into a hug.

"I'm not going to tell you it's perfect, but they care. I promise," urged Jackson, holding her tighter. "And you've got friends. You've still got so many things to live for. I'm going to be there for you, okay. You're my kid sister, remember."

"Can you not tell them about this?" begged Sienna. "Please. I didn't actually do anything."

"Promise you won't do anything like this again. I don't want to pick up bits of you off the rail line. Yeah?"

Sienna nodded, her fingers crossed behind Jackson's back.

Stephen and her parents left on Sunday morning. Sienna waved them off feeling guilty for the relief spreading through her. Walking back inside, she saw a large photo album on the dining table. She rushed back to the front door, but it was useless. They were gone.

Janice had brought it out at Stephen's request. To prove some point Sienna still didn't get.

"You took basically all those photos," he'd said, flipping through the pages. "I always loved looking at them. The way you captured things. It was like you were in all the photos."

"Except I'm not. I could've not even been there according to this," Sienna muttered.

"I know. We felt bad when we got them developed. But you don't understand how small and silent you were."

"Of course, I was silent. All I did was get in trouble. They yelled at me all the time. I never did anything right."

"You never did anything. You looked at the rides with wonder and longing, but we couldn't get you to go on any of them."

Sienna scoffed at the memory. That's not how she remembered it. The first ride she asked to go on, her parents refused. It was the biggest rollercoaster in the park and no one had wanted to join her. Yet when Stephen had wanted to go on something, they forced her to go with him.

The sound of her phone got her to her feet. She sighed, knowing the reason for the call.

"Sorry, Dad, only saw it after you left."

"What?" Arthur replied.

"You know, the photo album."

"Just post it back," he huffed dismissively. "I want to talk."

"Right, just not in person," Sienna retorted bitterly.

A heavy sigh. "It must seem like that to you, but it's not. You should've told us what happened from the start. You couldn't have expected us to be happy when we saw that." Silence. "I'm sorry we didn't give you a chance to tell your side of the story."

"Thanks," muttered Sienna.

"We spoke to Jackson."

"What'd he say?" asked Sienna anxiously, her heart thrumming.

"We just wanted an update on the case. We want those kids hit with the full weight of the law. Don't want them believing they can attack our family and get away with it," said Arthur. "But Jackson mentioned that you don't feel like you're a part of our family. Is that true?"

Sienna considered lying, but the honest answer slipped out first. "I always wanted to, but …"

"Wanted to or want to?" asked Arthur in a firm voice.

"There's no point. It won't work."

"There is a point," argued Arthur. "You're our daughter. Of course, there's a point. We want you to be a part of our family."

"I'll just ruin it. I'm better as a Smith. A nobody." Sienna's voice trailed off as she spoke. She didn't want to have this conversation.

It seemed Arthur didn't either. There was just silence and long, deep breaths on the other end of the phone. "You're somebody to us," he said eventually.

Sienna slept badly and woke with a throbbing headache. It was going to be a bad day. The sight of a police car out the front of the school when she arrived only confirmed that fear. Morning classes were cancelled; the senior grades pulled into an assembly where Ryan proceeded to lecture them about the taking and distributing of sexual images. Sienna was seated at the back of the hall, but all eyes turned on her. Ryan didn't mention her by name. He didn't even refer to Sam's party, but everyone knew what it was about.

"Richie Snitch," someone hissed.

"Can't believe you brought the cops in."

"Need daddy to fight your battles?"

"Won't stop here."

Sienna kept her eyes down as she left the hall. In class she moved to the desk furthest from people, but that didn't stop the snide comments.

"I don't know why you didn't just let it go," said Karina, falling into step with Sienna as she walked towards the gates at the end of the day. "Why'd you get the cops involved?"

"I didn't," snapped Sienna. "Why don't you blame whoever went to the press. Nothing would've happened if it didn't turn up in the paper."

Karina said nothing, but it didn't escape Sienna's attention that she wouldn't look her in the eye.

The front door closed softly. Sienna had been waiting for the sound, so even half asleep her eyes snapped open. Ten o'clock. Uncle Cole had not been home before nine once since the weekend of Sam's party. She'd left him a cake on the bench. Creeping to the door, she saw him grab the plate and shove it in the fridge.

"Busy day?" Sienna asked from the doorway.

"Go to bed. It's late," Uncle Cole huffed without turning around.

"So you're never going to forgive me? For one mistake?"

"That wasn't a mistake. You lied. Knowingly and purposefully."

"Yeah, and I paid the price."

Uncle Cole's shoulders slumped, but he didn't turn around. "Go to bed."

Sienna slammed the door, flopping on her bed, rogue tears escaping her eyes.

The magnitude of her mistake in getting Uncle Cole offside was highlighted by the weekly calls from her parents. They were so regular she was sure they had them booked into their schedules.

"So how's school been this week?" Arthur asked brightly.

They always started with that.

"Yeah, okay," Sienna replied.

"That's good. You know if you feel like you're not covering enough, we'll arrange for a tutor," he said.

"One from Sydney," Janice added. "They can video call you."

"No, it's fine," Sienna assured them.

"Any plans for the weekend? You and your friends have anything organised?"

And that was how they wrapped up. A serious question, as if they had no comprehension of the decimation of her social standing during their visit.

"No, just gunna study," Sienna replied flatly, not prepared to talk about the social isolation inflicted on her at school.

"That's good, Sen," Arthur said brightly. "Just focus on your studies. We'll talk to you next week."

Hanging up the phone, Sienna looked at the pile of books on her desk. Her head fell into her hands before she could even reach for them.

I don't care what you want to do. I said you're going to be a lawyer and that's the end of it!

The voice of Flynn's father – clearer than Flynn's – swirled through Sienna's mind. Flynn had been almost fifteen before he'd found the courage to tell his mother he didn't want to be a lawyer. She told him to bury his dream of being a teacher. It wasn't an option.

When his father found out about his confession, his reaction had been much more brutal. Sienna had only just managed to hide in time when Mr Matthews came bursting into Flynn's room.

When Flynn argued that he had a right to a say in his own future, Mr Matthews replied with his hands. Flynn had told Sienna that his father hit him, but seeing it was something else entirely. After almost five minutes of cruelty, Mr Matthews held Flynn's head up by the chin, his fist clenched menacingly to strike. This time, when Mr Matthews asked Flynn what he was going to be, Flynn fell into line.

"We'll be lawyers together," Sienna had whispered, when Mr Matthews left, holding back her own tears as Flynn angrily brushed his cheeks with the back of his hand.

He hugged her tight, nodding in agreement. They didn't want that future, but they'd endure anything to be together. Sienna had planned on being a brilliant lawyer so Flynn could have any career he wanted. Occasionally he indulged that fantasy, but mostly they planned their futures around them both being lawyers.

What really changed that day was how recklessly they lived. They no longer cared if their actions endangered their lives. They invited death so frequently it finally came, just not with a big enough appetite.

Starting on her homework, Sienna tried to figure out if being a lawyer now was betraying Flynn or fulfilling his destiny. He would have been a great lawyer. Skilful. Cunning. If she could emulate that, then perhaps she could bring him to life within her.

But Sienna knew she could never succeed at school if she continued to ignore her only strength. Pushing away the maths textbook that was only taunting her anyway, she grabbed a sketch book and pencil, drawing for the first time since Flynn's death.

For the first half an hour she did nothing but cry. Not attempting to stem her emotion, she closed her eyes and let her hand work, drawing the emotion from her heart on to the paper.

The pictures that emerged weren't a surprise. There was only one moment aching to be expressed. Often, she could only get an outline done before another part of that night pushed down on her pencil. Back and forth, she slowly added the detail.

"That's pretty haunting."

"It's not finished," muttered Sienna, looking up briefly from the lounge. She didn't mind Jackson visiting, but wished every cop in the town didn't have a key to her house. It would've been politer to knock.

"It'll be less haunting when you've finished?" asked Jackson.

"I doubt it," replied Sienna, shaking her head slowly. "Might haunt me less though," she added in a voice so low she wasn't sure Jackson heard.

~10~

VISITATION

"I want you to sign this."

"What?" Sienna asked.

Uncle Cole stomped forward and thrust a piece of paper in her face. It was a declaration stating that she wouldn't leave the house during the holidays.

"You're kidding, right?" she asked, not reading past the first line.

"I don't trust your word," Uncle Cole replied.

"But you trust my signature?"

This was a new low. Sienna signed without bothering to read the rest of it, tossing it back at Uncle Cole and turning away. It proved to be a stupid mistake when she left to go grocery shopping the next morning.

"Get inside now!" growled Uncle Cole.

Sienna stood on the path, staring at the front gate, willing herself to turn around. She hadn't tried to sneak out, but now wished she had. "What?" she asked defiantly. "I'm just getting food. Surely that's not banned."

"I said you weren't to leave the house and I meant it."

"I have to eat."

"Get inside."

"No!"

Sienna knew Uncle Cole wouldn't like the public nature of their argument, so with another comment about her rights, she turned and walked towards the gate.

It shouldn't have come as any surprise how strong Uncle Cole was. Sienna fought against him, but that only resulted in him marching her back into the house with her arm pinned behind her back. She couldn't even sneak out once he left.

Sitting on the verandah with her sketch book, Sienna was

disheartened by the hourly drive-by of a police car. Every time they passed, they earned a finger. When the car drove past at four, a hand emerged from the window, returning her gesture. Sienna smiled; her displeasure momentarily overridden by the connection to another living soul.

Five minutes later, Sienna's phone beeped.

What u doing?

Sienna replied to Jackson's text message, but not very politely. Jackson didn't respond, but he didn't drive past again either.

When Uncle Cole arrived home just after six, he brought dinner with him. Hamburger and chips. He didn't stay long and once he was gone, she threw it out. She wasn't desperate enough to eat it.

It was a stupid decision. Uncle Cole found the uneaten food in the bin the next morning. He was livid. She was sure he only just managed to hold himself back from slapping her again.

He didn't bring any food home that night.

Sienna ran out of food the next day, despite having rationed what she had. When Uncle Cole again came home without dinner for her, she had to get creative with what remained in the kitchen. Uncle Cole's house wasn't the kind to have stores of long-life foods. No baked beans. No eggs or flour. Soon there was nothing left but milk, sugar and coffee.

The milk got her through, but when it ran out Uncle Cole replaced it with single portion UHT milk. Then there was only water and coffee left. Sienna avoided the coffee, wondering if there would be any way of dying of starvation before the holidays ended.

Sitting on the verandah, Sienna contemplated whether it was worth trying to exploit Jackson's neglect of his duty and sneak down to the shops, but that idea was thwarted by the police car stopping in front of her house.

"Didn't want to have lunch by myself today," Jackson smiled, as he strolled up the path.

Sienna drank in his smile, savouring the sight over the image of Flynn's panicked eyes and lifeless body fixed in her mind.

"Hope you're not planning on having it here. There's nothing to eat," she replied flatly.

"You always say that and we always find something to cook. Come on," mocked Jackson, tapping her on the shoulder and walking inside.

Sienna followed Jackson to the kitchen, but stood in the doorway, leaving him to discover the emptiness of the cupboards. He looked at her questioningly, but she just turned away.

"What's going on, Sienna?"

"Fuck off, Jackson," she snapped. "Like you don't know. You're the one ordered to drive by every hour. I'm not allowed to leave the house."

"So what did you eat this morning?" he asked. Sienna didn't answer. "No, screw this."

Jackson stormed out of the house. Sienna curled up on her bed and closed her eyes, willing the world to end. The sound of the front door opening and closing made her stomach drop. She was going to pay for Jackson's interference.

"Hey, I've got food for you." Jackson sat on her bed and rubbed her arm. She didn't move. "Come on. You'll feel better when you eat." Taking her hand, Jackson led her back to the kitchen. There were two bags of Chinese takeaway. "I got a few different dishes. This should see you through."

"Thank you," replied Sienna, throwing her arms around his neck. Tears burned her eyes, but she forced herself not to cry. "How much was it?" Jackson refused to answer, walking away as she tried to pushed fifty dollars into his hand. "Please. Take it. For later. When you go shopping. Just get me some essentials. Things that don't go off."

"I'm going to sort this out, okay," Jackson said firmly, as he left.

Sienna was so sick with fear she couldn't eat. She just curled up on her bed, waiting for Uncle Cole. The sight of Jackson at her bedroom door three hours later was not comforting.

"You here to warn me about Uncle Cole?" she asked tentatively.

"I'm here to take you shopping," smiled Jackson triumphantly.

"What?" she asked, jumping up from her bed. "How?"

"Ryan wanted me to work back. I kinda made a fuss about needing to go shopping cos I was cooking dinner for a date tonight. The Chief walked out of his office and told me you needed to go shopping, so I could take you. I whinged a bit and he lost it, insisting I take you shopping – if I wanted to keep my job in this town," Jackson added, with a remarkable impersonation of Uncle Cole.

It was a big shop. Sienna made sure she bought lots of basics that would see her through any future period of unexpected house arrest. Jackson also contributed to her trolley, throwing in foods she'd never considered buying with a promise that he'd teach her how to cook with them.

"Call the Chief," said Jackson, as they carried all the groceries into the kitchen. "Tell him you'll cook him a great dinner to make up for being a pain lately."

Sienna was sure it was useless, but called anyway. She'd knew how to grovel, but Uncle Cole sounded unconvinced. It surprised her when he eventually agreed. Jackson stayed to help cook, but left well before Uncle Cole was due home.

Walking back to the kitchen after seeing Jackson to the door, Sienna found it a much darker place than it had been a moment ago. It left her without the smile she needed to greet Uncle Cole. She managed to counter his disappointment by claiming to be worried how the dinner would turn out; she'd never cooked lasagne before.

Uncle Cole smiled warmly. "Well it smells great," he said, hugging her tenderly. "It's a very nice thing to do."

Dinner was pleasant. It was quiet, but there was no anger or resentment hanging over them.

"I'm going to try and disappoint you less," said Sienna, when their plates were empty. "I'm trying, but you have to give me some room to move." Uncle Cole didn't answer. "It'd be nice to do this more often. Maybe if we have a chance to talk – see each other – we might get on better."

"It's not that easy, Sen. I'm not out all the time because I want to be. We're understaffed by two. I'm waiting for the extra men, but until we get them I can't just drop everything and run home to you for dinner."

"I know," Sienna nodded. But she didn't. Westloch covered all the night shifts. Most evenings Uncle Cole was finished by seven. There was always one more excuse for her family not to actually spend time with her. "What about shopping?"

"You'll have to do more than cook dinner to earn my trust," Uncle Cole said, before sighing heavily. "You can go with Jackson when he shops."

"But he's a cop!" cried Sienna, trying Jackson's tactic, but it made her wonder who Uncle Cole thought he was punishing.

"You didn't have any problem shopping with him today."

"I was hungry today," Sienna muttered.

"When you get hungry enough, you can go with him. I don't trust you by yourself and Jackson's the only one of my men who can handle being around you."

Despite getting what she wanted, Sienna went to bed deflated.

Sienna looked over at the clock. Eleven-forty-two. She'd been sitting at her desk since breakfast, determined not to move until she'd caught up, but she was starting to think she would die of old age first. Nothing about maths made sense to her brain. Numbers and formulas swirled in her mind in a way that meant she never combined them correctly.

Straining her ears, Sienna hoped to hear a knock at the door. An unexpected visitor would provide a legitimate excuse to escape her desk, but that was just wishful thinking. She hadn't seen Jackson since he took her shopping, and though Uncle Cole was less angry with her, he was still rarely around to talk to.

Before Sienna knew it, she was dialling her mother's office. It went straight through to Janice's secretary. Sienna immediately hung up. She'd only spoken to that woman once – long enough to be told not to bother Janice with unimportant calls. Sienna never got the chance to say why she'd been calling and always wondered if Janice had asked her secretary to prevent her calls from being put through.

Despite that, Sienna's fingers hovered over her mother's mobile number. She hit the dial button. The sound of the phone ringing made her heart stammer. She was about to hang up when Janice answered.

"Sienna? What's happened? Are you all right?"

Sienna couldn't answer. She didn't have a good reason for calling, certainly not the emergency Janice was expecting.

"Sienna? What's going on?"

"Nothing, everything's fine," sighed Sienna. "Sorry, I shouldn't have interrupted."

"Sienna, what's wrong?" demanded Janice.

"Nothing. I'll leave you alone. I just called to say hi, okay," she replied.

There was only silence. Sienna closed her eyes. She held on to the sob that was building in her chest as she went to hang up.

"Is it cold out there today?" asked Janice. Sienna gasped, trying to swallow her sob as she answered in the affirmative. "It's been freezing here. Cold and windy. I think that's why we work so hard in the winter. It's too nice and cosy in the office."

They spoke about non-descript things for the next five minutes before Janice suddenly asked Sienna about the weekend. When Sienna relayed her study plans, Janice asked if she would like a visitor.

"But I'm grounded."

"No one grounds my child to stop them from seeing me," said Janice fiercely. "I'll be there Friday afternoon."

"Um, maybe you should talk to Uncle Cole first," replied Sienna tentatively. "He's still really mad at me about that weekend. I'm not supposed to leave the house at all these holidays."

"Sen, do you want to spend the weekend with me?"

"If I'm allowed."

"That's not what I asked. Do you want me to come out so we can have a weekend together? Just the two of us?"

"Yes," replied Sienna, too scared to answer differently.

"Then I'm coming. I'm never going to be forced to ask permission to see my own child again."

That phone call was all it took to destroy the tentative truce one lasagne dinner had forged between her and Uncle Cole. He was cynical about the reason for Janice's trip. Sienna was too. She didn't know why her mother would come out to see her. They'd never shown any interest in her life. Then she realised she'd been telling them how much study she'd been doing. Perhaps they wanted to check up on her to confirm she wasn't lying.

Knowing she would never be able to impress Janice with her achievements so far, especially not compared to what Stephen had done, Sienna worked harder and longer. Uncle Cole walked in on her at two am on Friday morning. She was still studying at her desk.

"Don't know why you're pushing yourself like this," he muttered. "Won't make them love you. If they knew you at all they wouldn't be pushing you to be a lawyer."

"But I want to be a lawyer too," replied Sienna tentatively.

Uncle Cole looked at her sceptically for a long moment before speaking. "Jackson has a date in Westloch tonight. He said he'd take you to the airport to meet Janice."

"What do you have planned for the weekend?"

"Work. I have to work," Uncle Cole answered aggressively. "Some of us don't have the luxury of jetting off every other weekend. Some of us have to work hard for our money."

Sienna didn't reply. It wasn't fair how much money her family had, but she could never say her parents didn't work hard. They worked so much that she was just an afterthought.

Uncle Cole didn't say anything else and was gone by the time Sienna emerged from her shower. It wasn't until after breakfast that she saw his note on her desk.

Have a good time

The handwriting was scrawled, like it'd been forced from his fingers and there were pen marks below it, as though he'd been on the verge of saying something more. Sienna wondered if he was scared she would pick her family's money over him and if he believed that was what had lured her away before. He needn't have worried. She had never felt entitled to her family's money.

It was Arthur's parents who had the money. Old money. A long line of prominent judges, politicians and people of influence who had been collecting land and wealth since colonisation. Sienna only met her paternal grandparents a few times in her childhood; enough to know that their preference for Stephen was more extreme than her parents'. Never had they referred to her as their granddaughter and Sienna had never received a minute of affection from them. She didn't expect a cent from them when they died. She wasn't even sure she expected anything from her parents.

When the world looked at Sienna, they saw a spoilt heiress. As Sienna looked at Uncle Cole's note, she realised she didn't see herself that way and didn't want to be that girl. She wanted to be the daughter of a police officer. Uncle Cole's life, with all its faults, was much closer to the life she wanted to lead than her parents'.

The knowledge that she would never belong to her parents' world did not make packing easier. It was one more thing that divided them; an unforgivable transgression in her parents' eyes. For now, it would have to be a secret she kept, until she could release herself of financial obligation to her parents.

"You looking forward to your mother's visit?" asked Jackson, strolling into the house behind Sienna, having knocked for once.

"I'm still waiting for her to cancel," Sienna replied honestly. "Still don't get why she's coming out. Maybe I've done something wrong and they don't want to tell me off over the phone."

"You don't think there's a chance your mum's really excited about spending a weekend with you?"

"No."

"You're not taking all that with you, are you?" asked Jackson, as Sienna picked up a large bag of books and a small bag of clothes.

"You don't know my mum. She can't switch off. She'll be working the whole time she's out here, so I'd better have stuff to do."

Jackson didn't say anything. He just took the heavy bag and walked out to his car.

"We picking up your date?" asked Sienna, as Jackson headed out of town. "Or you meeting her in Westloch."

"I don't have a date," smiled Jackson sheepishly. "Your brother may've told me about your mum coming out and I may've lied about having a date."

"Why?"

"Well, I don't exactly plan on not having a date the whole night," said Jackson. "I'm meeting up with some guys after I drop you off. It'll be good to get away from Fortune. I've spent way too many Friday nights at your place. I hate it."

"Sorry," said Sienna automatically.

"It's not your fault," Jackson laughed. "It's just the way the Chief runs things out here. I don't know that I could stay the way Ryan has and Ian wants to, but they're made from the same mould. Well Ryan less so. I think he has more heart."

"You can just drop me at the airport then," said Sienna. "I'll hang until the plane arrives."

"And what happens if the plane's cancelled?"

"Probably know by now," shrugged Sienna. "And Uncle Cole won't mind rescuing me. He's never as angry when they stuff up as when they try and do something nice."

"So you're just going to send me packing without so much as a coffee to say thanks for the ride?"

Sienna was mortified. She hadn't been planning to do anything more than say thanks as she jumped out of the car. Jackson assured her he'd been joking, but she wasn't sure.

"Now this is how you make friends," said Jackson, when she placed a coffee and a large piece of cake in front of him as they sat down at a café in Westloch. "You having some or planning to take me out with a heart attack?"

"No, no. I got it for you," Sienna replied, sitting back and waving her hand.

"Seriously, it's practically half a cake. Eat some."

Not wanting to be lectured on her eating habits, Sienna dutifully wiped her spoon and cut off a small piece of the cake. Jackson laughed, but said nothing. He just took another spoonful, silently inviting her to have more whenever she stopped.

"You're good. You never seem to eat sweets, despite constantly cooking them for us at the station."

"I used to. Uncle Cole likes sweets. We ate a lot when I was a kid," said Sienna. Jackson smiled broadly and Sienna shrugged. "Wasn't allowed to have it at my parents' house. Taught myself not to like it."

"Why'd you live with Chief to begin with? Your brother ever live with him?"

"No," Sienna scoffed. "They love Stephen. Wouldn't ever ship him off and pretend he didn't exist." Jackson didn't respond. Sienna sighed heavily. "I don't know," she confessed. "No one's ever explained. From as early as I know I lived with Uncle Cole and Aunt Daphne. Didn't live with my parents til I was ten. Hardly had anything to do with them."

"So what happened when you went to live with them?"

"Nothing. They still didn't want me. All they wanted was to win me from Uncle Cole and I was stupid enough to be sucked into letting them. That's why Uncle Cole's so hard on me now – thinks I'll go live with them again. Never forgave me for leaving."

"What about now?" asked Jackson.

"Who knows. Only time I see them is when I've stuffed up," Sienna said bitterly. "They barely spoke to me after the accident. All I ever wanted was for them to like me and I could never make them. They're all brilliant and I'm not. I'm just a nobody. Maybe they always knew – could tell from the start – and that's why they gave me up. Just don't know why they keep up the charade of wanting me round. If they'd just told the truth then maybe we would've had some kind of relationship. Uncle Cole could've been my dad like he always wanted and they could've just been my aunt and uncle – never dealing with the difficult stuff."

Jackson stayed quiet. Sienna knew there was nothing to say. There was no way to adequately explain her parents' rejection of her.

With the mood effectively ruined, Jackson suggested they head to the airport.

"You don't have to stay," Sienna insisted, when Jackson pulled into a parking spot. "I've got this, seriously." Jackson followed her into the terminal and flicked his finger towards the little coffee shop that had opened for the arriving and departing flight. Sienna brought him back another coffee.

"Tell me about your aunt," he said, as he drank. "I can't imagine the Chief married."

"I liked her. She was a lot like Uncle Cole, but sunnier. The early years, they were good. When it was just us – just living – no fights about my parents – that's when I was happiest. Changed in the later years though. They fought more. Got bitter."

"Being a cop's a tough job," said Jackson softly.

"I know. He used to talk to us about it sometimes. He was different back then. Always really protective, but he wasn't always this distant. Aunt Daphne was able to reach him in a way no one else could. She could make him really smile. I used to think they were really good together."

"Used to?"

"The last two years weren't very good. Really bitter. Horrible, horrible fights. She left after I went to live with my parents."

Jackson nodded, but no one spoke. They just sat in silence until the plane landed. Janice was the third person off the plane. Sienna swayed on seeing her, unsure whether she should rush forward and throw her arms around her, hoping Janice would reciprocate as enthusiastically, or act coolly the way she always had. Janice's smile faltered slightly on seeing her. Sienna held back, cursing herself for continuing to believe things would change.

"Mrs Hollingsworth," said Jackson formally, holding out his hand. "Jackson Halley."

"Thank you for bringing Sienna to meet me. I hope we haven't put you out," replied Janice, shaking Jackson's hand.

"I'd planned a night out here anyway."

"That's very convenient. I fly out on Monday morning at seven. I got the impression my brother would be working. You wouldn't happen to have another engagement here then, would you? Perhaps on Sunday night? I'd be happy to pay for you to stay the night if you could take Sienna home in the morning."

Jackson looked mystified and Sienna felt a strange sensation as her lips curled into a slight smile.

"Yeah, I think I do have to meet a mate here Sunday night. I have a late start Monday morning, so that would work fine," replied Jackson hesitantly.

"That's wonderful," smiled Janice. "We'll book you a room where we're staying. Perhaps you can join us for dinner or supper."

"I'll let you know how things go with my mate," smiled Jackson. "Can I take you anywhere now?"

Janice politely refused, indicating that they would hire a car. As soon as Jackson left, Janice put her arm around Sienna's shoulders and led her out of the airport. They went straight to the hotel. Sienna was gobsmacked by the room. It was a two-bedroom apartment that felt only marginally smaller than Uncle Cole's house.

"You don't mind just eating at the hotel restaurant, do you?" asked Janice.

Sienna shook her head, not daring to mind anything. It was a quiet meal. Sienna wasn't sure what she could talk about, but asked the initial questions about how things were at home. Janice responded in great detail. Sienna noticed that their lives didn't seem any different to when she'd been there. There was no hole caused by her absence or wistful memories of when she'd been around.

When Janice asked about life in Fortune, Sienna's answers were very short. They had to have known her social standing had been destroyed during their last visit.

"Jackson seems very nice. Do you spend much time with him?" asked Janice. Sienna shook her head. "He reminds me of Flynn a bit. I don't know why." Sienna's head snapped up, her eyes bulging. "Makes me think Flynn would've turned out all right in the end. Settled down."

Sienna felt her lungs compressing, leaving her gasping for breath. She didn't know how to control them or the tears burning her eyes.

"Hey, shhh. Sen, what's wrong?" asked Janice.

Sienna shook her head, not daring to speak. Janice continued to question her, but she couldn't answer. When Janice's hand reached out and squeezed Sienna's, she lost control, a painful sob bursting from her lungs. Janice pushed immediately from the table. Sienna realised how much she must've embarrassed her, so dashed back to their room, but that only left her sobbing at the locked door.

Janice came up behind Sienna and guided her inside and on to the lounge. Sienna curled up in her arms, unable to contain the grief that had been released with one simple comment.

"I'm sorry, Sen," said Janice, stroking Sienna's hair. "I shouldn't have said anything. I assumed you would've seen it too."

"I did. I do," gasped Sienna. "He has Flynn's smile."

"Does that make it easier or harder?"

"Both."

Janice didn't ask any more questions. Sienna shifted out of her arms, hurrying to bed. She'd never displayed such emotion in front of her parents before.

Sienna heard Janice talking on the phone and was sure she was telling Arthur she regretted wasting her time coming out. Even Janice's sigh was audible as the lights flicked off.

The isolation of the last few months started to squeeze Sienna, even more so knowing human contact was just a room away, but still out of reach. She stared up at the ceiling feeling like there was another heavy blanket pressing down on her. If she closed her eyes, it felt like she was sinking. She would've let it swallow her if she thought it would take her to Flynn.

Slipping out of bed, Sienna listened for any sign that Janice was still awake. She grabbed her quilt and snuck into the other bedroom. Janice was sleeping peacefully. The sound of her rhythmic breath was calming. It reminded Sienna of sleeping next to Flynn. Spreading her quilt on the floor, she laid down and pulled it around her body.

Pain speared through Sienna's leg as a scream filled the air. It took a moment for her to realise that it wasn't her who'd cried out. The bedside lamp switched on.

"Sienna, what are you doing?" cried Janice. "You scared me half to death."

"Sorry," Sienna replied tersely.

"Is there something wrong with your bed? What happened?"

Sienna didn't reply, feeling stupid and childish. Janice kept staring at her, silently demanding an answer.

"I said sorry, okay," Sienna muttered, grabbing her quilt and stalking back to her cold bed.

Janice followed, turning on the light. "I want you to tell me why you were sleeping on the floor in my room."

"I was just lonely," Sienna answered defensively, curling her body away from Janice.

"Then why didn't you hop into the bed?" asked Janice softly, sitting on the edge of the bed.

"Only little kids sleep with their parents. You would've thought I was a loser."

"I'd never think that," said Janice, stroking Sienna's hair. "Ever."

Sienna closed her eyes, hoping to hold back the tears. She'd never thought of her mother as soft before. Or even kind. But the way she lied, just to protect her feelings, and laid next to her until she fell asleep made her more grateful than she could express.

It was late when Sienna woke. Janice was already dressed and sitting on the lounge with a pile of documents. Sienna scurried to the bathroom and under the shower.

"Sorry, I should've set an alarm," said Sienna, throwing on clothes and rushing back out to the lounge room.

"I curse the fact that I can't sleep-in," said Janice, putting the papers in her bag. "Too many decades of getting up at five-thirty. The best I've managed in years has been seven. So what would you like to do today? Have you seen much of the district?" Sienna shook her head. "What about the times you came out to visit during the holidays?"

"I mainly hung out at Uncle Cole's farm. Or helped at the station."

Janice didn't look happy with that answer and Sienna suddenly realised she expected her to be their guide on this trip. She'd never once considered it as she crammed more and more study into fewer and fewer hours. Walking through the hotel lobby, Sienna grabbed all the maps and tourist material she could find. She sorted through it in the car, but really didn't know her mother well enough to suggest where they could go. She didn't want to stuff this up.

"There's a winery about fifteen minutes out of town. Should we go there?" asked Sienna, quickly looking up from the map to gauge her mother's reaction.

"Sen, I didn't come out here for a winery tour. I want us to do something together," said Janice, stopping the car. "But I'm not going anywhere without breakfast and a good coffee."

Janice looked over the maps as they ate. Whatever she suggested, Sienna agreed with, but the plans changed so quickly she'd agreed to ten different things within five minutes.

"Can you stop agreeing with everything I say," Janice snapped.

"I don't know what's the best things to see," said Sienna defensively.

"Then we'll just have to find out, won't we."

Sienna didn't answer, staying silent as they finished breakfast and drove out of town. It was awkward. She didn't know how to talk to someone who was so familiar yet also a complete stranger.

"Will you tell me what it's like living out here?" asked Janice, after twenty minutes of silence. "Do you like it?"

"I didn't think I was supposed to," Sienna replied sceptically. "I was sent here as punishment, not to have a good time."

"That's not true. You said you wanted to come out here."

"What was the point in saying I didn't? Wasn't like I had a choice."

Janice looked at her curiously before turning her gaze back to the road.

"Did you bring your camera with you today?" asked Janice, when she stopped the car.

"I don't have a camera," replied Sienna agitatedly, feeling like these conversations were designed to test her.

"What are you talking about? What about the camera we got you? You were always using it."

"That's yours. You let me use it, but I couldn't take it. It doesn't belong to me."

"Where is it then?" asked Janice accusingly, before her voice softened. "I assumed you took it with you. I bought another camera after you left. I've been having lessons," she smiled proudly.

"It's in your office," mumbled Sienna. "I packed it up before I left."

"Well why don't we test out this new one," said Janice, hopping out of the car.

Sienna looked around and noticed they were at the start of a small track that led to a lookout. Following Janice to the boot, she watched her pull out her new camera.

"Wow!" gasped Sienna. It was ten times more impressive than the one they had let her use.

"I thought you'd like it. You want to test it out?" asked Janice. Sienna shook her head. "You going to teach me to use it then? I think I overextended myself. Your photography was a little too inspiring."

There was something clumsy about the way Janice handled the camera. It was so unlike the way Uncle Cole had taught Sienna to scan the scenery and find her image. When Janice asked about one of the functions, Sienna briefly explained its use, but didn't go into detail. Janice was already turning to take another picture.

"You have a go," insisted Janice, placing the camera in Sienna's hands. "I can't get a feel of this thing."

Sienna immediately engaged the manual settings. She'd learned on older cameras and though she liked many of the newer functions she could only settle herself in by fixing all the settings herself. Over time it had become almost instinctual. Uncle Cole had encouraged that. He and Aunt Daphne had taught her that art was something you felt your way through.

Sienna looked over the landscape, immediately finding the scene she wanted to capture. She moved around constantly, even daring to take a photo of her mother when she wasn't looking.

"You ever thought about doing this sort of thing as a career?" asked Janice.

"I thought you wanted me to be a lawyer," said Sienna, wondering if it was a trap.

"We do," said Janice firmly. "I just wanted to know what you've thought of."

"Nothing," replied Sienna seriously. "You and Dad want me to do law, so I've just been focusing on that."

"But you must've had your own thoughts about your future."

"Nope," shrugged Sienna, not prepared to discuss the lives she and Flynn had dreamed of. Those futures were gone. They'd never really existed and Sienna knew it was easier not to fight when she had no chance of winning.

"I ended up enlarging and framing some of your pictures," said Janice thoughtfully, watching Sienna move into a different position. "We gave a picture of Flynn to his parents. They really liked it. And the photo we gave them for the funeral."

"Which pictures?" asked Sienna, her voice breaking.

"One was by the water somewhere. The other in a park. They were really beautiful. You have a good eye for this stuff."

The camera dropped from Sienna's eye. She moved down the track, trying to see the beauty that minutes ago she'd wanted to capture forever, but everything looked darker now, washed out, as if clouds had come across the sun. When Janice mentioned seeing a nice photo opportunity, Sienna handed her the camera.

To keep her mind occupied, Sienna talked Janice through the technicalities of the camera. Janice took photo after photo, lamenting that she'd never remember what setting she'd used for each.

"You think we should go back the way we came?" asked Janice, looking at her watch. It was after one. "Did you read the sign? How long did it say the walk was? Maybe it wasn't a circle. I think we should go back."

"It's a circular track," said Sienna immediately, before stopping. She hadn't read the sign properly and didn't want to give her mother the wrong information.

"Tomorrow, let's pack food and water. Thank goodness I had a substantial breakfast."

Sienna's stomach rumbled in response. She'd only had toast. They kept going, but Janice constantly glanced behind her, sure they should turn back. She even started claiming they were lost.

"I'm sure this will lead us out sooner than turning around," said Sienna uneasily, although she was tempted to just give in and go back. "I think we've just been walking slow."

Janice looked up at the sky just as the sun went behind a heavy cloud, darkening the ground. "Can you imagine the headlines? Your father won't let me go anywhere by myself if we have to be rescued." She laughed darkly, but Sienna wasn't sure she was joking. It would be just her luck to be blamed for her parents' divorce. It made her anxious to get to the end of the track.

"Oh look, Sen, you were right!" cried Janice, suddenly spying the end of the track a few minutes later. "Thank goodness I listened to you. Would've been walking forever if we'd turned back."

Sienna wasn't sure that was accurate either, but said nothing as they jumped in the car and headed back towards Westloch.

"They do dinner," said Sienna, pointing at winery.

Janice didn't slow. She looked at Sienna curiously. Sienna felt her heart pounding, wondering what it was her mother was searching for.

"Ooh, look, Sen. Honey farm. Let's check that out."

Sienna had never cared much for honey, but her mother looked like a kid in a candy store. Sienna really didn't know her at all. The café was still open and Janice pulled her to a table, collapsing heavily into the chair. Janice studied the menu intently. Sienna watched curiously. Janice had always been very strict on their diets. It surprised Sienna then that her mother was paying no attention to the health content of the food, just whether she felt like it or not.

When the honey banana bread her mother ordered arrived, Sienna was shocked by the size of it and the fact that her mother spread the butter happily over its toasted face before cutting it into squares and eating joyously.

"Mmm, you should really have a piece," said Janice, pushing the plate towards Sienna. "It's nice." Sienna picked up the smallest piece and took a tiny bite. "You can eat more than that. You must be starving. You hardly ate at breakfast."

"You know how bad banana bread is for you, right? It's practically the kilojoule count of a meal."

"One, I'm on holidays," said Janice with the hint of a lecture. "You know we don't eat like this every day. Two, we just got ourselves lost and disorientated on a perfectly good bush trail. I think that warrants banana bread." Sienna wasn't convinced. "It's just food, Sen, not black magic. Just enjoy it."

Sienna had enjoyed food once, but her parents had lectured her out of it. When Janice's hand reached out and squeezed hers, she tried to believe those days were over. It would be nice to just enjoy the moment. Sienna took another piece of the banana bread and was relieved when her mother smiled.

"Did you want to go back to that winery for dinner?" asked Janice, when they returned to the car laden down with bags of honey-based products. "Or head back to town?"

"I just really want a shower," Sienna replied guiltily.

"Great minds think alike."

Sienna tried not to dawdle when they got back to the hotel. If they were going to find somewhere nice to eat, they would have to go out again soon. However, Janice appeared to be in no rush and Sienna was dressed and ready well before her.

"How attached are you to going out for dinner?" asked Janice, walking out of her room in very casual clothes. Sienna had made sure she was dressed properly, so shrugged, unsure where this was going. "How would you feel about going down to the supermarket, grabbing some popcorn, ordering room service and watching a movie in bed?"

"Really? You'd want to do that?" asked Sienna sceptically.

"You wouldn't?"

"No, it sounds great. I just wouldn't have thought you …"

"Well, I don't think there'll be much difference in the quality of food," sighed Janice. "Can't exactly expose you to a better class of people or standard of living out here. Might as well relax and spend a quiet night together."

Sienna was sure Janice hadn't meant to insult her, but it still felt like a rejection of who she was.

~11~

PATH TO NOWHERE

"Let's not get ourselves lost today, hey," said Janice, nudging Sienna gently as they hopped out of the car near another walking track. "We want to make it back in time to have dinner with Jackson."

Sienna nodded eagerly. The flashes of tenderness Janice had shown her yesterday made her want to experience more. It gave her hope that if she could be a better daughter – be the kind of daughter they wanted – she might know something close to love from her parents.

To show that she really did want to make them proud, Sienna asked all the questions she'd never cared much about before. They discussed the business, its history and their vision for the future. Sienna asked where her place in it would be and what they ultimately wanted from her.

"Well, I guess company and contract law would be the most useful," answered Janice. "If we get sucked into a bad agreement, it costs us millions."

Sienna didn't ask why she needed to have a law degree when Janice, Arthur and Stephen all had one. Janice and Stephen also had business degrees; Arthur an arts degree. What use they were in property development was also beyond Sienna's understanding. As far as Sienna had been able to tell, the only thing her parents' company made was money.

"Once you join the company and settle in, your father and I want to pull back a bit. Start transitioning it over to you and Stephen."

"But surely there're other people who could run it," said Sienna.

"We've built this company from the ground up," said Janice firmly. "You don't do that and then give away the profits to strangers."

"So that's the only reason you want me to do law?" asked Sienna, feeling more unsure of her future by the minute.

"Mostly. It always had to be something that would advantage the company, but you had other influences pointing you towards law."

Flynn. A strange misconception. He'd always hoped Arthur and Janice would consider law unsuitable for her and thus sanction another career path for them. Anything but law. Anything to avoid following in his father's footsteps. Arthur and Janice had some sway with Flynn's parents, but perhaps Flynn's parents had had more.

When Sienna stayed silent, Janice started listing other possible career paths within the company. Business. Finance.

"What do you want to do?" asked Janice. "I mean, it's really up to you."

"I want to do law," mumbled Sienna, not daring to confess her inability to do anything that required even a hint of maths.

Janice smiled warmly. This was the one avenue Sienna had to make her parents proud, and possibly even love her. It would be hard, but she was more determined than ever to be a lawyer.

"Got the camera?" asked Janice. Sienna nodded. "Will you take some photos of me today?"

"But you hate having your photo taken," replied Sienna, having learned that from bitter experience.

"I'm getting over it."

Sienna nodded and started walking towards the track. The sign claimed it was only a twenty-minute round trip to the lookout, and this time Sienna read all the information before trotting after Janice.

Janice asked where Sienna wanted her for the photos. Sienna was hesitant at first, but Janice turned out to be the perfect subject. She did whatever Sienna asked. And she was beautiful.

"I think I got a few good shots," said Sienna, as they looked out over the surrounding countryside.

"Just a few?" laughed Janice, though her eyes looked wary.

"I'm not a professional," replied Sienna defensively. "Can't take a great shot every time."

Janice pursed her lips and Sienna knew she was unhappy with that reality. So was she. She wished she could be great at something, even if it wasn't what her parents wanted her to excel at.

"Will you be my subject?" asked Janice, reaching out for the camera. "I need to get better at using this thing."

Sienna smiled at her mother's use of the word 'thing'. Janice didn't make Sienna move around like she had. She seemed content to find a nice spot for her to sit and moved around her. It was not Sienna's way, but it was nice to not have to do anything but stare out to space.

"I think I've got enough," said Janice. She looked downhearted. Sienna wondered if she made an ugly subject. "Shall we find lunch?"

"We should've packed a picnic. Then we could've eaten wherever we liked," mused Sienna.

She wished she hadn't. Her mother's disappointment was horrible. Sienna had thought about it, but hadn't dared suggest it. Aunt Daphne and Uncle Cole had often taken her on picnics, but her parents always avoided doing anything associated with Uncle Cole.

Janice suggested they find a deli and then search for a nice spot to eat. It didn't transpire that way. Nothing met Janice's standards. So after almost an hour and a half of driving, they settled on a pub that had a nice beer garden and decent food.

"Do you know what time Jackson finishes his shift today?" asked Janice, as they walked back to the car. Sienna shook her head. "Then let's head back now. I don't want him waiting around for us. We'll have to find somewhere nice for dinner."

Their timing was perfect. Jackson was just getting out of his car when they pulled into the hotel car park. He looked very unsure.

"Jackson," smiled Janice, walking over and shaking his hand. "What are your plans for tonight? We were just talking about dinner."

Jackson seemed ill at ease as he spoke to Janice, but smiled warmly at Sienna when she joined them. Although his room had already been booked and paid for, Janice went with him to check him in. He was in the room next to theirs.

"Come by once you've settled in. We'll have some tea," said Janice, opening the door for him before handing him the card. It was like he was a guest in their own house.

Sienna took the opportunity to head to the shower, standing under the hot water as she reflected on the weekend. She couldn't call it a success, but found that she liked Janice more than she ever expected. She might be critical of her, but she was company. It was so unlike the absent disapproval of Uncle Cole.

So caught up in her thoughts, Sienna was shocked to see Jackson sitting on the lounge when she walked out of the bathroom with just a towel around her. Jackson smiled as she passed, but quickly turned away and resumed his conversation with Janice, for which Sienna was very grateful. When she returned to the lounge room, he gave no hint that he had just seen her semi-naked.

"Jackson had some ideas on where we could go for dinner. He said there's a nice Italian restaurant nearby. That sound good to you?" asked Janice, as Sienna looked for a place to sit. Janice was on one lounge and Jackson on the other, but both lounges were small and Sienna felt awkward sitting with either of them.

Waiting for Sienna's answer, Janice held out her hand and pulled Sienna to sit next to her, asking again if she was happy with the dinner plan. Sienna sighed and nodded, before slipping back into the lounge. Jackson and Janice continued their conversation, talking around her with the kind of ease Sienna could only admire.

It didn't surprise Sienna when Janice invited Jackson back to their apartment for supper at the end of dinner. They'd barely stopped talking all night. Sienna kept quiet, knowing she couldn't contribute anything useful, but she did watch, hoping to learn how to communicate with her mother.

"Did you like your dinner, Sen?" asked Janice, as they waited for the bill.

"Yeah, it was really nice," Sienna replied truthfully.

"You didn't eat much," said Jackson.

He and Janice had helped finish her entrée and main.

"Doesn't mean it wasn't nice," retorted Sienna defensively. "And you and Mum both made me try some of yours."

"So it wasn't just cos you were worried it was too fatty?" asked Jackson sceptically.

Sienna crossed her arms over her chest, feeling exposed. Despite her best efforts, she'd still not found the right way to eat to please anyone. In an attempt to ward off any more comments, Sienna made sure she was the first to take a chocolate when Janice put the plate in front of them back at the apartment. Janice then reached out and offered the plate to Jackson. Sienna sighed with despair. Now she looked rude. Perhaps it was easier living with Uncle Cole.

By the time Jackson finally retired to his room, Sienna was on the verge of tears. Janice watched her with cautious eyes, forcing her to keep it together.

"I'll be up early for my flight tomorrow, but you can sleep in if you like," said Janice.

Sienna understood. Her mother had had enough of her.

Sleep didn't come quickly. When the door creaked open, Sienna shut her eyes. The feel of Janice slipping into her bed made her heart beat erratically. When Janice's hand gently stroked her head, she could pretend no longer and curled into her mother's chest.

Jackson eyed Sienna warily as they got in the car. She wished she'd been able make her own way home. It was ridiculous the number of times Jackson had seen her cry. He'd come to her room an hour after Janice left to find her on the lounge curled up in a ball and sobbing relentlessly. The pressure of the weekend – of trying to make Janice like her – had become too much.

"You okay?" asked Jackson, as they drove. Sienna nodded. "Your mum sounded like she had a really nice time."

"Sure," muttered Sienna.

"Why do you doubt that? She told me."

"Of course she's going to lie to you," spat Sienna. "I'm the one who knows her. Not your fault. I used to believe what they said once too."

Jackson didn't respond. It left Sienna free to mentally list off all the things she had to do when she got home. The most important was to return the camera. She'd been sure she'd given it back to Janice, but even her best intentions were failing her.

The whole morning was dedicated to going through the photos. Sienna was impressed by them, but knew her parents wouldn't be as easily pleased. Focusing on the ones of Janice, Sienna picked three and worked on them to make them just right. Attaching them to an email, Sienna promised she would send the camera back as soon as possible.

It must've been an issue. Arthur called three minutes later.

"Hi, Dad," she sighed, waiting for the barrage.

"Hey, Sen," Arthur replied cheerfully. "Thanks for sending those photos through. They're wonderful."

"Mum's too pretty to take a bad photo of."

"How'd the ones of you turn out? The ones your mum took."

"Yeah, okay."

"That good, huh?"

"She didn't have a great subject."

"Can you send them to us? Put them on a USB. Yours too."

Sienna tapped her head with her palm. Why couldn't she think of even the simplest things? "Yeah, I'll put them in with the camera," she replied. "Can you tell Mum I'm really sorry I forgot to give it to her."

"You did give it to her. She left it for you," said Arthur. "She really never got the hang of using that thing. First thing she did this morning was go find the old camera. Practically hugged it. She wants you to use that camera." Sienna could only nod. She didn't know how to react to such kindness from her parents. "You have a good time?"

"Yeah," Sienna replied, her voice crackling slightly. "It was great."

"Even with your mother trying to convince you that you were lost on a perfectly good track?"

"She told you about that?"

"Of course, she did."

"But she said you wouldn't let her travel alone again if you knew."

"And I'm not sure I will. At least not out to see you. I feel like I missed out on too much fun."

"Really? Mum didn't hate it?"

"Sen, why would you think that? You know we love to see you and spend time with you."

"But you never do."

"It's a bit hard at the moment with you living so far away," said Arthur, a hard edge to his voice.

"But you never did. The only time you spoke to me when I lived with you was when I was in trouble. I know that was all the time, but … that's how I knew you guys never wanted me around."

Sienna pulled up short, shocked that she'd said so much. She waited for Arthur to react – to contradict her – but there was nothing but silence. Sienna swallowed her sob and took a deep breath. "I'm going to work real hard this term – for my exams. I can make things better. Make you proud. A little bit."

"That's good, Sen. It's great your studying hard. I am really proud of you. We all are," Arthur replied. Sienna could hear the hesitation in his voice and knew what it was that was making him lie. "I'd better let you get back to it. Don't forget those photos, hey. Your mum's really excited to see them."

The rest of holidays passed with little excitement. Jackson didn't come by and Uncle Cole refused lift his ban on her leaving the house. Foreseeing that possibility allowed her to ration her food more accurately than before. She learned to cook from basics rather than relying on packaged foods, so that when she ran out of bread, she baked damper. It was a victory, but perhaps a self-sacrificing one; Uncle Cole wouldn't arrange a shopping trip until she was desperate.

Thankfully, school started before Sienna reached that point. She would be able to restock the pantry and stash additional food in her bedroom, but Uncle Cole had other ideas, insisting she needed a chaperone. She wasn't to go anywhere but school on her own.

Sienna was determined to test that restriction. Uncle Cole must have realised that by the sigh that escaped him as he left the house. Sienna followed several minutes later, even releasing a similar sigh as she closed the door behind her. She may have done little besides study all holidays, but knew it wouldn't make class any easier to understand. The taunts and teasing that were thrown her way also did nothing to enhance the experience. The only reprieve came in history when Amber sat next to her, but that was because they teased her instead.

Amber didn't last out the lesson. When they were given quiet time to work through the exercises, Amber packed up her things. "Sorry," she mumbled. "I need to do well. Just want somewhere quiet to work."

Sienna nodded, managing a slight smile, as she watched Amber move to a spare desk at the front of the class.

By the end of the day, Sienna was much less keen to test her uncle's authority. She didn't want more trouble.

"Hungry?"

Sienna looked around, caught short by the voice. Flynn's smile shone back at her. She had the immediate compulsion to reach into her chest and pull her heart from her body.

"Chief must think you are. Gave me an early mark to take you shopping," said Jackson, walking towards her.

Jackson was still in uniform, but Sienna was glad he'd put a t-shirt over the top. She followed him towards the shops, but struggled with conversation. Even when they shopped she only grabbed the bare necessities. It surprised her then that her trolley was so full when she went to pay. Jackson said nothing, just watched her cautiously.

"You okay?" Jackson asked, as they unpacked the groceries. Sienna nodded without looking up. "What you want to cook?"

"I don't really care. I'm not really in the mood for food."

"I am. Don't I get a free dinner for taking you shopping?"

Sienna's gut twisted. She had to try hard not to cry. It struck her that it was all she seemed to do now. Her crackled apologies were quickly dismissed, along with her dinner suggestions. Jackson grabbed a whole lot of things from the cupboard and put them on the bench.

"You want me to make something out of that?" asked Sienna.

"I guess I'll have to settle for teaching you how to make something out of this. Didn't you ever learn to cook?"

Sienna turned away. "Privileged existence," she muttered.

"What about before?"

"Where do you think I learned to cook at all?" Sienna asked. "But I never felt at home enough to raid the cupboard at my parents' place."

"Awesome, a student to mould in my very own image," replied Jackson dramatically.

He didn't wait for Sienna to work out how she was supposed to respond, telling her immediately what she needed to do. She liked that he didn't probe, but sometimes wondered if he cut her off because he thought her self-indulgent.

"Hey, keep stirring," said Jackson, gently prodding her.

Sienna smiled and focused on rousing her mood. She was more successful than she expected, finding herself chatting and laughing happily with Jackson as they ate. But when Jackson left, so did the cheerfulness.

Jackson soon became a regular afternoon visitor, though Sienna never knew when to expect him. She had no idea what shifts he worked, but doubted that would have much impact on his availability. Jackson's mutterings about last minute roster changes were all she needed to know that Uncle Cole could exert his influence in multiple ways. Yet Jackson's visits represented more than just the ability to shop. He was company. Even his smile tortured her a little less each visit.

"So how's school?" asked Jackson, while she cleared up after dinner.

"Shit," muttered Sienna. "Don't get it, specially maths. Hate it." That was an understatement, but she liked that she could speak that truth while still sounding like every other teenager.

"Well if you want help, I could always tutor you."

"Seriously? You did good at school?"

"What the hell's that mean?" snapped Jackson. "Why wouldn't I have gone well at school? Cos I'm Abo?"

"Huh?" asked Sienna, taken aback. "No, I … I wouldn't —" Sienna hesitated, reluctant to admit what she'd been thinking, but Jackson was staring at her with crossed arms and raised eyebrows. "I was thinking cos you were a cop."

"Great, so you're comparing me to apes like Ian, just cos we're both cops," laughed Jackson, seemingly over his agitation.

"I wouldn't ever think of you that way," said Sienna, trying to reverse the damage of a moment ago.

"What way?" asked Jackson distrustfully.

"Aren't I just a girl to you? Am I always a white girl?" asked Sienna tentatively, realising she should've dropped the conversation as soon as Jackson laughed. "Don't you ever just see me as me?" He turned away and she cursed herself for speaking. "Sorry, Jackson," she said, kneeling down in front of him. "I didn't mean to upset you."

Jackson looked in her eyes, his smile a bitter grimace. "You're sorry for being less racist than me?"

"You're not racist."

"I think of you as a white person."

"But I am. Always gunna to be. Just doesn't mean anything."

"Means something to me," said Jackson, a hard edge to his voice. "I see all the connotations that come along with being white."

"Like what?" asked Sienna confusedly.

"Beer-swilling, racist, privileged bogan who wears an Australian flag as a cape. Narrow-minded bigot who thinks people are coming here to steal their jobs and ruin their way of life, but won't admit they stole our land. Loves guns and violence."

"They're rednecks," said Sienna, hating that she was being conflated with that image. "All rednecks might be white. Doesn't make all whites rednecks. You think I'm one of them?"

"I guess I sometimes have a hard time telling them apart."

Jackson smiled tentatively. For the first time, Sienna thought she saw his true smile without any hint of Flynn clouding it. He moved forward, his hand cupping her head as his thumb stroked her temple. His eyes were intense, making her heart skip a beat. She was sure he was going to kiss her, but her head moved past his face and into his neck as he pulled her into a warm embrace.

"You're awesome, you know that. You make this town almost bearable."

"Ditto."

But almost was the operative word. When Jackson wasn't around, Sienna found everything much harder to handle. If he'd been at school with her, she was sure things would've been tolerable. As it was, if she wasn't being teased mercilessly, then she was ignored as wholly as if she didn't exist.

"There's gotta be someone you get along with?" said Jackson, astounded by her off-hand comment that she didn't have any friends.

"Nope," shrugged Sienna, not wanting to elaborate. "You've gotta have more friends than me in Fortune. Isn't it sad that you're hanging round a school kid half the week?"

"I so regret getting posted out here," moaned Jackson. "I get the worst shifts. I'm forced to spend my spare time with the guys I work with. Got nothing in common with them. We don't even really like each other," he added with a smile. "If I'd had more of a chance to get out then I might've met more people."

"Sorry."

"For what?"

"For having to settle for hanging with me."

"That's not how I meant it. Geez, Sienna, you've gotta stop doing that. Hasn't anyone ever told you how amazing you are?"

"Flynn."

Something flickered in Jackson's eyes. Both his hands moved to her face, gently holding her cheeks, forcing her to look into his eyes. She tried to turn away, but he wouldn't let go.

"I think you're amazing."

Jackson didn't smile. Sienna kept looking into his eyes. They seemed to stretch on forever, like looking down a well. They were beautiful. Sienna's heart twisted and warmed in a way it never had before. It was the first time the idea of moving on without Flynn truly crossed her mind, but it was short-lived. Flynn was the one person she couldn't live without. Jackson was the one she would have to.

A noise drew Sienna's eyes up. Uncle Cole was standing in the doorway. Jackson's hands were still on her cheeks. The look in Uncle Cole's eyes was close to murderous, yet Jackson didn't move. He kept sitting determinedly with Sienna under Uncle Cole's watchful gaze and even insisted on helping her wash up. When the last of the dishes were done, Jackson finally bade them goodnight.

***

Sienna heard the click of the door and her heart sank. They didn't even try to sneak in. They wanted her to know they were there. That they could be there any time and there was nothing she could do to stop it. It was Uncle Cole's punishment; sending his officers over at all hours just to make sure she and Jackson weren't alone together.

Ian strolled into the kitchen as Sienna cooked. Her heart pounded, but she tried not to let her fear show.

"You gunna cook me dinner?"

Sienna turned. Ian was right in front of her. He wasn't pressing himself on her, but he stood over her in menacing way; threatening, but never doing. There were footsteps in the hall, but Ian wasn't fazed. He kept smiling, as if daring her to complain.

"You right, Sienna?"

Sienna couldn't see Jackson, but was glad he was close by. "Yeah, I'm fine."

Ian smiled smugly. "You're nothing," he hissed, leaning forward so only she could hear him. "Your name and rich parents don't mean shit here. You're less than nothing." Sienna couldn't stop herself from looking into his eyes. It was an intimidating sight. "See you around."

Ian stepped back. Sienna instantly relaxed. Ian turned towards the door. He made no attempt to walk around Jackson, banging heavily into his shoulder. Jackson turned, but Ian was ready, rounding for a fight. Jackson didn't engage, despite Ian's racist taunts.

"You sure you're okay?" asked Jackson, hugging Sienna before checking her over. "He didn't touch you or anything, did he?" Sienna shook her head. "Good. The guy's a freaking psychopath."

They were quiet as they cooked. Jackson kept his arm around her. It was comforting and she knew there was no reason to read anything more into it. Jackson would never want her that way. He was her big brother. And after Liam, she knew there was no one for her but Flynn. It made her wonder if the only reason she kept Jackson close was so she could keep the last living reminder of Flynn with her.

Dinner was on the table when the front door opened. Sienna sighed with relief recognising Uncle Cole's footsteps. Greeting him with her friendliest smile, she offered him dinner, but he refused, heading to the lounge room and turning on the TV.

"You should go in there too," Sienna said to Jackson, sitting down at the kitchen table. "That's what he wants."

"Not what I want," he replied, before smiling. "I'll go if you do."

Sienna shook her head. "Trust me. Might make things better for you."

"Maybe after dinner," replied Jackson.

Sienna wasn't convinced by his conviction, but as soon as they'd finished washing up, Jackson grabbed two beers from the fridge and headed out to Uncle Cole.

"I don't want you here alone with her," said Uncle Cole, drawing Sienna's head up from her maths book. She crept quietly out of her room and into the hallway next to the lounge room door.

"What does that mean?"

"Exactly what it sounds like. Don't think I don't know what you're up to."

"And what's that exactly?" asked Jackson, although it sounded as if he knew precisely what Uncle Cole meant.

"She's sixteen. Practically a minor. I see the way you look at her. I know what boys your age want. There's only one thing on your mind. You've already gone through half the girls in town and now you want Sienna."

There was a long, strained silence.

"I keep her company because she's a nice kid," said Jackson, his voice wavering just slightly. "We get along. And when everyone else has abandoned her —"

"I have not abandoned her!" growled Uncle Cole ferociously.

"When was the last time you spoke to her? When was the last time you asked her how her day was? Do you know if she's okay after her break up with Liam?"

"If she'd listened to me, she never would've gotten into that mess. Any of it."

"Yeah, shock, a teenager who didn't take an adult's advice."

Sienna slid down the wall, curling her legs into her chest as the arguing became more intense and bitter. Jackson was unnecessarily antagonistic, but generally truthful. Uncle Cole continued to blame someone else – anyone else – for their relationship breaking down so quickly after her arrival.

"You can either make your life in this town easier or a hell of a lot harder," Uncle Cole snarled viciously.

"You're threatening me?"

"This is my town, my house, my police station. Cross me and I promise you'll never get a promotion. Anywhere. Ever. And I'll make sure your life here's a living hell."

"Yeah, because you've always been so welcoming," Jackson retorted. "You're a sad, pathetic bully, you know that."

Sienna jumped to her feet at the sound of footsteps. Jackson wouldn't meet her eyes as he stomped the front door. It slammed angrily behind him.

"Get to your room."

Sienna turned to see Uncle Cole at the lounge room door glaring at her. She instantly complied.

Curled up in a ball on her bed, Sienna felt like her ten-year-old self again. Lost. Alone. Confused. Argued over endlessly. But despite those terrible times, she'd always thought of Uncle Cole with fondness. He introduced her to art, supported her and taken her in when no one else wanted her. But he wasn't that man any more. He'd become bitter and resentful. Angry and disconnected. Just like her.

~12~

SEVENTEEN

With so little to distinguish the days, Sienna was caught short by the nightmare that tore her from her sleep to remind her that she had existed long enough to live through to another birthday. Gasping for breath as tears flowed down her cheeks, she tried to work out how it was possible she had not foreseen this.

Her mind travelled back to this day one year ago. Nothing when she had woken then had marked the day as anything but normal. Her only plans had revolved around avoiding her family. They would only ignore the occasion anyway and she wanted to spend as many minutes as possible with the only person who truly celebrated her birth.

Sienna made it to the shower before she broke down completely. She sobbed unrestrainedly, her tears turning the water salty. Trying to compose herself only made her sobs burst out more violently, but eventually she managed to contain herself to silent tears.

Uncle Cole was sitting at the kitchen table when she emerged from her room dressed for school.

"Happy birthday," he said, his voice gentler than usual. "I won't be home until late tonight. I wanted to wait til you got up so I could see you."

"Thanks," replied Sienna softly, touched by the gesture. "Would you like me to keep you some dinner tonight?"

"Look, Sen, it's probably better not to worry about food for me. I prefer just grabbing something at work or on the way home."

"But that's not healthy," Sienna replied without thinking.

"Your cooking's not exactly the epitome of healthy eating either. I've given up telling you how to live your life. How about you show me the same courtesy."

Uncle Cole nodded, wished her happy birthday again, then left. Sienna slumped down at the kitchen table. She didn't bother with breakfast. She just stared at her hands, forcing herself to keep her mind blank, until a glance at the clock told her she was late.

No one said anything as she entered the class with red and puffy eyes. No one noticed the agony every breath was causing her. She was ignored today as wholly as she had been for the past three months.

"Sienna," called her English teacher, beckoning her to his desk. "You have a delivery at the office. You can go now if you like."

Dread washed over Sienna, her worst fears confirmed when she saw the large bunch of flowers sitting on the benchtop at the office.

"There's a cake as well," said the office lady cheerily, placing it next to the flowers.

"Thanks," Sienna replied, though the sincerity was missing. "Um, can I leave these here until the end of the day?"

"Don't you want to take them with you? You can share the cake at recess. I'm sure that's what your parents wanted."

The office lady turned the flowers to display the card. Sienna tried to contain her glare. This lady either had suspiciously little insight into what happened at the school or a sick sadistic streak.

With a resigned sigh, Sienna grabbed the flowers and the cake. The cake was not large and the plastic bag helped mask its appearance. The flowers were a different matter. They were big. And bright. There was no way of reducing their visibility.

"Hey, look, Richie Snitch sent herself flowers," sneered Sam.

The whole class laughed. Even the teacher smirked, before quickly frowning and asking for quiet. But the snide comments continued. Muttered across classrooms, hallways and grounds. All day.

"You reckon she wants us to think she has actual friends?"

"Just wants people to ask who they're from."

"Such a loser. Who sends themselves flowers at school?"

Sienna looked forward and ignored every comment.

When she got home, it took all her strength not smash the flowers against the wall. She managed to contain herself to throwing them and the cake heavily on to the kitchen table. Stomping outside, she gave herself a minute to let the anger and hurt wash through her before sucking in the heaving sobs pushing on her lungs.

Her parents had spent time, money and effort on her gift and she was going to be grateful. It didn't matter that they had such woeful insight into her life that they would torture her this way.

Wiping the tears from her eyes, Sienna rummaged through the cupboards until she found a container that could pass for a vase and stuck the flowers in it. She put them in the bathroom, not wanting to think about the countless flowers Flynn's family would have received because of this day.

One present handled, Sienna considered what to do with the other. She had no intention of eating the cake, certainly not by herself. She didn't even bother opening the box.

It took longer than it should have for the most obvious answer to plonk into her mind. Grabbing the plastic bag, she headed to the police station.

"Hey, how you doing?" asked Jackson.

Sienna looked tentatively at his face. He wasn't smiling.

"Is Uncle Cole here? I brought something for him," said Sienna, holding up the cake.

"He's already finished for today," replied Jackson, his face crinkled with concern. "He and Ryan left about an hour ago."

"Oh," Sienna gasped, tears burning her eyes. "You should have this, then. It's real nice. You'll like it."

Sienna pushed the cake across the counter and ran out, ignoring Jackson as he called after her. In the street, she took a deep breath, forcing her tears to stop and her feet to slow. She looked past the people and ignored the whispered comments that trailed after her.

"Sienna, hey, wait." Sienna had no choice. Jackson's firm grip was impossible to break without fighting him. "What's with the cake? It's not the Chief's birthday, is it? I thought his was in November."

Sienna sighed and shook her head. She tried to tell Jackson to forget about it, but the words only came out as a mumbled mess. Jackson must've guessed the truth, because he started swearing under his breath and pulled her into a hug, but she didn't want him feeling sorry for her. Pushing out of his arms, she rushed home. Her phone was ringing when she arrived.

"Hi, Mum!" she said enthusiastically, even as tears dripped down her cheeks. "Thanks for the flowers and the cake. They were great."

"Did your friends enjoy the cake?" Janice asked cheerfully.

"Yeah, it was really nice. I saved some to take home for Uncle Cole. Everyone commented on the flowers."

"You and your uncle do anything nice today?"

"Yeah, he went in a bit late so we could have breakfast together and then I went into the station to share the rest of the cake with him."

"That sounds really nice. I wish we could've been there too. Maybe next year if you're still out there we'll all come out. It's a big year next year."

Sienna couldn't answer. Her parents' lies and half-truths were excruciating. "I miss you, Mum," she said in a strangled voice before she could stop herself. Perhaps she could deal with her parents' persistent disappointment better than this crushing isolation.

"We miss you too," replied Janice. "So much. I don't think you understand just how much."

She didn't. If it was even half as much as she missed them, why hadn't they dragged her home? When Arthur arrived on the phone minutes later to give his own birthday wishes, Sienna felt almost tortured by their kindness. They always seemed to like her more when she wasn't living with them.

"Happy birthday, little sis," said Stephen, ringing almost as soon as she'd hung up from her parents. "How'd you like your presents?"

"They were okay. Really nice," Sienna modified quickly.

"Yeah? I thought it might've embarrassed you a bit having them come to the school. Mum thought it'd be nice."

"It was really nice and thoughtful," insisted Sienna, determined not to discourage their kindness.

"You copped shit, didn't you?" asked Stephen, mirth in his voice.

"Just a little," confessed Sienna, feeling less guilty about being able to say so.

"What'd you tell Mum? You didn't tell her you had issues, that's for sure."

"I just said that everyone commented on the flowers."

Stephen laughed loudly and for much longer than Sienna expected. "I love the way you're able to lie by telling the truth. It's such an awesome skill. You really should be a lawyer."

"It's not like you tell Mum and Dad the truth about everything," countered Sienna.

"I know! But I always just have to straight out lie. You somehow manage to make it so that people just assume the lie and ignore the truth. Doesn't anyone ever pick you up on it?"

"Flynn did," replied Sienna slowly. "He could always pick it."

"Yeah," sighed Stephen. "I know."

Sienna doubted that was true. Her family had never wanted to understand her relationship with Flynn. The best they had done was tolerate it. They would never comprehend the pain pressing down on her chest making it hard to breath or the nightmares that took her back to her last birthday and the end of the only life she had learned to want to live.

A new pain settled in Sienna's body. One year she had survived Flynn. Another now loomed. Nothing good awaited her. Her exams had passed in the haze that had brought her blindly to her birthday. Now she faced the agony of judgement. It wouldn't be pretty.

Performing poorly in exams was nothing new. What disappointed her was that no amount of preparation could improve her performance. The first two exams had promised better things may lay ahead, but it was just a trail of false hope. Her maths exam proved that. It was a disaster. The only question Sienna had any confidence in getting right was her name, but with Uncle Cole insisting she use his surname, there was even doubt about that.

Things didn't get any better in the next two exams and as the last week of term approached, Sienna began dreading her return to school.

Arthur, Janice and Stephen wouldn't invest in her concern. No matter how she tried to warn them, they were convinced she'd blitzed her exams. Then Sienna realised they just didn't care. They started talking about how busy they were going to be. Their weekly calls might be a little irregular or haphazard. Things were crazy at work.

"But you need anything, you call us," Arthur added quickly, as if trying to backtrack his position.

"Anything at all," Janice added to their three-way conversation. "We're never far away."

"Thanks," murmured Sienna, wondering if speaking those lies made her parents feel better.

Wishing for a new way of passing the time that would allow her feel vaguely connected to the world, Sienna's eyes fell on her mother's camera. She'd packed it in a corner after Janice's visit, never trusting they would let her keep it. Uncle Cole didn't know she had it, but if he caught her out with it she could claim it was for homework.

Walking tentatively to the front door, Sienna was tossing up whether going out with the camera was worth the trouble when there was a knock at the door. Typical, she scoffed internally. Uncle Cole had probably sensed her plans and sent someone to stop her.

"Thought you might want to do an exchange," smiled Jackson, holding up a small cake box. "You gave me your birthday cake."

"It's your birthday?"

"Twenty-one today."

"Shouldn't you be celebrating with mates?" asked Sienna, feeling insufficient for the task.

"My mates are a five-hour drive away," replied Jackson. "I'm going back in a couple of weeks. Me and Marty are having a joint birthday. No one here knows when my birthday is. And I'm not telling them."

"You told me."

"So you going to celebrate with me?"

"You know you're not allowed to hang out with me."

"You're going to make me celebrate alone? Seriously?" cried Jackson. Sienna shrugged. "Were you going out? You allowed?" he asked, noticing the camera in her hands.

"No."

"No you're not going out? Or no you're not allowed?"

"Both, I guess. Was thinking of taking photos for art class. You could pose for me," she added, suddenly inspired.

"How could I resist?" Jackson smiled broadly.

Sienna had to swallow the cry that pushed up her throat at the sight. Closing her eyes, she followed Jackson out the door and down the street. They didn't speak. They just kept walking until they found themselves by the river.

Moving downstream away from people and man-made structures, Sienna lifted the camera to her eye. Without thinking, she positioned Jackson on the bough of a tree overhanging the river. It was so natural that it wasn't until she caught sight of his curious look that she started to feel like a fraud. She thought about explaining what she was doing before realising it would only expose her more. Jackson closed his eyes and put his hands behind his head, leaning back in the tree. Free from his gaze, Sienna was able to focus purely on taking photos.

Occasionally Jackson would open his eyes when she moved him, but he quickly closed them again.

"What's up?" he asked, when he noticed she'd stopped taking photos.

"Can you sit by the river?" asked Sienna hesitantly. Jackson jumped from the tree and sat on the river bank. "With your shirt off?"

Jackson turned his head slowly, his eyebrows raised and a slight smile on his face. Sienna tried to stop herself from blushing as she explained the scene she was trying to capture, but her explanation only made Jackson smile more broadly as she blushed more fiercely.

"Get what you want?" asked Jackson, when he put his shirt on.

Sienna sat next to him, looking at her watch. She'd been taking photos for over an hour. It reminded her of how easily time passed when she had a camera in her hands. "They're okay. Not exactly what I'd imagined. Light's not quite right."

"Too dazzling, am I?" asked Jackson with a smile.

Sienna couldn't help but smile in return. It felt foreign. "I think I need dawn light," she said, returning to the only sphere where she could make sense of things.

"What about dusk? Don't have to get up as early."

"Yeah, maybe."

"I should take you out for a drive. There're some really great places around here if you like nature photos."

"I like people and nature."

"How was I?"

"You know you're perfect," replied Sienna, trying to conceal her frustration with her own inadequacies.

"Perfect," cried Jackson. "That's a big call. I definitely have to help you now."

Sienna crossed her legs and packed her camera away, not knowing how to respond.

"I think it's cake time," said Jackson, placing the box between them. He opened it towards Sienna to reveal a large chocolate cupcake decorated with a small tower of green icing and mini M&Ms.

"Did you buy that in town? It looks really good," said Sienna.

"I made it," said Jackson. Sienna looked up to see him blushing slightly. "Happy birthday, Sienna." Jackson put a candle in the top of the icing and quickly lit it before she could argue about whose birthday it was. "Make a wish."

"You make one too," she replied, pushing the cake between them.

On three, they blew the candle out together. Jackson immediately held out the cake, but she refused to take the first bite. Jackson jokingly questioned if she thought he'd tried to poison her. She dismissed his fears, but he was still forced to break off pieces so she'd eat it.

"You eat the rest," said Sienna, pushing the remaining cake towards Jackson. He tried to argue, but she wouldn't be swayed. "It's your birthday."

Jackson smiled and shoved the last of the cake into his mouth in one go. Sienna plunged her hands into the cold river to wash them before moving up to the tree branch. Jackson quickly followed and sat facing her.

"You doing okay, Sienna?" he asked, taking her hands in his. Sienna looked up in shock. Had she really allowed him to see just how sick of life she was? Did he know what she'd wished for? "How's school?"

"School sucks," replied Sienna. "Get my exam results this week," she added, knowing that was a legitimate caveat.

"You seriously worried about that?" laughed Jackson. "I've never met a bigger nerd. All you do is study."

Sienna's stomach rolled over. "I need to get into law, remember," she said, wishing she was what people believed.

"Only if that's what you want. You don't have to do it just because your parents want you to."

"I want to." The only way she had survived to this point was keeping her head down and following the path laid out for her. If it disappeared, she had no idea where that would leave her.

"Still think you're being too hard on yourself," said Jackson. "I know people like you. They worry so much about doing badly and then they come back with ninety percent or something ridiculous. You're smart and you've worked really hard. I know you'll do well."

Sienna could only shake her head. She wasn't one of those people. The best mark she could remember receiving was in the low sixties and that was in primary school when everyone else got near-perfect scores. The memories of Uncle Cole and Aunt Daphne trying to teach her to read and help her with her homework were still painful. In class, it had always been easier to muck up than admit that she had no idea what was going on. It had been a relief when they introduced her to art. She finally had a medium through which to express herself.

But none of that would be good enough now. Sienna needed that much-promised hidden intelligence to shine through. She needed to be in the top one per cent of the state to get into a good law school.

"Look, have you ever worked this hard before?" asked Jackson. Sienna shook her head. "Then you might be pleasantly surprised. Trust me, the time you walk out of the exam thinking that you've aced it is the time you failed. I reckon you'll get your best marks ever on these exams. You won't have a problem getting into law."

Sienna was on the verge of vomiting. The teacher was halfway through giving back their English papers. If it was bad, she was prepared to walk out and never return to school.

"Well done," said the teacher, placing the exam upside down on the table.

Sienna was thrown by the comment. It didn't sound sarcastic. She turned over the paper and nearly choked. Seventy-six per cent. The number rolled over and over in her head. It was amazing. Jackson had been right. This was her best mark ever. She was even above the class average. It was the most extraordinary feeling she'd ever known and made walking into her maths class easier than ever.

Then reality hit.

Thirty-eight per cent. Not even close to passing. Holding back the tears of disappointment, Sienna tried to follow as the teacher went through the questions and showed the correct working. It still made no sense. She was lost within five minutes.

Expectations gone, Sienna wasn't too glum when she got her art mark. Sixty-three per cent. If she'd received that mark first, she would've been impressed, but she'd expected art to be her best subject. It was disappointing, but gave her some hope for improvement. Same with the sixty-five she received in legal studies. It was history that really blew her away. Eighty-one per cent!

Bounding home, Sienna hopped straight on her computer and put her marks through an online program that promised to accurately calculate her university entrance score.

Thirty-five-point-three.

Sienna read it again, sure it couldn't be right. That was impossibly low. She needed close to ninety-nine.

Ramping up her marks, Sienna tried again. It was better, but fifty-two-point-seven-five was never going to get her anywhere. She'd struggled to get into any course with that mark. Bulking up her grades to the point of impossibility left her fifteen marks shy of the lowest ranking law course in the country and almost twenty-five away from her goal.

Sienna didn't know what else to do. She was in a state of shock. She's never conceptualised just how poorly she ranked against other students. Thirty-five-point-three! The best marks she'd ever received left her languishing at the bottom of the state. She tried to convince herself she could do better, but she'd given everything she had to these exams and she wasn't even close. Any improvements in the future could not possibly bridge that gap.

The thought of having to confess the truth to her parents was terrifying. They would finally realise she had no value to them. The smiling façade they had put up since the incident with Liam would shatter and they would cast her off permanently.

Perhaps if she'd been left with Uncle Cole from the start – never claimed or fought over her – she wouldn't care about being discarded now. But she'd always wanted the love her parents promised and had thought she'd finally found the way to it, only for it to disappear right before her eyes.

Hands over her face, Sienna threw herself on her bed. There were no tears. It was beyond that. She didn't know how to find another trail to her future. Everything was lost and so was she. The pressure on her chest made it feel like she was drowning.

The light faded. The house was completely dark when Uncle Cole crept into her room. Switching on the light, he mistook her for asleep as he crept over to her desk.

"Oh, Sen, this is great!" Uncle Cole cried, moving to her bedside. "I'm so proud of you."

Sienna couldn't help it. The sobs burst from her chest as the tears overflowed. Uncle Cole sat on the bed and turned her to face him.

"What's wrong? These are the best marks I've ever seen. Eighty-one, Sen! That's terrific. Why are you acting like you failed?"

"I did fail," sobbed Sienna.

Uncle Cole shuffled the papers. "Oh. Maths. Sen, you know you've always struggled. But look at the rest. All above sixty. When have you ever done that well before?"

"But it's not good enough!" cried Sienna.

"For what? Your parents?" snapped Uncle Cole angrily. "If they knew you at all they wouldn't be burdening you with these unrealistic expectations! You need to snap out of this."

Sienna's tears started to dry, but only because she didn't want to anger Uncle Cole more. He didn't understand. He'd never understand. She was worthless. He just wouldn't accept it.

"Are you going to come to the pub for dinner with me to celebrate how well you've done?" asked Uncle Cole, his voice kind but firm.

"Not going to celebrate being pathetic," muttered Sienna.

Uncle Cole glared at her before storming out of the house. A sob pushed at Sienna's throat, but she managed to swallow it, her sadness sinking through her body. It was heavy, filling her stomach and making her feel full despite having not eaten for over eight hours. Closing her eyes, Sienna felt it spread through her body so that by the time she woke she was so heavy it was almost impossible to drag her body out of bed.

It was the last day of term. Sienna wondered if she should bother going, but knew Uncle Cole would be angrier if she wagged. She'd slept in her clothes, but didn't care. Stripping them off to shower, she threw them straight back on again before walking out to the kitchen. Her whole morning routine had been thrown off kilter, making it even harder to move through each step in the process. She got as far as reaching for the bread before realising she didn't want to eat. Hunger rippled through her stomach, but it didn't change her mind.

Meandering so slowly she was almost late, Sienna flopped down at her desk and just sat there. She didn't get out her books or pens. She didn't listen to anything the teacher said. Even when he stood in front of her and asked her to get her things out, she didn't respond. He only waited a moment before walking off and leaving her in her own world.

Class after class was the same. Sienna didn't pay attention to anything that was said and didn't participate in any form. Most of the teachers didn't even seem to notice.

Uncle Cole's words swirled around Sienna's brain. They'd barely spoken for months and yet he'd said he was proud of her. Despite all her mistakes, she'd proved herself worthy in his eyes. She tried to make it mean as much as it should have, but he'd raised her most of her life. Been the one to always take her in. He'd always loved her. It was her parents she needed to prove herself to and it was never going to be possible.

It was time to face the music. Sienna's whole body was shaking as she picked up her mobile. Sitting at her desk in her room, she thrummed her fingers anxiously deciding who to call. If she and Stephen were closer, she might have dared to ask him for help softening the blow, but she meant nothing to him either.

The softness of Janice during her last visit convinced Sienna to call her. It wouldn't change the outcome, but maybe she would reject her kindly. The phone rang twice before going to message bank. Arthur's didn't ring at all. Sienna didn't leave a message. They probably already knew how badly she'd done and didn't want to speak to her. Maybe Uncle Cole had told them.

Everything was falling apart.

Sienna's hand twitched. She instinctively reached for a pencil, but quickly dropped it and grabbed for a pen. A letter. She could have her say – explain her failure – without any confrontation. The pen hovered over the paper, but the words wouldn't come.

So agitated she couldn't sit, Sienna paced her room, the pressure increasing with every step. She was trying to do the impossible. Justify the indefensible. She dashed to the bathroom. The urge to vomit subsided, but still her body shook. Opening the bathroom cabinet, she spied Uncle Cole's stash of sleeping pills. He always kept bottles of them in the house. Grabbing the open one, she went to the kitchen and took two pills. Maybe everything would make more sense after a long, black sleep.

But sleep didn't come. Not quick enough. The anxiety was building again. And sleep wouldn't help. Sienna knew she'd wake to the same nightmare. Maybe if she could convince herself things would be okay, she could sleep more peacefully. Grabbing her phone, she dialled again. This time it was answered.

"Uncle Cole."

"What's wrong now, Sienna?" he asked in a frustrated voice. "I don't really have time for this."

"Okay."

Sienna hung up. Wouldn't have mattered. Uncle Cole couldn't have made this right. He'd never be able to make her parents love her. Despair washed through her. Why wasn't she asleep yet?

Walking back to the kitchen, Sienna grabbed the bottle of pills and shook three more into her hand. She took a bottle of bourbon from the cupboard and washed down the pills. That should make her sleep, but just in case, she took them back to her room.

Nothing happened. Sienna sat on her bed watching the clock. She was still awake. There was nothing she could do right. She turned away, but her eyes were caught by Flynn's photo. He was smiling at her. Really smiling. It was like he was trapped in the photo. Sienna grabbed it and stared at him. For the first time since his death she felt his presence.

That was why nothing made sense. She wasn't supposed to be alive. She'd been fighting fate since the accident. She should've died with Flynn.

The words were flowing now. Sienna dashed to her desk to write her goodbyes. They would understand this way. They'd know why it had come to this. They'd even be relieved. Uncle Cole would take it hard, but it was still better this way. She'd caused him nothing but trouble since coming back into his life.

Everything in order, Sienna swallowed four more pills with another swig of bourbon.

Jackson! She'd forgotten about him. They were supposed to go out early on Sunday to take photos of the sunrise. Fumbling for her phone, it rang and rang until message bank finally picked up.

"Jackson. Sorry. Can't do Sunday no more. Thanks for everything. Sorry I caused you trouble. It'll all be better now," said Sienna, the words sounding right in her mind, but strange to her ears.

A sense of peace washed over her. Falling asleep and never waking up. It had to be the best way to go.

But what if it didn't happen that way? What if she woke up? Cheating fate once had been bad enough. She didn't want to do it again. Stumbling off the bed, Sienna made it to the bathroom for the full bottle of sleeping pills and grabbed another bottle of bourbon.

She threw a handful of pills in her mouth, then sculled what was left of the first bottle of bourbon. She turned back to the clock. She still wasn't asleep. She tried to remember what time she took the first pills, but couldn't.

The more pills Sienna swallowed, the more alcohol she drank, the more aware she became of the fact that she was still awake. Still alive. It made her anxious. She couldn't fail at this too.

She spied scissors sitting on her desk. It was harder than expected, getting up and walking to them. It even took two tries for her to grab the scissors. At the foot of the bed, she had to crawl along it just to get to the other end. Turning over slowly, she knew she didn't have much time left to make sure she was dead before she fell asleep. The scissors weren't sharp. The cuts didn't bleed the way she expected. Her skin was tougher than she thought, but she wasn't going to stuff this up.

The phone was ringing. It was Stephen. Sienna's finger slipped over the screen. She needed to say goodbye while she still could. And sorry.

"Stee – fen," Sienna slurred, her mouth not able to work properly with all her focus on running the scissors across her wrist.

"Sienna! Shit, Sienna, what's wrong with you?"

"I'm going."

"Going? What are you talking about? What's wrong? What've you done?"

"Can't let youse all down … no more … better – without me."

"Oh my god, Sen, no! Where are you? Sen? Are you at home? Sen?"

Sienna couldn't answer. Flynn had arrived. He was standing next to her, taking her hands in his. He looked just the way she remembered. The scissors fell from her hand.

"Flynn," she gasped.

Flynn's arms cradled her. "I love you, Senna."

"I love you. Forever, Flynn. Together forever now."

The blackness closed in on Sienna, but this time she welcomed it. It wasn't threatening like it was when she was alive. Things would be okay now.

She was finally dead.

Finally at peace.

Finally with Flynn.

~13~

AFTERMATH

Heaven is white. Calm. Easy. Sienna truly smiled for the first time in over a year. Flynn was next to her. It was blissful, finally being at peace. Sienna took Flynn's hand and curled into his arms. He stroked her hair. When she looked out, they were on the beach. The sun was rising.

Spending every night sneaking in and out of each other's bedrooms had meant a lot of early mornings. Sunrise was one of their favourite times. Sienna would talk about the light and show Flynn how subtle changes could dramatically alter the mood of an image. It was during those times that she took her favourite photos of Flynn. He took the occasional picture of her. He always made her develop them. He kept one in his wallet. Out of sight. Sienna had once questioned him about it. Asked if he was ashamed of her. He'd always wanted to keep their relationship a secret.

"You're my heart," he'd told her. "No one can see my beating heart. Why should I show them my real one?"

"You're my heart too," Sienna had confessed.

Flynn had hugged her, holding her tight as his body shook. "We're never going to be apart, Senna. No matter what they do to us. They can't cut out our hearts."

It turned out to be a lie. But as Sienna buried her head against his chest once more, she chose to forget the year they'd been forced to bear apart. They were together now. That was all that mattered.

"I have to take you back now," said Flynn.

"What? No! What do you mean?" cried Sienna, watching the sun rise with unnatural speed.

"You almost died, Senna," cried Flynn. "I couldn't let that happen."

"Almost? No, Flynn, please. I have to die. I have to be with you. Don't make me go back. Please."

Flynn walked towards the water as the day rapidly darkened. Sienna chased after him, knowing she had to catch him before things went black again.

"You can't stay here, Senna. You have to go back. You have to live."

"Flynn! No! I have to be with you. Let me die. Let me be with you."

"I am with you," called Flynn, but his voice was unnatural, like a faded echo.

A second later he was gone.

Sienna screamed. Everything was getting dark again. Life was dragging her back, but she wouldn't go. She couldn't leave Flynn. Not again. Racing into the water, she tried to drown herself, but every time she opened her mouth her screams pushed back the water. She screamed for Flynn. Begged for mercy, but that was one thing she'd never been granted. The darkness had found her and it was taking her back to the world she'd desperately wanted to escape.

It took a while for Sienna to properly register her surroundings. She heard the muttering first. The voices were clear, but it sounded like they were speaking a different language. She could hear them, but not understand them.

Touch came next. There were hands on her body. Head. Shoulders. Face. Hands. It felt as though there was an octopus hovering over her, tentacles splayed in every direction as it spoke its strange language.

Sight came last. Heavy dread flooded Sienna's body as her parents' grave faces came into focus. There was no making up for this mistake. They'd never forgive her for surviving this time.

"Oh, Sen," cried Janice, holding Sienna's hand to her cheek.

"I'm sorry. I tried. I swear I tried as hard as I could," choked Sienna, unsure how many more pills she could have swallowed.

"It's okay. We know you tried. We know. It's okay," sobbed Janice.

They would deal with her survival. Just as they had tried to deal with her existence previously, they would deal with this.

"We're going to take you home once you're released," said Arthur. "We'll get you the right kind of help so this won't happen again."

"It's no use," sighed Sienna. "Nothing can make me better."

"Don't say that," snarled Arthur. "There's always hope. Let us help you."

"No," replied Sienna, tears slipping down her cheeks. "No, I can't disappoint you any more. It's too hard. I'll never be good enough. Not for you. You deserve more than me. Please, let me go."

"I told you she wouldn't want to go back with you."

Sienna looked around with her eyes, not game enough to sit up, but couldn't see where Uncle Cole was.

"I didn't exactly hear her say that," snapped Stephen.

Sienna recoiled.

"We have time to work it out," replied Arthur, his hand gripping Sienna's shoulder.

Sienna felt detached. Words and stares continued to flow over her, but she couldn't understand why. What was the point of fighting over scraps? But despite the worthlessness of their prize, they continued to argue until they were ordered to leave.

No one came back. Sienna was left to lie in her hospital bed alone. She wondered why she was still in hospital. She was alive. There was nothing left to do for her. Pulling the bandages off her wrists, she noticed that most of the cuts had been so shallow they'd barely drawn blood. Only two on her left wrist and one on the right required treatment, but she couldn't believe they were enough to justify her continued incarceration. None of the nurses or doctors who came to check on her said anything about being released. Perhaps it was like bail. If there was no one to vouch for you, there was no going home. Maybe no one was prepared to take her in this time. Uncle Cole had finally had enough. Her parents would take her back to the city, but not home, and leave her in some sort of institution.

"Sienna? Can I come in?"

Sienna turned to see Amber standing in the doorway looking small and timid.

"What are you doing here? You visiting someone?" asked Sienna.

"I came to visit you," replied Amber, stepping cautiously into the room. "I heard what happened. My mum's a nurse here."

Sienna nodded before stopping. "Um, where's here?"

"Westloch Base Hospital. Didn't anyone tell you?"

"I don't even know what day it is," said Sienna.

"It's Thursday," replied Amber. "You were in intensive care for two days. They were almost going to fly you to Sydney, but then you started responding. Took another two days for you to wake up properly.

My mum said I couldn't visit until you were better."

"It's really nice of you to come," said Sienna, expecting Amber to leave.

"Do you ever think that if I'd stayed sitting next to you in history that maybe you wouldn't have done … what you did?" asked Amber with a wavering voice. Sienna was thrown by the question. "Three people in my family have killed themselves. We still wonder what else we could've done. We never saw it coming. Just like you. You never seemed worried by anything."

Sienna couldn't answer and wondered if she was capable of relating to people. Perhaps there was something more fundamentally wrong with her.

"I shouldn't have done what I did," said Amber, looking guilty. "I shouldn't have abandoned you after Sam's party."

"You didn't do anything wrong," reassured Sienna. "It's not like you were my friend."

"I thought I was," sniffed Amber, tears falling down her cheeks. "Before – at the party – I thought … I guess not. It was pretty pathetic moving away when you were getting bullied. I hated … it wasn't fair. I should've stuck up for you. Not just left you to deal with it all."

"That's not why – you're not the reason I did this. None of that is. I've never been popular. I'm used to the teasing. It's not fun, but I wouldn't kill myself over it."

"Then why'd you do it?" asked Amber accusingly. "What is worth killing yourself over?"

"I just don't have anything to live for," replied Sienna. She was surprised how easy it was to admit that truth to Amber. "I want to be with Flynn. I don't want to be useless and crap at everything. I don't want to be a constant disappointment to my family. There's only ever been one person who really understood me. Liked me. I want to be with him."

"I probably don't understand you that well. Not yet. But I like you. I haven't been a good friend, but I am your friend. If you still want me to be."

"That's really nice, Amber, but … I'm not – it's not worth … I'm trouble. It's just not worth it."

"I think it is," smiled Amber. "You'll see. If I hadn't been so intimidated by how awesome I thought you were, you might realise that I've always thought you were amazing. I was just always so scared to talk to you. I thought you had all your shit together. Turns out you're just like the rest of us."

"Like what?"

"Fucked up and struggling through," Amber replied with a half-smile. "You're not the only one. Trust me."

Sienna was surprised by the rush of emotion that swept over her when Amber took her hand. In that moment, the isolation she'd been lost in dissolved slightly. Like a lightening of thick fog. It made her consider Amber's previous question more seriously. Would she have tried to take her life if there'd been just one person to hold her hand?

The next day doctors finally started talking about discharging Sienna, but not without throwing around terms like psychiatric assessment. Uncle Cole was indignant. He was refusing to have her subjected to anything like that. According to him, she just needed to move on and accept life as it was, not strive for a fantasy world that didn't exist. Arthur and Janice were just as insistent that she needed professional help. It left them fighting once more, arguing over who had the right to determine her fate. The doctors' compromise of a referral to a psychologist, who she would see after her discharge, meant everyone left unhappy.

Sienna was left to get ready on her own. She felt empty. Dressed to go, she sat on her bed not knowing what to do. When a nurse came in, she asked if she should leave by herself.

"Oh no, dear. Don't worry. Someone's coming for you. They're just organising it now."

Sienna waited. And waited. It was an hour before Uncle Cole stomped into the room. He had scrunched up papers in his hand and was muttering angrily. Sienna didn't listen to what he was saying. She just followed him through the corridors towards the car park.

Her parents and Stephen were nowhere to been seen. Sienna took a deep breath. They'd obviously gone home. They would've wasted enough time here already. The drive was equally silent. Uncle Cole was gripping the steering wheel fiercely before letting it go, then squeezing it tight again.

"Arthur and Janice want to take you back to Sydney," said Uncle Cole, when they were halfway home.

"They're still here?" asked Sienna, looking around. There was no car behind them.

"I'm surprised too. They've never cared before. Now they want to swoop in as if they've always been there for you." There was silence. It was tense. "They blame me."

"Why?" asked Sienna, shocked by the accusation.

Uncle Cole glanced at her sceptically. "Because I told you I didn't want to speak to you last Friday," he muttered. "Because I didn't want to indulge your selfish, self-absorbed state over your exam marks. It isn't something you should go killing yourself for. You understand that, right? You realise how selfish what you did was, don't you?"

"Yeah," Sienna replied softly. "I'm sorry."

"Yeah, well, you'll have to make it up to Jackson as well. He's the one who found you. I warned you to stay away from him. I don't know why you had to call him. Why you had to involve him. He's really torn up about what you did. I don't know what you were thinking, Sen."

"I just thought it'd be easier – for everyone else. All I do is cause problems."

"Unfortunately, that's very true. But the reality is that you thought it'd be easier for you and didn't give a shit about how it'd affect anyone else. And now I'm copping the blame from Arthur, Janice and Stephen. It's not the way I expected to be repaid for taking you in this year. When no one else wanted you, I might add."

Uncle Cole's lecture lasted the rest of the way home. It helped Sienna prepare the words she would need to face her parents. She'd been wondering what to say.

Arthur and Janice were waiting on the porch when Uncle Cole pulled into the driveway. They rushed and opened the car door for Sienna and held her between them as they walked inside. Stephen was waiting in the lounge room. He looked pale. When he glanced up, Sienna realised he was crying. She'd never seen him cry before – not without something hitting him first.

"Why'd you do it, Sen?" Stephen asked, his voice breaking. "I called you back five minutes after you called."

"I was just being selfish. I'm sorry," replied Sienna, looking between Stephen and her parents, who had moved to stand on either side of him, though she didn't meet their eyes. Her voice was calm as she mustered her uncle's words. It was harder than she thought it should be. "I know bad marks aren't worth killing yourself over. I was just thinking of myself. It was a really selfish thing to do."

"Really?" asked Stephen angrily. Arthur placed a calming hand on his shoulder. "Did he load you up with this shit on the way home?" Sienna was confused. "That's why you insisted on picking her up? Scared we'd take her home and find out the truth?"

"And what truth would that be?" snapped Uncle Cole, moving around Sienna until he was in front of her. "That you pressured her to the point of breaking? Look at them." He threw Sienna's test papers on the coffee table. "She worked day and night for that."

Despite Uncle Cole acting as her shield, Sienna could see the shock on her parents' faces as they passed the papers between them. Stephen looked perplexed.

"But you worked so hard," said Janice.

Worthlessness swamped Sienna as her parents comprehended just how pathetic she really was.

"If you knew your daughter at all, you'd know those are the best marks she's ever received," said Uncle Cole.

"But she's never worked at school before. She's barely done a day of study in her life before this. Of course, we expected more once she finally started working," Arthur cried.

"Even though she's barely literate?" asked Uncle Cole.

"What?" growled Arthur, anger swelling his body.

"Your daughter can hardly read," Uncle Cole replied, enunciating each word. "Get her to read something out for you. Better yet, get her to write something and see how long it takes her."

All eyes turned on Sienna. She slumped down on the lounge, her face in her hands, as if that would somehow hide the shameful truth.

"How long's this been a problem?" snapped Arthur.

"Forever," replied Uncle Cole sarcastically.

"And you never bothered to tell us. Never thought we had a right to know?" Arthur stepped closer to Uncle Cole.

Uncle Cole closed the gap, leaving only a foot between them. "But you've always told me how you were the best parents for Sienna. Insisted that she'd be better off with you. And yet, you know nothing about her."

"You manipulative bastard," hissed Janice.

Sienna felt herself being pulled to her feet and out of the house. She twisted her wrist, whimpering softly. Stephen immediately released her, but pulled her close, wrapping his arm around her waist.

"Got somewhere nice we can go?" Stephen asked softly.

There was only one place Sienna knew. With the weather starting to warm, the river wasn't as empty as if often had been. Stephen led them away from a group of kids swimming and swinging off the overhanging branches, finding them a tree to lean against.

"Will you explain it to me now?" asked Stephen. "Tell me why you did it?"

"You know why. I wrote it in the note," mumbled Sienna, looking out over the river to avoid his desperate gaze.

Stephen pulled a piece of paper from his pocket. He rubbed his face before speaking through his hand. Sienna appreciated that he read what she'd tried to say, not the misspelt scrawl she'd actually written.

"Mum, Dad, Stephen and Uncle Cole, I'm sorry," gasped Stephen, before steadying his voice. "You've all been so nice. More than I expected or deserve. I let you down. Always let you down. Will be easier now. Better. Wish I could be the daughter you deserve. I wish I could've been the daughter you wanted. But I appreciate all you did. Can't have been easy to always try. Now you know it's a lost cause. I'm a lost cause. I can't ruin your lives no more. This is the only good thing I can do for you. I hope it's enough." Stephen tried to read the note in a flat, toneless voice, but it broke several times before finally failing him at the end. "Why would you ever think we'd prefer you dead?"

"I've never been anything but trouble," cried Sienna. "You know that. Mum and Dad, they've never wanted me around. You and the business, that's all they care about."

"That's such crap!"

Sienna turned her body away from Stephen. "Then why didn't I live with you? Why was I shipped off when I was just a kid and never allowed to come home?"

"Because of me!" yelled Stephen, drawing Sienna's eyes to him. "It was my fault, okay."

"What do you mean?"

"Because I was always so sick."

"You're not sick. You've never been sick," retorted Sienna, turning back to the river, tired of everyone's lies.

"Don't you remember?" asked Stephen incredulously. Sienna shook her head. She really did live in a separate universe. "I was born with kidney problems. They were slowly shutting down and I was going to need a transplant. Mum and Dad aren't compatible. Mum's A positive. Dad's B negative. I'm O negative."

"Is that possible?" asked Sienna.

"Yes," replied Stephen with a watery laugh. "They must be both heterozygous. You're B positive. You were tested at birth. Doctors thought you'd have the best chance of being compatible with me. Didn't work out."

"That's why they didn't want me?" Sienna gasped. "Cos I couldn't give you my kidney?"

"No, Sen. They loved you. They'd been so scared that you'd end up sick like me. But I started to get real sick after that. I was on dialysis. I was in and out of hospital. We were on the list for a donor kidney. Mum was trying to keep the business running. Dad was always at the hospital with me."

"And I was in the way," murmured Sienna unhappily.

"No, Sen, no! Aunt Daphne offered to help out. You spent so much time with her and Uncle Cole. Everything was so disrupted that Uncle Cole suggested you live with them until I was better. By the time I got better you were so used to living there you didn't want to come home."

"Yes, I did," retorted Sienna. "You guys didn't want me. The three of you were happy together. I was just in the way."

"Who told you that? Bet it wasn't Mum or Dad," snapped Stephen, before calming himself. "They missed you so much. They worry all the time about how much they missed and always wondered if they did the right thing. You have no idea how much they fought with Uncle Cole over you. When you did come and visit, Uncle Cole would pick you up, acting as if it was some kind of custody arrangement. You were always upset and he'd blame Mum and Dad. Say it was their fault and threaten not to let them see you again. Mum and Dad had to go to court in the end to get you back. Uncle Cole fought them the whole way. I think that's why Aunt Daphne left him."

Sienna sat in silence. That was not the childhood she remembered. She vaguely remembered having to talk to a lot of people about how she felt about her uncle and parents. She remembered Uncle Cole telling her that she needed to tell those people about how upsetting she found going home and how much she liked living with him. It was true, but more than anything, she'd wanted to be wanted by her parents.

"I'm still not good enough for them," said Sienna after a long pause. "I see it. I see the pain I cause them."

"I don't think you understand why it hurts them," replied Stephen sincerely. "They don't know how to relate to you. I got everything and they feel like they've given you nothing. All they ever wanted was to have you home with us."

Sienna considered that against the life she'd known. No matter how hard she tried, she couldn't make it fit.

"Will you come home with us?" asked Stephen "You don't owe him anything."

"When are you going home?" Sienna replied, avoiding the question.

"We're staying as long as we need to. We're not being pushed out this time."

"We should go back. We can't let them keep fighting."

Stephen rolled his eyes as he nodded. "You know I always resented you coming back," he said with a guilty grimace. "It was nice being an only child. But at the same time, I felt really guilty about being the reason you never lived with us. I was always scared that if you ever found out it was my fault you'd hate me."

"I could never hate you."

"So you didn't answer the phone just so I could listen to you die?"

"I wanted to say goodbye," replied Sienna, her voice breaking as her eyes widened. "You'd been so nice to me."

Stephen laughed, choking on his sobs. "You're not right in the head. Reward for being a good big brother isn't listening to you say goodbye as you try and take your life. Hearing Jackson come in – screaming at him to tell me what's happening. Listening to you vomit."

Sienna looked at Stephen in horror. It had been so peaceful on her side. She didn't know how to reconcile those two truths.

"Mum and Dad were in a meeting. When they saw you'd called, they sent me out to call you," continued Stephen. "Dad thought you must've done really well and wanted to tell us. 'Just make sure she knows we're proud of her' he told me.

"I don't know how I looked when I burst back in, but I remember Dad's face. I couldn't tell them what I'd heard. They asked if I'd spoken to you and I nodded. 'She called to say goodbye' was all I could say. Mum understood immediately. She just snapped into action. Rang the airport, gathered our things. Was like when I was young. She was the one who could function. When she focuses on one thing, she can ignore everything else. But she started crying on the plane."

"I want to go home, Stephen. Let's go, okay."

They walked in silence. Stephen didn't hold her close this time. Sienna hated what she'd put her family through. If she'd got it right, their pain would've been short-lived. Now it was never-ending.

Arthur and Janice were walking out the front door when Sienna and Stephen arrived. They appeared upset. Uncle Cole was at the front door glaring angrily. Sienna looked between them wondering what she was supposed to do.

"I don't think we should go yet," said Stephen, walking over to his parents, leaving Sienna standing between them and Uncle Cole.

"I think we need to," said Janice tensely.

Uncle Cole was looking at Sienna expectantly. She wanted to speak to her parents and ask them about Stephen's story. It seemed strange that she would never know anything about him being so sick. There was something close to pleading in Stephen and Arthur's eyes, but Janice was more resolved. When Sienna just stood looking between them and Uncle Cole, Janice urged Arthur and Stephen to leave. There a slightly smug smile on Uncle Cole's face as he watched them.

"I knew they wouldn't stick around," said Uncle Cole, as they walked inside. "They never really cared. Like to use their money to make a show, but they always end up leaving you with me."

Sienna didn't find comfort in that thought. She wanted her parents to stop abandoning her when she needed them most.

Walking into the house behind Uncle Cole, Sienna was not sure what she was supposed to do. Uncle Cole muttered something about being hungry and she tentatively offered to cook him dinner. It was nice the way he smiled as he accepted the offer.

The actions of cooking were mechanical, but soothing. Uncle Cole was even complimentary when she served up. Sienna was not sure she wanted to eat. Food didn't hold much allure, but when her stomach grumbled she dished up a small serving. She was about to sit down to eat when her father walked unannounced into the kitchen.

"Did you cook?" asked Arthur, looking at Uncle Cole, who was sitting at the kitchen table, his dinner almost finished.

Sienna nodded, tilting her head towards the stove. "You want some? There's still some left."

Arthur's face turned into an angry snarl. Sienna dropped her plate on the table and rushed to her room. The smell of vomit hit as soon as she opened the door. It made her stomach turn. Her scissors were on the floor. She grabbed them as she pulled at the bandages on her left wrist.

"No, no, no," said an urgent voice. Arms seized her from behind and pinned her arms to her body. Sienna fought against them as they pried the scissors from her hand. "Sen, please. Don't do this. Please."

Tears wet Sienna's neck as Arthur's face buried itself there.

"I just offered you dinner," cried Sienna, her tears falling on her father's arms. "Why can't I do anything right? Why do I always have to let you and Mum down?"

"Oh, hell, Sen. I wasn't angry at you," gasped her father, holding her tighter. "Your uncle should've been cooking you dinner."

"That's not the way it works."

Arthur pulled Sienna tighter into his chest, turning her until she was curled in a ball in his lap. When her tears had dried, he lifted her to her feet and took her back to the kitchen. "Can I still try some of your cooking?"

Sienna nodded, taking her uncle's empty plate from the table and dishing the rest of the dinner on to a clean plate. She scrapped the bits of her meal from the sides of the plate back into the centre.

"This is really nice," said Arthur, squeezing Sienna's hand.

"It's just stir-fry. Jackson taught me to cook it."

"You spend a lot of time with Jackson, don't you?" Sienna shook her head. "He always seems to be around. I've heard a lot about him."

"We get along, but he's better off not spending time with me. I'm bad for him," said Sienna. Arthur raised his eyebrows. "And Uncle Cole thinks he's just trying to crack on to me."

"How old is Jackson?"

"Twenty-one."

"Probably is then," Arthur smiled.

"You don't think that's a bad thing?" asked Sienna.

"You worried he wouldn't take no for an answer?" asked Arthur seriously. Sienna shook her head. "Then I don't think it's a problem. You're beautiful and smart – no matter what the test results say. I'd think less of him if he didn't think you were worth cracking on to."

"I don't think he is," said Sienna. "It's not like that. He's my friend."

Arthur smiled and they finished eating in silence. When they were done, Arthur wouldn't let Sienna wash up. When she argued, he let her dry and put things away.

"Dad," Sienna said tentatively, not turning to look at him. "Do you really think I'm smart?"

"Sen, you don't have to be able to read or write to be smart. And if you find it as hard as your uncle says, then what you achieved is pretty impressive. But like I said before, tests don't tell you how smart you are. They can't tell you if you're a good person."

"Won't ever be smart enough to be a lawyer though."

"Maybe you can't get into law straight away, but you could do it later if you wanted. Is that what you want?"

"I don't know. Maybe. Just wanted to do whatever would make you and Mum like me."

"What is that supposed to mean?" cried Arthur angrily.

The trill of Arthur's mobile saved Sienna from answering. She rushed to her room, but was hit by the overwhelming smell of vomit as she opened the door. There was a large patch of dried vomit on the floor near her bed. Stepping past it, she reached out for her quilt, thinking she could sleep on the lounge, but it was stuck. Yanking it with more force, she was met with more vomit and large patches of blood.

The sight was more confronting than Sienna imagined. This wasn't her memory of that night. Backing away, she smacked into something warm that grabbed her tightly.

"Let's clean this, hey," breathed Arthur in a shaky voice. "You go start the washing machine. I'll get this."

Arthur had the bed stripped by the time Sienna returned from the laundry with a basket. His face was white and his hands shook as he put everything into the basket and walked out of the room. Sienna quickly got started on cleaning the carpet. She scrapped the vomit into a plastic bag before covering the carpet in cleaning powder. While she scrubbed at the carpet, her father tried to remove the stains from her mattress.

"We can just flip the mattress for tonight," said Sienna, holding up a musty-smelling sleeping bag. She'd scrubbed and vacuumed the carpet twice and it was as close to clean as it was going to get.

"You're not staying here tonight," replied Arthur angrily, before calming himself. "You're staying with us."

Arthur didn't give Sienna a chance to argue. He grabbed her school bag and tipped the contents on to her desk, then went through her drawers and wardrobe, grabbing everything she needed. Zipping up the bag, he threw it over his shoulder and took her hand.

"Where do you think you're taking her?" demanded Uncle Cole, stomping up the front steps.

Arthur pushed past him without answering. Sienna suddenly found herself pulled out of her father's grasp.

"Get your hands off my daughter," said Arthur angrily. Uncle Cole gripped Sienna tighter. "She's coming with me. Did you honestly expect her to sleep in her own blood and vomit or was cleaning it up supposed to be her punishment?"

Arthur grabbed Sienna's arm and pulled her to him. Uncle Cole resisted for a moment before releasing her. Sienna couldn't help but turn and watch Uncle Cole as they drove away. She held up her hand, but wasn't really sure what the gesture signified. Right then, she wasn't sure about anything.

~14~

APOLOGIES

Things were almost amicable by the time Arthur, Janice and Stephen returned to Sydney. Uncle Cole managed not to look too annoyed by Sienna's decision to ride with her parents on the way to the airport. Stephen drove. Janice and Arthur sat on either side of Sienna on the backseat. They each had one arm around her shoulder, their other hand holding one of hers. No one spoke until the airport came into view.

"We're going to come back for Christmas," said Arthur. "Then maybe you can come home with us for couple of weeks in the holidays. You don't have to decide yet."

"Just for a visit?" asked Sienna.

"For anything you want," replied Janice, her voice showing no sign of the tears welling in her eyes. "We're not – we're okay with you staying here to finish school, but you're welcome in our house any time for anything. You want to stay a night, a year or a lifetime, then that's fine with us. That's not just for now. That will be the same no matter how old you get. We're your parents and we'll be there for you. For everything."

Sienna turned to her father, who nodded in agreement. "Even if all I do for the rest of my life is stuff things up?"

There was a collective intake of breath and a second of painful silence.

"Even then," Arthur said tenderly. "We're sorry you never knew that before."

Arthur, Janice and Stephen were the last to board the plane. They held on to Sienna as long as they could and it hurt her more than she would ever explain to watch them walk away. She wondered if it would've hurt her as much to walk away from Uncle Cole.

As soon as they were out of sight, Uncle Cole's arm was around her shoulders. "Your parents won't agree, but I think there's something you need to do before we can really put all this behind you."

Sienna didn't ask what it was. She already knew.

There was nothing comforting about Uncle Cole's arm as it led her to Jackson's apartment. She'd expected to be facing him at the police station. It seemed too intimate visiting him in his own home and it was clear Jackson wasn't expecting them. He looked horrified by her arrival.

"You can call me once you've smoothed things over," said Uncle Cole, pushing Sienna into Jackson's apartment before leaving.

Jackson closed the door behind her and walked away. She followed him to the small kitchen. He put on the kettle, acting as if she wasn't there. Sienna wasn't sure what to say. Jackson had never treated her like this before.

"I'm sure the coffee's not really up to your standard, but —"

"It's fine," said Sienna quickly. "Jackson …"

Jackson turned away. He was leaning over the sink, his body shaking. Stepping tentatively towards him, Sienna put her hand on his back. He spun around to face her, his eyes immediately drawn to her still-bandaged wrists. Before Sienna could even think of how she could make things up to him, he was wiping his eyes and forcing a smile on to his face. He quickly set about making the coffee. Sienna sat down at the small kitchen bench.

"How you going?" asked Jackson, sliding a coffee towards her. It was a flat, joyless voice she had never heard from him before.

"I've been worse," shrugged Sienna. She took a sip of the coffee and almost spat it out. "Urgh, that's horrible. How can you drink it?"

"You're such a snob," replied Jackson, grabbing her coffee and tossing it, cup and all, into the sink. He then took a defiant sip of his own coffee. Sienna hunched her shoulders against the rebuff, wrapping her arms around her body. The sound of another cup being thrown into the sink made her flinch. "Why'd you come here?"

"To make things up to you," replied Sienna meekly.

"And you're going to do that by cowering in my kitchen?"

"I don't know how to make it up to you." Sienna looked up. Jackson's eyes softened. "I don't know how to live through the day right now."

"Don't say that," breathed Jackson. He took her hand and squeezed it gently. Sienna watched as his eyes flicked away then back. "I mean, you can say it if it's true. I just don't want it to be. I don't think I've seen anything worse than that."

"What did you see?" asked Sienna. Jackson shook his head firmly. "I need to know."

"No, you don't."

"Did I speak to you?"

"No," breathed Jackson. "You were unconscious when I found you."

"So I never said anything?"

"No. Why?" Sienna shrugged and shook her head. "Your wrists were bleeding. I grabbed what I could to wrap around them. Your brother was screaming from somewhere in the room. Ryan held your head when you started vomiting. That's how you would've died. Choked on your own vomit. Not exactly peaceful."

"It was for me," whispered Sienna, unsure if Jackson heard or not. "I'm sorry. I never expected you to find me like that."

"No, I guess not," sighed Jackson. "What was with the phone call then?"

"I didn't want you to think I – wanted to let you know I wouldn't be there on Sunday."

"Cancelling appointments before you die. How thoughtful."

"You think I was being selfish too?"

"I just don't get how those two headspaces could possibly exist at the same time!" cried Jackson, throwing his hands over his head as he strode to the adjacent lounge room behind Sienna. She turned to watch him pace. "So there you are, swallowing you pills, slashing at your wrists, and you think, crap, better tell Jax I won't be able to make it Sunday."

"I didn't want you to be upset with me!" cried Sienna, jumping off her stool.

"You thought I'd be mad at you for not showing up on Sunday, but not for killing yourself?"

"At least if I was gone I wouldn't keep messing things up for you."

"I told you you're the only real friend I've made in this town and you think I care how much shouting the Chief does?" asked Jackson incredulously. "One word from you and I would've told him to stick it. The only reason I never forced the issue was because I didn't want to cause problems for you. I loved hanging out with you."

"Really?"

"Shit, Sienna. Why didn't you tell me you felt so alone?" asked Jackson, stepping forward and hugging her. "Some of these entries, it could've been me writing them."

Jackson stepped away, turning back around with her diary in his hand. Sienna took it from him, glancing momentarily at the entries. Her handwriting had always been very neat in her journals. Keeping her sentences simple and not needing to structure coherent arguments made it look like she was actually literate; another façade to hide the terrible truth. Jackson didn't look ashamed by his intrusion into her personal thoughts. Sienna didn't seek to make him so. It was nice to be understood for once.

"It's not always easy being around you," she whispered.

"Because I remind you of Flynn?" asked Jackson. Sienna nodded. "Unbearable?" She shook her head. "Worth being friends, then?"

"Amber wants to be my friend too."

"You can be friends with both of us," laughed Jackson. "Can't you?"

Sienna nodded. She took one step forward, before stopping. Jackson was watching her cautiously. Bowing her head, she stepped forward again, throwing her arms around his neck and burying her head there. "Thank you. I'm still not sure I wanted you to, but – you saved my life."

"Yeah," replied Jackson flatly, wrapping his arms tightly around her. "He's why you did it, isn't he?"

Sienna nodded, breathing deeply to control her tears. "He's the only place I belong."

"It's a dangerous thing belonging to someone besides yourself. Leaves you pretty lost when that person goes away."

"You ever belonged to someone else?" asked Sienna, pushing out of Jackson's arms.

"Yeah, my ex-girlfriend," nodded Jackson, sitting on the lounge and inviting her to join him. "Kinda like you, I guess. Met her when I was young and everything good in my life was tied to her. I felt like I could do whatever I wanted when I was with her. She helped me realise I could do this job. Problem was that this job took me away from her. First the academy and then out here. She resented that. Resented me in the end. It was hard having that person turn on me."

"Worse than them dying, you think?" asked Sienna.

"You can't compare those things."

"But you didn't try and kill yourself over it."

"No, but I had lots of family support. Some support from the guys here." Sienna looked at Jackson questioningly. "Yeah, not personal support, but when it comes to doing the job the Chief and Ryan are actually pretty good. And I had you."

"Me?"

"I was pretty cynical about girls when I met you. I was pretty cynical about you when I met you," added Jackson with a smile. "Knew you were coming. The princess niece of the Chief. You were every bit the spoilt brat we thought you were. Perhaps just quieter. But you were also stubborn and strong and defiant. Yet friendly and sweet. You were fun. Worth getting to know."

"How'd that help you?" asked Sienna, unsure Jackson's assessment of her was particularly complimentary.

"You made time here go a bit faster – when we got to spend time together."

They were quiet for a long time. Sienna wasn't sure how long she should stay or when Uncle Cole would consider her forgiven.

"You ready for school tomorrow?" asked Jackson eventually.

"Amber said she'd come by in the morning so we can walk together," said Sienna. It was the one thing giving her the courage to return to school. "She reckons everyone knows what happened."

"Small town. Chief's niece. Everyone knows."

Amber came by at eight. Amy met them at the school gate. The tears in Amy's eyes as they approached surprised Sienna. As did the heartfelt hug Amy gave her.

"So Amber said you're not very good at recognising friends," said Amy, as they walked through the gates. "Well, Amber's one. I'm one and I think we roped Luke into being one too."

Sienna couldn't help feeling like Amy was making fun of her.

"He's in," said Amber, with a shake of her head.

"That's what he's hoping," smirked Amy.

Amber went red and hit Amy in the arm. Sienna was confused until Luke arrived. Thinking they would find her rude for never realising

Amber and Luke were a couple, Sienna tried to act like it wasn't a complete surprise. She wasn't sure it worked, but no one called her out on it. And none of that mattered when they made their way to class and the taunts started. It only got worse when the teachers became involved. Apparently, they felt the need to use Sienna's suicide attempt as a discussion topic, reminding students that school marks aren't everything and there are better ways to deal with exam stress.

"Geez, coming back here would be enough to make you want to top yourself, huh?" said Luke at lunch. "Can you believe they talk about you like you're not even in the classroom?"

"You get used to it," shrugged Sienna, trying hard not to let it get to her. Amy had been helping by running a sarcastic commentary through most classes.

"We could boycott in protest," suggested Luke.

Sienna smiled genuinely this time. It was a good suggestion, but Amber wasn't keen.

The conversation moved easily around Sienna. She was glad they didn't make her join in. It gave her time to settle herself. Socialising wasn't something she'd had a lot of practice at.

"So you do anything interesting in the holidays?" asked Luke casually, turning to Sienna.

"Luke!" hissed Amber.

"Oh, shit! Sorry. Don't know how – shit," gasped Luke.

"It's okay," smiled Sienna. "Interesting, no. But the second week – after I got out of hospital – that wasn't so bad. My parents were being super nice to me. Maybe scared I'd try and kill myself again."

"You get along with your parents?" asked Amy.

"It's hard to tell," shrugged Sienna. "I don't know them."

"I don't get along with my folks. At all," said Amy. "I can't wait to finish school. I just hope I can get into uni and get a job and enough money to get away from them."

"I just want to get out of Fortune," added Amber wistfully. "You don't know how lucky you are, knowing you're getting out of here at the end of next year."

Sienna found it odd they all assumed she'd move back to Sydney once she finished school. It had been her assumption too, but now that university was out of the question, she wasn't so sure.

"I don't mind it here," said Luke.

"Yeah, of course not," sighed Amber. "You know you can get a job out here. What about the rest of us?"

Luke shrugged in a disaffected manner. There was something more than was being said, but Sienna didn't understand the politics of Fortune well enough to know what it was. It made her feel incredibly self-absorbed.

"I'll meet you after school," Amber said encouragingly, when the bell rang.

Sienna and Amy headed off to English. The teasing began as soon as they were in hollering range. It made Sienna nervous that Amy would abandon her, but Amy stepped in closer and even stood a little in front of her as they waited outside the classroom.

"Quick, better pack away all the scissors," teased Liam.

"Nah, give her a pair. Maybe she can finish the job," retorted Sam.

"Imagine not even being able to kill yourself," laughed Karina. "Maybe if she'd done bio, she would know where her veins were!"

"You're such losers," countered Amy.

"Go have a drink, Amy," snapped Sam. "Oh, that's right, you can't. Your dad's already drunk the town dry."

Amy's face burned with shame. Sienna wished she could've said something, but witty remarks had never been her forte. The teacher brought the class to order, as he marshalled them into the room, but ignored the snide remarks that shot across the class at Sienna and Amy, only shushing them when they became too disruptive.

"I'm sorry," Sienna finally squeezed out when the class ended.

"Yeah, like I've never copped shit from those dickheads," snapped Amy. Sienna didn't respond. Amy sighed heavily. "Don't worry about it, okay."

"Are you doing anything this afternoon?" asked Sienna. "You can come over to my place if you want."

"I don't need your pity," snapped Amy. "I thought you got that."

"Pity? I don't – what do you mean?"

"Being the town drunk's daughter."

"Oh," said Sienna, wondering if that was what she was supposed to have been thinking about. "No, I was actually being more selfish than that. I can't be home alone, so if I don't make friends then I have to spend my time outside school at the cop shop. And I'm not real good at the whole friends thing."

"You're okay," smiled Amy. "But I can't do today. Tomorrow?"

Sienna was about to agree when she remembered that she had her first appointment with the psychologist tomorrow afternoon. She wasn't looking forward to it. Thankfully Amy and Amber promised to hang with her on Wednesday afternoon. It gave Sienna something small to look forward to as she walked into the police station.

"Hi, Sienna. How are you feeling?" asked Ryan kindly, though there was something haunted in his eyes as he looked at her.

Sienna could only mumble a response, knowing what he saw when he looked at her.

"You got work to do or you want me to give you something?" asked Uncle Cole gruffly, walking out of his office.

When Sienna indicated she had homework, he led her to the kitchen. He immediately moved to the drawers and took out all the knives and sharp implements.

"Is that really necessary?" asked Sienna.

"From where I'm standing, yes, it is."

Sienna put her head down and pulled out her books. She wasn't sure why she was even bothering with homework, knowing how little impact it would have.

"You still determined to see that shrink tomorrow?" asked Uncle Cole, forcing Sienna's eyes up. She nodded tentatively. "It won't help. You'd be better off focusing on school than going there."

"I tried that before, remember. That's how I ended up here."

"You need to realise your parents don't know everything," growled Uncle Cole. "You worked really hard and it paid off. Only you don't want to see it that way. You want to turn yourself inside out to be something you're not just to please them and damn the rest of us."

Sienna opened her mouth, but Uncle Cole was already gone. It left her conflicted. She wanted to believe the things he said, but she wanted to believe in her parents too – more so because they were the unfulfilled promise of her life. Yet Uncle Cole's belief that continuing to try at school had some point gave her the courage to do so. She just wished it got easier, but reading today was as slow and tiresome as it always had been.

"Where're all the knives?"

Sienna looked up to see Jackson rummaging through the drawers.

"Uncle Cole has them," murmured Sienna.

Jackson spun around, surprised by her presence. "What, he thought you'd top yourself in the kitchen?" he asked mockingly.

The realisation of how true a possibility that was must've shown on her face, because Jackson suddenly became very serious as he sat down at the table.

"You need help, Sienna," he said, squeezing her hands. "You can't keep thinking like this. Those thoughts – they shouldn't even be in your head."

"I see the shrink tomorrow, okay," said Sienna defensively, pulling her hands out of Jackson's grasp.

"Okay, well let's eat at your place then. You ready to go? Got something we can cook?" asked Jackson, jumping up from the table. Sienna huffed and crossed her arms. "Chief doesn't finish til eight at the earliest and I can guarantee he'll buy you take-out. Your choice."

"Fine," snapped Sienna, packing up.

The lack of anger on Uncle Cole's face when Sienna let him know what was happening was a thankful reprieve and made her think it hadn't all been Jackson's idea.

"Does Jackson have to stay until you get home?" asked Sienna tentatively.

"No," replied Uncle Cole. "But if you need – if you feel – go for a walk with your camera." Sienna nodded. "Sorry. I should've always made you do that."

Sienna's heart warmed. These were the moments of understanding she wished she had with her parents. It made her feel like life with Uncle Cole might not work out so badly after all.

"So how was the first day back at school?" asked Jackson, as he washed the dishes. It had been a very quiet dinner.

Sienna could only shrug, but that just made him more insistent for an answer. "What do you expect to hear?" she asked seriously. "I wasn't all that thrilled to wake up alive. You think that's all gone away?"

"But I thought you sorted through things with your parents. You still don't think they're going to disown you because you don't ace your exams, do you?" Sienna stared at Jackson questioningly. "They came to see me," he confessed. "We chatted about stuff. Nothing bad. They asked questions about your life here. About the Chief."

Sienna crossed her arms angrily. "You shouldn't have told them nothing about him."

"No, I think I should've," countered Jackson. "I get where you're coming from. They were looking for a fight, but let's face it, the Chief isn't up for any parenting awards at the moment. And they just wanted me to ignore the Chief's orders and be friends with you."

"That's it?" asked Sienna sceptically.

"Yeah, I promise. And it only cost me a stack of late night-early morning shift combinations."

"Jax, don't," sighed Sienna. "It doesn't make me feel better knowing I'm messing up your life."

"Being banned from seeing the one person in this stupid town I actually get along with doesn't make me feel better either!" cried Jackson. "Screw the Chief, okay. I hate it! I didn't get posted out here to have my freedom and social life taken off me. So will you ease up on me hanging out with you? Unless you don't really like it, of course."

"No, I want to hang out with you," replied Sienna in a soft voice, her eyes not meeting Jackson's.

"Good, then we need to start doing stuff together. I'm guessing you're going to make me continue my modelling career in the name of art. So that means you need to do something I like. You run?"

"Run?"

"Yeah, you know, put one foot in front of the other at an accelerated rate."

"Not well," replied Sienna with concern.

"Then we'll have to change that," smiled Jackson.

Sienna didn't expect that to mean the next morning. His reminder call at six-thirty was not the way she'd been seeking to wake up.

"I didn't sign up for this," Sienna grumbled, stomping out on to the footpath. Uncle Cole had looked something between concerned and amused when she'd told him what she was doing.

"Yes, you did," countered Jackson.

Sienna stifled a yawn. It didn't matter that she was up and dressed, she could have gladly gone straight back to bed.

"I thought you were talking about afternoons," Sienna muttered.

"Can you please trust me," sighed Jackson, nudging her forward. "I promise, you'll enjoy it."

Sienna started jogging. Jackson smiled and trotted next to her, but he was soon metres ahead. By the time he reached the end of the street she was over twenty metres behind. Sienna watched as he stopped and sighed, waiting for her to catch up. The process was repeated again and again, tearing open wounds so violently Sienna was surprised she wasn't visibly bleeding.

Refusing to put herself through this torture, Sienna turned around and stomped back towards home. Jackson caught up with her minutes later, a look of confusion on his face. That only angered Sienna more.

"I never said I could run," she snapped, continuing to march home.

Jackson jumped in front of her, blocking her path. When she tried to move around him, he restrained her, forcing their eyes to meet.

"Oh shit," breathed Jackson, quickly pulling her into a hug. "I'm going to teach you to run, okay. No more just expecting." Sienna shook her head. "Trust me. Tomorrow morning, okay. I think you'll need it."

***

"So what am I s'pose to say?"

It was the question that had been swirling through Sienna's head all day. By the time she'd reached the psychologist's office it was twirling so fast she thought she'd be sick.

"We can talk about anything you like," replied Dr Chousalkar.

"Shouldn't you have stuff you want to ask me? You're the one trying to sort me out. I'll just tell you what you want."

"Is that what you always do?" asked Dr Chousalkar. "Tell people what they what to hear."

"Usually better than dealing with me telling them stuff they don't want to know," replied Sienna flatly, moving to the window.

Dr Chousalkar had offered Sienna a seat, but didn't force the issue when she remained standing. Dr Chousalkar might have been nice enough, but Sienna realised she didn't want to be here. Maybe Uncle Cole was right and this was a bad idea.

"It's often better to let people know what you're really feeling and thinking," said Dr Chousalkar.

"Not in my life," muttered Sienna. "Never caused me nothing but trouble."

This back and forth conversation continued for a while before Dr Chousalkar started asking Sienna questions about the day she tried to take her life. They weren't particularly probing questions. What she did; all the mechanical things.

Then the real questions started. Dr Chousalkar wanted to know how Sienna had felt. What she'd been thinking. Why the lead-up events had affected her so badly. Sienna didn't have the answers. Just considering them made her feel like she was being stripped naked against her will. The acute feelings of worthlessness crept back into her body, making her hate herself and her life.

The session ended right when Sienna felt herself stripped bare, leaving her feeling horribly exposed and vulnerable. Uncle Cole shook his head as soon as he saw her and muttered the whole way home about how useless these sessions were and how they'd cause more harm than good. Right then Sienna was inclined to agree and was determined to say nothing next week.

"I didn't agree to this," snapped Sienna, stomping out the front gate to where Jackson was waiting for her in his running clothes.

Jackson didn't respond. He just smiled and started running. The pace was slow. They didn't talk. It was a pretty morning and Sienna soon found her mind pleasantly engaged as she took in the colours of the sky. But all that changed when she caught sight of Jackson's smug smile. Suddenly all the anger and resentment she'd been holding on to after being left in such a vulnerable state last night exploded to the surface.

"Screw this," Sienna snapped, turning and striding in the opposite direction.

"What's up?" asked Jackson, jogging in front of her and placing his hands on her shoulders.

"Screw this, okay. Screw you. I don't want to do it!" cried Sienna, throwing off Jackson's hands.

"Okay, we'll do something else," Jackson replied softly, trying to mask the hurt in his voice.

Guilt stabbed through Sienna, making her angrier than before. This was his fault and now he was making her feel sorry for him. She hated her life. She hated herself. And she hated that Jackson was standing in front of her making her feel all that.

Sienna's arm swung out before she knew what she was doing. Jackson's reflexes were fast. He held her fisted right hand firmly in his. Her left fist flew towards his face. He caught it as easily as he had her other arm. She tried to free herself, fighting against his restraint until he finally pushed her away from him.

"Hit me then," said Jackson angrily. Sienna didn't move. He raised his eyebrows and held his hands behind his back. "Come on. You want to hit me, then hit me."

Sienna turned and punched the trunk of a nearby tree. The rough bark cut into her knuckles. It hurt, but not enough.

Before she could attempt to drown out the pain, her arms were pinned to the side of her body. Jackson's arms were wrapped around her chest, his head in her neck.

"It's okay," he said in a shaky voice. "I'm not here to fight you. We'll do whatever you want."

The warmth of Jackson's embrace was comforting. Sienna's arms curled up and hugged his arms as they crossed her body. He held her tighter as her chest began to shudder. She didn't want to cry in the middle of the street. Sick of being weak and vulnerable, Sienna's anger began to rise again. Jackson must have noticed, because he was gripping her wrists firmly.

"Try something for me?" he asked. It took Sienna a long time to nod. "Run. As fast as you can. When you feel like you're going to collapse and die, push it harder. Just got to make it home."

Sienna didn't want to comply. She was sick of running, but she did want to get home and forget this whole morning and the fastest way to do that was to do exactly what Jackson said. Roughly pushing his arms off her, Sienna sprinted towards her house. It didn't take her body long to tire. Her lungs were burning as her legs became heavy and leaden. It didn't stop her. She pushed through until she reached her fence and her legs collapsed beneath her.

Jackson arrived just as she sat, gasping for breath, on the porch. "How you feeling?" he asked, sitting down next to her. "Too tired to think and feel?"

Sienna looked up, thrown by his question. She thought he wanted her to run because he believed her unfit and uncoordinated. "That's what you wanted?"

"Yeah, kinda," replied Jackson. "So am I coming back tomorrow?"

"No," replied Sienna seriously. "I'm want to sleep in tomorrow. But you can come on Friday if you want."

Jackson quickly enveloped her in a hug. She thought she'd seen him smile, but it wasn't Flynn's smile. It was his and she wished she'd seen it properly.

It took a while for Sienna to realise, but her life had fallen into a manageable routine. Jackson came by on Monday, Wednesday and Friday mornings for them to run. She didn't ask how it was that his shifts never clashed, assuming Uncle Cole wasn't completely against them running together. Jackson mixed up their runs, from leisurely jogs to sprint sessions. They always sprinted on Wednesday mornings and rarely spoke.

The psychologist appointments on Tuesday afternoons were not progressing the way Sienna thought they would. They continued to leave her vulnerable and agitated, which did nothing to improve relations with Uncle Cole. It wasn't a big surprise when Jackson replaced him as her driver to the appointments.

"You all right?" asked Jackson, as they pulled up out the front of Dr Chousalkar's office. Sienna nodded. "Okay. I'll be waiting here for you when you finish."

Sienna nodded again. The last couple of sessions had been very quiet. She'd spoken as little as she could and even now struggled to get the words out. Dr Chousalkar didn't seem to mind. She just asked questions Sienna could respond to non-verbally if she needed to. But keeping her mouth shut didn't prevent the memories from torturing her mind.

"Hey," smiled Jackson, causing Sienna's heart to twist as she walked towards him. "Been thinking that we should test out the food in Westloch. I hardly ever get to come out here and you should have a night off cooking every week."

"I don't like hamburgers," muttered Sienna, making her way to the car.

"Not talking about hamburgers," replied Jackson, grabbing her hand. "Come on, trust me."

Jackson took Sienna to a Thai restaurant. It was better than they expected, but it still did little to ease the twirl of emotions wreaking havoc in her mind. He must've understood, dropping her home with a reminder that she'd feel better after their run.

Better, yes, but never good. It took Sienna most of the week to return to some sense of normalcy.

"You coming over today?" Sienna asked as she, Amber and Amy walked towards the school gate at the end of the day.

They hung out after school as many afternoons as possible to reduce the amount of time Sienna had to spend at the police station. It was a good strategy, because they didn't have to stay all night for Uncle Cole to be content, though that was something they agreed to keep secret from her parents. Their promise to check-in rather than check-up was not being kept very well, meaning familial tensions were always high.

"I can't," replied Amber apologetically.

"I can come over," smiled Amy. "Happy for you to feed me too."

Sienna smiled broadly. She loved it when Amy stayed for dinner. They never spoke about the reasons why she liked to stay so late. They just enjoyed each other's company, understanding how hard it was for each of them to part and return to their normal lives.

"Room for one more?" asked Jackson, as Sienna and Amy cooked.

"Always," smiled Sienna.

Amy smiled just as broadly. It was nice the way Amy and Jackson got along. It was like an extra light being switched on and Sienna felt more alive when they were around.

"Hey, look at that," said Sienna, placing the last of the dishes in the sink where Jackson was washing and Amy was drying.

"What?" asked Jackson warily.

"The contrast of your skin colours," Sienna replied. "It's beautiful. Just wait there."

Sienna raced to grab her camera. Moving Amy's hand atop Jackson's she tried to find the right image, but it eluded her. Something about the setting was wrong.

"This isn't working," muttered Sienna.

She moved Jackson and Amy around, their skin always touching, but she still couldn't get it right. Even photographing them alone didn't help. It was making Sienna anxious. Then she remembered what Uncle

Cole said. He'd told her to go for a walk with her camera.

"Come out the back," Sienna instructed, waving for them to follow her.

It was so much better in the backyard and the evening light was perfect. Sienna grabbed Jackson and stood him under the tree before positioning Amy in his arms. Neither said anything as she continually moved them and shifted about, taking photos from all angles. It was only the fading light that caused Sienna to realise how long they'd been outside.

"Sorry," she murmured.

"Nah, it was fun," smiled Amy. "And you looked like you were in the zone."

"So you going to show us?" asked Jackson.

Sienna nodded hesitantly. She tried to flick quickly through the images, but Amy and Jackson wanted to examine them more closely. They were very complimentary, but Sienna wasn't sure how sincere they were.

"I should really be getting home," said Amy, packing up her stuff when they returned to the kitchen.

"You want me to take you?" offered Jackson.

"Um, no, thanks," replied Amy, grabbing her bag and backing out the door. "Probably best my dad doesn't know I hang out with cops socially."

Amy waved goodbye, but Sienna was focused on what she'd said.

"You've had to arrest her father?"

"Let's not go there," replied Jackson. "You know I can't tell you that kind of stuff."

"But she's okay, though, right?"

Jackson scowled, sighing heavily. "I think it's good she spends so much time with you and Amber. It's good for both of you," he quickly added. "I should get going too. Can we do something Sunday night? Movies?"

"With everyone?" asked Sienna, feeling like she was getting the hang of this friends thing.

"Who's everyone?"

"Amy, Amber, Luke," replied Sienna, as though this was obvious.

"I don't really want to hang out with a whole load of school kids," Jackson replied with a grimace.

"I'm a school kid," Sienna replied defensively.

"They're your friends, not mine. I just want to hang out with you."

"There's nothing I really want to see," said Sienna. Dr Chousalkar had been trying to convince her to speak up about how she felt and what she wanted, but the way Jackson's face fell wasn't endearing her to the practice. "But I could do a rental. Watch it here."

"How about my place?" suggested Jackson with a smile. "We can order pizza. Please let me order pizza."

Sienna nodded. When Jackson hugged her, she reconsidered the virtues of telling the truth.

~15~

SPHERES

"We've hired a house just outside of Fortune for the Christmas break."

Sienna's heart stopped. She turned to Jackson who nodded and smiled supportively. Glancing at her watch, though it couldn't tell her it was the fifth of December, she tried to determine if she had enough time to prepare for her family's arrival.

"We're flying out the Monday after you finish school. We can pick you up straight from airport, if you like," Arthur continued.

"What do you mean pick me up?" asked Sienna.

"So you can stay with us," said Janice. "For Christmas. That's why we're coming out."

"Am I allowed to?" Sienna asked hesitantly, wondering if Uncle Cole knew about this or if they were planning on kidnapping her.

"You're our daughter! You're supposed to stay with us," snapped Arthur.

That was answer enough for Sienna. She wrapped her arms around her chest and curled her body up on her chair, waiting out the silence.

"Maybe you guys can discuss your plans with the Chief," said Jackson, his arm slipping around Sienna's shoulders. "Might be easier than getting Sienna to sort out when you can pick her up."

There was a long silence. Sienna buried her head in her hands. Her parents only ever called now when Jackson was around.

"Does that work for you, Sen?" asked Janice. "If we arrange it all with your uncle, would you be happy to spend the week with us?"

"If I'm allowed, yeah," answered Sienna timidly.

Jackson nodded encouragingly through the sounds of annoyance on the other end of the phone. He left soon after they hung up, but as she watched him from the lounge room window, she saw him put his phone to his ear. She would have bet her life it was her parents calling him and it made her dread her uncle's arrival.

"I guess I should be flattered they even consulted me," muttered Uncle Cole the following night. "I'll be working anyway, so I guess it doesn't matter if you go."

"Thank you," nodded Sienna quietly. "I didn't want to upset you."

"I don't want them upsetting you," he retorted. "Just remember their previous actions and why you're here. You might what to question what this sudden interest in your life is all about."

Uncle Cole stomped out of the kitchen and Sienna dashed to her room. She had been questioning her parents' motives. In her own mind and even in a couple of her sessions. She'd never been able to come up with many good answers, but a large part of her still wanted to believe her parents loved her. If she was going to decide on a future, she would have to find out sooner or later. This would be the first test and Sienna decided to start safe and call Stephen.

"Guess what?" she asked, as soon as he answered.

"Good what or bad what?" he asked.

"Um, good, I think," Sienna replied, hoping that was true.

"You're sick of country life and are coming to live back in the city?"

"That would be good?"

"What's your news, Sen?"

"Uncle Cole's letting me stay with you – you know, at Christmas – at the house you hired," said Sienna, only to be met by a wall of silence. "That's good, right?"

"Yeah, of course. That's great," Stephen replied unconvincingly. "Mum and Dad'll be stoked. It's just – is that what you were worried about? You didn't say yes before because you were worried Uncle Cole might say no?"

"You know he doesn't want me to go. Of course he wants me to spend Christmas with him."

"He's working, Sen. Just like last year."

"Yeah, but I hung with him at the station," she explained, hating that they never considered Uncle Cole's feelings even a little bit. "I hate having to choose between them. Doesn't matter what I do, someone's always going to be angry with me."

Stephen quickly changed the subject. It left Sienna feeling uneasy. Thankfully, Janice and Arthur were both thrilled with the news, not making any of the comments Stephen had.

"You're really looking forward to spending Christmas out here?" asked Sienna tentatively.

"Can't wait," replied Arthur.

"Me either," said Sienna, relief flooding her body.

"Good, because we're hoping you'll come back home – maybe spend the rest of the holidays with us," said Janice. "We've already spoken to your uncle," she added quickly. "He's fine with it, as long as it's what you want."

Sienna wondered how true that was, but it wasn't her only concern. "What am I going to do there?" she asked. "You guys'll be at work most of the time. I don't remember ever doing anything in Sydney that didn't …"

"Involve Flynn," said Janice, finishing the sentence. "What about your friends? Would Amber and Amy like to come with you?"

"I don't think they could afford it," replied Sienna scathingly. "The flights, somewhere to stay, money to do stuff."

"They won't need more than spending money," said Arthur. "We'll cover their airfare and they'll stay with us in the spare room. None of that's an issue."

"And if you pack food from the house you won't need to buy any when you go out," added Janice. "Think about it, okay."

Sienna thought about little else. The idea of going back to Sydney and Flynn's memory terrified her. Yet she'd been living with the ghost of his smile for a year. It couldn't be much worse than what she'd already endured. And perhaps it would be a whole new experience being in Sydney with friends – unless Amber and Amy didn't want to go. She wasn't sure what her decision would be then.

"So you going to tell us what's got you all worked up?" Amy asked at lunch.

Sienna opened her mouth, but the words wouldn't come out.

"Come on, spit it out," said Amber. "How bad could it be?"

Sienna sighed. Closing her eyes so she couldn't see their reactions, she detailed her parents' suggestion for the summer holidays.

"Are you serious?" asked Amber, shaking Sienna to get her to open her eyes. "Like really serious? Does your place have a pool?"

"Um, yeah," laughed Sienna. No one in Sydney had ever asked her that before.

"Urgh, I mean, my parents will insist on talking to your parents and stuff like that," sighed Amber. "But this would mean we get to be in Sydney for New Years'. Will your parents let us go out?"

"I think so," replied Sienna hesitantly. She was sure she could guilt them into it if Amy and Amber were there. "Probably won't let us drink, though." Amber just waved her hand dismissively. "Amy, I can get my mum to ring your parents too."

"No, that's okay," replied Amy casually. "As long as they don't have to do anything, they won't care. If I tell them what day I'm coming home, that'll be enough."

"But that's a yes you'll to come, right?" asked Sienna seriously.

"Yeah," smiled Amy. "I'm definitely in."

"This is going to be the best holidays ever," said Amber excitedly. "Maybe we can check out the unis and decide which one we want to go to. And look at where we can live!"

"Live?" queried Sienna, lost by the turn in conversation.

"We're all planning on moving to Sydney, right. If we get a place together, we won't have to shack up with strangers in a cockroach-infested dive."

Sienna smiled. She loved the idea, but didn't want to tell them there was no chance of that fate ever befalling her. If there was one thing her parents had always protected, it was their image. And they'd never been shy of spending money on her. If she'd really been Uncle Cole's daughter, she would've been in the same situation as Amy and Amber.

"You reckon Jackson will be there?" asked Amy with a sly smile, exchanging glances with Amber.

"Where?" asked Sienna, and she could see they thought she was a bit thick.

"In Sydney. When we are," replied Amber slowly. "You said that's where he's from."

"It's not like he'd visit us. He doesn't like hanging out with a group of school kids," replied Sienna.

"No, he likes hanging out with just one school kid," replied Amy, a deep blush hitting her cheeks.

"Do you like him?" asked Sienna, shocked she'd never noticed.

"No, of course not," cried Amy, but her face was flaming red now.

"Oh, you do!" cried Amber. "Man, that sucks."

Amy shrugged and smiled.

"Why's it suck?" asked Sienna, feeling like she needed to be born in Fortune to make sense of their conversations at times.

"Ah, because he's in love with you," replied Amy.

Sienna didn't respond, but Amy's theory only added to her anxiety about Tuesday afternoon.

"Want to talk?"

Sienna shook her head. Jackson took her hand and walked them down the street, his thumb rubbing her hand, enticing her to open up. If she hadn't been so scared she'd scream instead of talk, she might have. It surprised her that after eight weeks each new session could bring so much more pain. She was yet to feel even the slightest bit comfortable. She hated questioning her uncle's motive for taking her in. She hated questioning her parents' love for her. She hated trying to find the courage to believe in her own self-worth.

Sliding in a booth seat at the restaurant, Sienna noticed Jackson's proximity. There was plenty of space. The side of his body didn't need to press against hers. His arm curled around her shoulders. When she started to tremble, he held her closer and kissed the side of her head. It was only when the food arrived that she found the strength to move away.

"So how are things going with Jackson?" asked Amy, as they walked towards Sienna's place the next afternoon.

"Nothing's going on between us. I don't want it to."

"Man, why not?"

Sienna shrugged. "Am I asking too much, making you pose with him?" she asked, hoping Amy wouldn't force the conversation. "You gotta tell me if I am. You two just look so good together."

"Nah, I know he's never going to like me. But it's kinda nice being so close to him. Gives me something to dream about. Don't think he enjoys it much. Bet he's wishing it was you he was posing with."

Sienna laughed, but realised Amy wasn't joking when she hijacked the next photography session, asking to have a go at taking photos. Jackson's instant and enthusiastic response left Sienna little room to refuse.

"What are you doing?" Sienna asked frantically, as Jackson stroked her face and pulled her arm around his neck.

"You've had me doing this with Amy for weeks. You think I don't know how to pose by now."

Sienna's heart was racing. She'd never felt this way with Flynn. Being with him had never made her anxious or nervous. It was so natural it was like breathing. This was completely different. Her nerves were on fire. When Jackson looked in her eyes, she saw something more than friendship burning there. She didn't know how to process the feelings that were swamping her body, because all her focus was on the terrifying realisation that she could be attracted to someone other than Flynn.

"We should start on dinner," said Sienna, when she could no longer stand the internal conflict.

"How the photos turn out?" asked Jackson, smiling broadly.

"Yeah, not that well," shrugged Amy. "I've got nothing on Sienna. Might have to keep practicing."

***

Everything was getting dark. Sienna could feel it getting gloomier, yet when she looked up at the light it was shining as brightly as before. A feeling of dread washed over her. She was never going to finish this assignment. There wasn't any point in trying. Even if she did hand it in, she'd only fail.

Uncle Cole had confiscated her scissors, but there were still knives in the kitchen. Jumping up, Sienna's eye was caught by Flynn's picture by her bed. She grabbed it, tears spilling down her cheeks.

You almost died, Senna.

His voice was clearer now.

Her parents had been desperate to stress that they would sort something out no matter how poorly she did in her final exams next year, but she didn't want to be a failure. And any successes she had, she wanted to be because of her own hard work – not her parents' influence. Flynn smiled knowingly from the photo.

Sending Jackson a text to cancel their Monday run, Sienna pulled her books back towards her.

"How'd the assignment go?" asked Jackson on Tuesday afternoon, as Sienna slipped into his car.

"If I pass, I'll be happy," she replied flatly.

"Yeah, right. You're going to blitz it," laughed Jackson.

"Why can't you accept my word when I tell you that I'm crap at school and just passing is hard enough? You really think I have so many things going for me that I can afford to talk down being good at something?"

"Sorry," said Jackson. "Chief told us you were disappointed with your marks last term. Said they wouldn't be good enough for law. But said you did really well. Never done better. Just assumed —"

"That I'm a spoilt princess who was worried that one or two marks the wrong way would keep me out of law," retorted Sienna. "How about I clear that up. I worked my arse off. Had no friends, no life, did nothing but read books day and night just to feel like I had a clue in class. I did do better than I ever had before. And my best is crap."

Sienna crossed her arms and turned away. Her insides were churning and she wasn't even in Dr Chousalkar's room yet. She hated Jackson for not knowing her better. She hated that he still saw her as nothing more than a cliché; a spoilt rich kid going off the rails despite having everything in the world.

Jackson tried to apologise, but Sienna didn't acknowledge him. As soon as he stopped the car in Westloch she was out and pacing away.

The session didn't go well. Dr Chousalkar seemed to only stoke Sienna's frustrations, asking her why the way other people viewed her mattered, as if wanted to be understood by those close to her was ridiculous. Sienna could barely articulate answers. She was ready to explode. The internal pressure was so high that she felt as though she needed to a tear hole in her skin to release it.

"How'd it go?" asked Jackson warily, as Sienna stalked passed him and straight to the car, struggling angrily with the door. "What's going on? Don't you want to have dinner?" he asked, standing behind her with his hands on the car either side of her to prevent her exit.

"I just want to get out of here."

Jackson didn't argue.

They drove in silence. Sienna was so consumed by trying to control the ticking bomb inside her that she was surprised to find they had stopped at a small lookout she'd never been to before.

"Come on, get out," ordered Jackson.

Sienna got out of the car feeling only more explosive. She just stood there, not knowing what to do or where to go.

"Scream," said Jackson.

"What?" snapped Sienna.

"Scream," repeated Jackson. "Do whatever it is you need to do."

All of a sudden Sienna felt arms bound tightly around her chest as Jackson grasped her from behind. She was only a metre away from the fence separating her from a death-inducing drop, though she couldn't remember moving.

"Not that," Jackson growled.

Sienna tried to free herself, but Jackson wouldn't let go. Indignation fuelled her anger as she wrestled him, elbowing his ribs and kicking his shins. The next thing she knew, she was on the ground, gravel cutting into her legs and arms.

"I'm sorry," said Jackson, breathing heavily as though he was trying to control himself.

Sienna jumped to her feet and rushed at Jackson. He grabbed her easily, but she continued to wrestle him. The cuts in her skin were helping to relieve the intense pressure inside her chest and she soon found herself smiling as she tried to bring Jackson to the ground. He laughed at her efforts, his wrestling becoming more playful, but no less powerful. She tried to hook her leg around his to trip him, but slipped on a loose patch of gravel. Jackson caught her before she fell and righted her easily, pulling her against his chest.

Jackson smiled. For a split-second he could have been Flynn, and in that moment Sienna felt part of herself heal. The warmth of his embrace, his lips, his hands running through her hair; everything she'd been missing. Slowly opening her eyes, almost expecting to find them on a beach, the sight of Jackson in front of her jarred her conscience. She pushed him away, gasping frantically.

"What the fuck are you doing!" she cried.

"Sienna, I —"

"I thought you were my friend."

"I am!"

"Then why would you do that? I never wanted you to do that."

"You could've fooled me. I wasn't exactly kissing myself," Jackson replied, his eyebrows raised.

Sienna couldn't counter that. She could never explain how Flynn's smile had lured her in. All she could do was rush back to the car, her mind spinning frantically. Was it possible Flynn approved of her being with Jackson? Had Flynn somehow chosen Jackson? Would it be a betrayal if the answers were yes?

Flynn wanted her to live. He'd brought her back to life against her will. The memory of their moment on the beach was the only clear vision she had of that night. If Flynn had wanted her to live then maybe he would approve of her loving again. But even as she tried to convince herself of that, she couldn't believe her and Jackson could work, and her heart couldn't survive being broken again.

They reached Fortune before Sienna realised they'd spent the drive in complete silence. There were just a few minutes left to make this right. Waiting until Jackson stopped the car, she turned ready to apologise, but the words wouldn't come out. He wasn't looking at her with anger.

"Sienna, I'm really sorry I upset you," he said tenderly. "But you have to know how much I like you."

"Jax, it won't work."

"Why?"

"You don't know me. Anything about me. This afternoon proved that," cried Sienna. "We inhabit two different spheres, you and me. You're better off sticking to those in your sphere."

"And what sphere is that exactly? Black? Poor? Car not good enough for you?" Jackson snapped. Sienna stared in horror at his interpretation of her explanation. "You're such a princess! I never realised a poor Koori cop was so beneath you."

Sienna wanted to dispute Jackson's claims, but the way he viewed her only reaffirmed how pathetic she was. Rushing from the car, she ran straight to her room and collapsed on to the bed in tears.

"What's wrong?" asked Uncle Cole.

Sienna felt him looming over her and tried frantically to control herself. "Nothing," she sobbed, sitting up and wiping his face.

"Then why are you crying?" he asked. Sienna shook her head, as he sat down on the bed. "I told you these sessions were only going to bring you grief. You need to get on with things. Not worry about the past, running over it again and again. Focus on the future."

"It's not the sessions upsetting me," replied Sienna softly.

"Then why do I have to put up with your moods every Tuesday night!"

Uncle Cole stormed out of the room. Sienna followed him to the kitchen. In the back of her mind, she knew this was not something she would normally do, but the swirl of emotions engulfing her left her nothing like her normal self.

"Takes half the bloody week for you to get back to normal after these damned sessions!" snapped Uncle Cole.

"Maybe the normal me isn't that great," cried Sienna, despite agreeing with him. "Maybe I'm trying to find a better me."

"There's nothing wrong with you," he cried, his arms flinging away from his body. "You need to start accepting that who you are is perfect. Stop buying into all this crap."

Sienna couldn't understand how Uncle Cole believing in her could somehow feel like an insult. "I want to go," she insisted, though she wasn't sure why.

"And I need peace in this house! I'm sick of the mood swings and having our lives and schedules dictated to! I know what's best for you. I know how to raise you. I've raised you over half your life."

"They're my parents. Of course, they want to be involved."

"Only when it suits them."

"That's not true," countered Sienna softly, yet she didn't know that. Not really.

"Then where've they been most of your life? Where've they been when you needed them the most? I'm the one who's been there for you, not them!"

"Maybe you never gave them the chance to be there for me."

"Excuse me?" snarled Uncle Cole.

"Why'd you fight them when they asked for me to come back and live with them? Why'd you make them take you to court to get custody of me?" cried Sienna, desperate for answers.

"Because you weren't worth anything to them until someone else wanted you. You think we never tried to give you back? That we stole you from them?"

"But ..." Sienna gasped.

Uncle Cole's face went white. He'd always refused to tell her why her parents didn't want her. "You lived your first ten years with me," he sighed, his finger squeezing the bridge of his nose. "I was more of a parent to you than they were. We weren't just going to hand you over to people you barely knew."

"But they're my parents."

"And what am I?" cried Uncle Cole, storming from the room.

Sienna stood in the kitchen shaking. He stomped back in with a plate and an empty beer bottle, flinging them into the sink. They smashed on impact, littering the sink with glass. Sienna moved forward to clean up the mess.

"Leave them," sighed Uncle Cole.

"But they're all smashed."

"You want to see them all smashed?"

Uncle Cole grabbed a plate that was sitting on the bench and threw it on the ground, shattering it. Picking up the dish rack, he hurled it to the floor. Tears slipped down Sienna's cheeks as she stood not knowing what to do. Very slowly, she leaned down to rescue a couple of cups that had escaped the massacre. Uncle Cole shoved her back. When she moved forward again he threw her away with greater force, her body slamming into the cupboard. The unbroken cups shattered against the wall half a metre from her head.

Sienna sat there too scared to move. Uncle Cole was yelling at her, but she couldn't comprehend. He suddenly grabbed her arm and tossed her towards her room, ordering her to bed. She collided heavily with the kitchen table, before tumbling over a chair and on to the floor. Scrambling to her feet, she rushed to her room and closed the door.

~16~

DETENTION

The sun pushed into the room, burning Sienna's red and tired eyes. Wednesday morning. Normally Jackson would be waiting outside. She didn't need to get up to know he wouldn't be there. Her arms wrapped themselves around her body, slowly moving up to her neck. Her hands tightened their grasp. Did she have the strength to squeeze the life out of her own body? But for who? For Jackson? Uncle Cole? It seemed perverse. Her hands flopped beside her. Flynn was the only one who held her life. If she was to die, it would be for him.

Closing her eyes, Sienna imagined herself sitting on the beach. It didn't take long for Flynn to join her. He held her in his arms. Ever since her suicide attempt she'd been able to get him to join her there. He never stayed, but he would come when she needed him.

"Keep going, Senna," he whispered. "You have to live. I want you to."

Sienna nodded and he squeezed her tight. The next moment he was moving towards the water as the sky rapidly darkened. It was pitch black by the time he disappeared beneath the waves, whispering as he went, "run, Senna, run."

Flynn was impossible to ignore. Sienna rolled out of bed and threw on her running clothes. She would run. Not for Jackson. Not for her parents. Not for her uncle. She would run for Flynn and herself.

It was liberating running alone. Sienna liked the freedom to think about whatever she wanted and not having to explain where her mind wandered. She could push her body as hard as she wanted or slow to walking pace without any questioning eyes turning on her.

Walking into the house, Sienna felt her body stiffen. It was odd. She hadn't been sore after running for weeks now. She kept her eyes averted as she passed through the kitchen to the bathroom. It was there, looking in the mirror, that she found the source of her pain; bruises blossoming down the right side of her body, over her hip and thigh. There were no bruises to accompany her sore shoulder, but there was a scratch across her cheekbone. It was raised, red and sore to touch. There was light discolouration around it, as though it was threatening to bruise.

The bathroom door burst open. Sienna instinctively used her towel to cover the front of her body and turned her back to the door. In the mirror she could see Uncle Cole staring at her. She hurriedly wrapped part of the towel around the back of her body. He stood there several more seconds before storming out.

Sienna adjusted the towel around her body and rushed to her room. She moved a bedside table to the door before getting dressed.

When the front door slammed shut she had the courage to leave her room. The sight that greeted her was not cheerful. The kitchen was in the same shattered state as the night before. Sienna gathered the broken pieces of glass and crockery with shaking hands. It took longer than she expected to clean the room. Even running to school she was fifteen minutes late.

"You okay?" asked Luke as she sat down next to him in maths.

Sienna nodded, forcing a smile on her face. Luke didn't probe any further. He was good that way.

By the time lunchtime came around, Sienna felt like she could handle conversation – until she opened her bag and found it devoid of food. Her stomach growled angrily as she realised it had been a whole day since she'd last eaten.

"Just buy something," said Amy tenderly.

"I've got money if you need some," added Amber. Sienna shook her head. "You okay? What happened?"

Amy and Amber each took one of Sienna's hands. The genuine support in their touch was too much and she burst into tears. Sienna looked up just long enough to see Luke's horrified face before she buried her head in her hands. Amber whispered nearby. Sienna felt arms wrap around her waist. No one spoke until she stopped crying, which took so much longer with their continued kindness.

"Jackson kissed me," said Sienna, wiping her eyes.

Amber's uncontrolled confusion caused her to speak first, and Sienna tried to explain why it was such a bad thing without sounding crazy. She didn't mention Flynn's name once.

"I don't really understand why you feel that way," said Amber cautiously. "But, seriously, I think I would've taken what you said the wrong way too. That whole two spheres thing, it makes you sound really conceited. I know you're not, but – I'm really sensitive about being Aboriginal. Always lingers in the back of my mind, wondering if people see me differently because of it."

Sienna didn't say anything. Not once had she thought about race last night, yet both Amber and Jackson had taken it that way. Sienna couldn't work out if it was because of her or them. It wasn't as though she was blind, but she'd never considered that their lives could be so different just because of a few shades of colour.

"Maybe you should try and tell him that's not what you meant," said Amy. "Say you don't feel the same way. That you don't like him that way. It's a bit of a lie, but better than him believing you don't want to go out with him cos of his skin colour."

It might have been worth a try if Jackson would talk to her again, but the disgust in his voice last night was enough to convince her that they couldn't meet again under happy circumstances.

"You're a piece of work, you know that."

Sienna stopped dead. Jackson was storming towards them as they walked through the school gates at the end of the day.

"Do you really hate me that much?" snapped Jackson.

"I don't understand," said Sienna.

"I never laid a hand on you," Jackson growled. "I didn't force myself on you and I sure as hell didn't beat you up for rejecting me. How could you tell the Chief I would do that?"

"I didn't," gasped Sienna, shaking her head. "I swear."

"Then why's he accusing me of it?"

Sienna shook her head, wondering if Uncle Cole really thought the bruising he'd seen happened before he tossed her across the room.

"To think I even liked you," spat Jackson. "Should've known better. You are just a stupid, naïve, rich, white girl. You're right, we do inhabit completely different spheres and I thank God every day I don't inhabit yours!"

"Oi!" cried Amy, charging forward, but Jackson was already at the car door. He slammed it shut and sped off.

Sienna took a deep shuddering breath. She didn't look around to see who else had witnessed the exchange. Amber took her arm and started leading her down the street. Amy quickly followed, cursing loudly.

"Forget it," said Sienna. "It's not like it's not true."

"That's not the point," sighed Amber heavily. "You can't have it both ways. I don't accept people saying shit about me cos of my skin colour, so I never say anything about anyone else's. It just doesn't work otherwise."

Sienna just shrugged. They'd reached Amber's street. Amber hugged them both tight, waving as she reluctantly walked away. Sienna and Amy turned into the cross-street.

"Can we not go to my place this afternoon?" said Sienna, turning to Amy after a few metres. "Maybe we can go to yours." Amy couldn't keep the shock from her face. "I just don't want you coming to my place right now."

"Yeah, sure, whatever," Amy said, turning around. "I'll see you tomorrow."

"Where are you going?"

"Home."

"Can I come?"

"Listen, I know you're not – I don't have people over, okay. I thought you understood that," said Amy, before something registered. "Why'd Jackson say all that shit about hurting you? Why would the Chief even think that?"

"You promise not to tell anyone?" asked Sienna anxiously. Amy nodded. "Not even Amber?"

Amy looked grave, but finally agreed. Sienna quickly explained what had happened with Uncle Cole. Amy's eyes bulged as her mouth slowly dropped.

"Let's go to the park or something," said Amy.

They ended up at the local library in a secluded corner where Amy forced Sienna to show her the bruising. Its colouring had changed during the day, making it look worse than it was. Amy wouldn't buy that, but Sienna was glad her disbelief didn't come with cries to tell someone else what happened.

"Sorry you have to go home for dinner," said Sienna.

"Maybe now you get why I don't want you at my place."

Sienna couldn't help but wonder why it was that she'd never seen Amy cry or come to school distressed. All Amy and Amber had ever done was support her, yet Amy's life was probably worse than hers and she'd never been there for her.

Uncle Cole stomped in the door. Sienna flinched, looking around the kitchen. Something flickered in his eyes when she kept herself against the bench.

"You got enough for me?" he asked in a softer voice than usual.

Sienna nodded and Uncle Cole smiled slightly. They didn't talk. Sienna expected him to leave her to finish dinner, but he stayed in the kitchen. He even brought the plates over when she was ready to dish and when she turned around she saw the table had been set.

"So what happened between you and Jackson?" asked Uncle Cole in a deliberately calm voice.

"Nothing," replied Sienna unconvincingly.

"Why's he suddenly unavailable to drive you to your appointment next week?"

Sienna tried to control the flush of her face and the guilt churning in her stomach, telling herself the outcome would've been the same no matter what mood Uncle Cole had been in last night.

"You come home all upset, he's all defensive when I question him," he continued in a harder voice. "I told you I didn't want you involved with him. I told you how it'd affect his work. We had a nice, tight-knit team before you came." He sighed heavily. "I fought your parents to have you come here because I knew it was the best thing for you. You were only going to kill yourself in the city with no one looking after you." Sienna struggled to contain her surprise at his choice of words. "I don't appreciate you repaying me by tearing my team apart."

Sienna nodded and Uncle Cole sighed again. He reached out and squeezed her hand. "I guess I'm going to have to rearrange the rosters to take you next week."

"No, it's fine. I was going to just catch the bus, but they called this afternoon. My appointment's been cancelled," lied Sienna, thankful for the reprieve. "I probably won't go back til I start school next year."

"You made the appointment for next year already?" he asked after a long silence.

"No."

"Good. Don't. I think you should wait to see if you need to go back.

Don't let everyone continue to convince you there's something wrong with you."

"I won't," squeaked Sienna, throwing herself into his arms.

Uncle Cole held her tight, soothing her the way he had when she was young. As he stroked her hair, she was sure she even heard him apologise. It was difficult for her to reconcile this man – the man who'd raised her and always believed in her – with the angry, violent man she'd feared last night. So she held this man tight, hoping the other one never returned.

***

It was finally the last week of school. As the classes shrunk day by day, Sienna feared her release from the academic world would only trap her between warring relatives. Uncle Cole's mood soured as the arrival of her parents neared. Stephen was right, she wouldn't have done much with him, but she still hated the torment her parents brought him.

When Uncle Cole came home on Thursday night in an irritable mood, Sienna knew not to bother asking permission to skip the last day of school. Amy and Amber wanted to go to Westloch, but Sienna had been hesitant to agree with any plans.

"Looking forward to the last day tomorrow?" he asked gruffly, as they ate dinner. "They got something fun planned?" Sienna couldn't answer. She really didn't know, but her hesitancy had him suspecting the worst. "I hope you're planning on going to school tomorrow. There's no reason not to."

"I know," replied Sienna, careful not to promise anything.

Uncle Cole must've seen through her response, because he was eating breakfast in the kitchen the next morning. When he cheerfully offered her a lift to school, she had no choice but to accept.

The school gates loomed like prison walls, reaching out to lock her in. Uncle Cole wished her a good day as she stepped out of the car and into the school yard. He was still there when she turned to wave goodbye.

It was going to be a boring day. There was no way Amber or Amy would turn up. Their whole grade had been condensed into a single class yesterday. It was likely the whole school would fit in one today. With the gates locking ten minutes after the bell, Sienna knew that if she didn't leave before then, she wasn't leaving. Thankfully there were very few teachers out and about, but it wasn't teachers she had to look out for.

Reasoning that Uncle Cole would expect her to sneak out, Sienna walked back towards the front gates. After a casual stroll past confirmed no one was guarding the exit, she walked out of the school and towards Amber's place. Then she saw Jackson at the end of the street. Her heart was pounding. She had no idea what he would do. He was leaning against a wall, his arms crossed and his face a heavy scowl. She decided to walk straight past him. He would have to arrest her if he wanted to stop her.

"Going to ignore me?" sniped Jackson.

"Didn't think you'd wanted to talk to me again," said Sienna. "Not with what you think I think about you."

"I think you think? How about what you said?"

"I only said we belonged to different worlds, not what those worlds were. You chose those them. I never thought those things about you."

"What else could the spheres be?"

"Heaps of things! Me being a school kid and you being a grown man?" replied Sienna, holding out her hands. "You being a cop and me being the kind of person you'd have to arrest one day? You being amazing and me being worthless," she added softly, without the hint of a question in her voice. "Anything but this," she continued more strongly, holding her arm against Jackson's. He remained silent. "So what are you going to do? Force me back to school? Take me to the station?"

"Nothing," replied Jackson, pulling his arm away and averting his eyes. "I never wanted to be here. It's a waste of time. It's the last day of school and he has half the station out checking if you're wagging."

"He's just concerned," replied Sienna dismissively.

"It's controlling," snapped Jackson. Sienna didn't know how to respond. "Go, I won't tell him I saw you."

Sienna took her chance and ran all the way to Amber's place. They met Amy at the bus stop, but Sienna couldn't rest easy until they were on the bus. Even then she kept herself out of sight of the windows.

"So don't envy being the Chief's kid in this town," laughed Amy. "This is next level!"

"I can't believe he'd do that," said Amber. "We all knew the Chief had been coming down hard on us this year, but I reckon the others really thought you were playing snitch. You got it worse than all of us. He seriously been doing that the whole time you been here?"

"Your dad might act the same if he controlled the cops in Fortune," suggested Sienna.

"Oh gosh, no, I think he'd be worse!" cried Amber, smiling away her concerns. "But I'm glad we were able to outsmart them for a day."

It was a great thought and one they revelled in for the rest of the trip. Once they reached Westloch, the cinema was their destination. Sienna was surprised there weren't cops patrolling it. There were kids everywhere.

"What do you want to watch?" asked Amber.

Sienna didn't care. It'd been such a long time since she'd been to the movies. Amber and Amy appeared set on seeing the romantic comedy. It wasn't Sienna's thing, but knew they'd watch something else just for her and didn't want them to.

"So you think you and Jackson might be friends again?" asked Amy, as they sat in the cinema waiting for the movie to start.

"I don't think so," answered Sienna. "I don't think he believed me."

"Maybe it's for the best," said Amber. "The Chief didn't want you guys hanging out and what he said was really mean. You have us. Don't need him anyway."

When Amy immediately agreed, Sienna found herself nodding. It was true, but there was something wrong with anything connected to Flynn turning against her. Until Jackson stopped sharing Flynn's smile, she was sure she'd never stop wanting to impress him.

"That movie was great," gushed Amy, as soon as the credits started to roll.

Amber enthusiastically agreed, before turning to Sienna. "Sorry you hated it."

"It's okay," replied Sienna softly. "Any movie with a guy and girl in love is going to make me think about Flynn."

"But which one was he?" asked Amy. "The one you thought you loved or the one you end up being with?"

"The soulmate," replied Sienna in a thick voice.

Amber and Amy quickly jumped from their seats, pulling Sienna with them, each with an arm around her shoulders as they walked out of the cinema.

"I've started a list of the things I want to see in Sydney," said Amber excitedly. "I've always wanted to go to there."

"You've never been?" asked Sienna. "Ever?"

"We went once, but I was only five. Doesn't count. Amy's never been either. Hope you're a good tour guide."

"Oh shit."

Amy's soft mutter turned Sienna's eyes in mild panic, wondering what she thought was wrong with their Sydney plan, when someone suddenly grabbed her arm. Sienna assumed it was Amber until she found herself being dragged across the footpath.

Sienna didn't need anything more than a glimpse of the blue uniform to know who'd found her. Struggling against him in an effort to gain her feet only resulted in Uncle Cole hauling her up and pinning her arm behind her back. He then marched her the last few metres to the car. That's when she saw his face. It was beyond angry.

It was a deathly silent drive. When they pulled up out the front of the police station, Sienna remained in car. She didn't want to sit in the kitchen and be ogled at. Uncle Cole reefed open the door and grabbed her arm. She had just enough time to get her bag as she was dragged into the station. Two recently-arrived officers looked confused by the scene, but Ian just smirked as Uncle Cole hauled her past the kitchen and through to the cells.

"Get in," he growled, pushing her forward.

"You've got to be kidding," she gasped fearfully.

"You want to break the rules I lay down for you, then you face the consequences."

"Rules, not laws. You can't do this."

"Watch me."

Time moved in the strangest ways. If not for her watch, and the confirmation time was actually passing, Sienna was sure she would've gone insane. She'd never experienced minutes longer than those in her cell. Yet somehow all those torturously slow minutes made up the hours that marched defiantly by.

There was no light or dark, no external indication that the day had ended and the night was now upon them. Dressed for a warm day, Sienna shivered under the fluorescent light. As the time passed, she became more aware of the absence of any laces or belt in her clothing, her fingers running unconsciously over the scars on her wrist.

A clunking noise roused Sienna. She jumped from the little camp bed and rushed to the door.

"I brought you some food."

It was one of the new cops whose name Sienna couldn't recall. He didn't look mean, but she could see that he had no intention of defying her uncle. He handed her a plastic bag. Sienna already knew it was Uncle Cole who had ordered it. Burger, chips and soft drink. His staple diet.

"Thanks," replied Sienna, taking the bag.

"You need anything?" asked the officer kindly, making her suspect he wasn't completely on board with this.

"Blanket?"

He locked the cell when he left, even though he was gone less than a minute. He brought back two blankets and a pillow.

When the door locked again, Sienna looked at her watch. Eleven twenty-three. Less than twelve hours she'd been in the cell. It felt like a lifetime.

Lying on the bed, she pulled the blankets up over her head to block out the light, but sleep wouldn't come. She tried to imagine herself on the beach with Flynn, but couldn't conjure the scene. When she checked her watch again less than ten minutes had passed. Fearing the onset of a panic attack, she jumped up from the bed.

Pulling out the food, Sienna dismantled it and ate it bit by bit. She walked around the room between every bite, desperately teasing out the time to make it move more swiftly. Three hours later, the food was gone, but it was still the middle of the night and now she needed to go to the toilet.

A sweep of the room was enough to realise that privacy wasn't a motivating factor in the design of the cells. If the flap on the door opened, there would be nothing to shield her from prying eyes. She tried to hold, but when the pain became crippling she grabbed the blanket and wrapped it around her body. Then she realised the toilet paper had been stripped from the cell.

Tears of shame slipped down Sienna's cheeks as she collapsed on the bed feeling soiled. She was still crying when the door clanged open hours later. She kept her head buried. Uncle Cole or his men wouldn't care for her tears.

"Feeling a little sorry for ourselves?"

Sienna squeezed her eyes shut and curled her body into a tight ball. She could hear Ian walking across the cell. The footsteps moved closer. Seconds later hot breath peeled down her neck. She forced herself not to react. Ian kept hovering over her. She didn't know what he was waiting for.

The door slammed shut. Sienna's heart rate tripled, terrified Ian had closed himself in with her. It took many long moments of silence for her to find the courage to open her eyes. Even when she moved it was slow and deliberate, listening for any sign he was still there.

The cell was empty.

All Ian had left behind was another bag of food. Hamburger, chips and soft drink. Her breakfast.

Sienna didn't eat straight away. She didn't want to use the toilet again. Exhausted, she tried to sleep, but could only string together minutes at a time. When she finally gave up, her stomach growled with hunger.

Eating just as deliberately as she had the night before, she passed away three and a half hours. Then she collapsed on the bed, forcing herself to resist the bodily urges stabbing at her gut. It didn't matter how much it hurt, she didn't give in. She held and held, until the door burst open again.

It was Ryan with another bag of food. Sienna buried her head, unable to stop the tears. He knelt next to her and tried to soothe her. "What do you need?" he asked kindly. "Different food? I can get you whatever you need."

"Toilet paper?" squeaked Sienna.

Ryan jumped up and marched across the room, cursing softly. A second later he was gone, the door locked tight behind him. He returned almost immediately carrying three rolls. Sienna realised she would be here for a while. Ryan put two out of sight under the bed. He didn't explain, but Sienna understood. Ian's next visit would see the other roll stripped from the cell.

Able to relieve herself, Sienna started to think more clearly. Stephen and her parents were flying in on Monday. There was no way Uncle Cole would let them find her here. There was also little chance he would let her out early, which meant she had less than forty-eight hours left in her cell. That should have been comforting, but the day she'd already spent in it felt like a horrible lifetime. The concept of even another day without sunlight, fresh air or real human contact left her hyperventilating.

It was a long time before the panic attack subsided. When it did, Sienna was able to rationalise the other side of the equation. Her time in this cell was limited. It would come to an end.

Determined to make the minutes pass, she jumped up and deconstructed her lunch. A turn of the cell had to be completed before she could take another bite or sip. With her bites becoming smaller, she was able to waste more time, forcing herself not to look at her watch until the food was eaten. It was impressive. Another four hours gone.

But that was when the time stopped.

No food. No drink. Nothing left to distract her mind.

There was rubbish everywhere. And plastic bags too. Sienna emptied out one of the bags and tried to fit it over her head. It was too small. It was only once she tore it off that she realised she was looking for ways to kill herself. The empty soft drink cans caught her eye. Picking one up, she inspected it for a long time and still had it in her hand when her dinner arrived.

The routine began again, but she was more agitated now. The cans were lined up on the bench, constantly drawing her eyes. Every time she turned away her eyes flicked down to her watch to see how little time has passed.

Unable to finish the food, Sienna tore a can in half. The metal nicked the back of her hand, drawing blood to the surface.

It would be so easy. Sharp metal against soft skin. Sienna tore up all the cans, ripping the aluminium into large pieces, cutting her hands several times in the process. The scars on her wrists stared up at her. Tried and failed. Perhaps she would be just as unsuccessful this time. Then she considered another option. Her hand raised the jagged metal to her throat. One clean cut and it would be over in minutes.

A gasp escaped her as the metal sliced through her skin. Blood tricked down her neck as her heart stammered rapidly. It took her a few seconds to realise the cut hadn't been deep enough to kill. Just a surface wound. The relief at that realisation shocked her.

Sienna paced the room, first around, then up and down it. She counted every step, but lost count after seven thousand. Scared of what she would do if she sat idle, she started doing sit ups. Her stomach burned at the assault, but she kept going until she collapsed with exhaustion on the floor.

The door clanged open. Sienna didn't move – not until Ryan was on top of her, lifting her head to examine the wound on her neck. He dragged her to the bed and ordered her not to move before sweeping all the rubbish into a bag. Then he pushed her to the far wall and tossed the cell, collecting every piece of aluminium he could find.

"Any more?" Ryan asked angrily. Sienna didn't answer. "Shit!" He checked the room again, finding three more pieces she'd stashed. "This isn't a game! Someone else finds these and the next cop to come and check on them gets sliced. You want that on your conscience? You want your uncle ending up in hospital or the morgue because of you?"

Sienna stood unmoved for a long time. She didn't even want Ian's death on her conscience. It took her less than a minute to give Ryan all the stashed pieces, but he still checked the room twice more. He was about to leave – taking the full can he'd brought with him – when he turned back around.

"Hands against the wall," he ordered.

Sienna didn't move, so Ryan forcibly turned her and placed her hands on the wall before frisking her. His hands scrunched her pockets, cursing loudly when the aluminium cut through the fabric.

"Turn them out!" Ryan yelled. "Now, Sienna!" She didn't move. "Don't even think about making up some story about me feeling you up," he spat, pushing his hand inside her pockets to turn them inside out. "I'm not going to watch you try and take your own life again."

The cell felt both safer and scarier when Ryan left. He even took the plastic bag. There was no way left to harm herself. She considered beating her head against the wall, but knew she had a greater chance of disabling herself than dying.

This time Sienna didn't eat. When she curled up and closed her eyes, she instantly found herself on the beach with Flynn. She wanted to ask him if he was mad at her for kissing Jackson but didn't dare. He didn't mention it and held her as tenderly as he always had. Perhaps it was a good sign. It allowed her to contemplate if she ever could date Jackson, but she could never get past how much better than her he was. Flynn had been her equal in every way – equally flawed, equally jaded, equally bitter. She was no better a person now than she had been then and that could never be good enough for Jackson.

"You're not seriously eating your lunch in the cells, are you?"

Sienna's stomach lurched at the sound of his voice. He was the last person she wanted to see here.

"It's for the prisoner," scoffed the second voice.

"You can't give that to a prisoner. You give them a drink can and the next time you do a cell check you get your throat slit. What the hell's wrong with you?"

"Chill, it's just the Chief's kid. She ain't going to attack us. We've been feeding for like this for two days already."

The footsteps were fast and heavy. Sienna waited for release, but only the peep hole flung open. Ever so slowly, Sienna turned her head. Jackson was staring at her, waiting for their eyes to meet. When he said nothing, she turned away to the sound of the flap slamming shut.

"I'm not letting her out. I'm not going against the Chief. You want to lose your job, you do it," said the other officer as footsteps paced away from the cell.

"If I open that door, it will be with the damn chief commissioner by my side," growled Jackson. "You're all spineless bastards, you know that."

"If you're not letting her out, then how's she getting out?"

"The Chief's coming to do what he should've done – to reverse what he never should've done."

~17~
A VERY HOLLINGSWORTH CHRISTMAS

"You know why I did what I did, don't you?" asked Uncle Cole, as they walked into the kitchen.

It had taken him just ten minutes to release her, but Sienna wasn't sure the early release was in her best interest.

"You can't go around just deciding which rules apply to you and which don't. How do you think it makes me look?" he continued, as if urging her to understand. "I control law and order in this town and to have my own child disgrace me by truanting."

"It was the last day. They weren't even running proper classes," replied Sienna, wishing he would understand her point of view.

"I don't care if they start running yodelling classes and you're the only person who's turned up. If you're meant to be at school, then you go. And don't think Jackson's threats will stop me from teaching you the consequences of your actions. You're my child and I will discipline you the way I see fit. No one's going to interfere with that while you remain under my roof."

"Can I go?"

Uncle Cole waved his hand, before adding, "You're grounded until your parents come and pick you up. They already know. Don't bother trying to get out of it."

She didn't. She wouldn't have tried to get out of the cell and in some ways resented Jackson's interference, though she was glad he'd cared enough to stand up for her. But then she remembered he was just like that. He could still hate her and stand up for her.

As soon as Uncle Cole stomped out of the house, Sienna tore off her dirty clothes and shoved them in the bin. She showered so long the water ran cold, but she didn't feel completely clean and even wrapped in her warmest clothes, she still shivered on her bed. Her phone rang and beeped several times, but she didn't answer it.

Monday morning had never felt so bright. As soon as Sienna woke, she was up and packing. Uncle Cole was still home. He looked surprised as she placed her bags outside her bedroom door. "I'll be back home in time for Arthur and Janice's arrival," he said in a soft, gruff voice.

It could've been a warning, but Sienna had the strange feeling it was an apology. As Uncle Cole nodded and left, she wished she understood him better. Maybe he did love her so much, was so proud of her, that such a simple transgression was so hurtful. Sienna didn't ask, even when he came back home. They just waited in the lounge room in silence. His hand clutched the arm of the chair, clenching and unclenching as the minutes ticked by. When she'd been little, she used to sit on his lap and push her fingers through his, forcing them to unclench and hold her tenderly instead.

"Sen?" called Arthur, the front door tentatively opening.

"Hey, Dad," she said, jumping up from the lounge. "We going?"

Janice and Stephen walked into the lounge room behind Arthur. Sienna felt Uncle Cole move next to her. Her position between them made her nervous.

"We thought maybe we could all go out for a late lunch," suggested Arthur, his eyes shifting edgily to Uncle Cole.

"I have to work, actually," said Uncle Cole. "I took an hour to be here when you arrived."

The visible relief of her parents made Sienna turn to him, wishing he knew she cared that he was around. Maybe he did, because he smiled softly and pulled her into a warm embrace.

"You have a good time," he said with genuine kindness. "I'll see you on Christmas Day."

Sienna nodded, tears in her eyes. Uncle Cole kissed her cheek before wiping it softly away. He grabbed her bags and carried them to the car. The action reminded her of his angry words in the kitchen; his demonstration of the fact that he'd never stopped her from going with her parents.

"There it is, our home for the week," said Arthur proudly, as they reached the end of the long dirt track and stopped in front of a large farmhouse.

It wasn't like the place Uncle Cole had had just outside of Fortune.

This was neat and manicured, not closed in by bush. Large paddocks, empty of almost everything but grass, surrounded the house. The paddocks continued on to the left, feeding a few hundred sheep. To the back right was the start of a national park, while the back left rose to a rocky peak. Sienna was looking forward to what the light did to the setting and hoped she would be able to take a few decent shots.

They unpacked the car, dragging their bags into the lounge room. Arthur showed Sienna to a bedroom almost as large as her one in Sydney.

"Is this the master bedroom?" asked Sienna. "You and mum should have this."

"No," scoffed Arthur. "Ours is bigger than this and has an ensuite. Stephen offered to take the smaller bedroom. You'll have to share the bathroom though. Couldn't find a place with three bathrooms."

"I'm surprised you found one with two out here," said Sienna.

"It was difficult," laughed Arthur. "But thank goodness we did. Would've been forced to stay in a hotel otherwise. Don't think we'd survive the week, all of us sharing one bathroom."

Sienna tried not to grimace. Of all the reasons she'd thought she wouldn't survive a week, sharing a bathroom had never been one of them.

"What would you like to do this afternoon?" asked Arthur.

"Um, what's happening for Christmas?" asked Sienna tentatively, as they walked into the lounge room where Janice and Stephen were sitting.

"It'll just be a quiet day. Nothing too fancy," said Arthur.

"Your uncle has to work, but he's going to come by for breakfast with all of us," added Janice, her voice strained. "He wanted to see you to give you your present."

"Jackson's working the morning shift, so I invited him to dinner," said Stephen, turning Sienna's head. "It's a pretty poor consolation prize, but thought it better than being alone after his leave got cancelled last minute."

Sienna waited for Stephen to tell the rest of the story, but when he stayed quiet she knew he didn't know about Uncle Cole locking her in the cells.

"Um, we – are we doing presents?" asked Sienna.

"No more than usual," replied Janice. "Just a couple of small things. You know we've never made Christmas about presents."

"So I shouldn't give you anything?" queried Sienna, hoping to understand what Christmas meant to her parents.

"You can give us gifts," said Arthur with a tone of annoyance. "Just don't expect a room full of expensive presents for you."

Arthur's answer stung. Sienna had never expected anything of the kind. Uncle Cole and Aunt Daphne had only ever bought a couple of presents each year, but they spent half the year leading up to Christmas making presents. Their house had been a shrine to the art they made one another. Sienna suddenly realised Uncle Cole didn't display any of that stuff in the house and wondered where it had all gone.

"Can I do some of my own work this afternoon?" asked Sienna, feeling inspired.

"Sen, why are you still up?"

Sienna turned to see Stephen walking into the dining room where she'd been working since everyone went to bed.

"I have stuff I need to do."

"Mum and Dad didn't come all the way out here to visit you for you spend the whole time working."

"Why not? It's all they do when I visit."

"That's not fair."

"Either's this."

"You can be a real brat sometimes. I thought we'd gotten over this."

"I just have to finish this! Why can't you get that? I need to have something to give people on Christmas Day," cried Sienna, her voice breaking.

"Is that what you're doing? Why didn't you just say so?" Stephen asked incredulously.

"Why didn't you just ask? Why do you always assume the worst?"

Sienna angrily wiped away the tears slipping down her cheeks. They had let her work, but not without interruption, leaving her no choice but to get up when everyone was in bed.

"Sorry, Sen," said Stephen solemnly. "We would've left you alone if we'd known." Sienna didn't respond. "Can you show me?"

Sienna sighed heavily and turned her computer towards Stephen. She'd already completed presents for him, Jackson, and Uncle Cole, and was now working on the picture for her parents.

"Wow, Mum looks beautiful," gasped Stephen. "You take this? It's amazing. Dad will just love it."

"Not if he never gets it."

"Okay, point taken. What can I do to help?"

"I need to get them printed and framed. Don't think it'll be possible before Christmas. Should've thought about it before."

"Don't worry. We've got a couple of days. You'll get your photos."

Arthur and Janice didn't question Stephen when he said they needed to do some stuff on their own the next morning. Sienna shook her head as they offered to hire him his own car so he wouldn't be dependent on them. It was such a contrast to the interrogation she received about how late she'd stayed up. They only let it rest when Stephen promised it was okay and that the surprise would be worth it. Sienna wished they'd taken her word for that.

"They always that easy with you?" asked Sienna, when she and Stephen were alone in their new hire care. "They didn't ask where we were going or anything."

"I mentioned that we needed to do stuff without them," laughed Stephen. "Why? Uncle Cole make you give him an itinerary?"

Sienna hated the way conversations always got turned back to Uncle Cole. "They never let me do anything without asking a million questions."

"Yeah, but you were young. And let's face it, you weren't hanging out great people."

"Who?" asked Sienna.

"Um, Flynn. Remember him? The kid that almost got you killed," replied Stephen mockingly. "The only reason they tolerated you being friends with him was because he made you want to stay with us. He was the reason you stopped coming out here every holidays."

"You guys didn't like Flynn?" asked Sienna, her heart beating frantically. Their disapproval of him felt like a rejection of her.

"There wasn't much to like. He was a better kid around you. You were like his conscience. The way you were wrapped up in him was a little scary. It was like you were dissolving into him."

"You don't understand what it's like to be constrained the way we were. Locked in a world we were locked out of. We just wanted our parents to see us – who we really were. Even when Flynn got in trouble they just bailed him out and sent him on his way."

"I'm not saying he didn't have problems, but he was still an irresponsible jerk," replied Stephen firmly. Sienna's arms wrapped around her chest. "The trouble he got you into – getting you pregnant, almost killing you. That wasn't the first time. I know how many times you went joyriding. I know all the other stupid games you played. I read your diary. I know the shit you got up to. It was getting more dangerous, more criminal, and you knew it. You could see it all with clear eyes, but you wouldn't break loose. It was like he was the only thing tethering you to this life. In many ways, I think he was.

"We were there at the hospital when you first woke up. We heard you screaming Flynn's name, begging to stay with him. I sometimes think that Jackson, reminding you so much of Flynn, was the only reason you lasted as long as you did. I just hope that he's not your new rope."

"You just don't get us," Sienna whispered. The best and worst of them couldn't be separated the way he wanted.

"You're right, I don't," replied Stephen instantly. "I don't get your loyalty to Flynn and Uncle Cole and your distrust of me and Mum and Dad."

"Yeah, well, I thought we'd gotten better too, but all I've copped since you guys got here is distrust and suspicion."

Stephen sighed heavily. "Sorry, you're right. I'll stop. Come on, let's get these photos sorted and I'll show you I can be a good big brother."

Photos ordered and with a promise of being ready for Christmas, Stephen and Sienna met up with Arthur and Janice in Westloch for lunch. It was one of the swishest restaurants in town and relatively quiet. Arthur requested a table away from other patrons. Sienna didn't understand why until he spoke.

"Stephen mentioned that you weren't feeling completely relaxed with us. I think there have been a lot of misunderstandings about … our family. So perhaps it's time we discussed things openly."

"Like what?" Sienna asked tentatively.

"Well why don't you start by asking us what you want to know," suggested Janice.

"Okay, how come I grew up with Uncle Cole? Why didn't you want me?" asked Sienna with a hint of aggression.

"We always wanted you," answered Janice tersely. "Things were so difficult when Stephen got sick. We had to give him so much attention and you were so young. We felt like we were neglecting you. We needed help and Uncle Cole and Aunt Daphne offered us help."

Sienna waited for more. This explanation was falling well short of what she needed.

"I was at the hospital with Stephen and your mother had to work," said Arthur, picking up where Janice left off. "The donor list was so long here. There was a chance we were going to have to go overseas for treatment. Bills needed to be paid. Life wouldn't stop."

"Why didn't you ask your parents for help?" asked Sienna combatively, hating that she'd come second to money. "They're rich. They love Stephen. Even if they never cared for me, they would've done it for him."

"Yes, they would've, but I guess I was too proud," replied Arthur.

Sienna pursed her lips.

"It wasn't like that," said Janice, as if reading Sienna's mind. "You loved being with your aunt and uncle and they loved having you. We just never expected it would take so long to find a donor. Before we knew it, you'd been gone three years. You got upset when you stayed with us. You didn't want to live with us. So we decided to slowly transition you back."

"So you actually wanted me to live with you? Not just pick me up to show me off when you needed to prove I existed?" questioned Sienna sceptically.

Stephen's knife fell to his plate with a clang that made Sienna jump. Arthur and Janice both looked at him warningly.

"No, this is bull. I bet that's what he told you," spat Stephen.

"No, that's what I remember," replied Sienna in a halting voice. "I never saw you unless it was some special occasion. You'd pick me up, dress me up, and show me off, act like you really liked me in front of other people, then just send me back. You never spent any time with me. You never came to anything that was important to me."

"Your uncle never told us anything!" snapped Arthur. "We had to beg to be involved in your life."

"I told you," whispered Sienna, her broken voice unable to speak any louder.

There was silence. Long, strained, painful silence. This wasn't how Sienna had imagined this week. It was nothing like the conversations they'd been having over the phone, but they'd always avoided difficult topics and they hadn't been around to question and criticise her every move.

While they ate, Arthur, Stephen and Janice started a conversation, talking around Sienna almost like she wasn't there. They looked at her every so often, as if expecting her to jump in, but she'd said enough.

"Okay then, I guess we'll see you guys for dinner," said Arthur, pushing away from the table.

Sienna looked around to see who she was being palmed off to.

"Don't have to look like you drew the short straw," Stephen sighed, as they got back in his car.

"I am the short straw," countered Sienna.

"I know it probably seems like that from your point of view, but it's not true."

"Right it's my point of view that's the problem."

"Let's not fight. Please. I want to hang out with you. We'll find something fun to do."

It wasn't an easy task, quickly discovering they had little in common, but Stephen wouldn't be deterred. He eventually agreed to go back to the house to check out some of the bushwalks.

"We're going to get lost," he muttered when the house was out of sight.

Sienna sighed and assured him they were fine, but was convinced he didn't believe her. He muttered as they walked. It was distracting, but Sienna still managed to get her eye in with the scenery and mentally listed a dozen spots to take photos – if she was allowed out.

"Still don't think this is worth it?" asked Sienna, as they made it to the top of the hill at the back of the property.

"Yeah, okay, it's pretty," conceded Stephen with a half-smile. "But we're going to rest up here for a while, right."

Stephen immediately found a rock that had a good vista back down to the farmhouse. Sienna sat near him, wishing they could stay to watch the sunset, but knew he wouldn't want to risk walking back in the dark.

"Hey, Mum and Dad are back," said Sienna, pointing down at the house. "You reckon they can see us?"

"Hope not, they'd freak seeing us up here. Besides, I kinda wanted them to spend some time together. They don't get much time alone. Guess we should've brought your camera," said Stephen, obviously starting to appreciate the scenery. "Your photos are pretty amazing. Was thinking you could take some of me and Rachel when you come back to Sydney."

"Sure, just don't expect too much. I'm not a professional. I don't need you guys making heaps of this just cos I can take photos better than I can read."

"Seriously, take a compliment for once. We've seen your photos. They're good." Sienna didn't respond. "Come on, let's head back before we get swallowed in darkness."

Sienna looked confusedly up at the sun still sitting well above the horizon, but she didn't argue, not even when he shared his surprise at there still being light three hours later.

Sienna rolled on to her back. Christmas. In a couple of hours Uncle Cole would arrive and the house would be full of tension once more. To her parents' credit, they'd laid off her in the last couple of days. They'd even tried asking her questions rather than assuming the answers, though they never seemed very impressed by any response they got. It was tiring, but they were trying and it was what she'd always wanted, so she tried to be less bitter and more pleasing.

"Merry Christmas, sweetie!" cried Arthur, as Sienna walked into the kitchen. "We decided to go all out."

That was an understatement. There was enough food for five families. Pancakes, bacon, sausages, eggs, tomato, mushroom and toast.

Arthur hugged her warmly before guiding her to the dining table. He was insistent that she didn't help. It made her feel useless and thankful for Uncle Cole's arrival.

"Merry Christmas, Sen," said Uncle Cole with a hint of sadness, as he hugged her tight.

Sienna squeezed him in return. When they broke apart, they were met by unimpressed faces. Sienna made sure she took the seat next to Uncle Cole at the table.

Breakfast was predictably awkward. Stephen did a poor job of masking his dislike of Uncle Cole. Arthur was only mildly more successful, while Janice tried hard to keep a smile on her face as she forced the conversation.

"I got a present for you," said Sienna with a soft smile, looking only at Uncle Cole.

"I got one for you too," Uncle Cole replied.

Uncle Cole handed her a card. Inside were three movie tickets. He nodded just slightly. Sienna's eyes filled with tears and he squeezed her hand under the table. Stephen coughed. Sienna looked up to see her parents' bewilderment at the silent exchange.

"I'll get yours," she said, rushing to the corner of the room and grabbing one of the large, flat rectangular presents leaning against the wall.

It wasn't just Uncle Cole looking at the photo when he opened it. Both Arthur and Stephen moved around him, while Janice leaned in towards him. They all exclaimed how great a picture it was, but Sienna was more interested in Uncle Cole's silent response. His fingers were tracing over the lines of light from the sun as they pierced through the morning mist over the river. It was a black and white shot that seemed to match the sleepiness of the scene.

When Uncle Cole looked up, she could see the questions burning in his eyes. He wanted to know what the colour shot looked like and the shade of the light. They'd spent so much time discussing those things when she was young that he didn't even need to speak.

"I should get going," said Uncle Cole, quickly rising from his seat. "You okay here? You can come back any time."

"She's fine," snapped Arthur, standing to full height.

"I'm okay," nodded Sienna.

Uncle Cole stomped to the door. It slammed behind him, his car screeching off. Sienna excused herself to use the bathroom. The scene that greeted her on her return couldn't have been more different to the one she'd left. Arthur, Janice and Stephen were talking and eating freely, smiling and laughing, as though a great oppression had been lifted. Sienna resumed her seat feeling like an intruder.

Jackson arrived at five. Sienna heard his voice, but couldn't force her feet to the door. He hadn't been there when Uncle Cole had released her from the cell and though he'd come to her aid, she still wasn't sure they were on speaking terms. She looked over at his present. It was a small photo album of some of the shots she'd taken of him.

"You coming?" asked Janice, walking into Sienna's room. She nodded, but didn't move. "You okay?" Janice paused for a second. "Has something happened between you and Jackson."

"No," cried Sienna, before quickly catching herself. "Sort of, but … I just want to be his friend. I explained it all wrong and he got upset."

"And you haven't made up yet," surmised Janice. "Then this is the chance. Come on, it'll be rude if you stay here."

"Okay," nodded Sienna. "Let me just write on his card."

Sienna's pen hovered over the card. A few pictures wasn't going to be enough to change his opinion of her, but she could try.

Merry Christmas Jackson.

You've been my best friend. Couldn't have faced Fortune without you. I haven't been a good friend back. Sorry. I suck.

I know you want more. I wish I could do it. I just don't like you that way – not enough. Not the way you deserve. Sorry. I know we probably can't be friends, but I hope you like your present anyway and don't hate me too much.

You're my best model.

Sienna

Shoving the card into its envelope, Sienna rushed to the lounge room where everyone was gathered. The coffee table was laden with food, even though dinner would be ready in under two hours. Stephen was sitting on one lounge with Jackson, while Arthur and Janice sat on the other. Sienna looked between them, once more feeling like an intruder, eventually slinking over to sit next to Stephen. He handed her a drink and offered her food.

Everyone started talking. Sienna didn't know what to say or when to speak. Janice mentioned their family trek into the country for Sienna to take photos. Arthur and Janice posed willingly. Stephen much less so. But it had been nice – nicer than she expected – and yet Jackson seemed more a part of her family than she did.

"I should check on dinner," said Janice, pushing up from the lounge. "Arthur, can you help me. Stephen, maybe you should top up everyone's drinks."

Within ten seconds, Sienna and Jackson were alone.

"What's that about?" muttered Jackson.

"I just mentioned to my mum that I'd stuffed things up with you," Sienna replied. Jackson nodded. "Listen, thanks for not saying nothing about the weekend."

"You haven't told them?" Jackson gasped.

"They won't care about me – just that it's something they can use against Uncle Cole. Besides, it's done."

"I remember the look in your eyes when I found you there. How can you forgive him for that? It's illegal. Don't you get that?"

"I'm real sorry you getting involved messed up your leave," said Sienna sincerely. "You don't even like me and I'm still causing you trouble."

"Wasn't about you," muttered Jackson, before softening his tone. "There're some things you just can't ignore. I've ignored a lot since coming here. That was one step too far. He starts getting away with that and who's next?"

Stephen walked back into the room, followed minutes later by Arthur and Janice. Sienna again fell out of the conversation, though she felt a slight thaw in Jackson's mood towards her. It was something she hoped could be consolidated when Arthur suggested they exchange presents while they were waiting for dinner.

"And I would like to know who that big one's for," said Arthur.

"Um, that's for you and Mum," said Sienna, handing it to Arthur. "It's nothing special."

"Oh, Sen, it's beautiful," he said in a thick voice, looking at the enlarged photo of Janice from her weekend visit.

"Thank you, Sen," nodded Janice, tears in her eyes.

"Um, this one's for you," Sienna said to Stephen, handing him the other large present.

"Thanks, Sen," smiled Stephen. "And this is from us," he added, handing her a small rectangular present.

Sienna watched Stephen unwrap the landscape photo she'd selected for him. She wasn't sure he'd like it, but really had nothing else to give.

"It's great, Sen. It'll look great in my apartment. Now open yours."

The wrapping paper was so nice, Sienna almost didn't want to remove it, but as she pulled the present out her heart warmed. It was a leather-bound journal.

"It's just like the one Uncle Cole gave me last year, but this one's a bit larger and isn't lined so I can draw in it as well," said Sienna, ready to fling her arms around Stephen, but the crash of his framed photo landing on the coffee table pulled her back.

"So he steals presents as well as people," he snapped, shoving the coffee table out of his way as he stomped across the room. The picture frame fell to the floor, shattering against the floorboards.

"What? I don't get —"

"That present last year was from us! Us! Not Uncle Cole! You get that?" yelled Stephen. "All the nice things you've ever been given were from us, not him."

"Did he always do that, Sienna?" asked Arthur, as though it were an interrogation.

"How would I know!" Sienna cried. "It's not like you were there to give them to me yourself. We never said who gifts were from. They thought it was rude."

"Yeah, real rude, passing off expensive gift as your own," muttered Stephen.

"Stephen," chided Janice.

"I didn't grow up like you," yelled Sienna. "The kids I went to school with didn't always have food to eat. Uncle Cole never wanted me knowing who couldn't afford to give expensive things or even anything."

"Especially when he was the one hiding his poor presents next to our expensive ones," snarled Stephen.

"So what you really care about is getting credit for spending money," spat Sienna. "I don't care about any presents. Take it back," she cried, throwing the journal at Stephen. "If you really wanted me to know something was from you then you should've been part of my life from the start, not just turning up when it suited you and expect me to feel blessed."

Sienna ran to her room, slamming the door behind her. Tears streamed down her cheeks as her body shook. If Uncle Cole had still been in the house she would've begged him to take her home. It felt like her childhood all over again.

Footsteps raced towards her room. Sienna pushed the bedside table against the door, but Arthur was able to open the door enough to get his head through.

"Open this door right now," he commanded. Sienna didn't move. She had no compulsion to let him in and wondered what he would do if she tried to shut him out. "Now, Sienna."

She shifted forward. Her father wasn't moving out of the gap that remained. Stepping back, she looked for an escape, but before she could reach the window, Arthur was restraining her.

"Let me go! Just forget it, all right. I don't belong here. I never will. I'm sick of it."

"You're our daughter!" growled Arthur. "The one place you do belong is with us. Don't you dare tell me otherwise."

"I just want to go to bed, okay."

"If you just wanted to sleep then why the blockade?" he asked. Then his breath stopped. He released Sienna and dived for her bag. She tried to protest, but that only made him search more thoroughly.

When he failed to find anything incriminating, he dragged her back to the lounge room. "Jackson, I need you to search Sienna's room."

"For what?" asked Jackson, taken aback. "There's no legal reason for me to do this."

Arthur pushed Sienna to Stephen with instructions to hold her. Stephen complied. Arthur beckoned Jackson, who reluctantly followed him. They weren't gone long.

Jackson strode into the room, refusing to look at anyone. He grabbed his things, muttered a goodbye and headed to the door. Sienna broke free of Stephen to give Jackson his present. He smiled softly. It made Sienna's heart ache. It was the look Flynn used to give her when she had no choice but to return home without him.

When Sienna turned around, she found Arthur holding everyone's attention with the bottles of rum and sleeping pills in his hands.

"What the hell do you have these for?" yelled Arthur.

"Just in case," replied Sienna, her voice barely above a whisper.

"In case of what? I thought you didn't feel that way any more. I thought the psychologist was fixing that," he cried.

"It's not like that! It doesn't just go away!" cried Sienna.

"And a few days with us is enough to tip you over the edge," snarled Arthur.

"It's not like that!" said Sienna angrily. "I'm not looking for reasons to kill myself. I spend every day searching for reasons to live!"

Arms suddenly wrapped around her. If she couldn't still see her father standing angrily in front of her, she would've assumed it was him holding her. Janice's embrace wasn't warm and comforting. It was strong and protective. It was as if she thought she could keep her demons away, but they weren't external. They were internal and Sienna knew it was a battle she would have to fight alone.

"So you always carry them with you?" asked Janice.

"Lately," muttered Sienna.

"Since we've been around, huh?" asked Arthur bitterly. Sienna couldn't answer. "Where'd the pills come from?"

"Home," she said.

"But where? Where did you get them?" asked Arthur insistently.

"The bathroom," replied Sienna, not understanding the question. "That's where he always keeps them."

"So you got these before your first – before that time and, what, have just been hiding them since?" questioned Arthur.

"No. I used most of his that night. That's one of the new bottles," said Sienna.

"One … of?" Arthur stammered.

Sienna knew she'd said the wrong thing when her father's mouth began to open and close without words coming out. Janice's grip on her tightened. Stephen was just shaking his head as he slumped into the lounge. Arthur took one look around the room, grabbed the car keys and stormed from the house.

It was nice to wake alone. Sienna had feared her whole family would be watching her. She hadn't been left alone for one minute last night; Stephen even standing guard outside the door every time she went to the bathroom. She'd gone to bed without waiting for dinner or her father's return. The house was quiet, so she snuck to the bathroom, before rushing back to her room. When she finally had the courage to trek to the living areas, she heard voices whispering in the kitchen, but couldn't make out the words.

"Morning, sweetie," said Janice in an overly cheerful voice.

Arthur responded similarly, but was slow to turn – to display his black eye and bruised left hand. Sienna silently wondered if Uncle Cole fared any better.

"Sienna, can you help your mother with breakfast while Stephen and I have showers?" asked Arthur, though it was more of a command.

Sienna shrugged and pulled food out of the fridge.

"Don't be too hard on your dad," said Janice, as they cooked. "It's hard for him. He's an emotional guy. He feels like he has to hide it a lot, but when it comes to you and Stephen – especially you – sometimes the wrong emotions come out. He was so excited when you were born. I think all he ever really wanted was a little girl – his little princess. "

"And he got me," murmured Sienna.

"No, he didn't," replied Janice firmly. "That's the problem. He hardly got you at all. He's had to watch another man raise you – one he's never thought that highly of."

"That was really his choice, though. In the end, if you'd really wanted me to live with you, you would've just come and gotten me."

"It wasn't that easy. We made a mistake. We focused too much on Stephen. You were such a shy, timid child and when we dragged you home when you were four you were so traumatised. We contacted your uncle for help and he took you back. It was difficult after that. Things between us and your aunt and uncle – it became very strained."

"So why didn't you just leave me there?" asked Sienna.

"Because you're our daughter and you belong to us!" replied Janice in a raised voice, before continuing more calmly. "We tried to transition you back slowly, but every time you went home upset your uncle made it that little bit harder to see you. When you told your aunt you wanted to come and live with us we demanded it happen. When it didn't, we were left no choice but to go to court."

"But you got me and all I did was disappoint you. You didn't want anything to do with me. Never spent time with me. What was the point?"

"Sienna, we tried. You never engaged with us. You didn't join in anything we did. When Flynn came along you all but disappeared. Everything in your life was suddenly wrapped up in him. We couldn't compete with that."

FINAL MESSAGE

"Have you got your friends' numbers?" asked Janice at lunch on Sunday, finally bringing up their imminent departure to Sydney. Sienna nodded. "You want to ask them if they can stay in Westloch tonight. We're going to organise rooms since we have an early flight. It's best to be close. We can pick them up this afternoon or this evening."

Sienna felt sick. The original plan had been to stay in Fortune for the last night. The change was a pleasant shock to Amber and Amy, but Sienna was sure Uncle Cole would be less thrilled.

"Right, I'll take you to pick them up, while your mum and Stephen go find us somewhere to stay," said Arthur.

The drive home was tense. Sienna had never seen her father as worked up as when he was walking towards the house. She hoped Uncle Cole was at work. He wasn't. He was watching TV in the lounge room. There was a shadow of a bruise on the right side of his face. Sienna walked in to greet him. The first thing she noticed was her photo hanging on the wall between the two front windows.

"Pride of place," said Uncle Cole gruffly. Sienna hugged him tight. "Janice and Stephen out? What do you want to do for dinner?"

"We're staying in Westloch tonight," said Arthur.

Sienna felt Uncle Cole's arms go cold around her. He looked down, waiting for her contradiction. "Is that what you want?" he asked, though it was more of an accusation than a question.

"We have an early flight. It's just more practical," Arthur answered firmly, before Sienna could open her mouth. "Sienna, you'd better go pack. We still need to pick up Amy and Amber."

"So I don't get a single day with her these holidays, is that it?" spat Uncle Cole bitterly.

"You had last weekend," replied Arthur in a measured voice.

"She was in trouble last weekend. I could hardly do anything with her while she's being punished."

"That's your problem. You knew the deal. She's our daughter. We have the right to take her home. Whenever we see fit. You mightn't want to forget that."

"She's sixteen. She can decide where she wants to go," snarled Uncle Cole, nudging Sienna.

"And she did," Arthur replied, pulling her from Uncle Cole's arms and pushing her towards the door.

Sienna rushed to her room. She could hear them fighting, but tried not to listen. With shaking hands, she replaced the dirty clothes in her bag with some clean ones and threw in the assignments she needed for school.

"You packed already?" asked Arthur, bumping into Sienna as she hurried out of her bedroom. "Don't you need more than that?"

"Why? Did you chuck out all my stuff?"

"No, of course not," said Arthur, before seeming to understand. "What about those?"

Arthur picked up her sketch book that was lying open on the desk. Sienna watched him nervously. She'd been experimenting with her drawing. Trying to draw how she felt rather than what she saw. Arthur looked uncomfortable as he flicked through the pages.

"What's that one?" asked Arthur, putting down the sketch book and pointing to another closed one. Sienna liked that he didn't grab it. She opened it and passed it to him. "Is this me?" Sienna nodded. "May I?" Sienna nodded again and Arthur scanned through the book. He stopped at one of the middle pages and Sienna felt her stomach twist. She was almost certain she knew what picture he was looking at. "I remember that photo. Always thought you were in it," said Arthur. Sienna shrugged. "You've never really felt like a part of our family, have you?" Sienna didn't react, but Arthur waited for her answer. She eventually shook her head. "We're going to change that, okay."

Uncle Cole followed them out to the car. He took Sienna's bags from her shoulder and put them in the boot before walking her to the car door.

"You can come back anytime," he said, earning him a glare from Arthur. "Just call and I'll come get you if you need me."

Sienna was scared to nod, but did. It was crazy. Uncle Cole was moody and temperamental. He could lock her up in a police cell and yet he would still rescue her if she needed him. No matter how angry he was – for her leaving or doing something wrong – he would come to her aid. Sienna trusted him to be there for her and realised she didn't trust her parents the same way.

"We have to go," said Arthur flatly, slipping into the car and starting the engine.

Uncle Cole didn't rush his goodbyes, only infuriating Arthur further. Sienna was glad it was only a few minutes before they arrived at Amber's house, where she and Amy were waiting. Jumping in the back seat with them, Sienna detached herself from her father's anger and focused on their excitement.

"Wow," squealed Amy, when the three of them were shown to their room for the night.

"Sorry it's not flash," said Janice, following them in. "It was the only triple room we could get. We're over in room nineteen. Where we stayed before, Sienna. We'll go out for dinner about seven, so come to our room then."

"Is she serious?" asked Amy, when the door closed behind Janice. "Your mum's apologising for not getting a better room for one night. How rich are they?"

Sienna mumbled an answer, but Amy didn't seem to really care for it as she fell on her bed with a smile. It was the same question Sienna had asked herself a lot as a child. Her parents spent money in a manner she had never seen before. It was so unlike the measured consumption of Uncle Cole and Aunt Daphne. Perhaps it was why he saw her parents' spending as a way of buying her affections rather than just what they did.

Amy's eyes grew progressively wider over the next twenty-four hours. There was dinner, then breakfast. The airport. The plane ride. And, finally, Sienna's house. Even Amber, who lived in one of the best houses in Fortune, could not help but gasp as they got out of the car.

"Sienna, can you show the girls to their room," said Janice in a harried voice.

Janice was gripping her phone. Arthur was grabbing the bags, while Stephen had already rushed into the house with a promise that he would handle it. This was the family Sienna remembered. She didn't even have to answer. Janice was gone.

"It's upstairs," said Sienna, waving Amber and Amy inside.

Thankfully, they were still so captivated by the journey that they hadn't noticed being dumped.

"You're freakin' kidding me, right? This is my room?" asked Amy, when Sienna showed her to the guest bedroom.

"It's okay, right?" asked Sienna.

"You going to get all strange like your olds? Seriously, this is amazing. What else could we want?" laughed Amy.

"A chocolate on the pillow," Sienna replied sarcastically.

Amber laughed and put her arm around Sienna's waist. "We don't care that you have hotel rooms in your house," said Amber. "Now you gunna show us your room?"

Sienna nodded, but was struggling to control her frantic heart. Her bedroom. The bed she'd shared with Flynn. It felt like the first time she would be entering it since his death. Those few of days she had spent in it after leaving the hospital had been so unreal they practically didn't exist.

"We'll be with you," said Amy, standing on the other side of her.

It struck Sienna that her parents had never considered supporting her in this moment. She placed one hesitant foot in front of the other. Amber and Amy kept talking, asking about the rooms they were passing. It helped her keep the tears at bay, but only just. Opening her bedroom door was like tearing open her heart.

"Whoa," gasped Amy, releasing Sienna and walking dumbstruck around the room. "This is next level."

Amy's reaction reminded Sienna of how she'd felt on being shown the room for the first time. It was huge – easily twice as big as her room in Fortune. The queen-sized bed helped fill the space. A matching dresser and bedside tables gave the room an elegant look Sienna had never felt reflected her. Then there was the walk-in wardrobe and ensuite as big as Uncle Cole's bathroom in Fortune. It was all topped off by large bay windows with a view down towards the water.

"It must've been so hard going from this to the Chief's place," said Amber.

Sienna felt her parents' wealth carving out a gulf between her and Amber and Amy. "I actually found it harder going from my uncle's to this," she replied. "This doesn't feel real to me. Never has."

"Um, you have a phone in your room," said Amy, pointing to

Sienna's bedside table.

"Yeah. Used to have about five different lines, but they replaced most of them with their mobiles," explained Sienna. "Kept that one cos they didn't want me to have a mobile. Never realised Flynn gave me one of his old ones. Besides, never had many friends to call it. Only person to really call me was Uncle Cole."

"I think you have a message," said Amy, peering closely as the lights. Sienna waved her hand dismissively. "Want me to play it?"

"Probably just be someone hanging up," said Sienna.

"Senna!"

Sienna gasped as her legs weakened.

"You'd better not be answerin' cos you're already on your way," called Flynn's voice from the machine. "Gunna have the best time. Me, you and the open road, baby. Don't try and be my handbrake tonight. We're cuttin' loose. Lovin' you more every second."

There were so many thoughts racing through Sienna's brain that she couldn't comprehend them. She could feel her body shuddering and wasn't sure she'd be able to control it if she tried. Flynn. Her Flynn. For those brief moments he was alive again. Not a shadow or a hazy memory. Flynn in all his living glory.

It took a while for Sienna to realise she was sitting on her bed. Amy and Amber were on either side of her, holding her tight, as though they were literally trying to keep her together.

"That's Flynn?" asked Amy quietly. Sienna nodded. "So that was the night?" Sienna nodded again.

"You never saw it before today?" asked Amber.

Sienna could only shake her head.

"How are you girls settling in?" asked Janice, striding in the open door. "We're going to have to – what's wrong?"

Amber stood and spoke quietly to Janice. The next second the message was playing once more. Janice ushered Amy and Amber from the room. Sienna pulled her arms around her chest, waiting for the lecture.

"Sienna, I – are you okay?" asked Janice, even though there could never be more than one answer. "You want me to delete it."

"No!" cried Sienna, jumping up to stand protectively in front of the machine.

"Okay, calm down," urged Janice, sitting her back down.

"Why's it still hurt?" gasped Sienna tearfully, feeling like her body could be torn apart with the pain.

"It takes a long time to heal," said Janice, taking Sienna's hand. "We lost a child. Between you and Stephen. He was stillborn."

Sienna looked up, wondering if Stephen knew about their brother. It didn't matter that Janice's voice was stuttering as she spoke. All Sienna could feel was betrayal at yet another secret. More proof she'd never belonged.

"It took years before – I remember holding him. He was still warm, but so lifeless. Your dad held him for over an hour, stroking his face and his tiny head, holding his hand." Janice wiped the tears at the side of her eyes and took a long, slow, steadying breath. "It gets easier, but the pain never goes away completely. It's something you live with and hold on to. It shapes who you are, but it doesn't rule you. You move on. Some days are only just bearable. Others you feel guilty for not even thinking about it."

"I don't know if I want to move on," said Sienna, the words barely able to escape her constricted chest. "It's not right. I belong with Flynn. He's my heart. My life. I'm not real without him."

"Yes, you are," replied Janice urgently, grabbing Sienna by the arms. "Flynn wouldn't want you to think like that. He'd want you to move on and be happy."

Sienna's head shook, though she urged it to be still.

Arthur arrived at the door looking pale. He spoke to Janice quietly in the hallway. Sienna ignored them and hit the play button on the machine, soaking in Flynn's voice and regenerating his memory in her heart. This time, she wouldn't forget the tiny details that had slipped away before.

"That's enough, Sen," said Arthur softly. "Come downstairs."

It seemed like such an innocent request, and it was nice to be with Amy and Amber, but when Sienna was allowed to return to her room she noticed that it had been ransacked. Her parents had tried to cover their tracks, but everything was noticeably out of place.

Arthur and Janice tried to be subtle, but it was obvious they had devised a secret schedule to watch over her. Sienna was rarely allowed in her room; ushered out in the morning and kept from it until night. During the day, they were lured from the house with fully paid public transport tickets.

Amy and Amber had no idea of the significance of public transport in Sienna and Flynn's relationship – just like her parents – but that didn't last long. The tears in her eyes that too often rolled down her cheeks were enough for questions to be asked and for once Sienna wanted to answer.

"Do you ever talk about Flynn?" asked Amy. "You mention him, but not much."

"No one wants to talk about him," Sienna shrugged. "They want me to get over it."

"What about the shrink?" asked Amber.

"All she wants to know is how I feel about things. Why do I care what people think? Why do I think my parents don't like me?" muttered Sienna. She'd never spoken about this either. "Urgh, it's supposed to give me insight, but I'm not getting it."

"We know you loved Flynn," said Amber. "You don't have to avoid talking about him with us."

"I just think about all the plans we had – knowing we'd never be able to do any of it. Now I'm back here and we're talking about what we'll do when we finish school and I kinda think it's useless."

"You coming back to Sydney?" asked Amy.

"Don't know. Might not have a choice. Now I can't be a lawyer don't know what they'll want me to do. Might just leave me in Fortune with Uncle Cole."

"Well we know what you should do," said Amber.

"What?" asked Sienna.

"Ah, be a photographer," Amy replied mockingly.

"But as a job? How would I make any money?" asked Sienna. "I'm not that good."

"Yeah, well you're only seventeen," said Amber. "It'd be a bit depressing if you were already packing out galleries."

"And there's like a million photography jobs," said Amy. "Weddings. Portraits. Travel. Work for the press. Shit, I don't know, photograph rich people your parents know."

They all laughed at the last suggestion. Sienna was sure her parents had the power to arrange such a future. And they probably would too if she promised not to try and kill herself again. But that was exactly what she and Flynn had been trying to escape; careers credited to their parents.

When she and Flynn had dared to dream of the futures they knew they would never have, he always suggested she do something artistic. Sienna knew he believed in her, but like his desire to be a teacher somewhere far from the city, she'd buried that possibility with him. In their more realistic moments, they'd focused on making the most of their predestined careers as lawyers. It surprised Sienna now that he never told her she wasn't capable of making it. He had to have known. He was witness to her daily struggles. Perhaps he thought she was hiding her intelligence behind her misbehaviour too. Or maybe he truly believed she could be a lawyer despite her marks. He may have just had so much self-belief that he thought he could pull her through. If he'd told her that, she was sure she would've believed him too.

Now that future was gone as well, photography made an alluring career path. It was something she could imagine dedicating herself to. It also had a more serious air than simply being an artist.

"What are you guys going to do? You still think you're going to study in Sydney?" asked Sienna.

"I'm leaving Fortune at the end of next year whether or not I get into uni, have a job or a place to live," said Amy matter-of-factly. "I'll probably have to study part-time if I do end up at uni. I ain't got no million-dollar mansion."

"What do you want to study?" asked Sienna, trying not to feel guilty. There'd been little jealousy and no malice in Amy's comment, but there was no getting around the fact that her situation sucked.

"I've always considered teaching or nursing," replied Amy. "You know, jobs you can take anywhere. Every town has a school, most have a hospital."

"I've thought about medicine," said Amber. "Maybe science. Or economics," she added with a smile. "I don't know. My folks would be stoked with medicine, of course, but that's so hard to get into."

"But will you study in Sydney or in Westloch. Your parents want you to stay, right?" asked Sienna.

"They don't quite say that," replied Amber tentatively. "But, yeah, I reckon they'd be stoked if I stayed. I think they're torn between me chasing my dreams and having me around. They'd support me if I came here. But I'm not trying to run away from anything in Fortune.

It's kinda tempting to stay. Here's so big and scary."

"Hey, Amy," said Sienna tentatively, when they were alone that night. "You serious about leaving Fortune next year?"

"Yeah," replied Amy sombrely. "Can't stay. Thought it'd be better to wait til I had money – you know, so I could take the twins with me, but ever since Amber talked about us all living together – just need to get out. Something to look forward to."

"Would you live with me?"

"You're not going to live here?" asked Amy hesitantly. "I think your folks expect you to."

"I don't know what they'll say bout me being a photographer. Maybe it'll be okay, but I can't live with them. Don't think I ever could. Just really wanna get out on my own."

"And what happens when your parents convince you to live here and I'm left with nowhere to live?"

"If they wouldn't drag me home when I was a kid, don't reckon they'll do it now. Please. Don't reckon I could do it on my own, but if it was me and you, that'd be okay."

"Yeah, okay," smiled Amy. "Don't think I could do it by myself either. Be too chicken. But we can be reckless together."

Sienna was genuinely excited when she went to bed, but it felt like yet another secret she had to keep from her parents. They would never understand her need for independence. It would be hard enough to get them to agree with her desired career.

"Just get it over and done with," suggested Amy. "Your parents said they were sticking round for breakfast. Me and Amber will eat real fast. You tell them and then we'll run away to watch the fireworks."

"Yeah, don't let this drag into next year," Amber nodded.

Arthur and Janice smiled warmly as they sat down at the dining table, immediately asking about their New Year's Eve plans.

"Amy and Amber want to go into the city to see the fireworks," said Sienna.

"You might be a bit late for that," laughed Arthur, looking at his watch. It was almost eight. "Everyone would be lined up for the good spots by now."

"Seriously?" cried Amy and Amber simultaneously.

Sienna smirked. She'd mentioned that many times, but they hadn't believed her. They couldn't comprehend so many people and hadn't been keen on camping out for spots.

"You won't miss out. They're plenty of places you can still get to," Arthur assured them. "You get a pretty good view by the pool too if you don't want to travel."

"I don't think that's what they want," smiled Janice, quickly noting down a list of vantage points for Sienna.

"What are you guys doing?" asked Sienna.

"Your father and I'll be at work all day and will go out from there. We've booked somewhere for dinner," answered Janice.

Sienna couldn't help but wonder what they would've done if Amber and Amy hadn't come with her.

"Um, we're going to start getting ready," said Amber, pushing away from the table with Amy.

Arthur and Janice turned to Sienna. When she kept her seat, they nodded to dismiss Amber and Amy, then asked what she wanted to speak to them about.

"I don't want to work in your company," said Sienna, pushing the words out before she found a reason to keep quiet.

"Okay," Janice replied slowly. "Do you have another plan?"

"Photography," muttered Sienna, feeling her parents' judgement.

"That's not exactly a stable income," said Arthur. "I think it's fine as a hobby – maybe a side business – but I'm not sure you can make a career out of it."

"But isn't that my choice?" asked Sienna. "You guys were getting mad at me for just relying on you telling me what I should be, but now I tell you what I want, it's not good enough."

"Your father's just trying to point out that that kind of career won't be easy," said Janice soothingly.

"Reading and writing isn't easy, yet you want me to do jobs where I have to do that all the time," cried Sienna. "Least I know how to take photos."

Arthur and Janice exchanged grave looks. Sienna started turning the crust of her toast to crumbs. The minutes ticked by, but only silence remained.

"Don't worry, I'll think of something else," muttered Sienna, pushing her plate away.

When Arthur flicked his hand, Sienna walked out. But she didn't have another plan and didn't want one either. Amy and Amber were right. There were lots of ways she could be a photographer. She didn't need to earn lots of money and could work other jobs on the side if she had to. If Uncle Cole supported her then it could happen, though she feared it would ruin her chance to move to Sydney with Amy.

"We think it's a good idea, Sen," said Arthur, walking into her room with Janice half an hour later.

"Or you think I'll knock myself off if you don't agree with me?" Sienna replied bitterly.

"We never said that," Arthur snapped. "Stop twisting everything."

"We talked about it," said Janice calmly. "We stand by what we said, but you're right, you do have the right to make this choice. What we're saying now is that we'll support you."

"Thanks," replied Sienna, trying to be grateful, while wondering why they couldn't have said that from the start.

Arthur nodded and turned to leave before walking over and hugging Sienna. It was fierce and Sienna tried to return it in equal measure. Janice stroked Sienna's hair, then joined the embrace.

Amy and Amber insisted they try to find a vantage point in the city to watch the fireworks. It took the whole afternoon to convince them of the futility of it. Sienna didn't mind the waste of the time, especially as Amy and Amber were both deriving so much enjoyment from the atmosphere.

"We finally ready to concede defeat?" asked Sienna. "There're two lots of fireworks, so if you don't like the first spot, we'll find another for the midnight ones."

With an unhappy sigh, Amy and Amber finally nodded, but Sienna didn't have to worry about either being disappointed for long. They ended up by the water and when the fireworks exploded overhead, they were lost in awe. They'd never seen a spectacle of this magnitude and where they stood became inconsequential. Sienna watched Amy and Amber rather than the fireworks. There was little pleasure in Amy's life and Sienna took strength from the fact that she was able to struggle through and still find happiness in moments like these.

When midnight struck, Sienna closed her eyes and let the year wash through her. It was over. She was still alive. A future of some description lay ahead of her. It was daunting and terrifying, but when Amy and Amber started cheering and hugging each other, she joined in, embracing them as sincerely as they held her.

"Just a year to go," Amy cried in Sienna's ear over the roar of the crowd and the explosion of the fireworks.

Just a year to go, repeated Sienna in her mind. It built, chant-like, in her head. A mantra alternating between her voice and Amy's. Just one more year to go. To what, she didn't know. The next year. The next empty promise of something better to come. But perhaps she could drag herself from one year to the next, forever telling herself just one more year to go.

~19~

GIFT

There was something unreal about the four weeks Sienna spent in Sydney. There were all the fears, frustrations and family conflicts of her previous life living with her parents, and yet it was so different now. She wasn't sure she was the same person without Flynn. She'd lost her direction, and yet paving a new one often made her feel more lost. She needed Flynn.

Amy and Amber were great. In the first week of the new year, they were out and about so much Sienna barely saw her family. But the constant movement left Sienna spinning and the only way she knew to stop it was to draw.

"Then stay home and do some drawing," said Amber, when Sienna tearfully confessed to not wanting to go out again.

"But what about you guys?" asked Sienna.

"We can go out without you, right?" asked Amy.

"You wouldn't be mad at me?" questioned Sienna.

"Nup," laughed Amy. "Just as long as you promise to guide us home if we get lost."

They didn't get lost, but Sienna did. She was still drawing when they got back. They were impressed by her artwork and the progress she made as they days went on; though Sienna's family was much less inclined to approve of her activities. They didn't see the drawings. All they noticed was that she wasn't always with Amy and Amber. They didn't ask her what she was doing, rather spied on her to find out that she was listening to Flynn's final message and trawling through photos of him on her computer.

At first, they made off-hand comments about how she should be spending her time. Then they started arriving home unexpectedly.

"Shouldn't you be out with your friends?" asked Stephen, walking into Sienna's bedroom.

Sienna was sitting on the floor, her sketch book against her legs, the answering machine by her side and laptop next to her. She looked up briefly, before returning her concentration to her work. "They're doing their own thing this afternoon," she eventually answered.

"Because you're in here sulking. It's not good for you."

"Fuck off, Stephen. Don't pretend to know what I'm doing."

Sienna closed her eyes and pretended he wasn't there. Concentrating on releasing her anger, she hit the play button on her answering machine and imagined Flynn's face.

"Senna!"

Vibrations through the floorboards alerted her to the danger. Stephen was reaching for the answering machine. She jumped up to intercept him, struggling to push him away. "You delete that and I swear I'll never, ever speak to you again."

Stephen immediately stepped back. He stared at her for a second before storming from the room. Sienna sat back down, knowing she hadn't heard the end of this.

"This isn't healthy, Sen. You need to stop it now," commanded Arthur, as soon as he arrived home.

Sienna refused to respond – until Arthur reached for the answering machine. She pushed him away, but he was much stronger than Stephen.

"Get out! Go away!" she yelled.

"You're not well. You need help!"

"There's nothing wrong with me! Fuck! Don't you know me at all?"

"I know you far too well," Arthur countered, turning over her wrists.

"I hate you."

He released her, looking wounded as he slunk from the room.

Sitting back down, Sienna tried to block out the sound of the angry voices downstairs and more footsteps stomping her way. She took a deep breath. "Leave me alone," she said through gritted teeth, not looking up to see who was at the door.

"We need to talk." It was Janice.

"Talk? All anyone ever does is accuse me of things."

"We haven't accused you of anything," said Janice calmly. Sienna held her tongue. "We just don't understand why you keep torturing yourself with that message."

"Then why not just ask?"

There was a short silence before her mother spoke again. "Why, then? Why do you keep listening to that message over and over?"

Sienna hesitated. She wanted her parents to understand, but didn't trust them. "So I can see Flynn again," she eventually replied.

"What's that mean?" asked Arthur, his voice shaking. He wasn't mad any more. "You still want to – to …"

"No!" cried Sienna emphatically, though the truth wasn't that clear-cut. "I want to see Flynn the way I used to. I want to stop seeing him like this." She grabbed one of her art books and threw it on her bed. It contained images of Flynn from the accident scene that had tortured her for so long; a mixture of memory and photographic reality. Arthur and Janice were speechless. They flicked through the book and Sienna could see she hadn't helped her cause. "I want to be able to draw him alive again," she said, trying to keep her voice calm as she passed them another sketch book. "That's what I've been working on."

"You listen to the message to do this?" asked Janice.

"I need to remember him how he was. It's hard sometimes. Hard to fight against the other images," said Sienna. "That message. That's Flynn. Everything I love about him."

"But it upsets you," said Arthur.

"So does living," Sienna retorted so harshly even she thought she was a bitch. "Please, just leave me alone."

The tension in the house ultimately worked in Arthur and Janice's favour. Sienna needed to get out, though she never went anywhere without her sketch book and made several recordings of Flynn's message before leaving the answering machine unattended. They were saved on her phone and computer, sent as emails and text messages to herself, giving her peace of mind that she wouldn't lose the last living reminder of Flynn.

But inevitably, as soon as Sienna felt like she'd learned to manage one issue with her parents, another developed.

"Don't you like it?" asked Arthur, as Sienna stared at the mountain of new, and very expensive, photography equipment he and Janice had come home with.

"You should be grateful, Sen," muttered Stephen.

Amber and Amy slipped quietly from the room. Sienna watched them leave, wondering how this would change their opinion of her.

The look in Amy's eyes at the sight of thousands of dollars' worth of goods being presented as little more than a trifle was painful.

"Of course, I like it," Sienna answered, trying to keep her voice even. "But I never asked for it."

"We wanted to show you we were serious about supporting you being a photographer," said Arthur. "We asked them at the shop what you'd need to start up."

"But you didn't speak to me!" cried Sienna.

"We wanted to surprise you," Janice offered weakly.

"In front of my friends who could never dream of having parents who could afford all this," countered Sienna. "I wanted your support, not your money. Why don't you ever realise that?"

"That's what we thought we were giving you," Arthur muttered.

Sienna couldn't argue. She felt selfish and ungrateful, but wanted to be able to have a say in her future. What her parents had bought was everything she had ever considered she would need and then some. It was generous, but she couldn't help but feel that her future was once again outside of her control.

"So are we taking it back to the shops?" asked Stephen bitterly.

Sienna didn't look up or speak.

"You're right, Sen, we should've spoken to you first," said Janice. "But we thought we were doing the right thing."

"It is very nice," said Sienna, hoping her parents would finally understand. "But when you just throw money at me but can't speak to me … I feel like I'm being bought off. If I was really Uncle Cole's kid, you wouldn't want anything to do with me."

"That's not true. Of course, it would be different, but we would've supported you," said Janice, but Sienna didn't believe her. "Cole's my brother. I wouldn't have let you go without."

"What? By taking me out every so often? Letting me stay in your mansion occasionally?"

"Listen, we paid your uncle almost five hundred dollars a week to look after you when you were younger," snapped Arthur angrily. "Even more now that you're older and need more things."

"Yeah, right. That explains how we've been able to live in the lap of luxury," Sienna retorted sarcastically before she could stop herself.

Something clicked in Sienna's brain as she looked at her parents' shocked faces. That was the arrangement. Money. What it always came down to.

"Sen, wait," called Janice, as Sienna stormed away.

"No, I don't want your money, okay. I never wanted it. Don't you understand that?"

They let her go. She locked her bedroom door. Her head was spinning. Over twenty thousand dollars a year. Perhaps it was why Uncle Cole kept her around, but if he was taking the money for himself, she couldn't conceive what he was spending it on. He had nothing expensive or flashy. It didn't make sense.

A soft knock at the door drew Sienna's head up. Amy smiled softly when she opened the door, leaning against the door frame.

"Amber's talking to her parents. Was getting a bit mushy. They're so excited she's coming home in a couple of days."

"You looking forward to going home too?" asked Sienna.

"Well …"

"Just looking forward to leaving her, huh."

Amy smiled apologetically. "It's not like that. I guess it's just hard sometimes." Her eyes flicked down.

Sienna followed her gaze. The pile of photography equipment was in the corridor, looking even more obscene in the confined space. "I'm sorry," Sienna whispered, slumping to the floor.

"Not your fault your parents are crazy rich," said Amy, sitting next to her.

"It's not fair."

"Life's not fair," added Amy quietly. "But you should take the stuff. It's like the only way they know how to love you. Don't want to throw that back at them."

~20~

MAKING AMENDS

Amy and Amber's feet stuttered when they saw Uncle Cole waiting for them at Westloch airport, still haunted by him hauling Sienna into his police car outside the cinemas. Sienna only felt a rush of gratitude, propelling her into his arms. He squeezed her tight. His perpetual presence at moments like these was such a contrast to her parents. Despite spending most of the night before trying to convince her to stay in Sydney, dismissing every obstacle as inconsequential, they still couldn't find the time in their schedule to see them off; a chauffeured car turning up instead.

When they arrived home, Sienna set about making a large batch of brownies – enough for the house and the station. It brought a smile to Uncle Cole's face that was only wiped away by the sight of her new photography gear.

"You ask for this?" Sienna shook her head. "They take you with them to buy it?" Sienna shook her head again. Uncle Cole smirked and sighed. She knew exactly what he was thinking, but was glad he didn't say anything as he examined it. "Only the best," he muttered.

"Would've been happier to get cheaper stuff and get it myself."

"Treat this well and some of it you'll never have to replace," replied Uncle Cole gruffly. "You want to test this stuff out, just tell me when you're going and where."

He left her then. Sienna immediately packed her new camera bag and headed out. She was impressed by the results. The lenses were amazing and opened up new realms of imagery. There was so much to try that Sienna spent much longer than she expected out and about.

As she walked back towards home, she realised she was only a block from Jackson's place. Walking tentatively up to the door, she turned away three times before finally finding the courage to knock. The door opened seconds later, but Sienna was disorientated by the sight of a girl in the doorway.

"Oh, sorry, wrong —" Sienna's eyes flicked up to the number on

219

the door, then down the corridor, completely confused. "Um, I thought – sorry – Jax – Jackson, does he live here?"

"He's in the shower. And who are you?"

"Um, Sienna," she replied meekly. "Are you his sister?"

"I'm his girlfriend," the girl replied firmly.

"Oh," gasped Sienna, surprised by the pain that statement brought her. She'd never considered going out with Jackson, and he was always seeing someone, yet there was something very wrong with this situation.

"I'll let him know you stopped by," said the girl, closing the door.

Sienna hesitated for a moment before turning to leave. She walked slowly, wondering why she'd come.

"Sienna!"

The sight of Jackson striding topless towards her was physically painful. She'd never been convinced anything she'd felt for him was a product of anything more than his strange similarities to Flynn.

"What are you doing here? You okay?" he asked feelingly.

"Yeah, I just – last year – wanted —"

"It's okay," nodded Jackson.

"I – um – I got you a present from Sydney," Sienna said quickly, reaching into her bag.

Jackson smiled softly, just the way Flynn used to, and opened the small box to reveal a snow globe of Sydney's skyline.

"Thought you might be getting homesick."

"Well, I never will again."

Sienna nodded. "I guess I'll see you around."

"Wait, you going to the shrink on Tuesday?"

"No. Going Thursday. Might work better. Used to ruin my whole week," she replied, though she wasn't convinced the change in day would do much. She wasn't even convinced she wanted to go, but her parents had been so insistent, and so distrustful, that they made the appointment themselves before she returned to Fortune.

"How you getting there?" asked Jackson.

"Bus," Sienna replied, deciding against asking him to take her.

"He won't let you."

"He can't stop me. It's my choice to go," she lied.

"You want me to take you?" asked Jackson. "I'll talk to the Chief if you want. Make it okay."

Sienna wasn't sure that was possible. It was unlikely Uncle Cole had changed his stance on Jackson in her life, but he hated her going to the psychologist, hated taking her, so might be inclined to let Jackson do it for him.

"It's okay," nodded Sienna. "I'll talk to him."

"You been taking more photos?" asked Jackson quickly, pointing to her bag. "My mum loved the photos you gave me. Sent her pictures of them. Made me promise I'd bring them when I come home next."

"I can get you copies. Printed or digital. Whatever. Just let me know. No problem."

Jackson's girlfriend stepped out from his apartment and into the hallway. Sienna immediately started backing away, feeling like an intruder. When Jackson looked behind him, she rushed off.

Walking quickly towards the police station, Sienna felt like she was trying to race her decision to let Jackson drive her. Somehow Uncle Cole would know before she got there, but by the smile on his face she knew that hadn't happened.

"You might not be that happy to see me soon," said Sienna, hoping some forewarning might help her cause. Uncle Cole took her into his office. "I'm going back to the psychologist. Thursday. I can catch the bus, but I ran into Jackson while I was out. He was with his girlfriend. He said he could still take me, but I don't want to cause problems."

"You don't need to go there," said Uncle Cole in a low voice. "I told you before there's nothing wrong with you. You're perfect just the way you are."

It was ironic that the only person who could make her feel like she needed to see a shrink was the person most against her going. "I'm not," she replied, shaking her head. Uncle Cole opened his mouth, but she held up her hand. "I can't see the girl you can, but I want to. I want to be who you —" Sienna's throat strangled closed.

It felt wrong after all her parents had done for her and all the fights she and Uncle Cole had had to want to be the daughter he desired, but right then she realised she could be happy as that girl. Uncle Cole must've understood something of her dilemma, because his arms were suddenly around her, holding her tight to his chest.

"I'll sort it out," he reassured her, as he walked her out of the office, his arm around her shoulders. "Ryan, you make sure Jackson isn't rostered on Thursday afternoons again til I say so. Got it?"

"Yes, Chief," answered Ryan immediately.

Sienna couldn't help but wonder what Ryan was thinking as he agreed to that command. The last time she'd been here he'd been forced to lock her unlawfully in a cell. Now he was being asked to alter their rosters to suit her needs.

On Thursday morning, Sienna woke with a feeling of dread. For the first week of school, it hadn't been bad, but a session with Dr Chousalkar was certainly not her preferred way of ending it. She still didn't know if she should tell Dr Chousalkar about Flynn's message. She'd always planned to, but now wasn't so sure. The last thing she wanted was to have Flynn stripped from her again. To date, Dr Chousalkar appeared to want just what Arthur and Janice did. Sienna had never been able to articulate just how much Flynn meant to her, and to Dr Chousalkar he was nothing more than a childish infatuation, someone who would be replaced in time.

"You ready?" asked Jackson, when Sienna approached his car after school. He seemed to be steeling himself against her inevitable mood. Sienna nodded and got in the car. "Want to talk?"

"Dunno. Maybe."

"Don't have to if you don't want to. Not trying to pry."

Sienna's heart fluttered. When she thought about Flynn, any notion of Jackson being more than a friend crumbled to dust. But she couldn't deny the connection between them.

"I know. Didn't mean it like that," she replied. "Just that things changed over summer."

"How?" asked Jackson quickly. "With your parents."

"No," Sienna scoffed. "With Flynn. He left me a message."

"What?" cried Jackson, the car swerving as he turned to face her. He corrected, staring straight ahead as she explained. "Oh shit, Sienna, I can't imagine how hard …"

"Yeah," she nodded, trying to master her voice and hold back her tears. "Never realised so much had slipped away. Felt like he came back to me a bit when I heard it. I could see him proper again – all the things I forgot. I just don't want anyone to take that from me."

"No one should," said Jackson firmly.

Sienna turned. Jackson instantly met her eyes. He looked serious as he nodded. Sienna made up her mind. She wouldn't tell Dr Chousalkar about Flynn.

"I'll see you when you finish," said Jackson, when they arrived in Westloch.

He smiled when Sienna turned to him. It was Flynn's smile – another piece of him reaching out to her. She pulled it close to her heart, as though it could patch the wounds. It gave her the strength to go to her appointment, but by the end of it, she wished she'd been a coward.

The session focused on the events of the summer holidays. Sienna didn't mention Uncle Cole locking her in the police cell. As terrible as it was, she didn't need anyone to explain his motives. It was her parents she struggled to understand, and since they were demanding these sessions, she thought she should try and figure them out. Dr Chousalkar seemed to think it was her who needed sorting out. All the questions focused on why she felt, and reacted, the way she did. The result was Sienna feeling like she'd been carved open in the search of something worthwhile, but when Dr Chousalkar found nothing, she was left with gaping wounds.

Jackson was standing against his car as Sienna walked out. They headed straight back to Fortune. Sienna hunched over in her seat and wrapped her arms around her chest.

"You okay?" asked Jackson.

Sienna shook her head. She was so far from okay she didn't know what okay was any more. "Can we maybe pull over somewhere?" she asked, her voice quivering.

Jackson didn't answer and Sienna didn't look up until the car stopped. As they got out at the lookout, she wondered if this was the only place to stop between Westloch and Fortune.

"You okay?" asked Jackson again. Sienna nodded and breathed deeply, her arms still wrapped around her chest. It was a lie, but they shouldn't be here together. "Tell me about it. Tell me about the session."

If Jackson had asked her if she wanted to talk, she would've said no, but there was something about his command that made her speak against her will.

"You can't let your worth be determined by something outside of you," said Jackson seriously. "Your existence is worthwhile. You have to believe that no matter what other people think. Trust me. You can't survive as a cop if you take on board everything people say about you. You've got to believe in the traits that are core to you."

"Like what?" asked Sienna, not really understanding.

Jackson stared at her hard for a moment, as if she was asking to cheat on an exam, before finally answering. "For me, it's things like being a good friend, loyal, trustworthy. I'm my parents' child. That's important to me. I'm Aboriginal," he added, pacing thoughtfully. "I'm a cop and all the values associated with that."

Sienna waited for more, but Jackson didn't say anything. He was staring at her. She knew he wanted her to try and define her traits, but she couldn't. There weren't words yet.

It took a long time for Sienna to compile her list. She decided to start with an unfiltered description of who she wanted to be in the absence of any external influences. Flynn was the first word she wrote. He was her heart and soul and she didn't want that to change. Her heart had died with him and his heart was all she had left.

When she sought to define her core traits beyond Flynn, she had just enough courage to call herself an artist. No matter what job she had in the future, art would be at the core of her existence. Even photography was just a subset of that. She wanted to be kind and empathetic, compassionate and loyal. She wanted to be daring.

Then Sienna thought about what Jackson's other traits had been. His parents' son. Sienna closed her eyes as she wrote. Her heart ached as she read the outcome.

Uncle Cole's daughter

Arthur and Janice's niece

Sienna thought back to when she stopped thinking of Uncle Cole as her dad. It had been a painful decision and one she was sure had fractured something inside of her.

Quickly shoving the notes into her journal, determined never to leave them where anyone could find them, she wrote out the version she would let people see; the version that contained nothing about her family or Flynn. The version that was barely her at all.

Jackson was the first person she showed the list to. He read it silently before handing it back to her and starting the car. The drive to Westloch continued in silence. It made Sienna nervous.

"You haven't said anything," she said tentatively.

"I was thinking – about how your list compared to mine," replied Jackson

"Yeah, I know. I stole off yours a bit," she admitted.

Jackson smiled. "Not much."

"You think I'm soulless?"

"What? No, that's not what I meant. It's just interesting. When I said about being my parents' child, then being Aboriginal. They were almost the same thing. You don't have that." Sienna shook her head. "I kinda expected – after what happened last year – that you'd put white or Australian or something."

"I've never seen my race as a defining part of me," Sienna replied softly. "It's an accident of birth. Just like my family's wealth. Might shape me, but I don't want it to define me." Jackson stayed silent, his eyes on the road. "Maybe it'd be different if I was something special like you."

"How am I special?"

"You, being Aboriginal. It's special. There's nothing special about being white."

"Except all your inherent privilege," muttered Jackson.

"No, I mean nothing special personally. I'm just the default. You can't derive anything from that. I get that white supremacists think they're better than everyone, but I don't believe that. I know how pathetic I am."

"You seem better for doing it – writing the list," said Jackson, sidestepping the race issue. "You seem better since Christmas. More settled."

"Maybe," she said cautiously. It wasn't how she felt.

Dr Chousalkar was also impressed by Sienna's list. It was the first time she'd told her she was making real progress.

The sigh that escaped Sienna as she slid into the car at the end of the session was one of pure exhaustion. Jackson squeezed her hand and started the car. Sienna immediately disentangled herself. "You're a taken man," she said. Jackson smiled. "What's her name?"

"Alyssa," he replied with a smirk. "Probably should've told you I only have two brothers."

"Where'd you meet?"

"Met ages ago. Then we ended up at the same New Year's party."

"She was your midnight kiss?" grinned Sienna, feeling like she had to hide the jealousy she wasn't even sure she felt.

"Something like that," Jackson replied mockingly.

"Oh," Sienna murmured. "You seeing her tonight?"

"It's the only night I have guaranteed off. If they find out I've planned something, suddenly I'm needed to stay back or have to swap shifts."

"I'm sorry."

"For what? You're the reason I get a night off."

"Yeah, but I'm also the reason you're copping all this shit. If you'd have stayed away from me like Uncle Cole wanted, you would've been fine."

"If I'd suppressed my morality when I came here then maybe I'd be better off," Jackson countered in a hard voice. "Chief runs the station like he owns the town. His rule is law. I was having issues even before you came. I couldn't do it. At least with you leaving at the end of this year, I don't feel as bad about putting in for a transfer."

"What?" cried Sienna.

"I'm going back to Sydney. I don't care where. I'm not holding out much hope it'll be soon. They've told me mid-year at the earliest. My mum has some health problems and we may've made them out to be worse than they are, otherwise I don't know when I'd get out of here."

"But what about Alyssa?"

"What about her?"

"Does she know? She going with you?"

Jackson smiled broadly. "There's nothing to tell right now. And I don't see it being that serious by then that she'd come with me. Why?"

"No reason," Sienna replied quickly. "You know, just – she's your girlfriend. Can't just leave her."

Jackson didn't reply. He just looked at her curiously before turning his eyes back to the road.

"Your parents called," muttered Uncle Cole, as soon as Sienna walked in the door.

Sienna joined him in the lounge room, surprised by the smile that greeted her arrival. He didn't ask about her session. Maybe he knew nothing good could come from that conversation.

"You had dinner yet?" asked Sienna.

"Want to join me at the pub?" replied Uncle Cole.

It was the last thing Sienna wanted. She was tired and grumpy, but the dulling of Uncle Cole's eyes was something she hated more. "Can I come home after dinner?" she asked tentatively. Uncle Cole started to smile. "And order a salad?"

Uncle Cole laughed, leading Sienna happily to the car. When their food came, he offered her some of his steak in exchange for salad.

"You got me on to it," he confessed, forking a piece of lettuce. Sienna smiled and ate the steak. "Don't have it every day, but …"

"I didn't change that much," Sienna whispered, tears stinging her eyes. "I just stopped eating from the kids' menu."

Uncle Cole's reached out and squeezed her hand. "I turned around one day and you weren't my little girl any more."

"I just wasn't little any more," she clarified, terrified of saying more.

"And now you're almost a woman," chortled Uncle Cole, pulling back and clearing the seriousness from his face. "I was fighting a losing battle, keeping you from your salad. It's something genetic – on the X chromosome. That's why men only like salad half as much as women."

Sienna laughed, playfully chiding him for his sexism. She hoped it was a sign that things would be better this year – that an unspoken understanding had been reached. She could only hope so. She needed her ally back. However, with half a state between them and just a telephone for communication, Sienna found Arthur and Janice strikingly easier to deal with. And despite his raised eyebrows, Sienna knew that Uncle Cole would never expose the half-truths she told to keep her parents satisfied.

***

The first term trundled slowly into gear. With the exception of her therapy sessions, Sienna started to feel at ease with life, though there were still the days where everything seemed pointless. The only thing she wished for on those days was to be transported to Flynn. Art was what she relied on most on those darks days. She would listen to Flynn's message and draw him as he'd once been. Uncle Cole caught her listening to it, his face paling.

"You make sure you have copies of that somewhere else," he said in a gravelly voice. Sienna stared at him. "Phones get lost and stolen. Break. Make sure you've got it saved somewhere else."

"I will," nodded Sienna.

A week later Uncle Cole came home with a USB and an old video camera. He'd had it when she'd come to visit him in Fortune in the early years, but it disappeared a while later.

"Broke one night after the boys had a big one," he explained. "Forgot all about it til you showed me that message."

"We used it," Sienna gasped. "Me and Flynn." Uncle Cole nodded. "He used to take videos of us, but they were all on his phone. I never had them and couldn't ask after."

"I got them to make a few copies. You take this one," said Uncle Cole, handing her the USB. "I'll keep the others safe."

There were five videos in all. None were longer than three minutes. None were serious. And in all of them, they were so young. They had felt so old, their thoughts often on such serious things, but they had been little more than kids. Just fourteen-year-olds.

"You won't tell Arthur and Janice about this, will you?"

"You don't want me to send them a copy for safe-keeping?" Uncle Cole asked seriously. Sienna shook her head. "How'd they react to the message?"

"Not well," replied Sienna softly.

Uncle Cole didn't say anything, but Sienna noticed that when her mood dipped low, he would put a sketch book in her hands and quietly encourage her to draw. She was tempted to ask him to explain to Arthur and Janice everything he knew about her, but that plan would never work. They wouldn't listen to him any more than they listened to her.

"Ready for another week?" Jackson asked, as they slipped into his car on Thursday afternoon. Sienna shook her head. He stayed silent for a minute before speaking again, his voice light and chirpy. "How's your photography coming along? You doing that for your art project?"

"Photography's going fine," replied Sienna. "But don't know that I can make it work for my major art work."

"What do you mean? Your stuff's great."

"But it needs to be more than a nice photo. Need a story. Have been working on that black–white theme, but nothing's connecting."

"Why not? Socially, you could take it anywhere."

Sienna screwed up her face. "Yeah, that was never my angle. I liked the contrast. The visual aspect. Race relations, all that kind of stuff, I wouldn't know how to do that."

Jackson was almost incredulous, bringing up lists of issues she could address.

"You see that stuff, not me," murmured Sienna. "You saw my list. My skin colour isn't a defining part of me. I don't think I should try and pretend to know what it's like to be racially discriminated against. Or what it's like to not like someone because of their skin colour." Jackson didn't reply. "But been trying black-and-white photos – of other things – scenery – Amy … just can't find what I'm looking for."

"What are you looking for?" asked Jackson.

"The fog," Sienna replied before she could stop herself. Jackson looked confusedly at her, half-asking questions, as if knowing the answers were bad. "The place I go – it's black. Encasing. Like a fog of all your darkest thoughts and insecurities you've held deep inside leaking out into the world and then turning back on you – eating you alive trying to get back in. Eventually all you have around is black. It chokes you."

Jackson concentrated on the road, looking ahead. He was silent for almost five minutes before speaking quietly. "You need to draw it. Stop trying to find that picture. It doesn't exist. You have to draw it. Show that moment right before you took those pills."

The commanding way Jackson spoke triggered something in Sienna's brain. She hadn't considered drawing it. A photo felt safer, but Jackson was right, the only way to create that image was with her own hand. It was already coming together – her, trapped by fog – Flynn with her, but not really there – everyone else at a distance – and between them the fears that kept them apart.

All through her session, Sienna's mind swirled on that image. It left her distracted and Dr Chousalkar annoyed, but for once she didn't walk out feeling like she wanted the world to dissolve.

As soon as Jackson dropped her home, Sienna started mapping out the images. Uncle Cole watched her working furiously. He said something, but she didn't hear. The next time she looked up she was alone and a poor-looking sandwich was next to her.

~21~

EASTER

Time in Fortune had never moved so swiftly. Before Sienna knew it, Uncle Cole was asking if she wanted to take up her parents' offer of spending the holidays in Sydney.

"You be mad if I go?" asked Sienna.

"You're coming back, aren't you," Uncle Cole replied without a hint of a question. Sienna nodded. "Then you should go if you want."

"I'll see if Amy and Amber can come with me."

Uncle Cole smiled just slightly.

"So?" Sienna asked the next day at lunch. "Will you come? I have enough money saved to get us all there on the train."

"Sorry, but I have to stay and study," said Amber. "And Easter's real big in my family. Can't miss it."

"I'm in," said Amy, removing Sienna's need to beg.

"Yay!" grinned Sienna, glad she didn't have to come up with an excuse for not going.

Dropping her bag on her bed, Sienna called Arthur, thankful she finally had news he would be happy with.

"What do you mean pay for the train fare?" snapped Arthur. "Is that why you didn't tell us you were coming earlier?" The answer was worse than that, so Sienna stayed silent. "Your uncle put you up to this?"

"No!" she cried. "It has nothing to do with him! What's it even matter?"

"Then why catch the train? We would've booked tickets the minute you told us you were coming. And for your friends."

"But the train's cheaper," said Sienna.

"I don't care about that!"

Sienna hung up on the verge of tears, sending Janice a text to let her know it was best she didn't come. The returning call took much longer than expected.

"There's no issue with you coming by train," said Janice.

"Yeah, tell that to Dad," Sienna muttered spitefully.

"I have," replied Janice calmly. "I've always liked the idea of train journeys. We just seem to be in too much of a rush to do them. I'd like to know what it's like."

"So cos you want to do it, I'm allowed?" questioned Sienna. "Won't I ever be allowed to choose how I want to do something?"

"It's not like that, Sen," sighed Janice.

"Dad yelled at me for saying I'd bought train tickets to come home. You want me to come home. I do it. And I still get in trouble. Why do I even bother?"

"Please don't say that," said Janice. "We miss you so much. We don't want to miss more. Your dad, it's been so hard that even a couple of hours – in his mind, it makes a difference. And, your dad, he has the funds to spoil you. He wants to give you the best of everything. It's the only way he's ever known to show his affection."

"I don't care about money," spat Sienna.

"And either does your dad," replied Janice. "Just in the opposite way. He's never gone without."

"And you have," said Sienna sceptically.

"You forget that your uncle is my brother and we grew up together," Janice replied gravely.

Sienna said nothing. Janice never spoke about her childhood. Either did Uncle Cole, but he'd never dismissed her the way Janice had when she'd asked about it. He explained it was something he didn't want to speak or think about and asked that she wouldn't make him.

Janice sighed heavily. "Your uncle and I didn't have a nice – there's a reason you don't know your grandparents. We haven't spoken to them since we left."

"When was that?" Sienna asked tentatively.

"When your uncle was eighteen. He got a job. Got a place. Had just enough to support me as I finished school. He went to the academy as soon as I was done. Supported me even then. He must've lived on almost nothing – just to get me through my law degree. That's where I met your dad. I wanted to pretend I was just like him – rich – not a care in the world. Cole hated that. But I was running from that world. I wanted Cole to come with me, but the more I pulled, the more he dug his feet in. I think about it now. The resentment. You in that world I hate."

"It's where I belong."

"It's where you know," countered Janice. "Your father and I, we struggle to think of you belonging anywhere but with us."

"I can't change who I am."

"Either can we. So maybe we have to learn to meet each other at the border. Just keep meeting us. Even after we disappoint you. Please. We do love you."

Arthur came around a few days later, calling with a compromise; they could catch the train up and he would fly them home. Sienna agreed, wanting to avoid a fight. Amy didn't care either way – as long as the flight back this time wasn't as bumpy as their last one.

"Was actually pretty glad you suggested the train after that," laughed Amy.

"It was pretty bad," agreed Amber. "I seriously thought we were going to die when it did that big drop."

Sienna had been transported to Sydney from Fortune by plane so many times she'd stopped noticing how shaky the trip could be in a little plane. Uncle Cole had nearly always picked her up, but almost never dropped her off. He argued that if they wanted her back, they could come for her. Instead, a plane ticket always arrived and she was shipped back alone.

Blocking those memories, Sienna reminded herself that tomorrow was the start of two weeks of freedom.

"You seem happy," said Jackson, as she approached him outside the school. She'd been tempted to cancel her appointment, but her parents had asked about it just the day before, forcing her to keep it. "Looking forward to the holidays?" asked Jackson as they drove off. "Or just two weeks off from me?"

"I'd never be happy about not seeing you," Sienna replied truthfully, before she could stop herself. "No, just looking forward to the break. Sure I'll spend most of it arguing with my parents, but still."

"They coming out here?" asked Jackson.

"No," scoffed Sienna. "Ain't causing no scandal for them to fix. Nup, going there."

"Great," spat Jackson angrily.

"What?" asked Sienna defensively.

"I put in leave ages ago for Easter. Supposed to leave tomorrow morning. Come back next Friday. But something's going to 'go wrong'. Shit! My brothers are going to hate me."

"I don't get it. What's that got to do with me?" asked Sienna. "It's not like we'd be hanging out. He can't think that."

"I've given up trying to figure out what the Chief can think," muttered Jackson. "Fuck this. I'm so sick of this place."

"Go now. Just drop me off. I'll catch the bus home," urged Sienna, hating that she was in any way involved in this.

"Nice thought," smiled Jackson. "But they know I'm meant to bring you home. They'll time the call to make sure I haven't skived off. Don't worry. It's not your fault. I'll ring my mum, tell her I'm not coming."

Sienna could barely concentrate on what Dr Chousalkar was asking. Their sessions had deteriorated over the term as Sienna had become more reluctant to discuss Flynn, wanting to hold him close to her heart so no one could take him away, and determined not to question Uncle Cole. The world didn't need to know, but she was his daughter again and things made sense that way.

"Maybe we can come up with a plan," said Sienna, striding towards Jackson after her session.

"Don't worry," he answered in a terse dismissal. "I've already told them I probably won't be coming."

"You need to go home to pick up your stuff?" asked Sienna, ignoring Jackson's comment. It felt odd being the positive one of the pair. "Cos we do that before you drop me home. I'll jump out and you drive to Sydney. Don't stop. Don't answer the phone. I'll tell Uncle Cole you got a call about some emergency at home." Jackson stared at her. "Screw them, okay. You're not having Easter taken off you like your Christmas was. Not because of me."

Jackson nodded stiffly and turned the car towards Fortune, his foot to the floor. Sienna looked over at his speedometer and was surprised to see he was only just over the limit, yet he was driving so much faster than he usually did. The result was that, even with the detour, she was home a bit earlier than normal.

"Where's Jackson?" asked Uncle Cole, walking slowly out of the house to meet Sienna.

"He's gone. Got a call," replied Sienna, trying to sound ignorant. "Some emergency. Said he had to get home."

"Humph, his girlfriend probably broke a nail," scoffed Uncle Cole. "I'll catch him at his place."

Sienna only shrugged and headed towards her room. Uncle Cole never discussed work with her and would be suspicious if she started asking questions now.

"What home did Jackson say he was going to?" stormed Uncle Cole, bursting into Sienna's room fifteen minutes later.

"I don't know," replied Sienna, trying to sound causal. "He just said home. Why?"

Uncle Cole didn't answer. He just walked back out to the lounge room. Sienna heard him muttering to Ryan, who must've just arrived. She stayed out of their way. Uncle Cole didn't ask her to come to the pub for dinner with them.

Amy laid her head against the train window, gazing out at the passing scenery. Sienna moved across the carriage and pulled her camera up to her eye. The other passengers on the train looked at them curiously, but Sienna paid them no attention. Amy was getting better at that. She had spent most of the term being Sienna's model. Amber volunteered occasionally and Sienna had taken some great shots of the two of them that she planned to enlarge and frame for them.

"So what's the plan for this trip?" asked Amy, as they neared Sydney. "Going to make me model all Easter? Feels pretty strange staring out to space all the time."

"Ha, no … well maybe," smiled Sienna. "Actually, my dad called last night. He wanted to make up for getting mad at me for catching the train. Got us tickets to the Easter Show. Ride passes too."

"If only that's what happened when I ticked off my dad," scoffed Amy.

There was no malice in Amy's voice, but Sienna knew there was a serious edge to her thoughts. There was no violence in Arthur or Janice, never even the threat of it. Sienna reminded herself again that her life wasn't bad. She just wished she knew how to live it.

Stephen met them at the station and drove them home. He was dressed for the office, so Sienna wasn't surprised when he didn't get out of the car.

"Mum and Dad said they'd be late home, but to tell you there was plenty of food in the house," Stephen called, as he drove off.

"So your dad was mad that the train would get us here after they went to work?" asked Amy, looking down at her watch.

"Nup. Wouldn't have made it here in time," replied Sienna.

"They know it's a public holiday, right?" asked Amy, as they walked into the house.

"Don't expect to see them much," said Sienna. "I've come back. Probably think they've won some victory over Uncle Cole. They can go back to being themselves now."

"This is what they were always like?" asked Amy incredulously. "Just dump and run."

"Sometimes reckon they got so used to me not being around they forgot I was supposed to be here. They did once. Year after I came to live here. One Friday night they just never came home. Stephen neither."

"Serious?"

"Was going to call Uncle Cole. He was in Fortune, but knew he'd come. Kept thinking they'd be back before he got here and it'd only cause trouble. Didn't know what to do. Never been alone like that before. Flynn had told me his number, but we'd just hung out at school mostly. Eventually called him. Was crying. Thought he'd think me a real loser. I remember how he smiled when he saw me and laughed when I told him what happened, but there was this hardness in his eyes. For a moment he got real serious and he just said, 'You and me.'

"We hung out the whole weekend. He even stayed over so I wouldn't be alone. Told his parents some lie. They didn't care. He was here when my parents came home. You know what they said?" asked Sienna. Amy shook her head. "Said, 'Oh, Uncle Cole drop you off already?' Made me think I'd gotten it wrong, but they'd booked the plane ticket. Even had someone pick me up from the airport. Stopped trying to be part of things after that."

"You got us now," said Amy. "We've got your back too. And you might think it a drag coming back here, but your friends love the chance to stay in the amazing house – with the pool – and bedrooms made up like hotel rooms."

"Ha, yeah," smiled Sienna. "Glad to help."

Leaving Amy in the spare room, Sienna put her phone on her

bedside table. She hadn't heard from Jackson and was concerned that he'd been rushing home so fast he'd crash. More likely he hadn't even thought of her, but knowing she'd worry if she didn't confirm he was okay, she sent him a text message. Three minutes later, the phone rang.

"My saviour," he cried, as soon as she answered the phone.

"So you got home okay?" she asked.

"Thanks to you. In for it when I get back, but I don't care. Mum was hysterical for almost an hour last night. Or this morning. Don't know. We didn't sleep." Jackson was rambling like he was drunk as he recounted his drive, fearing the phone would ring, ignoring it when it did, and his family's surprise at his late-night arrival. "When you going home?"

"Don't know. My parents were booking the return flights."

"I'm heading back Friday. I can drive you and Amy, if you like. We can do some photo stops on the way."

"Can't. They already went mental I didn't fly up," said Sienna. "Don't need more trouble over transport."

"What are you doing tomorrow? Maybe we can catch up. I need to thank you for getting me out of there."

Sienna explained her and Amy's plans for the Easter Show and was surprised by Jackson's enthusiasm. His brothers were keen to go and tomorrow worked as well for them as any other day.

"How old are his brothers?" asked Amy with a broad smile, as they made their way into the Show. "I wonder if they're as cute as him."

They were due to meet Jackson near the rides. It was less than five minutes before they showed up and Amy's mouth practically fell open at the sight.

"Less obvious," said Sienna in a laughing whisper.

"I bags brother on the end," smiled Amy.

Jackson did the introductions, first his youngest brother Austin, who was sixteen, then his middle brother Avery, who was nineteen. Amy was shy, but one smile from her was all the encouragement Avery needed, and they were chatting like old friends in under a minute.

"Should we start with the rides?" asked Avery. "Jax, we'll get the day passes like the girls."

"Um, actually, you can have mine," offered Sienna. "I'm not really the thrill-seeker type."

It was a lie, but no one called her out on it. She and Flynn had always gone for the biggest, fastest rides – and loved them. It was a memory she wasn't ready to face.

"I don't have to do rides," shrugged Austin.

"Go do rides," said Jackson, pushing him towards Avery. "Here, take this," handing him a hundred dollars. "We can meet up at lunch."

A minute later Sienna and Jackson were alone. They walked off in the opposite direction, but she noticed him looking back over his shoulder.

"It's a little demoralising watching someone who's had a crush on you for ages, dump you within a minute of meeting your little brother," he said.

Sienna laughed. Jackson smiled at her. It made her stomach twist and her cheeks flush. There was something alluring about seeing Flynn smile at her like that; the combination suddenly attractive to her in a way it hadn't been last year.

They wandered aimlessly, neither of them having a destination in mind. The place was packed and after they got temporarily separately, Sienna found her hand in Jackson's, his grip tight. She grasped back, hoping for a sign that Flynn approved.

"Come on, Miss No Thrill-Seeker," said Jackson, pulling her towards a long queue. "Let's see if you can survive this."

"No, no, Jax, seriously. I'm okay. I don't want to go on rides," she said anxiously.

"One ride. For me. Come on. It'll be fine."

Sienna was so anxious she thought she would vomit. Tears burned her eyes, but she kept them at bay as they shuffled towards the front of the line. Jackson chuckled every so often, clearly misinterpreting her anxiety. When they were finally seated in the round cage of the sling shot that would fling them high in the air before bouncing them slowly back to earth, Sienna's heart cracked open.

"You scared?"

"Uh huh."

"Why?"

"We might crash and die."

"But we'll die together. So hold me tight, okay. You ain't goin' nowhere without me."

Flynn's arms seemed to wrap around Sienna's body, as if he was the harness holding her in the chair. She gripped it tight and closed her eyes, hearing their cheers in her ear as they accelerated straight up. Adrenalin coursed through her, and the joy of being back with Flynn brought a genuine smile to her face.

A groan caught her ear. Jackson's hands were over his face as they bounced up and down in ever-shorter rotations. The sight was jarring against the feelings that had swamped her body moments ago. Sienna held her harness tighter, trying to feel Flynn's arms around her once more.

"I think I'm gunna puke," Jackson muttered, as he stumbled from the ride.

Sienna placed a guiding hand on his shoulder and led him to a bench where he proceeded to hang his head between his knees. The sight made her chuckle. It was clear he shared nothing else with Flynn but his smile.

"Will take your unaffected state to mean you were lying before," Jackson groaned, lifting his head.

"Was that a lie detector test?"

"Yeah, something like that," he replied, coughing up a laugh. "Urgh, you could at least pretend to feel as bad as I do."

"How bout I promise not to tell anyone how bad you look."

Jackson took it, before asking if she'd brought her camera. It was a pointless question. She rarely went anywhere without it. This wasn't quite her scene, but it was an interesting challenge.

When lunch time came around, they all converged on the arena, seeking out a place to sit. Jackson went with Avery and Amy to find food, dismissing Austin's ability to buy Sienna food she would eat.

"You a fussy eater?" asked Austin.

"Guess," Sienna shrugged.

"You can say no," Austin replied, causing her to turn.

"Just don't like take-away food much."

"Better that way round," he said, surprising her with his lack of retorts. "Um, we'd better move – unless you brought sunscreen. You're already looking pink."

Sienna felt her face. It was hot. Austin led her around to another section of the arena. He made the conversation, chatting endlessly. It was easy, but it could not stop her attention being caught by the stares and pointed fingers stabbing her. It should have been enough to keep her eyes forward, but she turned and found herself face to face with a group of kids from her and Flynn's old schools.

Nobody spoke. There were no smiles or scowls. Just stares. Ashton's girlfriend Keisha Wells was at the centre of the group, tears filling her eyes. Moments later, the group closed in around her.

"This way," said Austin, leading Sienna to seats in the shade. "You okay?" Sienna couldn't answer. "If it's any consolation, they looked just as shocked to see you."

"You know them?" she asked, surprised.

"Saw the crash on the news. Knew all bout it even before Jax met you. You guys are only a year older than me."

"Don't tell no one," said Sienna desperately. "Please. They'll freak and make a big deal. I just – please."

"Sure," shrugged Austin. "Just get the panic off your face or they'll know something happened."

Sienna became even more stressed. Austin tapped her leg and pointed to the stunt bikes that were performing in the arena. He drew her attention to details she'd never considered before – the rev of the engine, the position of the wheels on the ramps. Jackson and Amy still knew something had happened, but Austin covered it smoothly with a story about her freaking out about a rider almost falling off his bike.

"I'm sorry you got stuck with Austin," said Amy, as she and Sienna slumped down on Amy's bed.

They had arrived home much later than they expected. Sienna had intended to be home for dinner, but Avery insisted they stay so Amy could see the night show and fireworks. Yet once they had seats saved, he and Amy ducked off and missed half the show.

"I don't mind," replied Sienna truthfully. "Austin's nice"

"Didn't cramp your style? Jax looked like he could've done without the company."

"He has a girlfriend and I don't like him like that."

"Yeah. Right," laughed Amy.

"How bout you tell me what happened with you and Avery," retorted Sienna. "Since you were so keen to lose your third wheel."

"Just kissed," smiled Amy, her cheeks flushing.

"So you going out with him?"

"We live five hours apart," replied Amy. "Reckon we'll stick to the holiday fling."

"You okay with that?" asked Sienna, taking Amy's hand.

"Yeah," Amy nodded convincingly. "Couldn't happen back home. They'd know my family. I get to just have the good bits this way."

Amy's phone buzzed, a blush rising up her cheeks. Sienna smiled and excused herself. Lying down on her own bed, she closed her eyes and put in her earphones. She had Flynn's final message on loop, serenading her to sleep. When she dreamed, it was of Flynn, but during the night he slowly morphed into Jackson. Only Flynn's smile remained.

INSIDE OUT

If Amy wasn't on the phone with Avery she was out with him. She tried to be apologetic, but it was clear she was having too good a time. Sienna wasn't resentful, just lonely. Her parents and Stephen worked all weekend. They came home for late dinners and talked mainly about work. Occasionally they asked about her day, but they were always more disturbed by her art than supportive of it.

"Jackson!" cried Janice warmly, practically dragging him into the lounge room when he turned up at the house on Monday night with Amy and Avery. "It's wonderful to see you again. Please, join us for supper."

Jackson couldn't have refused if he wanted to. Stephen had an arm around his shoulder, leading him to the lounge, while Arthur and Janice were setting drinks on the coffee table. Sienna looked around, but Avery and Amy had disappeared.

"How's it been having Sienna back?" asked Jackson.

"Wonderful," cried Arthur. "Things don't get better when your family's complete."

"Absolutely," said Jackson. "So what've you been doing together?"

"Dinner," Sienna answered, her answer probably too bitter to be passed off as a joke.

"Brat," Stephen muttered under his breath, before starting a conversation with everyone but her.

"How long are you in Sydney?" Janice asked.

"Drive back Friday," said Jackson. "So I can take Sienna and Amy back with me, if you like."

"I thought you were staying the whole holidays," said Arthur, turning on Sienna.

"I never said yes to him," cried Sienna.

"Sorry, I didn't mean to cause problems," said Jackson quickly.

"There's no problem, Jackson," said Janice. "It makes sense for Sienna and Amy to go back with you. We'd just been hoping to spend more time with Sienna."

"You taking time off next week?" asked Sienna.

Arthur didn't answer. Not in front of Jackson. They waited until Jackson and Avery had left before starting their argument. Sienna sat silently through her parents' displeasure, letting the words flow around her until it was decided she should go home with Jackson.

"Want me to cancel my plans with Avery this week?" asked Amy, when they retreated to her room.

"No," sighed Sienna. "Want me to get my dad to fly us home at the end of next week?"

"Nah, Avery's got stuff on next week. Wouldn't see him much anyway," smiled Amy.

Amy left the house early the next morning. Sienna was thankful her phone rang fifteen minutes later.

"Bored? What to catch up?" asked Jackson.

"Yes!" replied Sienna.

"City. One hour."

The sight of Jackson and his smile flooded Sienna with emotion, her dream of Flynn slowly transforming into Jackson playing across her mind.

"Bring your camera?" asked Jackson. Sienna nodded. "Harbour then. My mum wants more photos."

That idea filled Sienna with dread. She hated expectations, but photographing Jackson was so easy she soon forgot her concerns. There was something about his face and the depth of his eyes that made him the perfect subject.

"How's um … your girlfriend?" asked Sienna, as he rested against the trunk of a tree in the Botanic Gardens, the harbour sparkling in the background.

"Alyssa?" he asked with a curious smile. "Yeah, she's okay."

"Yeah, Alyssa, that's right. Missing you?"

"Desperately," smirked Jackson

"You miss her?"

"Yeah, sure," he laughed. "Why?"

"I care," Sienna answered defensively.

"Just not enough to remember her name. I know your boyfriends' names. Even get to know them."

"There's only been one and you didn't know anything about him," she snapped.

"Probably knew him better than you think. I just never gave you my opinion of him."

"How would you know the first thing about him? Sharing his smile doesn't give you some secret insight into him!"

"I was talking about Liam," said Jackson.

Sienna stopped. She'd never thought of Liam as a boyfriend. It was difficult to explain why. They'd done all the things boyfriends and girlfriends did together, yet in her mind he'd been reduced to nothing.

"Sorry," said Jackson sincerely, taking Sienna's hand and drawing her into his lap. "I'd want to forget him too."

They stayed silent for a long time. It took Sienna a while to notice Jackson's hands were stroking her arms. He wasn't looking at her, but past her down to the harbour. When she shifted her body, his eyes returned to her, a smile beaming across his face.

"You reckon I could convince you to take some other photos?"

"What kind of photos?" Sienna asked fearfully.

"My mum's always wanted family portraits. Was thinking you could come by – take some photos on Friday morning before we drive back to Fortune. I'd pick you up."

"Jax, no, don't. I'm not – too much – I —"

"I can pay you," Jackson retorted, pulling away from her.

Sienna shuffled back, sitting on her knees, her hands clasped. "Not that! Me – I can't. I'm not that good. I can't give you what you want. Don't make me let down your mum."

"You wouldn't," smiled Jackson. "I told you, she loves your photos. She wants what you do."

Sienna tried to refuse. Many times. But Jackson wouldn't listen. Nor would anyone else.

"They're pretty excited," said Amy on Wednesday night. She was going to spend her last day – and night – with Avery, so made the effort to be back for dinner.

"And being nervous is perfectly normal," said Arthur.

"Just doesn't give you an excuse for not doing your job," added Janice. "You're not going to cut it as a photographer if you refuse to take photos."

Stephen snickered. Sienna glared at him, but he just shrugged.

It made Sienna wonder if their plan was to organise jobs designed to set her up for failure, just to show her she couldn't make it. Though she was determined to prove them wrong, she was still terrified this wasn't the job that would do it.

"What's going on?" asked Arthur, walking into Sienna's room at five am on Friday morning. He was dressed in running clothes.

"I look all right?" asked Sienna, stepping away from her closet. She was in a dress. It was too cold for it, but it was the best smart casual outfit she had.

"Very pretty. What's it for?"

"Today!" cried Sienna.

"You're just taking some pictures."

Sienna groaned and threw her hands in the air, angrily dismissing him before heading back to her closet. Arthur grabbed her and sat her on her bed.

"You take all your clothes to Fortune?" he asked, going through her cupboards and drawers.

"No, left most of them here."

Arthur didn't respond. Her collection of clothes was very limited outside of school and formalwear.

"Here, how about this?" suggested Arthur, laying out a pair of jeans, a white shirt, black vest and black jacket. "Hopefully it all still fits you. I'm sorry we didn't realise you had so little."

"It's enough," said Sienna, grabbing the clothes and heading to the bathroom to change.

Arthur was still in her bedroom when she emerged. She moved in front of the mirror.

"Wow, Dad, that looks good," said Sienna sincerely.

"So maybe I'm useful after all?"

"You're great, Dad."

"Thanks, Sen," replied Arthur, pulling her into his arms. He held her tight, his chest heaving. "I'm sorry we're not what you want us to be. But we do love you." Sienna was suddenly swamped by guilt. "Got time for a run with your dad before you leave?"

"Heaps now I have something to wear," smiled Sienna.

It was a nice and Sienna made a mental note to suggest they go for runs on her future visits. It was good to have an activity they didn't fight about.

"You look really nice," said Jackson, as they drove towards his house. "But you didn't need to dress up. It's a favour not a job."

"Yeah, but they're your parents. Of course, I have to look nice," replied Sienna. Jackson stared at her for a moment before looking away and she suddenly realised how that must have sounded to him. "How was Amy last night? I wonder if anything happened."

"Not under my parents' roof, it didn't," replied Jackson. "You don't do that there. It's why I always stayed at my girlfriend's place."

Sienna didn't say anything. Her parents had accepted Flynn under their roof – and in her bed – from the age of thirteen.

When Sienna started asking Jackson more about his family, he painted a picture of his mother as a very foreboding woman. Sienna had always considered Janice frightening, but she sounded mellow compared to Jackson's mum. It left her on the verge of vomiting as they approached his house.

It was wasted anxiety. Sienna had never met anyone as welcoming as Mrs Halley. It made her wonder if Jackson had frightened her on purpose or if it was the way he saw her. Jackson's father was much more reserved. There was a shyness about him that Sienna could relate to.

Mrs Halley didn't have any suggestions for what kind of photos she wanted. She loved the photos of Jackson so much that she wanted Sienna to decide everything. Sienna wanted to vomit again.

They all left her alone in the lounge room. Sienna put down her bags and took out her camera. Holding it up to her eye, she tried to find the scene in her head, but no matter how she adjusted the light, she couldn't make it work. Moving to the next room, she took a deep breath to keep the tears at bay. She couldn't do this.

Lowering the camera, Sienna let her eyes take in the scene. The house reminded her of where she'd lived with Uncle Cole as a child. It was old, but the care taken with its interior helped to defy its age. It was so homely and comforting, yet every time she lifted the camera to her eye, the visions in her mind dissolved.

Resolved to telling Jackson she was out of her depth, Sienna wandered through the house until she came to a bedroom where all three brothers were getting ready. Austin was already dressed, while Avery was straightening himself up. Only Jackson was half-dressed, his top in his hand.

"Hey, photo girl," smiled Avery. "Going the candid shot?"

"I was just looking for where we could do the shoot," replied Sienna nervously, knowing she wouldn't find anywhere.

Jackson turned away from her.

"You find somewhere?" asked Austin.

"Um, maybe," Sienna lied. A brief flash of inspiration hit and she quickly lifted her camera to her eye. Ignoring the evaporation of the vision, she clicked the button and hoped it would turn out better than was she saw through the lens.

"We starting?" Avery asked cheerfully. "Want us half-naked like Jax?"

Avery didn't wait for an answer. He stripped off his top and, with a nudge, Austin was similarly undressed. They immediately struck a pose. Sienna didn't think. She just took photos. They would be terrible, but they would be something.

It took some coaxing, but Jackson soon joined in the frivolity. Sienna was just starting to get comfortable with the setting when Mrs Halley came in and ordered everyone to get dressed.

"Sienna," called Austin. "Amy's in the backyard. I think she wanted to talk to you before we started."

Sienna nodded and rushed out, hoping Amy could help her out of this mess. Amy must have seen how frantic she was, because she immediately had an arm around her shoulders. "It's fine. You'll find a spot," she said consolingly. "What about out here? Have you looked here yet?"

Wiping her eyes, Sienna looked around the backyard. There was a cluttered chaos about it, trees and scrubs lining every fence, while every patch of concrete was covered with pots filled with plants and flowers. Sienna suddenly felt at ease. She lifted her camera to her eye and started taking photos. Moving Amy around, she judged the light and scenery.

"Better?" asked Amy. Sienna nodded. "I'll go get them."

Jackson and his family arrived a couple of minutes later. The boys were all dressed in jeans and white t-shirts, while Mrs Halley was in a black-and-white dress. Mrs Halley tried to get the boys in order, fussing over their hair and the way their t-shirts sat. Sienna moved around them, quietly capturing the scene. Avery soon noticed and posed in the background away from his mother's eye.

Sienna insisted Mrs Halley describe the types of photos she wanted. Most important were some serious ones, which Sienna did quickly. They mixed up the combinations of parents and children. Sienna then moved on to some of her own inspiration, making sure she took a number of shots with Mr and Mrs Halley together and some of Mrs Halley alone. The final photo was of the family linked in a huddle, looking down at Sienna as she took the photo from the ground.

"Can you do a couple more?" whispered Amy, rushing to Sienna's side as they started to pack up. "Of me and Avery."

Avery was quick to agree with the suggestion. Sienna moved them to a corner of the yard under a tree. She expected romantic poses, but they were much more interested in playful shots. Sienna convinced them to take one serious picture, but it was the best she could manage.

"I'd better get started on lunch," said Mrs Halley, dashing towards the house.

"Not for us, Mum," said Jackson quickly. "We've got to go."

"But it's eleven-thirty. You'll be hungry in an hour. Won't take long," insisted Mrs Halley.

"Gotta get back. Having dinner with Alyssa," replied Jackson. "We'll pick something up on the way."

"Oh yeah, Alyssa, the girl you talk about all the time," Austin said sarcastically.

Jackson shoved Austin hard in the shoulder before walking inside. Sienna was confused, but followed Jackson into the house and quickly packed up. Amy was much slower. By the time her bags were in the car, lunch was on the table, but Jackson was adamant. They had to go.

Sienna jumped in the car immediately, concerned by Jackson's dark mood. Amy took her time, saying a private goodbye to Avery, but when they parted there were only smiles.

It was a silent drive. Jackson didn't look Sienna's way, keeping his eyes forward. They stopped two hours later for food and petrol.

"I told you I wasn't a professional," she said to him, when Amy went to the bathroom. "You shouldn't have promised your mum good photos."

"The photos are fine, Sienna. Don't worry," Jackson replied tersely.

"Then what did I do wrong?" she asked, realising she had offended Jackson with more than her substandard photography skills.

"Nothing, but you're right. Should never have taken you there. I should've found somewhere else to take photos."

"I don't get it. The backyard was nice. Gave it a real homey feel," said Sienna.

"Yeah, that was the look on your face. All homey," snarled Jackson bitterly. "Wouldn't have taken you so long to find places to take photos in your mansion."

Sienna's breath hitched. She tried to conjure the right words, but she didn't know why it'd been such a struggle. Jackson just glared at her and shook his head. The same hatred she'd seen last year burned in his eyes.

Sienna sat in the back with Amy on the rest of the drive home. Amy appeared completely unaware of the tension surrounding her as she gazed out the window, a soft smile on her face. It wasn't until Jackson pulled up in front of Sienna's house and dumped their bags on the footpath that her head snapped up.

"Thanks for the lift," said Amy sincerely. "And thanks for letting me spend so much time with your family. It was really great. You're real lucky."

"Yeah, sure," Jackson muttered, before jumping back in the car and screeching off.

"What's going on?" asked Amy.

"Nothing. Don't worry about it," smiled Sienna.

Amy nodded and smiled, apparently too happy to worry about anything.

~23~

BLACK AND WHITE

Sienna locked herself in the house for the second half of the holidays. She needed to start on her major artwork. The basic design was mapped out, along with drafts of some of the images, but there was something terrifying about starting the real thing. It felt like she was cutting herself open so she could imprint her soul on the paper.

Needing more space than her room provided, Sienna set herself up in the lounge room. She intended to pack it up before Uncle Cole arrived home, but once she started she became so engrossed that time escaped her.

"What's this?" asked Uncle Cole, stomping into the lounge room. Sienna explained without looking up. "They tell you to do this? Part of your therapy? Dwelling on it won't make things better."

"Was my idea," Sienna replied defensively. "And it's not dwelling." Uncle Cole stepped forward and looked at the draft sketch of the full image. His fingers traced over it. "Besides, this is for school. Gunna be judged against the whole state. Gotta give 'em what they want."

"Yeah, they'll want this," replied Uncle Cole. "You still on the drafts or you started?"

"Something's holding me back. Dunno what."

Uncle Cole laid the draft image on the coffee table and questioned the intention of each section. They started talking technique and tested out their ideas in her sketch books. It was midnight before they even looked at the clock.

"Just make sure you pack it away before anyone comes over," said Uncle Cole, as they made their way to bed. "I'll let you know if the guys are coming by."

Something of their old relationship rebuilt that week. Uncle Cole always had time for her art. It didn't matter how late he arrived home or how early he needed to get up, if she spoke to him about her artwork, he would stop what he was doing and turn to her. His ability to sketch what she described was phenomenal. Sienna knew he had to be still drawing himself to be able to do such things, but whenever she alluded to it, he moved the conversation on.

Sienna made a lot of progress with her artwork, but by the end of the week there was a deep feeling of unease in her stomach. She couldn't quite place it, but assumed it was the result of spending all the hours she wasn't drawing working on the photos of Jackson's family. There were a couple that had captured Jackson's disgust. Sienna often found herself staring at them, trying to erase his scowl and replace it with Flynn's smile.

When the first day of term arrived, Sienna surprised herself by waking with a sense of steely resolve. She felt she was returning to the girl she'd been before Flynn's death. She didn't take things to heart and could ignore what pained her – unless she was working on her art project.

That strange dichotomy of strength and vulnerability made her even less enthusiastic about attending her psychologist appointment, and she determined that if someone wasn't waiting to take her, she would go straight home.

The sight of a clear street that afternoon made Sienna sigh with relief.

"Hey! Aren't you going today?"

Sienna took a deep breath and turned to face Jackson. He was a few metres behind her, half-out his car door. She'd only made it a block from school.

"I thought I was taking you," he added as if she'd rejected him.

"You weren't there and I haven't heard from you in two weeks," Sienna replied.

Jackson shrugged and muttered something about being busy. He didn't insist she go with him, but he waited until she felt awkward enough about their mid-street conversation to get in the car. If she didn't go, it would get back to her parents and they would blame Uncle Cole.

Reaching into her bag, Sienna pulled out the USB of photos and handed them to Jackson. "I would've sent it to your mum, but I didn't have her address."

"You could've got it off Amy," replied Jackson, dropping the USB into the middle compartment.

Sienna had never considered that. Closing her eyes, she accepted that Jackson wouldn't forgive her transgression, but she didn't have to continue to expose herself to his anger. "I'll catch the bus home," she said, as soon as he stopped the car in Westloch.

"You don't want me to take you home?"

"You don't want to take me home," she said. "And I hate these sessions enough without adding another level of torture."

Jackson was waiting for her at the end of the session. He said nothing as they walked to the car and stayed just as silent on the drive home. Sienna kept her gaze out the window until they pulled up in front of her house.

"Thanks," she said, as she got out of the car.

Jackson only nodded before speeding off.

"You didn't talk to him about spheres again, did you?" asked Amber, when the topic of Jackson came up the next day and Sienna again couldn't provide any information on how he was going.

"No," answered Sienna. "All I know is it's got something to do with the photos I took at his place."

"That's crazy," said Amy. "Avery told me his mum was real happy. And he had a great time. Thought you were real good. They can't wait to see the photos."

"So what could've happened?" asked Amber.

"Jackson made out like I acted too good for his place," admitted Sienna guiltily.

"What?" cried Amber.

"Aww, shit. I think I know," said Amy. The look on Amy's face made Sienna want to vomit. "You do this thing. Remember dragging me through your house to take photos? You kept trying to find – I dunno what – but you never found it. You had this look on your face – real unimpressed. As soon as we got outside, you were fine. Wasn't until you dragged me back inside that I worked out you don't like taking photos indoors."

Sienna was shocked. When she thought about it, she realised Amy was right, but she never would've figured it out herself.

"I did that at Jackson's house?" asked Sienna mournfully.

"Yeah," nodded Amy apologetically. "Avery noticed. Asked if you always made a rotten egg face when you took photos. I didn't know what he meant so snuck a look at you. We laughed when I explained. Told him to wait 'til you figured out you needed to go outside."

"That's why Austin told me to go outside looking for you?"

Amy nodded. "He thought it was mean we didn't just tell you. I'm sorry. I didn't think it would be an issue. Just thought they would've told Jackson as well."

"Screw it," said Sienna, even though she felt sick to the stomach. "We're leaving at the end of the year and I won't see him again. He can hate me. I don't care."

But she did care. Flynn's smile lived on in Jackson. She hated that she'd lost it and knew she'd take almost any opportunity to see it again.

Flynn's hidden smile was the only thing that got Sienna in the car with Jackson the following Thursday. It stayed hidden the whole trip to Westloch and tainted her session with a sense of loss, though she tried hard not to speak about it. Taking a deep breath as she walked outside, she prepared herself for Jackson not to be there, but he was sitting on the bonnet of his car, speaking on his phone. He waved as she approached. It was the friendliest gesture she'd received from him since their return to Fortune, but she couldn't trust it.

Waiting in the car, Sienna kept her head down. It wasn't until he nudged her arm that she realised he was holding his phone out. "It's my mum," he muttered, when she didn't move.

Sienna put the phone tentatively to her ear. "Hello?"

"Oh, Sienna, dear, thank you for the photos. We got them on Monday. They're just wonderful. We can't wait to get them printed."

"You liked them?" asked Sienna, unsure of Mrs Halley's sincerity.

"Oh, yes. Thank you so much. I've only ever dreamed of having such beautiful photos of my family on the wall."

"If you let me know which ones are your favourites, I'll get them enlarged," urged Sienna.

"Oh, no, you've done enough," replied Mrs Halley cheerfully.

"Please. I want to."

"Okay, dear. We'll let you know," said Mrs Halley in a gentle voice. "Thank you again, dear."

Sienna nodded and handed the phone back to Jackson. He spoke to his mother for a few minutes before tossing his phone into the middle compartment and screeching off. There was something angry about his silence and Sienna was glad the trip felt shorter than usual, jumping out as soon as the car slammed to a stop.

"The photos were fine," said Jackson, stepping out of the car as Sienna turned in half-circles. He'd pulled over at the lookout. "You didn't have to make a thing about it with my mum. Now she thinks something's wrong."

"Something is wrong!" cried Sienna. "I told you I wasn't a proper photographer. I couldn't give you what you wanted. And now you hate me."

"No, I took you into my home, introduced you to my family, and you turned up your nose at them," spat Jackson. "I know I don't live in a mansion. I know there wasn't lots of great places to take photos, but I thought you were better than that."

"I don't live in a mansion either."

Jackson turned away. Sienna shifted her bag on her shoulder and started walking towards Fortune.

"So I'm s'pose to believe Austin's fanciful story about you not being able to take photos inside," Jackson called after her. She didn't answer. "You're the best photographer I know. It can't be true. There's no fucking difference!"

Sienna refused to defend herself. It'd never made any difference, and it was clear Jackson, like her parents, was determined to believe his own truths about her.

Jackson's car stalked her down the road. Sienna kept her eyes forward, but she couldn't avoid him when he pulled the car across her path and jumped out. "Get in," he demanded. Sienna stood her ground. "Get in. You can't walk."

Not waiting for her assent, Jackson grabbed her arm and pulled her towards the car. Sienna didn't resist. But for the second time that night she jumped out of the car expecting to be home, only to be thrown by her location.

"Why are we here?" she asked, looking up at Jackson's apartment block.

"Because I want you to prove to me it wasn't my house you were disgusted with," he answered. "Got your camera?"

Sienna didn't move and again Jackson took her by the arm. She was shaking by the time he released her in his lounge room. He walked to the other side of the room and stood there staring at her, his arms folded.

"What do expect me to take photos of?" she asked, thinking she would have to remember to leave her camera at home next Thursday.

"Anything! Me. The pot plant. I don't care. Just do it!"

"I can't!" she cried, tears filling her eyes.

"Why not? You can take photos anywhere. Take them here," snapped Jackson. "Where do you want me? Come on, position me like you normally do."

Sienna fumbled for her camera, determined to take a couple of pictures then run from the place and never look back. But even that wasn't easy. She wasn't used to lifting the camera to her eye and taking photos she didn't like.

It didn't matter. Whatever test Jackson had set for her, she passed. Within minutes there was a smile on his face and his arms were wrapped around her. "What's wrong with you?" he asked. "You're a photographic genius. How does this stump you? And why didn't I know?"

Sienna didn't answer. Jackson's reversion to pleasantness was as disturbing as his transition to nastiness and all she wanted was to go home.

"We'll take photos today," said Jackson, when he picked up Sienna after her session the following Thursday.

Sienna tried to quell the distrust in her stomach. He'd been nothing but lovely all week, joining her for two runs, and now he was smiling as though there hadn't been weeks of hostility between them.

Jackson chatted jovially as he drove. Sienna tried to respond in kind, but was struggling. Hopefully a photo stop at the lookout would help quell her agitation, but he didn't take her there.

"I can't take photos here," she growled, following him into his apartment.

"How's that even possible? You take amazing photos. How much difference can it make being inside or out?"

"Heaps!"

Jackson walked over to her. There was something approaching compassion in his expression. "Try," he urged.

Their eyes met. His gaze was hypnotic, and when he smiled softly, Sienna felt Flynn reach out for her. She nodded slowly, moving away to inspect the apartment, trying to silence the part of her brain that was screaming out at the ridiculousness of this attempt.

"Find anything?" asked Jackson, joining her at his bedroom door.

Perhaps she'd been there too long, because she couldn't deny the answer. She had found something. She just wasn't sure she could make it work. "I was thinking about the bedroom," she confessed reluctantly. Jackson grinned. "Don't be foul."

"Okay, I'm sorry. What do you want?" he asked. Sienna didn't know. The frustration was crippling. His arms were tender but firm as he restrained her. "What about this?" he asked, looking down at his arm pressing against hers. "Your black–white theme. Can't you use that? Help you find what you're looking for."

"Sure, but who's going to pose with you?" asked Sienna.

"What about you?" asked Jackson.

"I have to take the photos, remember."

"Camera has a timer. You have a tripod. Better it's just me and you, don't you think."

Jackson turned her to face him, Flynn's grin drawing her into his crazy plan.

"You don't need to do anything. Just lie there," said Sienna, waving Jackson away.

They'd been at it for over an hour, but she still wasn't sure she had the light right. Jackson was surprised by how much she was investing in the shoot, but if she was going to try and make it work, then it couldn't be a half-arsed job.

The white sheets were crisp against the black of Jackson's skin. Sienna had him dressed in just a pair of white underwear. It had been confronting seeing him strip, but now she was behind the camera his near-nakedness was almost inconsequential. Jackson kept asking her to join him, convinced she wouldn't get a real feel for the shot until she was in it, but she knew she had to make the shoot work with him alone first.

It took three weeks, but Sienna was finally ready to join Jackson. She was dressed in a tight black t-shirt and short black tights. Getting the focus right while using the timer was the next challenge. That took another two weeks. Then Sienna found herself in Jackson's arms.

The realisation took her breath away. Up until that moment, her focus had been solely on the photography, but now she was the subject and she couldn't keep taking photos of her concerned face. The black and white of their limbs needed to be entwined. It was so easy to envisage from the other side of the camera, but to be a part of that embrace was something else entirely.

Jackson's touch was electrifying and terrifying all at once. It was something Sienna didn't know how to process and wouldn't make the next stage of the photo shoot any easier.

Thankfully, the winter holidays provided a legitimate escape. Arthur and Janice all but insisted she come back to Sydney for the break. With the time she and Uncle Cole were spending together on her major artwork, it was easier to discuss the topic. Uncle Cole was still sceptical of their desire to appear so involved in her life, but raised no objections.

"You going to come?" Sienna asked Amy. "My parents are happy to pay your airfare. We have to fly this time."

"Uh, the pain," laughed Amy. "I want to, but ..."

"But what?" asked Sienna. "Cos Amber can't come?"

"No, it's ... okay, don't hate me, but if I went back, I'd want to spend most of my time with Avery. There's only so many days you can swan around a mansion."

"Sorry, you should've told me."

"No, not like that," cried Amy, grabbing Sienna's hand. "You're different there. On edge. Go into yourself. But when you do that, you draw. I don't have that escape."

"Well, you do now," said Sienna. "Come. See Avery. It'll be fine."

"But I want to keep it secret," grimaced Amy. "Even Amber doesn't know about Avery – except that I met him as Jackson's brother. I want to keep it like that. I just – it's —"

"It's okay. I get it. Just come back in time for dinner and no one will ever know."

~24~

DEMONS

The week in Sydney went by so fast Sienna felt it like it didn't happen. Arthur and Janice tried to insist she stay another week. They wanted to spend more time with her, but it would never matter how much time she spent there if they never took the time away from work to see her. Thankfully, she had the excuse of needing to study and work on her art project, and so she was allowed to return to Fortune with minimal opposition.

Sienna's major artwork was starting to take shape, but that created issues she'd never envisaged. Perhaps she drew her demons too well, because every time she put her artwork up in the lounge room it felt like they leapt straight off the page, stalking her as she worked.

In a way, she was grateful for their presence. It made it easier to create the cloud of darkness that had surrounded her during the months leading up to her suicide attempt. She sat in the middle of it; Flynn with her, but not really there – forever kept from her in heaven.

The urge to join Flynn grew by the day, even though she knew she had things to live for and it scared her. Going to Uncle Cole was out of the question, and seeing her in this state would frighten Amy and Amber. It left Sienna no choice. She rushed to the bus stop and headed into Westloch, but Dr Chousalkar didn't provide the relief she was looking for.

"If you're worried about what you might do to yourself, we can admit you," said Dr Chousalkar. Sienna imagined Dr Chousalkar was trying to be supportive, but that was the last thing she wanted. "Just for a couple of days."

"No!" cried Sienna, rushing from the room.

She ran from the office, hoping Dr Chousalkar wouldn't chase her and commit her against her will. The bus came almost immediately. Sienna boarded, her heart hammering. She couldn't go back home. It left her with only one place.

"Hey, what's going on?" asked Jackson hesitantly, as he opened the door to his apartment.

"I need your help," Sienna stuttered. She tried to explain, but Jackson shushed her, pulling her into the apartment and to the lounge.

"If I gave you a knife right now, what would you do with it?"

Sienna looked up in horror. The images in her head created such a contrast in desires that she didn't know what would happen. Maybe Jackson hadn't forgiven her. Perhaps he wanted her dead.

"You're going to stay with me, okay," said Jackson, holding her tight. "You want to talk?" Sienna shook her head. "Okay."

They stayed silent. Jackson shifted his body, moving her into his lap and holding her against his chest. He stroked her hair, urging her to rest. She closed her eyes. Tiredness swamped her body.

It was warm and cosy, but when Jackson shifted Sienna jerked awake.

"Shh, close your eyes. You're fine."

"Uncle Cole?"

There was a chill around Sienna's body and she realised she was being slipped into her own, cold bed. Uncle Cole pulled the quilt over her, tucking her in. He stroked her hair and held her hand, promising to stay until she fell asleep.

"How you feeling?" asked Uncle Cole, when Sienna tiptoed out of her room the next morning. She shrugged half-heartedly. "I have to go to work. Let me show you something first."

Uncle Cole walked towards the lounge room. Sienna followed reluctantly. She was scared of facing her artwork, but pulled up short when she saw it rolled and clipped so only a part of the full image was visible.

"You can't let it overwhelm you," he said. "Break it down. One little section at a time. Focus on the technique. It's just art."

"No, it's not," gasped Sienna, tears spilling down her cheeks.

Uncle Cole turned her so their eyes met. "It has to be. Or you need to stop," he said feelingly. "You have an amazing gift. But you need to detach from it."

"I can't."

"You can," he said firmly. "Imagine you're looking at it through your camera. Break it down and view it through a lens."

"I'll try," she whispered, and Uncle Cole pulled her into a tender embrace.

Life was like a see-saw. Sienna's mood could change with the minutes, not just the hours or the days. It made her fear her return to Dr Chousalkar, worried she wouldn't be able to hide her demons well enough to prevent her from being committed.

"Sienna, you okay?" asked Uncle Cole anxiously, when she walked into his office.

"I don't want to go," she gasped, tears falling down her cheeks.

"To school?" he asked confusedly. Sienna shook her head. "You don't have to."

"But they'll ask – they want me – if they find out why —"

"I'll handle it."

"I don't want you to fight," whispered Sienna.

"I haven't fought enough for you," muttered Uncle Cole. "Trust me. You're not going. Head to school and I'll sort it out."

Sienna nodded, but her fears about a fight were well-founded. Uncle Cole didn't back down. Sienna was impressed that he didn't mention anything about the traumas her artwork had been causing her, sticking to the story that she just didn't like Dr Chousalkar.

"Then find her someone else!" growled Arthur.

"Or just let her focus on her studies," retorted Uncle Cole. "These appointments have caused her nothing but stress and now you want to submit her to more with just months left before her exams."

"And if she kills herself?" asked Arthur sardonically.

"Even you can't be naïve enough to believe that one appointment would be enough to prevent that," snapped Uncle Cole.

"We're just worried about her," said Janice.

"Then trust her when she says she wants to stop," said Uncle Cole.

Arthur finally conceded, but not without insisting on hearing Sienna speak the words herself. Uncle Cole sat next to her, his arm around her shoulders as she stutteringly explained how much she disliked her sessions with Dr Chousalkar.

When they finally hung up, Uncle Cole pulled her into a warm embrace. "Don't be afraid to come to me. I'll back you up."

"Only against my parents?"

"No. Even against me," he replied. "I've made things harder than they had to be for you here. You being taken away from me – the things that happened over those years – it wasn't your fault. I'm not a perfect parent."

"But you're my parent," replied Sienna without thinking. "I mean – no – just —"

"Our secret," whispered Uncle Cole.

That promise was reassuring, but Sienna was glad she didn't have any expectations of it changing anything. Life didn't suddenly become easy to live and there was no quelling of the usual familial tensions. The only reprieve was Uncle Cole's grudging acceptance of her friendship with Jackson, though he never masked his disapproval.

"Don't listen to him," said Amber. "Your olds are going to either love or hate your boyfriend. Definitely more likely to hate if he's older."

"Jackson's not my boyfriend," said Sienna.

"Right, and how are those naked photo sessions going again?" asked Amy, trying to keep a straight face.

"We're not naked yet," said Sienna.

"Yet?" questioned Amber.

Sienna had lost her nerve during the last shoot. When Jackson's hands had moved up her waist, it had taken all her control not to slap it away. The last thing she wanted was to be attracted to him. But if she could teach herself to slowly detach from her major artwork, then she could learn to detach from him as he held her in front of her camera.

"So what's the plan for today?" asked Jackson, as they ate an early Saturday breakfast.

"More photos," replied Sienna.

"Yeah, got that. Same thing?"

"Bit different."

"Really? Hope we're not losing more clothes," he laughed. Sienna's face fell. "Oh, we are." He took a deep breath and nodded.

"Not you," Sienna murmured.

"Oh." Jackson tried to hide his smile.

"This isn't – just promise – I know you wouldn't, but —"

"Sienna, trust me," said Jackson seriously. "I'd never hurt you."

Sienna couldn't finish her breakfast. By the time Jackson was in position on the bed in his underwear, her heart was hammering so hard it hurt. Slipping off her top, she was down to her bra and undies. It was a fact she tried to forget, telling herself it was no different to swimmers, but when she moved on to the bed, the camera timer ticking down and Jackson's arms snaking around her body, it was hard to be convinced.

"How're they going?" asked Jackson, when Sienna took the camera off the tripod.

They'd been at it for over two hours. She didn't let herself really look at the shots as she went, rather changed things just a little each time, hoping something good would be captured.

Jackson was suddenly behind her, peering over her shoulder at the images. "We look good together," he said, his arms wrapping around her waist.

They did, but Sienna had so few pictures of herself that she struggled to believe she was the womanly creature he was holding so intimately. It was impossible not to think of herself as the young girl grasped in Flynn's arms.

"Are you still seeing Alyssa?"

"Nup," replied Jackson, unmoved. "And if I were, one look at those photos would end it real quick."

"But we're not doing anything. It's just modelling," said Sienna.

"Yeah, just modelling," repeated Jackson, before taking a deep breath and stepping away. "So maybe now's a good time to tell you I got my transfer," he said casually, as he dressed.

"What?" cried Sienna. "But you said it'd take ages."

"It's felt like ages."

"When?" she asked, her voice barely above a whisper.

"Week after my birthday."

Sienna could only nod. Less than five weeks. "Then you'll be gone forever," she whispered to herself, trying to comprehend the loss of another piece of Flynn.

"Forever from Fortune, yeah."

PARTY

The ticking of the clock boomed in Sienna's ear. Seconds, minutes, hours, all marching her towards another birthday without Flynn.

"Sen, you're going to be late," called Uncle Cole from the kitchen. She didn't move. "Don't get up and I'll assume you're terrified of your parents coming out today. I'll call and tell them not to."

Sienna groaned loudly and rolled out of bed, stomping heavily so he could hear. Since her parents insisted on coming out to celebrate her birthday, she insisted it not happen on her actual birthday. The weekend before was the closest she could accept.

"You have to keep moving, Sen. It's the only way forward," said Uncle Cole in a gruff impersonation of supportiveness when she trudged into the kitchen.

"Don't want to," she muttered, heading for the bathroom.

"I'm not asking you to enjoy it. I'm telling you to survive it."

Sienna turned. He was leaning against the bench, coffee in hand. There was no smile on his face. He was deadly serious, but there was compassion in his eyes – as though he knew just how much she wanted to rebuff him. She tried to take on the advice. It was practically Uncle Cole's motto – get on, get moving, go towards the future. It was a tactic her parents would no doubt endorse – if they didn't know who it came from – though she always felt their view on moving on was to bury the past. They wanted her to bury her feelings for Flynn like they had his body. Perhaps it was what they'd expected her to do with her confusion over their absence from her life.

Sitting at her desk, dressed, but not ready to face school – or the weekend the end of the day would bring – she reached for her computer and recklessly clicked on a video. Flynn immediately came to life in front of her. Nearly two years he'd been gone and yet her heart yearned for him as if it were only yesterday.

"We'll walk home with you," said Amber, when the final bell rang.

Amy nodded in agreement.

"I don't need you guys witnessing the calamity of my family," Sienna replied glumly.

"We never said we were coming in," Amy chuckled.

Amber laughed and Sienna couldn't help but lift her lips slightly, but that faded when Uncle Cole's patrol car pulled up in front of the school gates.

"Your parents are coming in on the last plane," he said, hopping out of the car and speaking over the roof. "I need to work late. Arranged to be home for an hour now when they were supposed to arrive. You girls mind keeping her amused?"

"Sure, Chief," Amber replied compliantly.

"They should be here by eight-thirty," Uncle Cole added gruffly. "I'll be home by nine hopefully."

Sienna sighed and nodded. Uncle Cole looked at her for a moment before sliding back into the car and driving off.

"Milkshakes!" exclaimed Amy, dragging Sienna towards the shops and away from her dark thoughts.

"Oh, Sen, gosh, we've missed you," cried Janice, pulling her into a hug as soon as she opened the door.

Arthur quickly followed, expressing the same sentiments. As did Stephen. It was a lot of missing from people who always claimed they'd be on the first flight of the day. They immediately started asking about her major artwork, hoping they could see it, forgetting that she'd told them the submission deadline was two weeks ago.

"I have photos though."

Sienna set up the laptop and went through the images, starting with the whole and moving into the close-ups of the different sections. Stephen, Arthur and Janice huddled around. Feeling more confident, Sienna started to explain the different techniques she used, but stopped when Arthur suddenly grabbed the laptop. He flicked rapidly through the images, back and forth, zooming in on the ribbons of writing – her fears and insecurities – that created the black fog that encased her.

"This is what you think of us?" questioned Arthur. "You submitted this, slandering the family, for the whole world to see."

"Arthur," Janice chided, but he started reading from the screen, quickly pulling her and Stephen to his point of view.

Uncle Cole walked into the room. Sienna turned and saw the pleasant mask fall from his face. "What's going on?" he asked gruffly.

"Have you seen these?" asked Arthur, pointing furiously at the screen.

"I'll do you one better. I saw the real thing. Quite a masterpiece. I hope that's what's stunning you," replied Uncle Cole.

"Masterpiece? You're kidding me," spat Arthur. "You should've shown us what she was drawing."

"Why?" asked Uncle Cole.

"I don't think we would've agreed to Sienna stopping her therapy sessions if we knew she'd been working on this," said Janice.

"I was more confident letting her stop because she was working on that," countered Uncle Cole. "Look at it. Really look at it. Your daughter has drawn about the darkest moment of her life – not just that moment, but all the demons that chased her to that point. You fear it because you can see them. Feel them. They're practically alive. Dancing off the page."

"Exactly!" spat Arthur.

"I challenge you to draw your emotions as superbly as Sienna has hers," said Uncle Cole. "Try putting on canvas not what you see, but what you feel. Sienna will never be able to put that into words, but in that one image she's all but written the history of her life."

"I think you're ignoring the words she did write," Arthur snarled.

"You're concerned about how your daughter feels or what someone else might think?" asked Uncle Cole.

"We're not concerned about our reputation," snapped Janice. "But what she's said …"

"What she felt," corrected Uncle Cole. "Are you going to sit here and blame your daughter for how she feels about her relationship with you? Blame her for her hurt and confusion? I can tell you it wasn't easy seeing her distress over our relationship, but I'm thankful for the chance to change it."

Uncle Cole seemed to suddenly realise he didn't speak about his feelings out loud. His gruff exterior returned as he informed Stephen that there was a bed in her room if he wanted to stay. Sienna was as surprised as Stephen. Walking into her room, she noticed a trundle bed next to her bed. It had new sheets on it; a pillow and quilt folded up on it.

"Have to confess, think he's doing better at keeping the promise to keep the peace than us," said Stephen. "Should probably stay here, then. No point offending him."

"You don't have to if you don't want to," spat Sienna.

"Didn't mean it like that."

Sienna wasn't sure how anything her family said was meant. It was like they spoke two different languages. The words were the same, but the meanings were different. There was only one person left who understood her.

"Thank you," Sienna whispered, creeping into the lounge room where Uncle Cole was watching television.

"Your artwork's one of the best things I've ever seen," he replied, pulling her into a hug. "If that doesn't get picked to go on display at the Art Gallery with all the other top entries, then those judges don't know what they're talking about."

"Why don't they get me?"

"I don't know," sighed Uncle Cole. "Maybe that's been the problem the whole time. We thought they didn't love you and really they just don't understand you."

"Maybe," replied Sienna.

"I'm working early tomorrow," said Uncle Cole, kissing the side of her head. "You spend time with your parents while they're out here. I'll see you at dinner."

The weather gods were on their side. Their picnic was set up under a crisp blue sky; fluffy white clouds sailing peacefully across it. The river provided a perfect backdrop. Sienna had her camera, but only took a few photos. She had promised herself she would try to get along with her parents, and photography had always been her way to escape them.

"This was a really great idea, Sen," smiled Janice.

Sienna accepted the compliment, but it wasn't what she'd envisaged. This was the most upmarket picnic she'd ever seen. They even had champagne for the occasion.

"So you looking forward to your party tonight?" asked Arthur.

Sienna shrugged non-committedly. She doubted she would ever enjoy her birthday again. But her tentativeness only spurred her family to increase their enthusiasm levels, as though that's what was missing.

As they walked to the restaurant, Arthur insisted on holding Sienna's hand, swinging it childishly. It was embarrassing and annoying, but she said nothing. Stepping off the curb at the main road to check the traffic, Sienna suddenly felt herself yanked violently back on to the footpath. Five seconds later a semi-trailer rumbled past.

"Oww," she cried, trying to pull her hand from Arthur's, but she was already wrapped in his embrace.

It was then she noticed his uneven breathing. She could feel his heart pounding against her chest. "Can't lose you. Not again."

"I wasn't standing in the middle of the road," said Sienna softly. "I saw it."

"Yeah, I know. Just panicked."

Sienna trailed behind them as they crossed the road. She wanted to slip even further back when they reached the restaurant, but Stephen pushed her in the door first. Their guests were already there. It wasn't a big group, but Sienna still found it overwhelming. All her childhood birthdays had been marked by a small family gathering with a few friends and a colourful cake. Sienna couldn't remember her parents making it to any of those events. They'd always promised something bigger and better when she came to live with them, but she'd stopped trusting their word by then.

That last birthday with Flynn was the closest she'd come to a celebration of the day since leaving Uncle Cole. The memory burned her eyes, almost blinding her as people descended on her.

"Next year it can be you, me and a blue and green cake," Uncle Cole whispered, suddenly appearing by her side. "This year, just hang with your friends."

Sienna looked around and found she was standing with Amber and Amy. They smiled brightly and each put an arm around her waist. They didn't say happy birthday. They didn't talk about it at all. They spoke about all the things they usually did and Sienna was able to forget for a while what the night was about.

When dinner came, Sienna took a seat between Amy and Amber. Jackson sat opposite her with Stephen, while Uncle Cole was next to Janice. It was a surprising move and one Sienna watched with interest as the night wore on. There was a civility between them she had never witnessed before. It didn't seem to extend as far as Arthur, but it was a vast improvement on the all-out war that usually occurred.

The most strained relations appeared to be between Jackson and Uncle Cole. They barely spoke all night. With Sienna's movements and friendships being less restricted this year, she had actively avoided knowing anything about station politics. Even when she had visited Uncle Cole there, she'd kept herself blinkered. It left her unsure which side the tension was on and how the team was dealing with Jackson's impending departure.

"Happy birthday to you! Happy birthday to you!"

Sienna turned in horror to see a waitress walking towards them with a huge cake covered in sparklers. Worse, the whole restaurant joined in the singing. Arthur and Janice were beaming. Sienna noticed Uncle Cole looked somewhere between concerned and amused, so she tried to wipe the horror from her face.

"Hippip, hooray! Hippip, hooray! Hippip, hooray!" everyone cheered.

Sienna's face exploded into flames of embarrassment. Amy and Amber giggled on either side of her.

"Make a wish," said Stephen eagerly.

Sienna shook her head, putting the knife into the cake and pressing it right to the bottom.

"Won't come true now," teased Arthur.

"There's nothing I would wish for that could come true," replied Sienna, thinking of Flynn.

Arthur, Janice and Stephen exchanged wounded glances. Sienna felt a guilty knot in her stomach, realising they must have somehow related her comment to them.

"You cutting the rest of that or keeping it to yourself?" asked Jackson.

Sienna immediately started handing out pieces of cake, smiling thankfully at Jackson as she did. When Amber and Amy asked if they should suggest they needed to get home as soon as they finished their cake, Sienna realised she'd made some pretty good friends in Fortune.

"I should go too," smiled Jackson, when Amber and Amy rose to leave. "You got plans for next weekend?" he whispered, walking around to Sienna's side.

"You mean besides study, study and more study?" she laughed.

"Can you skip that? Please. One weekend. Celebrate our birthdays together."

Sienna looked down. Her hands were in Jackson's. When she looked up, Flynn's smile was waiting for her, beckoning her towards adventure the way he always had. Without any conscious thought, she found herself nodding.

"Great," smiled Jackson. "I'll give you your present then."

~26~

EIGHTEEN

Sienna woke with a start. That wasn't Flynn's playful call on her answering machine. It was the voice of terror – the cry he never got to make two years ago in the moment they were torn apart. Sienna could barely breath through the heaving sobs. Her arms wrapped around her chest, trying to keep herself together.

How she made it to school was beyond her. Amy and Amber had arms around her as soon as they saw her, but if they spoke, she didn't hear them. It wasn't until Sienna found herself in the school office, Jackson kneeling in front of her, that she realised she wasn't in class.

"Chief asked me to take you home," he said softly. "Had the day off."

Sienna nodded but didn't move. Jackson pulled her into his arms and that's where she stayed. Sometimes they comforted her. Other times they restrained. It didn't matter that she'd survived the celebrations of her eighteenth birthday, the urge to join Flynn on this day of all days was so strong she wasn't sure how she'd overcome it.

"I can't, I can't. Please, Jax, let me go. I can't do this any more. I want it to stop. I want it to all go away forever. Please."

Perhaps realising that his previous attempts at comforting her weren't working, Jackson stayed silent.

Uncle Cole came to collect her in the late afternoon. She tried to keep it together in front of him, but was barely successful.

"Let's cook tonight," said Uncle Cole, as they walked into the house. "I'm sure you've had enough birthday dinners out for one year."

Sienna had no idea what to cook, but she didn't have to worry. He had it all planned. Everything was even already chopped up. It wasn't until later that she suspected it had been to keep knives from her hands.

They ate in the lounge room and watched television. Sienna was sure she cried the whole time. She just didn't know what to do next or how to build the desire to live to see another day.

"Here," said Uncle Cole, handing her two tablets and a hot chocolate. "You need to sleep. You need to survive until tomorrow."

Sienna nodded and swallowed the sleeping pills. Uncle Cole didn't say anything else. They just kept watching television until her eyes slid shut.

Uncle Cole lifted her into his arms. She murmured that she needed to brush her teeth and change, but he told her not to worry about that for one night. When she was tucked into bed, her eyes remained open long enough to see Uncle Cole laying himself down on the trundle bed. She liked that he trusted her enough to set it up on the other side of her bed to the door.

It was late when Sienna woke. She could hear Uncle Cole moving about the house. He didn't ask how she was when he saw her, only letting her know that he had informed the school that she would be late. When she curled into his embrace, he promised they would come up with a better plan for next year.

"I think we need to stop seeing this as the day you mourn Flynn's loss and instead celebrate that you had him in your life."

"But I miss him so much," gasped Sienna, tears tracking down her face.

"You always will," said Uncle Cole seriously. "I'm not trying to change that. I'm talking about finding a way to keep loving him and living at the same time."

"You think that's possible?" asked Sienna. "You don't think I need to stop loving Flynn."

"Not if you want to keep living."

Sienna wandered home on Friday, her mind a numb twirl. The exhaustion from her birthday had not completely subsided. She was trying to implement Uncle Cole's advice about Flynn, but with his loss still so close and raw, she wasn't sure how to feel about this weekend. The sight of Jackson waiting outside her house made her check her steps. Then he smiled. It was like balm on her wounded heart. She hadn't lost Flynn. He was right here with her in Jackson. When he greeted her with a warm hug, she found herself returning it fiercely.

"You packed?" he asked, stepping back and stroking her face.

"Um, what? Aren't we leaving tomorrow?" replied Sienna.

"No. Come on, you won't need much."

"Where we going?" she asked, placing her suitcase on her bed.

"Camping," replied Jackson, instantly replacing the suitcase with a duffle bag.

"Like in tents?"

"No, like in swags," he smiled, laughing as concern flickered across her face. "Trust me." When he smiled like that, she would've trusted him with her life.

It was a quiet drive. Sienna looked around, trying to figure out where they were going. They were travelling in the opposite direction to Westloch, an area Sienna had never ventured to. When Jackson pulled over after more than an hour, she was left confused by their surrounds.

"We break down?" she asked.

"No, we're here," laughed Jackson.

"Where? There's nothing here but bush."

"Hence the camping gear. Didn't I tell you to trust me."

"Is it safe?"

"Yes," Jackson sighed dramatically. "We're heading to a spot about a ten-minute walk away. It's by the river. I promise, you'll like it."

Sienna nodded, helping Jackson load the gear on to their shoulders. When she complained about how heavy it was, he noted how much of it was her camera gear, but he wouldn't hear of her leaving it behind.

They reached the river after twenty minutes, slowed up mostly by Sienna. She felt unbalanced and was scared of tripping. The sight of a cleared patch of land and the charred remains of a fire surprised her. Jackson had obviously been here before and she wondered how many other girls he had brought to this spot.

"Why don't you make the most of the sunset while I get our camp set up," suggested Jackson.

The light was beautiful. Sienna traipsed along the river and into the trees, searching for the perfect shot. As the sunlight faded, the light from the campfire took a greater hold of the scene. Jackson sat staring into the flames. Sienna used him as the subject of many of the shots – until she realised how rude she was being and quickly packed up her gear.

"Welcome to the million-star hotel," Jackson smiled, when she sat next to him. "Come, I want to show you some things." He'd set up a large mat with two sleeping bags. Lying down on it, he pulled her against his body so her head rested in the curve of his shoulder. "See those stars up there?"

Jackson pointed and Sienna squinted. There were so many stars she wasn't sure which one he was trying to show her.

"Sorry. I'm ruining your story, aren't I?" she said, after five minutes of trying to find the right star.

"No. Doesn't matter about the star. Close your eyes. I can just tell you the stories."

Jackson told Sienna five different Aboriginal stories about the stars and animals. Some were similar to the stories she'd heard at school as a child, but it was the way he told them that she liked. He brought them to life, the imagery dancing across her eyes, lulling her into a peaceful sleep.

A rumbling ache woke Sienna. Opening her eyes, she noticed the sun pushing the first light into the eastern sky. Her body shivered against the morning chill, waking Jackson. He rolled from his sleeping bag and restarted the fire, having it crackling again in under a minute. When he shuffled back, he pulled Sienna close, hugging her tight as he closed his eyes.

The sun had fully risen by the time Sienna opened her eyes again. Jumping out of her sleeping bag, she tried to capture what was left of the misty morning, but Jackson was soon calling her back to the fireside.

"Breakfast first," he said. "You didn't eat last night."

Sienna couldn't argue. Her stomach growled angrily, the noise rippling across the quiet air. Jackson smiled, loading her plate with food. As soon as they were done, he insisted they go out to take photos. Sienna tried to assure him they could do something else, but he was adamant and volunteered to be her model.

It didn't take long before she forgot all about her concerns. The scenery was stunning, particularly where the bush opened up to give a view of the expansive open land around them.

"So how bout some of us together," called Jackson. "Don't tell me that timer doesn't work."

Sienna set up the tripod she'd been using intermittently and chose her scene. She doubted it would work well, but was happy to appease Jackson.

"Do they all have to be so serious?" he asked, after the fifth shot of them together.

Sienna shook her head. This time he pulled her into his arms before striking a ridiculous pose. It took her much longer for her to lower her inhibitions and act foolishly, but he eventually pulled it out of her. Then he took things too far and stumbled off the rock he'd jumped on.

"You okay?" Sienna gasped, dropping to her knees next to him.

"Am now," he smiled.

For a second, Sienna saw Flynn all grown up; handsome and mature. The next thing she knew, she and Jackson were kissing.

"Sorry," Jackson whispered, pulling his lips away, though his hand continued to stroke her cheek.

"It's okay," she replied, her voice so soft she wasn't sure he heard.

"It's okay, I can do it again? Or just, it's okay."

"It's just okay," whispered Sienna, but it wasn't. Her heart was pounding. She enjoyed kissing Jackson, but wasn't sure if it was him she was really kissing.

Jackson nodded and moved away. He smiled just slightly and squeezed her hand. Sienna took a deep shuddering breath and collected her camera. She wasn't sure what to do next. Her mind was no longer on photography. The rumble of her stomach saved her from any decision. They walked back to the camp and re-started the fire.

"You bring your swimmers?" asked Jackson when they finished cleaning up after their late lunch. "We should swim." Sienna shook her head "Skinny-dipping it is then."

"Or I can just use my underwear. It's pretty bikini-like in design."

Jackson's eyes sparkled. It was alluring and after months of photoshoots, she was no longer embarrassed. Part of her even wanted to throw herself into his arms, feel him hold her the way Flynn had – and watch Flynn smile back at her.

"It might be cold," said Jackson, taking her hand and leading her into the river.

It was beyond cold. It was only because he kept pulling her in that she immersed her body. She would've stopped at ankle-deep. Smiling as he let go of her hand, Jackson swam across the river. Sienna felt compelled to follow, despite her muscles aching from suppressed shivers.

"Oh, shit, Sienna, you're freezing," gasped Jackson, when he swam back to her.

He dragged her back to the fireside and piled on more wood. The wind was picking up so he sat behind her and rubbed her arms, but he couldn't compete with the storm that was brewing around them.

"We might need to find shelter," said Jackson, looking at the rapidly darkening sky.

Heavy rain drops started to fall as they packed up their camp, which felt like it had doubled in size since they arrived.

"I saw a cave from where we were this morning. I think I can find it," said Jackson, as they trekked into the scrub.

It felt like forever before they stumbled across it, the rain having hardened into a downpour within minutes of them leaving their campsite. It made the shelter of the cave the most welcoming thing Sienna had experienced in a long time.

"Stay here," commanded Jackson. "I'll get wood for the fire."

A second later, he was gone. Sienna stepped out of the cave. There was plenty of tinder nearby, so she grabbed what she could and set it in a small pyramid. The kindling smoked as it burnt off the dampness, but she kept it going until he returned with the larger pieces of wood.

"I didn't know you knew how to start a fire," said Jackson, failing to hide his surprise.

"You'd be surprised what Uncle Cole taught me," replied Sienna. "I'm not good at reading and writing, but that doesn't mean I can't do anything."

"I didn't mean it like that. Actually, just don't know many girls who can light fires."

"That's pretty sexist."

"Not if it's true."

"Anyone bother to teach the girls? Or you just act surprised when girls can't do things they're never taught?"

"Oooh, burn," laughed Jackson. "Here, quick, get changed before you freeze to death."

Sienna grabbed the clothes Jackson threw at her. She was still looking for a place to change when he began stripping in front of her.

"What are you doing?" he asked, looking up to see her watching him.

"No – nothing – just – nothing."

Sienna huddled into the darkest corner and changed into the dry clothes. She felt instantly warmer, but there was a deep chill in her body the clothes couldn't touch and she shivered even as she moved close to the fire.

"Quick, jump in," said Jackson, already shuffling into the sleeping bag.

Jackson had zipped the two sleeping bags together, so there was no avoiding being close to him, though she tried. She moved to one side of bag, but he immediately pulled her into his arms.

"You know if we were doing this properly, we'd be naked," he said, holding her close.

"What?"

"Getting warm," he laughed. "Though while we're talking about being naked, why don't you tell me why you were staring at me getting undressed, then go and hide in the darkest corner."

"I didn't ask you to strip in front of me."

"I thought you were changing too. Turned my back. Expected you to do the same."

"Guys get to check out naked chicks all the time," she replied, refusing to meet his eyes.

"Where?"

"There're photos of naked girls everywhere. You don't have any reason to look at me."

"And you've never seen a naked guy before?" queried Jackson disbelievingly. Sienna shrugged and turned away. "Just one, huh."

"Pretty much."

Jackson rolled her on to his chest, making himself a warm mattress. He held her tight as he kissed the top of her head. The way he stroked her hair was mesmerising. She didn't dare look at his face, too scared to see Flynn's smile when she felt so vulnerable.

"Try and get some sleep," he murmured from time to time, but neither of them closed their eyes until the wind died down enough to let the fire take hold and warm the little cave.

The day broke cold and rainy. They struggled to restart the fire with the wet wood, but managed to scrape together something for breakfast before packing up their camp one final time.

"Next time, I check the weather forecast," sighed Jackson.

"You didn't check it?"

"Well apparently you didn't either."

"No. I trusted you. Amber told me it was supposed to rain, but I thought you must've known something she didn't."

"Just how to ruin a weekend."

"You didn't ruin it," cried Sienna, grabbing his hand. "It was one of the best weekends I've had out here."

Jackson smiled and stroked the side of her face. It set her on fire. She couldn't understand the effect he was suddenly having on her, but every time Flynn smiled at her, she felt more comfortable with Jackson's touch.

"Let's get back. Get warm," said Jackson.

It was a short drive. Jackson insisted she have the first shower and laid out some of his clothes for her as he dried out the rest of their belongings.

Sienna made hot drinks while Jackson showered, hoping to warm them back up from the inside.

"Sorry about the weekend," said Jackson, moving behind her as she stood by the window watching the pouring rain. "I made a cake. Good thing I forgot to pack it. Want me to get it?"

Sienna turned to say yes, but didn't realise how close he was. She was immediately in his arms. When Flynn smiled at her, she realised Amber and Amy were right. Flynn was okay with this. He had to be or he wouldn't keep leading her to Jackson.

This time, when their lips met, Sienna didn't pull away.

~27~

END OF FORTUNE

A sense of dread filled Sienna's stomach as she looked over at Jackson. His arm was draped across her body as he slept peacefully. They'd shared a wonderful moment, but she couldn't help but regret it. She'd been drawn to him almost as if he was Flynn, but all trace of Flynn had disappeared from his face and a sense of betrayal now filled her body.

"Hey, beautiful," said Jackson sleepily. His hand stroked her face tenderly. Sienna closed her eyes as the tears built in them. "I wish I didn't have to take you home. Why couldn't we have reached this place sooner?"

Sienna had to fight to hold in her sob. It would have been easier if Jackson had just dismissed her as a conquest, because he was a good guy and she couldn't be with him if Flynn wasn't there, shining out from his lips.

"At least we don't have to deal with the Chief," Jackson continued. "You can keep a secret for a week, can't you?" Sienna nodded. "And the long-distance thing won't be too bad. I'll be starting a new job. You'll have exams. By the time we have a chance to breathe we'll be in the same city again."

Sienna tried to control the frantic beating of her heart that was making her breathing shallow and erratic. Jackson brought in her clothes from the dryer and she dressed hastily. She watched him carefully, waiting to see Flynn smile at her, telling her this was okay, but when Jackson smiled it was his smile, not Flynn's.

"I can't, Jax. Shit, I can't," she cried, rushing out of the bedroom.

"Can't what?" he asked, following her to the lounge room.

"You and me. It won't work."

"This better not be that spheres crap you were pushing before. I don't care about any of that. You're not sixteen any more. The age difference, work, it doesn't matter and you said yourself the race thing isn't an issue."

"It isn't."

"Then what? We aren't going to be here. We'll keep it secret until I go. After I go. Chief never has to know as far as I'm concerned. We'll be in Sydney."

"I can't be with you in Sydney!" cried Sienna.

"Why not?"

She couldn't answer, but the truth was obvious enough. Jackson's eyes turned hard in an instant. He glared at her as tears slipped down her cheeks.

"Flynn's gone, Sienna," he said, his face softening with his voice. "He's gone. You can't keep holding on to him like this. Don't you think he'd want you to move on?"

"No," she sobbed, her head shaking slowly back and forth. "We never wanted anyone else. I still don't want anyone else."

"So what the hell was this?" cried Jackson. She opened her mouth, but he yelled over the top of her. "Fuck off, Sienna. Just get out." She hesitated. "Get out!"

Sienna rushed from the apartment, frightened by Jackson's anger, and ran the whole way home. She was soaked through by the time she pushed open the front door. Uncle Cole was in the bathroom long enough for her to dash to her room and claim the need to change.

"Didn't hear you pull up," he said, when she walked out to the kitchen, his voice less gruff than usual.

Sienna loved that he missed her so much and threw herself into his arms. When he asked about the trip, she spoke only of the hours before arriving back at Jackson's apartment. He accepted her story of them huddling in the cave all day in the hope that the rain would ease without question, and thankfully agreed to wait until she'd looked through the photos before seeing them. It hadn't been until she'd been describing one of the shots that she realised she'd come back empty-handed.

"Sounds like a good weekend," said Uncle Cole, ruffling her wet hair.

"Yeah, but it's all over now," she replied mournfully. Uncle Cole looked at her with concern. "Nothing to save me from study," she added, pushing a smile on to her face.

"Well come and have one last dinner with me at the pub," he said.

"I'll drive you straight back after we eat. Even go shopping tomorrow and fill the house with food."

Sienna burst into tears. Uncle Cole immediately pulled her back into his arms and held her tight. "Where were you last year?" she sobbed, grasping his shirt.

"In a bad place," he murmured. "Just like you."

"You blamed me?"

"Blamed everyone," he said. "Including you. But it wasn't your fault. Of course, you wanted your parents to love you. Wanted what everyone else had. What they promised. I'm sorry you never got it."

***

"Seriously, when are you going to tell us what really happened?" Amy pleaded, as they walked to Sienna's house on Monday afternoon.

"Nothing else to tell. Nothing happened," Sienna replied, trying to keep her voice light and playful.

"Two nights alone with Jackson Halley huddled around a campfire, even with me something would've happened," said Amber.

Sienna turned in surprise and Amber laughed. Amy smiled, her face blushing. Sienna wondered if it was because of Avery, and hoped her feud with Jackson didn't impact their friendship.

"Yeah right nothing happened," Amy whispered loudly to Amber.

It was then that Sienna noticed Jackson's car out the front of her house. As soon as he saw them, he was out of the car, unloading her bags on to the footpath. He placed the camera equipment gently, but showed no care with her duffle bag.

"Hey, thanks for dropping this off," said Sienna, hoping they could appear friendly in public. Jackson glared at her. "You want to come in?"

"What, Flynn not here today?" he asked acidly. Sienna didn't respond. "I never want to see you again." He jumped in his car and sped off.

Amy and Amber turned to her. "I stuffed up, okay," Sienna sighed. "Ruined it with both of them."

"Both? You mean Flynn?" asked Amy.

Sienna nodded, tears leaking down her cheeks at the memory of her betrayal. As she detailed what happened, Amy and Amber tried to gently persuade her that she was allowed a life after Flynn, even if she did still love him. Sienna couldn't convince herself of that and knew she couldn't fix the situation with Jackson, but hoped there was a way for him to leave Fortune without hating her.

Grabbing her camera, she decided to try and find a photo of him she could give as a parting gift. The screen was blank. She toggled the settings, wondering what she'd done wrong, but no matter what she did, she couldn't find the photos she'd taken. She checked the memory card. It was still in the camera. Connecting it to her computer, she searched for the photos again. It was blank.

Sienna couldn't understand what had gone wrong.

Rummaging through her camera bag, she found the memory card that had been in her camera at the start of the weekend. She'd had to change it on Saturday morning. Placing it into the camera, her heart sank as the photos of the misty morning appeared on the screen. There was only one explanation. Jackson had wiped the other memory card.

The revelation left Sienna wavering widely between anger and sympathy. She was feeling sympathetic on Sunday morning as she walked towards Jackson's apartment, even though part of her was hoping he'd already left. As she turned the corner, she saw him packing his car.

"Don't bother," he spat. "I don't want to talk to you."

"I just wanted to say goodbye," said Sienna meekly. "We used to be friends."

"You got that right. Used to be," Jackson replied bitterly. "You were right when you said we lived in two different spheres. So fuck off away from mine. I don't want to know you."

"I'm sorry. I never wanted to hurt you."

"Just get lost, Sienna."

Sienna took one last look at Jackson, grateful there was no hint of Flynn's smile on his lips. It made it easier to walk away; the memories of Flynn's real smile, his spirit and love wrapped around her heart, stitching it together. Once more, Flynn was her heart and soul and she would not change that for anyone.

***

Study, study and more study. Even after the term finished, that was all Sienna's life comprised of. Amy came over every day, while Amber joined them when they were all revising the same subject. Their presence made the whole process just bearable.

Uncle Cole was also helping out, his parenting skills improving exponentially. Yet it was inevitable that the one topic that had the potential to destroy everything good they had built would eventually arise. Sienna just wished it didn't have to be the night before her first exam.

"Your mother keeps saying you're going back to Sydney after your exams. When do you leave?" he asked.

"Haven't got an exact date yet, but probably a couple of weeks after exams finish," replied Sienna, keeping her head down.

"Can't wait to get away, huh?"

"As long as I'm here, I'll be something you guys fight over. I can't do that any more."

"So you're going to live with them because you think I won't fight for you?"

"No. I'm going back to Sydney because it's the only place I know how to live independently."

"They won't let you move out."

"They'll have to. Me and Amy are going there to get jobs and our own place. Amy can't do that here. You know that."

"They're not the only people who can help you."

"No. You can give me everything I need but one thing. They offer me that one thing as if it's all I could need. I've never asked for money before and I never will, but to help Amy, I won't refuse it this time."

"What do they know of your plans?" asked Uncle Cole seriously.

"That me and Amy are coming to stay after our exams," replied Sienna.

"If it doesn't – not that I want – but just in case …"

"I know," smiled Sienna. It was the one thing she'd always known.

"First one down," sighed Amy the next day, as they walked out of the school hall.

Sienna could only nod. She had no idea how she'd gone. It wasn't a disaster, but there was a definite limit to her optimism. Amber was just as pessimistic, though with much less cause, while Amy was determined not to care.

The whole process was repeated the next day. Then again the following week. Except when Sienna exited her maths exam, she was holding back her tears. No one followed her as she sprinted home, but there was someone waiting for her. Uncle Cole met her at the door and took her straight out to the backyard. There was a canvas waiting.

"You should do more painting," he said, speaking for the first time after more than an hour of silence.

"Was never nowhere to do it," replied Sienna softly.

"Expensive carpet everywhere?"

"Yeah," she laughed. "Never told you. Painted on the dining table once. Tried to be neat. They didn't appreciate it."

"I can imagine. Make sure they don't talk you into renting a place like that."

Sienna looked over at Uncle Cole. He smiled ruefully, but she felt more at ease now than she had in so long. He wouldn't fight her decision to leave. Though most of her choices this year defied him as much as the year before, he was standing by her now. Perhaps he'd been right all along. She didn't need a shrink. She needed him.

There was just one more exam to go. Sienna finished with legal studies in just two days, while Amy and Amber finished this afternoon. Sienna set an alarm for five minutes before the end of their exam and rushed down to the school.

"Congratulations!" she cried, as soon as Amy and Amber emerged.

Amy bounded forward and hugged her tight. Amber's approach was much more sedate.

"Look at her," sighed Amy. "We finish our exams and she's more worried about one of the questions she thinks she got wrong."

Amber tried to insist she was wrong, but it was clear she wasn't. "You didn't have to come down," she said. "Can't be any fun when it's not your last exam."

"Makes it closer," smiled Sienna. "And it means you guys will have to come meet me after my last exam."

"I can't believe we only have two weeks left in this town," smiled Amy.

"Can't believe you guys are leaving me here alone the whole summer," replied Amber.

"You'll have Luke," offered Sienna. "And someone has to find a place for us to live next year."

Amber smiled broadly, but they knew it was unlikely she would join them. There was no doubt Amber would go to university and be successful. It was a different path to the one they were going down.

After a celebratory milkshake, Sienna trekked home to study. It was difficult to get back into the groove, but she refused to let herself up from her desk. She had under two days left and could endure this pain a while longer. She refused to leave Fortune a failure.

She had just started to find her rhythm when there was a knock at the door. Sighing heavily, she pushed away from her desk, wondering who was ignoring Uncle Cole's ban on visitors during her exams.

"Amy? You okay? What's going on?" asked Sienna on seeing her tear-stained face. She quickly pulled Amy inside, where the bruises on her arms became evident. They were grip marks and Sienna could only imagine how hard she would have to have been held to bruise her like that.

"I can't go," gasped Amy, more tears tumbling down her cheeks.

"You can't stay either," said Sienna, grabbing her hands. "You can't keep copping this."

Sienna had only ever seen a couple of other bruises, but knew from Flynn that that was never the full extent of it.

"I can't leave them with no one to protect them," sobbed Amy, shaking her head. "Thought I had two years. Get set up and they'd come live with me as soon as they turned sixteen, but if I'm not there he'll go – they won't —"

"Yeah, I know," nodded Sienna.

She took Amy to her room. Perhaps they would be staying in Fortune after all. Sienna knew she wouldn't go to Sydney without Amy. The problem would be getting enough work to save for a place of their own. Jobs just weren't as easy to come by in the country.

"What if they came with us?" asked Sienna, trying to think through every possible solution.

"Don't have enough money."

"We might if we both get jobs. Won't be forever. Just til we get settled. Then you can go to uni – be a teacher or a nurse. Together, me and you, we can afford it."

"But what if you get sick of us? You'll just go —"

"No, I won't," said Sienna firmly. "Of all the places I'd go, that's the last. I can't – you don't get – it's so different to what you have to deal with. Maybe I'm weaker than you, but I can't live with them. I'd come back here first. We can do this. I promise."

Amy was just starting to believe Sienna when there was a knock at the bedroom door.

"She okay?" asked Uncle Cole gravely. It was clear Sienna wasn't going to have to explain anything.

"Not really," she answered.

"We need to talk to her," Uncle Cole said, placing his hand gently on her shoulder.

Amy nodded and Sienna stepped aside to allow Uncle Cole and Ryan into her room. Sienna waited in the kitchen, feeling the minutes tick by. When the door finally opened, Amy walked out in front of Ryan and Uncle Cole. Sienna was shocked by the bruising that had started to blossom across her face.

"We're taking her to the hospital," said Ryan quietly.

"Can she come too?" asked Amy in a broken voice.

Ryan nodded and Sienna immediately took Amy's hand.

It took many hours to clear Amy of any severe injuries. Her father had been arrested, but her mother was refusing to take out a restraining order. That left Amy in the uncomfortable position of being the one to lay the complaint against her father. In the end she couldn't do it.

"We can proceed with the charges even without your complaint," said Ryan. "You want Matt and Michelle thinking this is okay?"

"We know it's not okay!" cried Amy. "But charges won't get him out of the house. I just want to keep them safe, okay. So just take me home."

"What if we got the twins out?" asked Uncle Cole, placing a lightly restraining hand on Amy arm. It was clear he wasn't keen on taking Amy home. "You can stay with us and we'll get them into care."

"I can't abandon them to strangers," gasped Amy.

"Won't be forever, remember," said Sienna. "Don't forget our plan. We'll get jobs. Get a place."

Amy finally nodded.

The social worker was sympathetic to Amy's situation and promised to do everything in her power to keep them together. Matt and Michelle were placed with a family in Sydney. When Amy got herself set up, they would assess her for custody.

"As soon as we get to my parents', we'll start looking for jobs and houses. Me and you, we can share a room if we need," said Sienna determinedly.

"Thank you," sobbed Amy, breaking down in a way Sienna had never seen before. "I'm sorry I stuffed up your study."

Sienna laughed. "It's already part of the past," she said. "Doesn't mean anything to me."

FINDING THE FUTURE

Sienna slumped on her bed, exhausted. She was asleep before she even thought to close her eyes. It was only the sharp sound of her alarm that got her moving the next morning.

"You make me feel bad when you look like that," said Amy, when Sienna yawned her way around the kitchen.

"Wouldn't swap if you paid me," Sienna smiled tiredly.

"But they do pay me. A lot," replied Amy. "It should've been your job. Not mine."

This was probably the hundredth time Amy had said that.

Sienna had mentioned nothing to her parents about their plans on returning to Sydney, but they already knew. Uncle Cole, the most unlikely of snitches, told Janice everything. Sienna still wasn't sure who he did it for.

If it was Amy, he achieved his goal. Within a month they were in a four-bedroom house in the inner city and Amy was working directly under Janice earning a salary most eighteen-year-olds could only dream of. Amy's income alone was able to keep them. It was made easier by the fact that they didn't pay any rent. Sienna owned the house – a property her parents had bought in her name when she was ten. A welcome home present she'd never known about. If Amy hadn't needed it to secure custody of Matt and Michelle, Sienna wouldn't have accepted it.

What Amy didn't know was that Sienna didn't have to work two jobs. Arthur was continually pushing her to accept his offer of an allowance; an amount very much in excess of what she was earning herself. His reasoning was that she would then have the time to pursue her photography, but she was determined to do this on her own. She accepted the photography jobs her parents arranged, knowing there had to be a limit to her stubbornness, but so far her plan for independence was working and she wasn't giving it up – even for sleep.

The first job Sienna got was at the local supermarket. It was a strategic move. It was open eighteen hours a day and offered enough shifts to keep her going. The second job was less about money and more about opportunity.

Of all the things Sienna liked about her new house, it was that it was in the middle of an artist's hub. There were small galleries nearby and cafes that encouraged their staff to express their creative sides. Sienna spent weeks scouting them, finding the one that suited her. She secured weekend work and they got artwork for their walls that changed with every piece sold. Over three months she sold ten pieces, but there was one photograph that was still on the wall. It was a crowd favourite, and had many offers, but it was not for sale.

Having a picture of Flynn with her as she worked made her feel safe. There was something radiant about the image. That sunrise had been special. Not for any particular reason, just one of those moments they felt better for experiencing – one that had made them, for a moment, thankful for their lives. That was what Sienna captured; Flynn, sitting on the sand watching the sun rise over the ocean, a slight smile on his face.

Sienna loved the way Flynn's playful voice rang out from the photo. It brought him back to life in a way that didn't hurt as much as it had before. She was finally learning to cope with his loss.

It had only been possible with the help of her new psychologist. She had never intended on seeing one, but at the end of her first phone call to Uncle Cole, a week after arriving back in Sydney, he suggested she see someone. He'd already checked them out and was sure they'd be a better fit. Perfect was closer to the truth.

Dr Cheng allowed Sienna to feel safe in her own mind and taught her to accept her life for what it was, but beyond that, she gave her the courage to accept how she really felt about things. And the first thing she did was book a train back to Fortune.

"You don't mind me visiting, do you?" she asked, when Uncle Cole collected her from the station, though his hug was answer enough.

They went home and immediately set up a canvas to work on as they caught up. He surprised her by mentioning that he had off the couple of days she was in town.

"Unless there's an emergency, of course," he added.

"I know," smiled Sienna. "And just in case there is, can I ask you something now?"

"Sure, Sen."

"Why won't you tell me what happened when I was a kid? Why I lived with you."

Uncle Cole sighed heavily, a grimacing smile settling on his face. "Guess I should've expected that." He sighed again. "Because you never stopped wanting your parents to love you. And I wanted you to believe it was possible."

"You don't think it's possible?" she asked, turning to face him.

Uncle Cole put down his paint brush, his fingers pinching the bridge of his nose. "Not in the way we expect of them – though I'm trying to be more understanding, knowing I never stopped loving you all those years when I did a very bad job at showing it."

"But you were there! Every time I needed you."

"Not the time you needed me most," he murmured. "And I'll live with that forever. And I will always owe Jackson for saving your life." His voice faltered.

Sienna threw herself into his arms. "I need to ask you something else."

"Anything."

"Can I go back to calling you papa?" she asked, pulling back so she could see his reaction. "It's not quite the right word, but I'm trying to learn to get along with them – be their daughter. But I realised that even if I do that, it won't change that I was your daughter first. Always. I'm more you than anyone and I wish I never lost you." Uncle Cole just stared. "So can I?"

"Of course, Sen," he replied, just managing to squeeze the words out as he held her tighter.

"And we can keep it a secret?"

"Absolutely."

Almost overnight, Uncle Cole returned to the man who raised her. It made her realise that their separation had broken him too, but the reunification made them stronger and closer than ever. Barely a day went by that they were not in contact. They worked hard to devise ways for her to get along with her parents, but after five months, Sienna was beginning to think it was a lost cause.

"I think you've proven your point, Sienna," said Arthur, as they sat around the dining table.

He and Janice had come to dinner at her place. Sienna could hardly mind their presence. She still thought of the house as theirs.

"What's my point?" she asked, trying to keep her cool.

"That you don't need us," Arthur replied.

"I don't want your money," Sienna corrected.

"Take some advice, then," said Arthur. "Focus on your career. Your artwork was judged the best in the state. You have talent and you're wasting your time in a supermarket."

"I can change my name to Smith. Then no one will know the great Hollingsworth name is being disgraced in such a way."

It was something she had seriously considered, particularly after her artwork had been judged so favourably. Arthur and Janice both argued that it was too realistic – too dangerous – to display, claiming it was practically a suicide manual. They denied their stance had anything to do with fears for their reputation, yet their objections all but disappeared when she informed them that it would be attributed to Sienna Smith, not Hollingsworth.

"It's got nothing to do with that and you know it!" yelled Arthur.

"That's not fair, Sienna," said Janice, her voice dripping with disappointment.

"Either's being shamed for trying to make my own way in the world. I appreciate everything you've done – especially for Amy – but I'm sick of not being allowed to do anything my way. Stop being so disappointed in who I am."

"We're not," said Arthur.

"You act like it," replied Sienna. "You don't trust me to do anything. Every time I speak to you about an idea, you either dismiss it straight away or take it from me and do it yourself, like I'm not capable."

"We just want to get you set up," said Janice.

"And when do I learn to do stuff?" cried Sienna.

"If you're so capable, then why haven't you spoken to Jackson about getting his consent to use his images?" asked Arthur. "Some of your best work is locked up because you won't do what needs to be done. That's why we don't trust you."

"But that's my choice!" cried Sienna.

"Just because things didn't end well in Fortune is no reason to limit your future," countered Arthur.

"How would you know things didn't end well?" asked Sienna.

"You can't keep away from each other at your birthday, but never speak a word of him when you come here," replied Arthur.

"Stephen told us," Janice said over the top of Arthur.

"And what would Stephen know?" cried Sienna.

"He and Jackson are friends," said Janice delicately. "Stephen only told us so we wouldn't ask about it." Sienna nodded, half-accepting her explanation. "But your father has a point. Just because things didn't work out doesn't mean Jackson wishes you ill."

Sienna assumed that meant they knew nothing about him deleting some of the best photos she'd ever taken. That, more than anything, was why she'd never sought his consent.

"We're having Jackson over for dinner on Sunday," said Arthur. "We expect you to be there."

There was no escape. Even Amy thought she should get it over and done with.

"He hates me," said Sienna.

"Time has a way of softening feelings," smiled Amy. "Trust me."

"Fine," sighed Sienna, assuming Amy's confidence was related to inside information.

Though Amy never spoke about Avery, Sienna had seen his name flash up on Amy's phone enough times to know they kept in touch. But despite Amy's assurances, Sienna's heart still pounded as she made her way to her parents' place. Jackson's car was out the front when she arrived.

The sound of chatter and laughter sent Sienna's nerves into overdrive. She could see the back of Jackson's head where he sat on the lounge. Her heart thrummed. Everyone but Jackson turned at the sound of her approach. He waited until she was in front of him to acknowledge her. It wasn't the glare she'd been expecting. It was a neutral gaze that gave nothing away.

"Hi," she said softly.

"Hey," replied Jackson.

"I'll get us more drinks," said Janice, quickly rising from her seat.

Arthur immediately followed her out of the room. Stephen stayed long enough to get the conversation going, before joining his parents.

"Subtle," said Jackson. "What's going on?"

"What, Stephen didn't tell you? I thought you guys told each other everything," said Sienna, being unnecessarily antagonistic.

"I didn't expect him to say anything," said Jackson. "But we're mates and he asked."

"So how are you so ignorant of what this is?"

"I was just hoping it wasn't some match-making scheme."

"Then you're in luck," said Sienna flatly. "As far as I know, my only task tonight was to ask you to sign a release so I can sell the photos I took of you. So there's no need to like me. Don't even have to say yes."

"You don't want to use my photos?"

"I'd love to. Those photos – there's something about you – it's almost magnetic. You're one of the best subjects I've ever had, but you hate me. I don't expect anything from you."

"I don't hate you," said Jackson softly.

Sienna didn't have the chance to respond, her stomach flipping at the hint of a smile that crossed Jackson's face just as Arthur, Janice and Stephen returned.

Dinner was awkward. Sienna hardly engaged in the conversation. Her eyes were seeking signs that Flynn had forgiven Jackson. If he could return to Jackson's lips, in this house of all places, she might believe he really was telling her he wanted her to move on.

"We'll get dessert," said Janice, rising from the table, pulling Arthur and Stephen with her from the room.

"How obvious do they get?" asked Jackson.

"Let me give you the form. Take it – make your decision. No pressure. Let's just do what they want so we can escape this madness."

Jackson nodded. Sienna rushed upstairs. The room was full when she arrived back. Not making eye contact with anyone, she handed the form to Jackson with sincere thanks for considering signing it. "I should probably get going," she added. "Have an early start."

"I can give you a lift," offered Jackson.

"No, it's fine. It's out of your way," she replied, already backing out the door.

"That would be really nice, Jackson," said Arthur. "We worry about her on public transport at night."

Sienna rolled her eyes. Taking Papa's advice and choosing her battles, Sienna made no further complaint and waited until everyone had taken their leave of Jackson before following him out to his car.

"You reckon they'd notice if you replaced me as their second child?" she asked, as they drove away.

"They've set you and Amy up. Given you everything. Don't you think that's a bit much?" asked Jackson incredulously.

"So money's everything? Never would've thought ..."

"What?" asked Jackson, turning to her as the silence extended on.

"Nothing. Just for someone who accused me of not wanting to date you cos you didn't have enough money, it's a bit harsh being told to just take my parents' money."

Jackson let out a short laugh, but said nothing. The rest of the drive was spent in silence, which left Sienna surprised when he got out of the car with her.

"We need to talk," he said. "And that wasn't going to happen with your crazy family around – no matter how many times they left the room en masse. Please."

Sienna nodded and allowed him inside. Amy's face showed her shock and amusement at this development, but she did nothing more than wave a greeting from the lounge room, where she was sitting with Matt and Michelle.

"We can go in my studio," said Sienna, leading Jackson to the back of the house.

"Wow, this is amazing," he gasped, walking around the room.

One corner was dedicated to sketches. There were several in progress, many others sitting in a large open file. Another corner was where she was testing her painting skills. It was her least developed skill, but one she was enjoying working on. There were several canvases on the wall and a stack more in the corner waiting for improvement or to be painted over. The rest of the room was taken up by her photography. There were two more large open filing bins with enlargements of her photos. One was of approved images she was looking to sell in some form, the other was of potential images – most of them of Jackson.

"Never saw how these came out," said Jackson, pulling out a photo of them together in his bedroom.

"Most were terrible, but there were a few good ones," said Sienna.

Jackson looked at her curiously. He was still holding the photo. It was so easy to imagine them back there, his arms around her.

"What do you think about when you look at this?" he asked.

"You."

"Which parts?"

"The good parts," she answered seriously. "I know I hurt you. Only fair I remember all the good things you did for me."

"Only the good parts," murmured Jackson, putting the photo back and flicking through the others. He pulled out a picture of him sitting by the campfire on the edge of the river. "How many did you lose?"

"Not sure," she shrugged. He held her gaze. "Couple of hundred maybe."

"And you can still think of me kindly after that?" he asked. "You know that's why I never came to see you. I wanted to. Haven't stopped thinking about you. But all I could imagine was how angry you'd be and I was too ashamed."

"You were upset."

"That's no excuse. Of course, it would've been hard for you – first time after Flynn. I should've understood. Not yelled at you. You take your first step at moving on and when you have a moment of hesitation I shoot you down. It was cruel."

Tears slipped down Sienna's cheeks as the pain of that weekend finally rose to the surface. She'd buried it so deep she'd almost convinced herself she was unaffected by what happened.

"I'm sorry, Sienna," said Jackson sincerely, moving slowly towards her. She held her ground, her heart thrumming, as he stroked her hair and wiped the tears from her cheek. When she looked into his eyes, she was reminded how mesmerising his gaze could be. "Forgive me?" he asked. Her breath stuck in her throat, fresh tears spilling from her eyes. "Impossible, huh?"

"No," she gasped, her head swaying from side to side. "But I can't, Jax."

"Can't what?"

"I'm still – you'll want to fix me."

"I don't want to fix you."

"Everyone does."

"Not me. I want to love you," said Jackson over the top of her. "Shit. I never wanted to say it like that, but it's true. From the first time I met you – there was something about you – you were – I don't – Sienna …"

"Jax, I can't go through that again."

"You won't. I promise." Sienna's head hung low. Jackson's hands gently grasped her cheeks, lifting her gaze to his. "I love you," he said, smiling softly. Her heart strained at the sight. It was as if Flynn was standing before her.

"Stay with me," she whispered.

"I'm never leaving you again," replied Jackson.

When he sealed his promise with Flynn's smile, Sienna's resistance collapsed. She stepped forward, her heart feeling whole again when his lips met hers.